Even Weeds Have Flowers

By Cherrie Burdeshaw

Daily Devotional Readings

Personality
INSIGHTS
PRESS

Even Weeds Have Flowers
366 Daily Devotional Readings
for those who hunger and thirst after God

All of the proceeds from this book,
except for the cost of printing, go to
The Potter's House For Women, Inc.
a faith-based ministry helping women
with shattered lives to be made
whole through the Lord Jesus Christ.

Graphic Design, Pedro A. Gonzalez
Cover Stock image ©123RF.com

Published by
Personality Insights, Inc.
P.O. Box 28592
Atlanta, GA 30358-0592
1.800.509.DISC

www.personalityinsights.com

Personality
INSIGHTS
PRESS

ISBN 13: 9781450544900

Printed in the United States of America

Table of Contents

Foreword

It takes a lot out of a person to be a giver. You can give and give and give of yourself – your time, your talents and your resources until you are completely drained. It is a worthy goal to be a generous person – one who knows how to give and bless others. Unfortunately, some people will drain the life out of you until there is nothing left. Jesus dealt with this same issue when he was on this earth during his earthly ministry. He would minister to those in need all day long, but finally he would stop. He told his disciples, "Come, let us go aside and rest for a while" (*Mark 6:31*).

I once heard Vance Havner say, "If you won't learn to come apart and rest for a while, you will eventually come apart for good!" Rest, knowing when to say "No", knowing who to help, when to start helping and when to stop helping are not easy tasks. The good news is the fact this kind of wisdom can be learned with years of experience and it can also be learned from seasoned, mature Christians.

Cherrie Burdeshaw is just that kind of person. She started the Potter's House Ministry in 2000, just after her own mother went to heaven. And she knows what it takes to give of herself, yet where to draw the line in helping too much! It has been my happy experience to watch "Mrs. Cherrie" develop the ability to welcome women to the Potter's House who are in crisis, to love them, help them, pray with them, feed them, heal them and get them started on the right road to recovery. That takes a lot of time, effort, energy and most of all wisdom. She has all of those qualities…and then some!

The devotional book you now hold in your hands was not written from an ivory tower somewhere in a remote village. It was written out of the years and tears of Mrs. Cherrie helping others and being the one who ministers to those who are hurting and are in need of a new life.

It is my prayer that the spiritual truths found in this book will be a blessing to the reader and give them guidance as to how to replenish their own fountain daily in order to have some good truths about life to give out to others when required to do so!

God bless you Mrs. Cherrie for all you do for the Kingdom of God and in the lives of the Potter's House women.

Robert A. Rohm Ph.D.
President of Personality Insights, Inc.

Introduction

Worthless…useless…without a purpose…a nuisance! That is what I had always thought about them up until this point in time. Never one time in my life had I heard anything good about them. Not once had I ever been told that they were helpful in any way. In fact, from all my experience, the only thing that people ever wanted to do with them was to get rid of them!

However, on this particular day, my whole perspective changed! I was walking through the woods, just enjoying spending time with my dear Savior, when they caught my eye. There before me were deep, rich purples; beautiful blues; vivid yellows; soft pinks; serene lilacs; and vibrant reds. I stood in amazement, silently enjoying the beauty before me, when the thought crossed my mind, "Even weeds have flowers!"

Perhaps your life is filled with "weeds." There are so many things you don't understand, so many problems and heartaches and disappointments. Just about the time you get on your feet and start to make some headway in your life, something else happens to pull you down. You are on a merry-go-round of circumstances, always moving but never going anywhere. Life is puzzling to you. You have questioned the Lord over and over about the way things are, but you have yet to figure it out. Why is it that you try to live right, do your best to serve God, and all these "weeds" still crop up in your life?

Friend, maybe you have always thought that weeds were just plain useless. You have looked at them as a nuisance, as worthless, as without purpose. However, if you will look again, you will see that "even weeds have flowers." For every weed in your life, God has put a beautiful flower on the end of it. God has a purpose for that "weed" that you don't know about. He has designed it specifically for you, to help you learn some valuable lessons that you need in your life. However, you have been focusing on the "weed" instead of on the flower.

Through this devotional book, you can begin to take a look at your garden of life. Sure there are some "weeds" that you would love to eliminate, but you cannot change or control everything that happens to you. So, why don't you look for the flowers instead? There is purple for royalty, red for the blood of Jesus, white for purity, yellow for the warmth and hope of the Sonlight, and blue for Heaven. Start counting these circumstances, these "weeds," these trials as all joy in your life. Remember: no matter how bad things get in your life, "even weeds have flowers."

It is my desire that, through this book, you will develop a closer, more intimate, more trusting walk with Jesus Christ by seeing the flowers rather than the weeds!

Cherrie Burdeshaw
Executive Director of the Potter's House Ministry

January

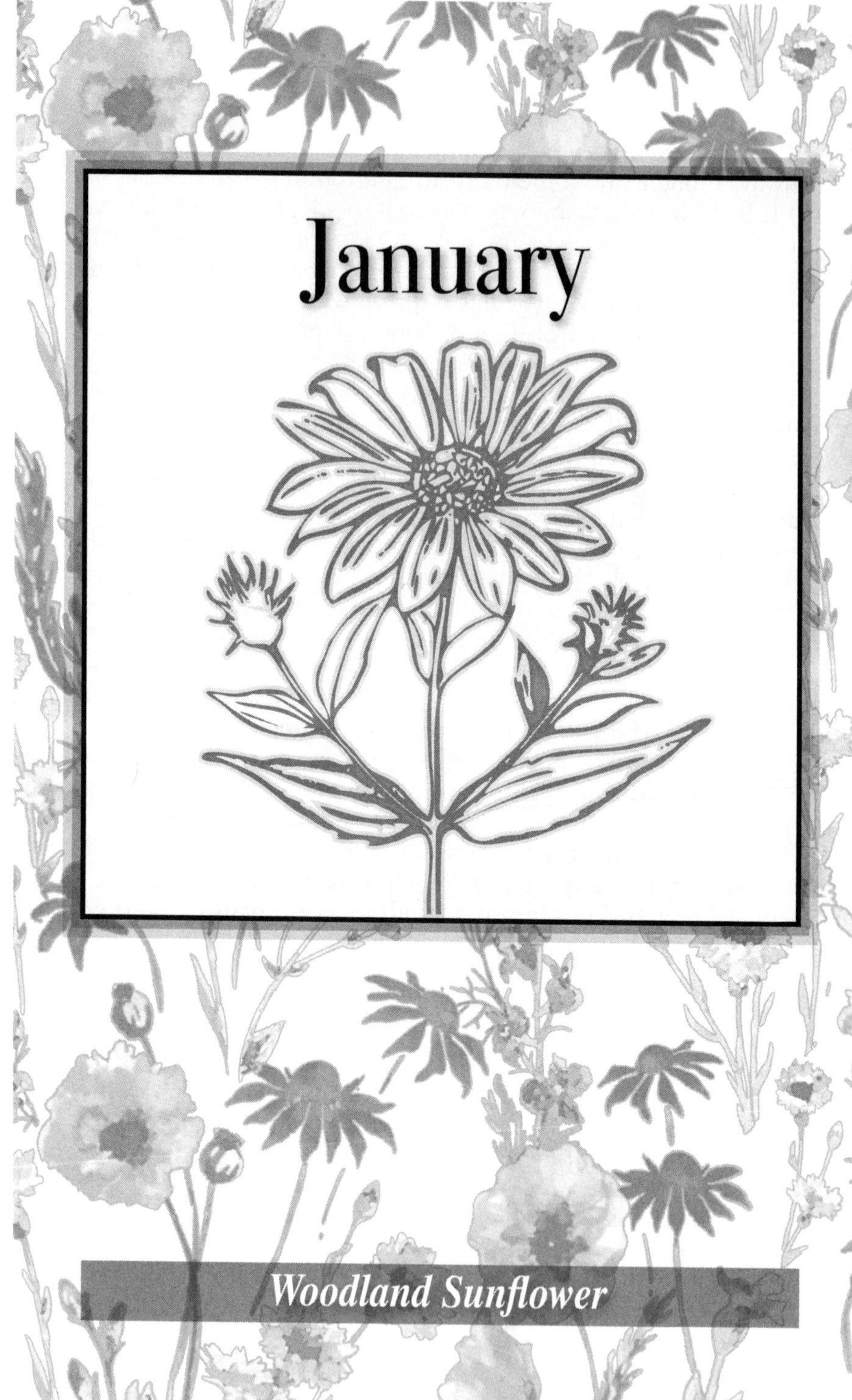

Woodland Sunflower

January 1

Taking Euroclydon into account

What a predicament to be in! Here they were in the middle of the sea, having seen neither sun nor stars for many days, much less land. Euroclydon had made sure of that! For days, this tempestuous, violent storm had come down upon them with all her fury and might. She had pounded and beat the ship mercilessly, thereby threatening to sink her and all her crew. Finally, the crew had nothing to lose, as they probably would never see land again anyway, so they began throwing the ship's cargo and tackle overboard. Just about all hopes of ever being saved were given up!

If they had only listened to the man of God, they would not have been in this predicament in the first place. Paul had admonished them not to sail. However, the centurion had believed the master and owner of the ship rather than believing Paul and had decided to sail in spite of what the man of God had said. After all, a soft south wind was blowing at the time, making Paul's advice appear groundless. Therefore, because of this deceptive appearance and because of the opinion of the majority, the decision to set sail had been agreed upon and carried out!

However, they all soon discovered that these two things are not always reliable. Neither circumstances nor the majority opinion took Euroclydon into account. Only God knew that Euroclydon was up ahead. Therefore, they should have listened to God through the man of God. Had they obeyed God, their lives would never have been in danger, and their ship would never have run aground and been torn apart. It would have been safe in port instead.

Friend, you are getting ready to embark on a brand new year, which will require many and varied decisions on your part. Often, a soft, south wind will be blowing, causing the circumstances and the opinions of others to appear favorable in a certain direction. However, in many cases, the Word of God will admonish you otherwise. Take it from the sailors on that ship in Paul's day…it always pays to listen to and heed the Word of God, because neither circumstances nor the majority opinion can take Euroclydon into account. God is the only One who knows where Euroclydon is. So, if you go ahead, in spite of the warnings from the Word, you will suddenly find yourself in a stormy tempest that you cannot handle. Your ship of life will be battered and tossed. You will not see sun or stars or land for a long time. And, you will eventually crash on the rocks somewhere. Your vessel will run aground and be torn apart.

Therefore, for your safety and protection, you would be very wise to begin this new year in the Word of God. Don't make your decisions based on circumstances, on feelings, or on the majority opinion. Instead, read and heed the Word of God. After all, Euroclydon is out there somewhere, and God is the only One who knows where she is!

ACTS 27:14 *"But not long after, there arose against it a tempestuous wind, called Euroclydon."*

January 2

It's worth leaving your windows open

He could have closed the windows! It would have been a whole lot safer under the circumstances. But, he wasn't really concerned in the least about the circumstances. Even though a decree had been signed by King Darius, forbidding anyone for thirty days to ask a petition of any god or man except the king, Daniel was unmoved. He knelt upon his knees three times a day, prayed, and gave thanks before his God, as he had always done previously.

With his windows open wide, Daniel's prayer was easily heard by those outside who had set this trap, knowing that nothing would stop this devoted, dedicated man from praying to his God. His strong love for the Lord moved him to such holy boldness, even though he knew full well that this action would result in being thrown to the lions. Nonetheless, Daniel had purposed in his heart long before this time that he would be steadfast, uncompromising, and faithful to his God. Without hesitation or remorse, this unwavering servant of God faced the den of starving lions.

Daniel knew not whether his God would intervene in his behalf. He knew his stand for God meant either deliverance by death into God's eternal kingdom or present deliverance from the lions. Either way, he would win! So, he triumphantly entered the pit! And every lion in that pit was suddenly stricken with heavenly lockjaw. Daniel passed the night unharmed and was removed from the pit the following morning. Because of Daniel's tenacious stand, King Darius signed another decree that all men tremble and fear before the God of Daniel. Everyone around saw the glory of God that day!

Had Daniel closed his windows, he also would have shut out God! Had he made that one little compromise at the beginning, no one would have seen the glory of God in such a powerful way! His stand affected a king and an entire nation!

Christian, like Daniel, leave your windows open. Be bold for Christ! Don't compromise! Take an unwavering, steadfast, unmovable stand for the Lord Jesus Christ! It may result in the lion's den, but there is a world at stake that needs to see the glory of God through some Daniels. If what you have isn't worth leaving your windows open for, then the world will think it's not worth having!

DANIEL 6:10 *"and his windows being open in his chamber.....he kneeled upon his knees three times a day, and prayed, and gave thanks before his God, as he did previously."*

January 3

It's midnight!

It was midnight! Without even a sliver of light anywhere around, Paul and Silas sat in the inner prison, shivering in the cold, black, damp darkness. Their feet had been put into stocks; therefore, they could not get up and walk around or even get comfortable. And besides that, they had been beaten before being thrown into prison. The blood that had poured from their wounds had become dried and crusted over, causing their clothing to adhere to the clotted blood. Their circumstances were anything but desirable.

Judging from the situation, Paul and Silas could have been moaning and groaning, complaining, fretting, worrying, and having a big old pity party. They could have been questioning God and even blaming Him. After all, this suffering was due to their stand for Him in the first place.

However, that is not what they were doing! Instead, they were singing praises to God and praying. They knew that all things work together for good to those who love God…so, they were acting on the truth, not on the circumstances. And, since God always inhabits the praises of His children, He showed up. When He did, His presence brought an earthquake, which shook the prison doors open and shook off all the chains with which the prisoners were bound.

The keeper of the prison, thinking that all the prisoners must surely have escaped, was planning on killing himself…..for anyone who allowed prisoners to escape would have been put to death anyway. However, Paul called up to him, telling him to do himself no harm…that all the prisoners were still intact. At this, the Philippian jailor sprang down into the inner cell and asked them what he needed to do to be saved. Right then and there, he received Christ as his Savior and Lord.

Friend, perhaps today, it's midnight in your life, too. Maybe, like Paul and Silas, there's nothing comfortable about your life right now. You feel that all is lost, that there is no way out of this inner prison of suffering you are in. You have been crying and mumbling, questioning God, and having a pity party. Well…..quit it right now! Start praying and singing praises to God! Perhaps there are some other prisoners nearby watching your life and listening to your talk. Perhaps there are bonds that need to be shaken loose. Perhaps there's a Philippian jailor around that needs the Lord. What happens from here on out depends upon what you do in your circumstances!

Remember, child of God…God inhabits the praises of His children. So, who cares if it's midnight? It's a good time for God to show up!

ACTS 16:25 *"And at midnight, Paul and Silas prayed and sang praises unto God; and the prisoners heard them."*

January 4

In word only

With your mouth watering, you jump into your car and head out for your friend's house. You wouldn't dare turn down an invitation like this, especially since apple pie is your very favorite dessert. It's not every day that a friend calls, asking you to come over for such an indescribable, scrumptious delicacy. As you walk through the door, your taste buds go into high gear, as your eyes quickly spot a covered pie dish sitting on the table. However, as your friend removes the lid, you receive quite an unexpected shock! Lying in the dish is a recipe for an apple pie. Oh, it's a apple pie all right…but it's "word only" and this "word only" apple pie doesn't do anything to satisfy your mouth-watering desire.

Arriving back home some time later with the recipe, you are still craving apple pie. So, you get out all the ingredients listed in the recipe and put them on your counter top. Now, you have the recipe and you have all the ingredients, but you still do not have a real apple pie. It's not enough to just have the recipe or even to have all the ingredients. You must mix all the ingredients together and apply power to them.....the power of a mixer and the power of an oven. Once the power is applied, a transformation takes place. The word and the ingredients now become a real apple pie. They are transformed from word into actuality.

This also applies to salvation. There are many today who have a word-only salvation. They have the recipe. Having been raised in church, they can talk the talk. They know several Scripture verses, even being able to quote some of the recipe from memory. They can carry you down the Roman's Road. But, in reality, they have a word-only salvation, having never genuinely experienced the real thing.

Then, there are others who know the recipe and have all the ingredients. They have said a sinner's prayer, squalling and crying alligator tears as they affirmed their belief in the Lord Jesus Christ. Yet, in actuality, they only have the ingredients without ever having allowed the transforming power to be applied. They have a word-only salvation and their spiritual taste buds have never been satisfied!

Are you truly saved? Have you allowed the hand of God to stir you and mold you? Have you allowed the fiery heat to be applied? Has there ever been a radical change in your life? Do not gamble with your eternity. A word-only salvation will not get you to heaven. You need more than the recipe. Make sure today that you have the Biblical recipe for salvation and the correct ingredients, and that you have allowed God's power to transform them into actuality.

I THESSALONIANS 1:5 *"For our gospel came not unto you in word only, but also in power..."*

January 5

Is there not a cause?

Standing on the mountain with a taunting, scornful attitude was Goliath of Gath, a mighty warrior, a champion of the Philistines. As he stood over nine feet tall, fully armed and equipped for battle, Goliath was a very commanding presence on the mountainside that day, striking fear in the hearts of the Israeli soldiers. Confidently defying the armies of Israel, he breathed out a challenge to them, asking for a real man to fight him. The outcome of the fight would be "winner take all. The army of the loser would become servants to the army of the victor.

Expecting Israel's best, most valiant, most experienced, warrior to face him, Goliath stood ready with undaunted faith in himself. However, much to Goliath's and to everyone's surprise, it was not a man, not an experienced warrior, but a youth that rose to this fearful occasion. The young boy stepped forward proclaiming, "*For who is this uncircumcised Philistine, that he should defy the armies of the living God?" I Samuel 17:26* Disgusted by the attitudes of all the other soldiers, David loudly asked, "*Is there not a cause?" I Samuel 17:29* He had recognized that God was being mocked and he wasn't the least bit intimidated. In fact, he didn't even see an invincible, frightening, well-trained, well-equipped giant. David saw instead the God of Israel who was bigger than Goliath ever even thought about being, the God whose cause he was ready, willing, and eager to defend. David, seeing by faith rather than sight and armed with the Lord rather than with human armor, marched right into the enemy's camp, used his trusty slingshot, and killed the Philistine giant with one shot!

Friend, perhaps there is a Goliath in your life today, too. He is quite impressive. He is fully equipped and armed and is breathing out threatenings to frighten and intimidate you. But, you just remember that it's your God he is mocking. He is really defying God, although he is doing it to you. If he can cause you to retreat, you will become his servant instead of God's.

"*Is there not a cause?*" Are you going to stand by and let him defy God by getting you discouraged? Are you going to cower down in fear and unbelief? Why don't you be a David today, seeing by faith rather than by sight? You just march right out against your giant, taking your shield of faith and your sword of the Spirit. You have nothing to fear, because all of heaven is behind you. Besides, your God tells you, "*You shall not need to fight in this battle...for the battle is not yours, but God's." II Chronicles 20:17, 15.*

Yes, there is a cause! There is a world out there that needs to see the living God. There's a world that will become Goliath's servants unless someone stands and calls his hand. Goliath is standing today on that mountain, taunting and scorning God's servants, just waiting for his challenge to be met! Won't you be the one to meet it? Friend, there IS a cause!

I SAMUEL 17:29 *"And David said, What have I now done? Is there not a cause?"*

January 6

I will stop you!

So, you call yourself a Christian! You say you love the Lord and you will do whatever He says. You say you belong to Him. You say He is in control of your life. Well, we'll see about that. I can stop you dead in your tracks!

Hey, I'm sly. I will not announce to you who I am before I come around. Pretending to be something else, I'll fool you. I'll mix up your emotions, because you always go on them anyway. I'll make you think that your problem is anxiety, worry, fear, discouragement, depression, etc. That will always keep you from recognizing me, the root of your problem; therefore, you'll never get any better, since you won't know what's really wrong. You'll live your life out under my deception. Oh, I am so good at my job that I surprise my own self. I just love it! You are so easy! Why, I can just put one small question, one little doubt in your mind, and you'll run with it. And pretty soon, I can even have you doubting the Word of God. That's really my whole aim anyway!

By the way, I have been around for a long time. I first showed up in the Garden of Eden and I've been around ever since. Did you know that I am a celebrity? I caused the fall of the entire human race. That's how powerful I am. And, I've also been responsible for other things down through the ages that are too numerous to count. I am responsible for the death of Lot's wife. I caused the children of Israel to wander in the wilderness for forty years. And, I am even responsible for stopping the Lord Jesus Christ once. I stopped Him in Jerusalem. He could do no mighty works there because of me.

Today, I am just serving you notice that I am after you, too. I love my work, because it hurts God. That's why I can't let you go forward. I must stop you, because you love Him, you want to serve Him, and you plan on being faithful to Him. I just cannot allow you to do that, and I am the only one who can stop you. I am coming after you. I will paralyze you. I will defeat you. I will entrap you before you even know what's happening. Ooo, I cannot wait for this! I love it!

Would you like to know who I am? Well, I have no fear of telling you. I can walk right up to you and even announce who I am and what I'm going to do… and you'll still hold out your hands anyway for me to put the handcuffs on. You haven't caught on to me in all these years…and you never will. Oh, by the way, my name is unbelief! I am after you. I will stop you! Just you wait and see!

HEBREWS 3:12 *"Take heed, brethren, lest there be in any of you an evil heart of unbelief."*

January 7

God showed up!

Have you ever noticed throughout the Bible what happened when God's children were in deep trouble or distress? Why, God showed up, that's what happened. When Daniel was thrown into the den of starving lions, God showed up! When Shadrach, Meshach, and Abednego were thrown into the fiery furnace, God showed up! When Paul and Silas were put into the Philippian jail, God showed up! When David went up against Goliath, God showed up! When Elijah stood on Mount Carmel against the prophets of Baal, God showed up!

These are only a few of the hundreds of examples in the Scriptures showing how God came through for His children in mighty ways. Taking a closer look at these, we can find several common denominators.

First, all these were servants who had made the Lord and His will the number one priority in their lives. They were not for sale. They could not be bribed or bought. They would not bend, compromise, let up, slow down, back off, or be deterred from obeying God. They had long before settled in their hearts Who their Master was and had decided to follow Him no matter the cost!

Second, these were all servants of great faith. They did not know what the outcome would be in each particular situation, but they knew their God was in control. They had determined that whatever God chose to do would be fine with them. They trusted Him completely, not to do what they wanted, but to do what He knew was best.

Third, these servants all faced impossible situations. Humanly, there was no way out. Yet, they did not look at the situation, get discouraged, and turn back. They looked at God instead and obeyed Him despite any feelings of fear or apprehension.

Today, you may be facing something in your life that is comparable to the situations these servants faced. You are in deep trouble and distress. So, what are you going to do? Why don't you follow the examples set before you in the Word of God? Plant your feet firmly. Make God's will the number one priority in your life. Trust God no matter what the situation looks like. Look, not at the impossibility, but at God. Submit your life to the Lord, step out in faith, cry out to Him in your distress, and leave the results up to Him. And guess what? God will show up when you do!

MARK 11:22 *"Have faith in God."*

January 8

A spiritual bubble bath

You step into the tub of hot water, filled with mounds of bubbles. Lying back in the tub, you let all your muscles go limp and completely relax. You just let go and let the warm, soapy suds do their thing. It feels so refreshing to your tired, worn, dirty, physical body.

Did you know that you can take a hot spiritual bubble bath also? It is very similar to a physical one. First, you must set aside time for your bubble bath. You cannot take a spiritual bubble bath amidst all the hustle and bustle of the world any more than you can take a physical one. So, you set aside a special time to get in the Word of God, as you are "*washed by the water of the Word.*" *Ephesians 5:26* Enjoy this special time....don't rush through it!

Second, get in your bubble bath alone. You don't take your family, your co-workers, or your neighbors with you when you take a bubble bath. Get alone with God without any interruptions, even if you have to get up in the wee hours of the morning to do so.

Third, take off everything you've covered yourself with when you get into your bubble bath. You need nothing interfering with the water doing its job. Remove all your pride, all your self-sufficiency, all your self-efforts, and all your excuses. Make yourself bare before God.

How about you today? Why don't you set aside some time for a spiritual bubble bath? Get in the Word of God, cease all activity, let your spiritual muscles go limp, and let the Lord clean you up. He will create in you a clean heart. He will renew a right spirit within you. You just get in His presence and soak in Him...and He will do the cleansing. And oh how invigorating and refreshing it will be to your tired, worn, dirty spirit!

Come on! Get in! The water's ready! Just let go and let God. You owe it to yourself to take a nice, long, enjoyable spiritual bubble bath!

PSALMS 51:10 *"Create in me a clean heart, O God, and renew a right spirit within me.."*

January 9

The biggest nation in the world

It's the biggest nation in the world. It has been in existence since the beginning of time. Being the most popular vacation spot on earth, it has had more visitors through the ages than any other nation has ever had. It is a very enticing nation to visit…but it's definitely not a good place to live. No one ever plans on settling here for life. Most just plan to make a quick trip, perhaps a day or a week at the most, and then return home. However, multitudes get caught here and never seem to escape!

It's difficult to leave this nation once you visit. The real estate agent here is the best agent of all times, offering deals that most cannot refuse. In fact, he offers his real estate for free. Yes…free! The deals are so cleverly offered and so ingeniously disguised that the buyer falls hook, line, and sinker, seeing only the immediate results rather than the long range ones.

The immediate results are somewhat gratifying. However, the long range ones are very, very costly. They often cost people their jobs, their homes, their relationships, their good standing, and even their families. But, there is something far worse than any of these. Settling in this nation could very easily and subtly cost people their eternity. This nation is called "procrasti-nation".

Procrastination has been one of the devil's main tactics since the creation of man. Most people do not plan on going to hell. They don't consciously think, "I am going to live like I want, ignoring God, and I'll just go on to hell when I die." On the contrary, most people plan on getting right with God sometime before their lives are over. They visit procrastination, planning only to stay for a short while. However, days soon turn into weeks, weeks turn into months, and months turn into years. And, finally time runs out, as they plunge from the land of procrastination into an eternal hell. With unquenchable flames engulfing them, they now know they should never have settled in the land of procrastination. The long-range results are tragic!

Friend, you are still alive. If you are dwelling in the land of procrastination, you'd better get out quickly. That lying real estate agent has sold you a piece of dangerous property, which will cost you your eternity if you continue to stay there. Do today what you know you should do! Get out of the nation of procrastination immediately and make things right with God! Don't put off any longer what you know to do about your soul! Behold, today is the day of salvation.....not procrastination!

II CORINTHIANS 6:2 *"Behold, now is the accepted time...now is the day of salvation.."*

January 10

Not now

As I gently pled with you to come
And at an altar bow,
You thought of all the time you had
And so you said, "Not now."

"Some day I will, when things are right.
Some day I'll make that vow.
But, I have to live in this ole' world,
And so I can't ... Not now."

You made a mess of things in life.
I tried to show you how.
But you said, "I'm not ready, Lord.
I will, but just not now."

I showed to you My nail-pierced hands,
The thorns upon My brow.
"These scars are all for you, My child."
You looked…but said, "Not now."

And finally, when your life was o'er,
You thought about that vow.
You called to Me, "I'm ready, Lord."
But I said to you, "Not now."

You lived your life just like you chose.
It's too late for you to bow.
Forever and ever and ever, you'll hear
Those tragic words, "Not now."

Did you know that you cannot get saved any time you want? It's a very foolish and dangerous thing to put God off! He said in His Word that His Spirit will not always strive with man. So, friend, if God is drawing you today, it's time to come….. He might ot ever call again. He's not obligated to give you another chance! Don't gamble with your eternity. If you tell God "Not now," then He may one day say the same to you!

HEBREWS 2:3 *"How shall we escape, if we neglect so great salvation..."*

January 11

What's your Delilah?

According to the Word of God, he was the strongest man who ever lived. He single-handedly defeated one thousand Philistines and slew a lion with his bare hands. Yet, Samson made one fatal mistake that robbed his strength and sent him to his death. He hung around Delilah!

Delilah had told Samson, "*Tell me...wherein thy great strength lieth, and where with thou mightest be bound to afflict thee." Judges 16:6* Her own words told him she was out to destroy him, yet he kept hanging around her. She knew exactly how to defeat him: persistence! She tried three times and failed. But "*she pressed him daily with her words, and urged him, so that his soul was vexed unto death." Judges 16:16* She kept pressing until he finally gave in!

However, Samson was defeated long before he actually gave in. He was defeated when he allowed her to coax him and press him to the point of losing his joy. *Nehemiah 8:10 says, "...for the joy of the Lord is your strength."* You see, once his joy was gone, his strength to stand went with it. He went down first in his inner self; then, he went down outwardly. His eyes were put out, he was bound, and he became a slave.

Perhaps there is a Delilah in your life today. She has come after you to destroy you and you know it. She is vexing you daily. She is persisting relentlessly. She is coaxing you and pressing you to the point of losing your joy. You are becoming depressed, angry, resentful, unappreciative, unforgiving, unkind, fearful, doubtful, and void of faith.

Obviously, you had better get away from Delilah as fast as you can. Once your joy is gone, your strength to stand will be gone too. Your spiritual eyes will be put out, keeping you from seeing things from God's perspective and preventing you from enjoying the Word of God, prayer, or the things of God any more. You will be bound and shackled by the enemy's ropes of defeat and discouragement. And finally, you will become a slave, a captive, a prisoner of the enemy of your soul. The only way out for you will be the same way as Samson's way out...death! He died physically...you will have to die to your flesh......to its desires, to its plans, and to its own ways. You will have to surrender completely to the Lord Jesus Christ in repentance.

Today, take a good look at your life. Perhaps there is a Delilah hanging around somewhere, something that is just bugging you to death. This Delilah is vexing you daily, thereby robbing you of your joy. You'd better get Delilah out of your life before she brings you down!

JUDGES 16:16 *"And it came to pass, when she pressed him daily with her words and urged him, so that his soul was vexed unto death..."*

January 12

An unusual bank

Every living, breathing soul on the face of the earth has me. Some have me longer than do others, but all have me. Every person in the world has the same amount of me during each day's span that everyone else has. No one, whether king or pauper, can get more of me in one day than anyone else. And, no one can buy me, work for me, or bargain for me. I'm not for sale. No one can live here on earth without me. However, how much of me you have is not nearly as important as what you do with me. What you do with me will affect you here on earth and will also affect your entire eternity. My name is time.

Time is like a bank. However, in this bank, you had nothing to do with the deposits. God deposited your entire allotment. It was determined even before you were born. You cannot make any more deposits. You do not know exactly how much you have in this bank or when it will run out. You are continually making withdrawals from your account until that final day when you will make your last withdrawal. Knowing all this, you should use your withdrawals wisely.

Every day of your life, you will withdraw exactly the same amount as you always have. It remains the same until death. Each day, you will withdraw 86,400 seconds. You will withdraw them whether you ask for them or not and you will use them in some manner. This bank gives to you no matter what you do with your withdrawals.

So, today, what are you going to do with your 86,400 seconds? How will you spend each of them? Once you spend them, you cannot take them back. You cannot store them up either. You spend each second as you get it. Since all this is true, doesn't it stand to reason that you should be very careful? Shouldn't you be investing each of these precious moments in eternal things? Would it not be dumb to invest these withdrawals in earthly things that will one day burn up?

Christian, take stock of your bank account. What are you investing in? After all, you only have one life. You have just one shot at it. So, why not make it really count? Take those 86,400 seconds each day and use them for the glory of God. You'll be eternally glad that you did!

PSALMS 89:47 *"Remember how short my time is..."*

January 13

Fuel of grumbling…or extinguisher of praise?

There's one thing about opposites…they cannot both be true at the same time. If something is up, it's not down. If it's out, it's not in. If it's new, it's not old. If it's fresh, it's not stale. If it's over, it's not under. Either something is one or the other, but not both simultaneously. Therefore, to combat and overcome one condition, you would use its opposite. Success is guaranteed that way!

Now, that seems simple enough, but we certainly haven't learned that principle very well in certain areas. For instance, when we get down and discouraged, we grumble, complain, and throw pity parties. We keep adding fuel to the fire, because grumbling does the same thing to the doldrums in our spiritual lives that adding gasoline does to a fire. It doesn't put it out, nor does it slow it down. Instead, it causes the fire to get bigger and more dangerous. It makes the fire spread. It even affects multitudes of others. The last thing you would want to do to combat fire would be to pour gasoline on it.

Well, friend, how come you grumble so much in your daily life? Why do you keep adding fuel to your doldrums? You'll never get rid of them that way. No wonder your Christian life is so ineffective. You need to learn about opposites. It's high time today to put up the fuel of grumbling and get out the extinguisher of praise. Grumbling keeps your mind on you and your problems…praise keeps your mind on God.

Our Father knows this. That's why He started and ended the last five of the Psalms (146-150) with the exact same phrase, "*Praise ye the Lord.*" He tells us how long to praise…"*while I live,*" "*while I have any being.*" He tells us why it's good and pleasant to praise Him. He tells us who is to praise Him, what to praise Him for, what to praise Him with, and what to praise Him upon. And, He ends it all, in the very last verse of the Psalms, with *"Let everything that hath breath praise the Lord. Praise ye the Lord."*

Do you have breath today? Well, start using it for something besides grumbling. Try the opposite. Both bitter water and sweet cannot come out of a fountain at the same time, so just fill your mouth with praise. Every time you open your mouth, think about what comes out…is it doldrum fuel or is it a doldrum extinguisher? You have both all the time…but it's up to you as to which one you will use!

PSALM 150:6 *"Let everything that hath breath praise the Lord. Praise ye the Lord."*

January 14

Excuses and weeds

We don't train them to do it. Somehow they are just born with it in them. I've never known a parent to sit down with a child and tell him, "Now, I'm going to teach you oday how to make excuses." Excuses are kind of like weeds.....they don't have to be planted, watered, or tended to in order to grow. Neither of them requires any effort, so we just allow them to grow unhindered, even though neither is profitable or desirable.

So, why have excuses? After all, isn't an excuse really just an attempt to hide something questionable? You've never seen anyone make an excuse for doing righteousness, have you? No child would ever come up to his parent and say, "Mom, I'm sorry I obeyed you and did right, but I have a good excuse for it." No excuse is ever needed for doing right. Excuses are used instead for doing wrong. Excuses are used to cover up something that we don't want exposed. Excuses are used to keep people from knowing the real truth of our actions.

Today would be a good day to examine your garden. Maybe there are some weeds growing there. Perhaps you've made excuses to God as to why you aren't faithful in church, why you don't spend time alone with Him like you should, why your prayer life is weak, why you're not a good witness, why you don't know any more about God's Word than you do, etc. Well, dig that weed up! What is the real reason you don't do those things?Is it because you just don't want to? Or perhaps you're just too lazy, too self-centered, or too undisciplined to do it? Or is it because other things are more important to you; therefore stealing the time you could be using for the Lord? What is the real reason? Just be honest. After all, God has already spotted that weed long ago. He knows it's just a weed...and He wants it pulled up.....now!!!

If there is anything in your life today that you are making an excuse for, then it's a weed. If it were right in God's sight, then there would be absolutely no need for an excuse any more than that child would need an excuse for obeying his parent. If you are living in accordance with God's will, pleasing Him, serving Him, and honoring Him, then you need no excuse for that! So, what does your garden look like today?

Mistress Mary, quite contrary,
How does your garden grow?With
obedience and faith and love Or
excuses all in a row?

ROMANS 1:20 *"...so that they are without excuse."*

January 15

As an ox to the slaughter

Everybody loves me, or at least they sure act like they do. I am probably loved and worshipped about as much as anyone or anything in the whole world. It just astounds me that people everywhere are so drawn to me, from babies all the way to great-grandmas. I have never seen anything like it. Why, they will sit facing me for hours on end, almost getting mad if someone interrupts them. I have their undivided attention.

I sit and watch their faces. They remind me of an ox being led to the slaughter. I laugh at them, at their ignorance of what I am doing to them. Poor things, they don't even realize what is going on. They will sit and allow me to pour out foul, profane language right in their living rooms and they will even laugh about it. Oh, they would deck someone else who came walking into their homes and poured out that garbage in their children's ears. But, they will let me do it.

They will sit and allow me to bring sexual acts right into their living rooms. Now, they wouldn't think of letting someone come into their homes and perform such sexual acts. They especially wouldn't allow their children to watch. But, they will let me do it.

They will sit and allow me to bring all sorts of perverted thinking, various derogatory ideas about the family, and multitudes of weird, perverted relationships into their homes. They will let me bring in rebellion against authority. They will even let me bring in violent, bloody, horrible torture and murder right there in front of their eyes. Oh, those unsuspecting creatures…they don't know that every single thing they see and hear will stay in their brains forever. Therefore, they continue allowing me to pour my garbage into their homes, as they all sit there comfortably eating and drinking.....just as an unknowing ox being led to the slaughter.

It amazes me to look in their faces. Why, I have them completely under my control. I can make them laugh, cry, feel sad, or feel hostile. I can make them want new things. I can mold their thinking and change their attitudes and opinions about things, thus allowing me to even shape the future of their families and their nation. In fact, I am really their god, because they devote more attention to me than they do to anything else.

Everybody loves me! So, they will keep on sitting before me for hours on end, letting me entertain them and soothe them and satisfy their flesh. And all the while, I will silently lead them as an ox to the slaughter. So, if you're smart, you'll not allow that to happen in your home. You'll decide to control me…or I'll control your family. And, by the way, in case you haven't guessed by now what I am…..I am a TV!

PROVERBS 7:22 *"He goeth after her straightway, as an ox goeth to the slaughter...*

January 16

Go find your Jonah

Like a toy, the ship was being tossed brutally about by the raging, tempestuous sea. It was in grave danger of being broken up. All the mariners, filled with fear, began casting some of the ship's cargo into the sea to lighten it. This, however, had no effect, because it had absolutely nothing to do with the real problem. The real problem had gone down into the sides of the ship and was fast asleep. His name was Jonah. He had rebelled against the Word of God, and had set off to do what he wanted rather than what God had told him to do.

This rebellion had brought on the storm. Rebellion always does that. Jonah told the mariners that the only solution would be to remove the problem.....throw him overboard! After trying all other methods they could think of unsuccessfully, they finally had no other option but to resort to Jonah's suggestion and throw him overboard. They did.....and, just as Jonah had predicted, the sea immediately ceased its raging!

Perhaps there is a sea raging in your life right now. Your world is tempestuous, tossing you brutally about, and you are beginning to wonder if you are going to make it through! Fear has overwhelmed you as you look at the endless waves and high winds! You have tried all you know to do to solve this problem; yet, nothing has had any effect at all. Why, you have even thrown some things overboard in your attempt to calm the storm.

If this is your present condition, now would be a good time to go down into the interior of your soul to see if the real problem is asleep somewhere. Perhaps there is something in your life that should not be there. Or maybe there was a time in your life that you rebelled against the Word of God in some particular area. Or it could be that God has been speaking to you about a certain matter, but you have been replacing it with something else, always avoiding the real issue.

Friend, the storm is not going to stop until you get rid of the real problem. You can substitute other things all you want, but they won't work. You can beg God all day long to remove the problem for you. But, He isn't! You are the one who must throw it overboard!

Today, go find your Jonah and get rid of him. He is there somewhere, hiding from God. He is not going to jump overboard on his own, so throw him off. Go ahead! It's not that hard. Just throw him overboard...and, when you do, your sea will immediately cease its raging!

JONAH 1:5 *"But Jonah was gone down into the sides of the ship; and he lay, and was fast asleep."*

January 17

Self-image or Jesus-image?

Speaking in the first person, the devil whispers in your ear, "I'm no good. I am a failure. I am not smart enough, or pretty enough, or outgoing enough. I have a poor self-image. So, I'm going to do everything I can to improve myself. I will have plastic surgery to improve my looks; I will start working out at a fitness center; I will get more education; I will take some courses on influencing people; I will go to some stress management seminars; I will do everything I can to be better equipped for life. Then, I'll feel better about myself. My self-image will be improved. I'll be worth more. "

Has the devil ever whispered any of his verbal trash in your ears? Well, if you're a Christian, you can jump with joy when he tries that on you. Just reply to him, "Oh, have you just now noticed that I'm no good? Hey, I've known that for a long time. Why do you think I need a Savior? If I were any good or if I could improve myself, I would not need Jesus! Hey, I don't need help, devil. I need Him! He came to inhabit me, to live through me, to be everything He is in me. He did not come to improve me.....He came to replace me. Ah, yes, devil, I'm no good! And I'm so glad I'm not!

By the way, devil, why would I want a self-image anyway? Why would I want something that I would have to work on constantly? Why would I want something that is always affected by what others think? Wouldn't it be dumb to want a self-image when I can have a Jesus-image? I realize that this old rotten, sinful flesh is no good, so I will put it to death. I will step aside and let the Lord of Glory take over. Hey, devil, thank you for reminding me that I'm no good. What a great opportunity to kneel at the cross again!"

Every time you are reminded of your failure or incapability, just let out a sigh of relief and admit it. That is a great time to yield to Jesus! It's an opportunity to run and crawl up in His lap, saying, "Lord, I can't, but You can! And I'm going to let You." Quit trying to improve your self-image; rather allow it to be replaced with a Jesus-image.

COLOSSIANS 1:27 *"Christ in you, the hope of glory..."*

January 18

She walked away

He watched her as she walked away. She didn't stay with the others. She always had this faraway look in her eyes. Oh, how he loved her! His heart broke as he watched her go to the far reaches of the field, gazing longingly at a nearby pasture. It hurt him so, because he had done everything for her. He had found her one day. She was a thin, undernourished little lamb, at the point of death. She had strayed away from her flock and had been left behind by an unconcerned shepherd. No one even bothered coming for her. She was so helpless. He had picked her up and tenderly nourished her back to health. With his whole heart, he loved her and longed for her affections. She was so special to him, so very special. He did everything he could to show her; yet, she had a yearning for other places. She just never seemed to care that he had done so much for her. She was restless and discontent, quite often straying away from the fold and even leading others with her.

Finally, he was forced to break her legs to keep her from straying again. However, very tenderly, he carried her on his shoulders the whole time her legs were healing. He was hoping she would grow to love him dearly after being so close to him for such a long time. But, now that her legs were well, it was time to put her down and let her do whatever she pleased. How he hoped she would cling to him, follow him, and love him! He had grown to love her so much during this time of closeness, during this time that she was always on his shoulders. His heart was filled with anticipation. After all, he had loved her so tenderly that surely she would never leave him again!

But, she walked away! As she had always done previously, she wanted to live as she pleased. Tears ran down his face as he watched her walk away. He knew she cared more about herself and her pleasure than she did about him. And, he knew she would find an opening again somewhere, some day, in the fence...and she'd be gone. She'd be gone, out from under his loving watch-care and protection and guidance. Oh, how he loved her!How his heart longed after her. How much better off she would be under his gentle care!

But.....she walked away!

Today, dear reader, is Jesus that shepherd and are YOU that lamb?

JOHN 10:27 *"My sheep hear My voice, and I know them, and they follow Me."*

January 19

A place called Wit's end

Dragging yourself to shore, you are completely exhausted. Your self-propelled boat, which you've always been in control of, has crash-landed on the shores of this foreign land. However, there are multitudes of other travelers who have run aground here just as you have. They, too, have gone as far as they can go. They have tried everything they know to try. They have done everything anyone could possibly do. Yet, just like you, they also have failed, landing here on the shores of this strange place called Wit's End.

As you stand on the shore looking around, you spot many good intentions that have been dashed on the rocks. You see multitudes of hopes, plans, and dreams lying in a big rubbish pile. You see a big open pit, filled with many aborted efforts to change things and people. This place, Wit's End, is an absolute wasteland. It is the back end of yourself. There's certainly no place left to go now.

But, wait! Right over there at the very end of this desolate place is something you haven't noticed before. It's an old rugged cross. You cannot see what's beyond it, but somehow you know that it's nothing even remotely similar to this wasteland. You get the feeling that this cross is not the end; rather, it's the beginning. Your heart is stirred as you begin realizing that you are standing on the brink of something wonderful. You suddenly become aware that you had to get to the back end of yourself, to Wit's End, before you could discover the front end of God. As long as you could do it yourself; as long as you could control your own life; as long as you could run things your way, you didn't need God. But, now since all that has failed and you have run aground on Wit's End, there's nothing else left to do.

Quietly, you kneel at that old rugged cross. You lay all your crumbled intentions, all your dashed hopes, and all your aborted efforts at the feet of Jesus. You give Him control of your life. You give up all rights to yourself, all plans of doing things your way, all your efforts of changing things, all your self-centered ways.....in other words, everything! You ask Him to take over your life. And suddenly, "*Old things are passed away; behold, all things are become new*," as you sail away from Wit's End into the Sonrise!

II CORINTHIANS 5:17 *"..old things are passed away; behold, all things are become new.."*

January 20

Oh, no!

One tragic day, while working on a high tower, a young man fell to his death. Normally, he fastened a safety belt around him, allowing him to use his hands more effectively. He could also lean back on the belt while he worked. But, as these precautions had become routine through the years, he began to take them forgranted. And, on this particular day, he did not fasten his safety belt.

As the young man began working, his mind became absorbed in his job. He methodically carried out his responsibilities, as he always had done before. However, he forgot about not having the safety belt on. Without thinking, he leaned back. At that split second, he realized what he had done. As he fell backwards, his last words were, "Oh, no!"

He had thought he was safe. He had put his trust in his own self that day. Little did he realize when he awoke that morning that it would be his last day on earth. He never dreamed that, in one split second, everything would change. Now, it was too late. He could not go back. His negligence cost him his life!

Today, millions of people are living just like this young man. Life has become routine. They have been safe for years, so today is just like any other day. They are trusting in themselves. It has worked so far, so they figure it will keep on working. Every day, they will go on just as they always have. They will ignore the pleas of their loved ones and friends to put on the eternal safety belt, which is Jesus Christ. They will shun the repeated warnings being sounded from pulpits.

But suddenly one day, without warning, they will lean back on their own security and it will be eternally too late. They will realize in that horrible moment that they never put on the eternal safety belt. They never accepted Jesus Christ as their Savior and Lord. They never committed their lives to Him. They were trusting in their own selves. Their negligence - not their sinful lives, not their awful thoughts, not their wasted time - their negligence to accept Jesus cost them their eternity.

Don't wait until it's too late! Today, put on your eternal safety belt! Commit your whole life to the Lord. Give Him total control of your mind, body, soul, and spirit. Once you have put on the eternal safety belt, you will never have to face that moment of horror and have to say, "Oh, no!"

PROVERBS 21:31 *"Safety is from the Lord."*

January 21

Others

Others! All around you, there are others! Everywhere you go, there are others! They are at work, in the stores, on the highways, in the malls, and in your neighborhood. You are in a sea of people no matter which direction you go. However, you can be in this sea, yet be focused totally inward and barely see or hear the countless others surrounding you.

Today, you may pass one who has lost all hope. Today, you may pass one who has been devastated and is in the throes of despair. Today, you may pass one who is so full of hurt and pain that he feels he cannot go on. What will you do if you pass one like this today? Will your eyes fail to see their pain, because of your own "I" sight? Will your ears fail to hear their cries, because they are clogged with your own problems? Is your life so "I" centered that you don't have time for the others around you?

What in the world do you think God left you here for anyway? For yourself? No.... you are here for others. God wants to live out Himself through you to others, so they will know He is God and be drawn to Him. He wants to speak to that hurting one today. He wants to love that one who is crushed and rejected. He wants to offer hope to that one who feels he can't go on. And, He wants to do it through you!

Will you yield to God today? Will you allow Him to do through you what He desires? Will you be open to the moving of God's Holy Spirit today as He guides you and speaks to your heart about the others all around you?

I see the tears behind your mask.
I hear the cries behind your laugh.
I see the pain behind your smile.
I feel your heart, oh fearful child.

I sure don't know just what to do
But I can be a friend to you.
I'll share your burdens and your tears,
Your heartaches, hurts, and all your fears.

So, take my hand! Don't go alone!
Together we'll go to the Father's throne.
He'll know exactly what to do.
For us, dear friend, He'll make all things new!

PHILIPPIANS 2:4 *"Look not every man on his own things, but every man also on the things of others."*

January 22

There's lots of activity, but no fire!

What is happening on Mount Carmel? This is the strangest sight I've ever seen! There are four-hundred and fifty men gathered around an altar with a bullock on it. They are crying aloud, calling on someone named Baal to hear them. Why, they are even cutting themselves with swords and lances until the blood gushes out upon them. They are leaping upon the altar. They are going through all this activity for nothing. Their god is not answering. He is not regarding them in the least. All their crying, cutting, begging, and leaping are not getting their god's attention. There's lots of activity, but no fire!

But, what's this? A lone figure is calling all the people to come near. He is around a water-soaked altar, calling on the Lord God to send fire. And, fire has fallen! This lone prophet, Elijah, has stepped right out of God's presence to face hundreds of people, all needing to know that God is the Lord! And they know, because the fire has fallen!

What is happening here? This is the strangest sight I've ever seen! There are hundreds of people gathered here in this building. It has a sign over the door, saying that it's a church. All these people are singing songs about someone they call Jesus. But, where is He? I do not see Him around anywhere. They keep calling on God, but He's not answering them. However, they don't seem to notice. They are all too busy to see that God isn't regarding them. They are involved in all their activities - trips, sports, showers, weddings, funerals, aerobics, gossip, classes, seminars, etc. There's lots of activity here, but no fire!

Oh, that a lone figure would rise up out of these masses of people and call on the Lord God! Why doesn't somebody rise up...somebody who isn't interested in all the endless activities, somebody who isn't fooled by all the empty cries to God with no results, somebody who so lives in God's presence that he can get in touch with the living God?

Today, we have a need! God has not changed. He is the same God now as He was in the days of Elijah. We need not ask, "Where is the Lord God of Elijah?" Rather, we should ask, "Where are the Elijahs of the Lord God?" Oh today that an Elijah might rise up to call down fire from heaven. There are millions needing to know that the Lord, He is God. How we need the fire! There's lots of activity, but no fire!

I KINGS 18:38,39 *"Then the fire fell...and when all the people saw it, they fell on their faces, and they said, The Lord, He is God; the Lord, He is God."*

January 23

Turn, oh backsliding America

Oh, America, I remember you when you were but a baby. How you loved Me then! You had come from many foreign lands, because you wanted the freedom to worship Me. You went through much peril, many heartbreaks, hardships, and wars just to worship Me. I was the love of your life. It stirs My heart to remember those early years. Oh, America, how you loved My Word then...and how you prayed! All your decisions, your Constitution, and your laws were based upon My Word and upon prayer.

Oh, America, what has happened to you? What iniquity have you found in Me, that you have gone far from Me and have walked after vanity? Why aren't you saying, "Where is the Lord, who brought us up out of bondage, who led us across the sea, and brought us into a plentiful country, to eat its fruit and its goodness?" But, when you entered, you defiled My land and made My heritage an abomination. The preachers are not even asking, "Where is the Lord?" And they that handle the law know Me not. The rulers transgress against Me; and the prophets prophesy by other gods and walk after things that do not profit.

Wherefore, I will yet plead with you and with your children. Has America changed her gods, which are yet no gods? Oh, but My children have changed their glory for that which does not profit. America, your own wickedness shall correct you and your backslidings shall reprove you; know, therefore, and see that it is an evil thing and bitter than you have forsaken the Lord, thy God, and that My fear is not in you. Your iniquity is marked before Me. You have forgotten Me days without number.

Return, oh backsliding America, and I will not cause My anger to fall upon you; for I am merciful. Only acknowledge your iniquity, that you have transgressed against the Lord, your God, and have scattered your ways to strangers and have not obeyed My voice. Turn, oh backsliding America!

This message to America is the message Jeremiah preached to Israel for forty years. They did not listen; therefore, they were taken into captivity. Is America any different? If not, what do you think will happen to us if we don't heed these warnings and return wholeheartedly to God?

JEREMIAH 3:12 *"Return, thou backsliding Israel, saith the Lord, and I will not cause Mine anger to fall upon you; for I am merciful...."*

January 24

Chained to these soldiers

Death lay at the door! King Herod wasn't playing games. He had already arrested James, the brother of John, and had him executed with a sword. Peter knew very well that his own arrest and imprisonment meant a similar fate. However, he wasn't overly worried about it. In fact, he was sound asleep between two soldiers. He wasn't about to lose a good night's sleep worrying over his future. Why, he knew his life was in God's hands, so he might as well go to sleep and let God handle things!

Suddenly, an angel of the Lord appeared and a light shone in the cell. The angel struck Peter on the side and woke him up. The chains fell off Peter's wrists. Following the instructions from the angel, Peter got up, wrapped his cloak around him, and followed the angel right out the prison doors. They went past the guards, through the iron gate, which opened by itself, and down one street. And then, when Peter was away from danger, the angel departed.

Coming to himself, Peter realized what had happened. It wasn't a vision after all. God had really delivered him! He started toward Mary's house where, unknown to Peter, many people had gathered and were praying for his release. How astonished they all were to find the very one they were praying for standing and knocking at the door! They discovered that day that God really does answer prayer!

We need to learn what those early Christians learned, because many of our brothers and sisters in Christ today are also in prisons. However, unlike Peter, these Christians are bound in prisons of their own habits, appetites, and desires. They are chained to these "soldiers," and cannot escape without help. They feel trapped, unable to break the chains, and have succumbed to defeat. They come to church, but alas, the church has practically no power to deliver them from the bondage they are in.

Church, it's time to quit pointing a finger and start bending a knee. Let's get together over at Mary's house for a prayer meeting! Let's pray...without ceasing...unto God...for the shackled! And we, too, can hear what Peter heard, *"Arise quickly. And his chains fell off from his hands..."* and God delivered him. *Acts 12:7*

PSALM 107:13,14 *"Then they cried unto the Lord.....He broke their bands in sunder."*

January 25

How much faith does it take?

Standing with much uncertainty on the banks of the river, you debate with yourself as to which course of action to take. In the middle of the lake, which appears to be frozen, is a one thousand dollar bill, which you desperately need in order to pay off some overdue bills. The only way to get this money, however, is to walk out on the lake and pick it up. But, you are not sure if the ice is frozen enough to hold you. So, you are faced with a choice…either walk off and leave the money or walk out and retrieve it!

In this situation, you must exercise faith to receive the reward. The amount of faith you have is not nearly as important as what your faith is in. You could have great faith, step out boldly, walk out on the lake, and fall through. Or, you could have a weak, shaky faith, step out cautiously, walk slowly, and make it to the money and back. In both cases, it was not how much faith you had, but the strength of the ice that mattered. As long as you stepped out, exercising whatever faith you had, even if it were no bigger than a grain of mustard seed, then the rest was left up to the ice!

Repeatedly in our Christian lives, God brings us to this same point. He holds out His abundant, blessed promises before us, but they always appear far away and out of reach. In fact, they look impossible to get. So, we are continually faced with the same choice over and over again. We can just walk off and leave the promises, or we can walk out and retrieve them. We can step out in faith, even though it's as small as a grain of mustard seed, disregarding all the feelings inside that are screaming out, "No," and claim those promises.

Today, God has made many promises to you. A promise is someone's word and is only as good as the promisor. Therefore, promises from the Word come from God…and that makes them only as good as God is…which is perfect! In fact, none of His promises have ever gone unanswered. He is Almighty God, faithful God, who stands behind all His promises. So, there is absolutely NO way for you to be disappointed. God cannot fail. God cannot lie.

So, friend, don't you think you can step out on His Word? The promise is there, but you can only have it by stepping out. Once you step out, the rest is up to God. Don't try to help Him fulfill it. Remember: it's not how much faith you have. It is taking the faith you do have and placing it in the One who always secures the promises He makes. The ice may break. It can fail. But, the God you serve never will!

MARK 11:22 *"And Jesus answering, saith unto them, have faith in God."*

January 26

Truth struggle

Apparently, you have the wrong information. You are struggling and fighting with every ounce of energy within you. It's as though you're trying to gain power and advantage over the enemy in this battle of life. Somehow you have the mistaken idea that this battle is a struggle for power. But, in actuality, it's a struggle for truth instead.

This earthly battle began in the Garden of Eden. Satan did not come in and overpower Eve. It wasn't a matter of who was stronger or more powerful. He just simply said, "*Yea, hath God said?" Genesis 3:1* The struggle was over truth. Would she believe God, or the devil?

As Goliath stood in defiance of the Israeli army for forty days, we again see a truth struggle. The Israeli army saw it as a power struggle, thinking no one was strong enough to defeat this nine-foot giant. But David, just a young man, saw it as a truth struggle. He went into the battle in the name of the Lord of Hosts, the God of the armies of Israel. He was not concerned with power. He just simply marched onto the battlefield saying, "The battle is God's," and truth prevailed. It always does!

The children of Israel wandered in the wilderness for forty years because they saw a power struggle. They saw walled cities and giants; therefore, they did not think they were strong enough to take the land. They failed to see that it was a truth struggle. God had said that the land was theirs. All they had to do was go in and take it. They did not believe the truth and they lost. That's the way it always is!

Christian, there's a struggle in your life right now. It is not a struggle for who is stronger or more powerful. You're not trying to beat the devil. He has already been beaten. Jesus did that on Calvary. Instead, it's a struggle for truth. The devil is lying to you, causing you to doubt God. He knows he is doomed if you get in the Word of God, believe it, and act upon it. Therefore, his tactics are, not to overpower you, but to keep you from the Word of God. Learn to recognize his tactic of casting doubt upon the Word, thereby causing you to retreat. Change your battle strategy. Just start reading, heeding, and obeying the truth. Remember: it's not a power struggle; it's a truth struggle.

JOHN 8:32 *"The truth shall make you free."*

January 27

The richest treasure you have

If you want to relay your thoughts to someone else, how would you do it? The other person cannot read your mind, so you must communicate your thoughts to them through some medium. That medium is words. Words are simply vehicles, carrying your thoughts to someone else. God Himself even used this same vehicle to carry His thoughts to us. We call this the Bible. The Bible is God's Word, His thoughts, His message to us.

God's Word is like a telescope. It brings into visibility things too high, too far off to see without aid. It brings heaven and hell into focus. We can see some things going on in these places that we could never see without God's magnificent telescope. In fact, we can see to the outer limits of the universe, the third heaven, through God's Word.

God's Word is like a microscope. It actually sees down into the human heart, bringing into focus things that could never be seen any other way. It even brings feelings, desires, and motives into visibility. It shows up the invisible realm all around us, which angels and demons inhabit, and allows us to see what's going on. It magnifies everything.

God's Word is like a time machine. It carries us all the way back to the beginning of time. It carries us all the way into the future, into eternity. You can get into this time machine and go forward or backward, depending on which direction you wish to go.

God's Word is like a prism. It takes the light of God and breaks it down for us to see. The light around us appears white, but a prism breaks it down for us to see that it is really composed of several colors. Likewise, we see God as one, which He is. However, His Word allows us to see that He is three.....Father, Son, and Holy Spirit.

Today, you have in your possession the very thoughts, desires, and heart of the King of kings and Lord of lords. He has chosen to communicate His thoughts with you through the vehicle of words, the Holy Bible. It's the richest treasure you have. Get it out and go on a treasure hunt. You'll strike it rich, as you search and probe this inexhaustible, unbelievable, heavenly gold mine!

PSALMS 119:161 *"My heart standeth in awe of Thy Word."*

January 28

Most unlikely to succeed

I'm just a nobody. I have a family and a few friends that love me, but other than that, I'm an unknown traveler here on planet earth. I have not achieved great success. I do not have lots of money. I am not one of the beautiful people. And, I am not outstanding in any talent or any endeavor I have ever undertaken. I'm just a plain, ordinary person.

However, as I look back through the corridors of time, I see something startling. I see a certain poor widow in the temple, putting two mites into the treasury. Jesus is praising her for her contribution, which totals one-fourth a cent. He's not applauding all the rich ones, the beautiful ones, or the talented ones. Instead, He is recognizing this "nobody," even recording her in His Holy Word forever. No one there, other than Jesus, even gives this poor "nobody" a second thought. They would all probably vote her "Most Unlikely to Succeed."

Looking further back through time, I see a demoniac from Gadara. He is wild, running naked and untamed, dwelling in the tombs. But, he sees Jesus and runs to worship him. Jesus is speaking to him. He even records his name in His Holy Word. He does not record anyone else from Gadara.....not the rich, not the prominent, and not the educated. Rather, He is recording this outcast of society; this Gadarene demoniac; this one who is now clothed, in his right mind, and seated at Jesus' feet; this one who would be voted, "Most Unlikely to Succeed."

Throughout the pages of God's Word, we find Him recognizing those whom the world would vote as "Most Unlikely to Succeed." His criteria, His standards of measurement are not at all like ours. So, you may not ever be recognized here on earth. You may not have lots of money or be one of the beautiful people. You may not ever be outstanding in any area. And, your name may never go down in the Hall of Fame. Oh, but you can be in God's Hall of Fame. The widow is, because she gave all she had to Jesus. The demoniac is, because he ran and worshiped Jesus. And you can be, too. Forget the world and its recognition, which is only for a moment. Just give your whole heart and life to the Lord Jesus Christ. You may be "Most Unlikely to Succeed" here on earth, but not in heaven!

EPHESIANS 3:8 *"Unto me, who am less than the least of all saints."*

January 29

The devil's bait

There he goes! He's reeling you in again! The devil threw out his bait and you swallowed it hook, line, and sinker. He has done it to you too many times to even count; yet you continue to strike as soon as the bait is cast before you. The sad thing is, though, that you never even realize you're being enticed by the devil. When will you ever learn?

It looks like you would notice the bait by now. It's always the same old bait, never a new color or a new shape. Of course, the devil does not need a new bait when this old one works so well. All he has to do is to cast one negative thought into the waves of your brain. You will bite that negative thought and run with it. Before long, you will have gathered up much negative scum from the bottom of the lake where your mind is running. Then, you'll drop that scum to others. Pretty soon, you are exhausted. The devil reels you in, depositing you in his bucket of depression and discouragement.

Maybe you've never realized that the devil is an excellent fisherman. That means you need to be a smarter fish. Quit biting his bait! Every time a negative, critical thought enters your mind, recognize it immediately as Satan's bait. Instead of biting it, turn the tables on the old crafty fisherman and begin thinking on and speaking of all the good, positive things. That'll teach him to fish for you!

In our world today, there is much complaining and very little appreciation. We are very quick to criticize, but very slow to thank. How many notes of appreciation have you written lately to just let others know how grateful you are for them? How many phone calls have you made to encourage someone, to praise them, to let them know you care? Think of what comes from your mouth! Is the majority of it helpful.....or critical? Remember: negativism is the devil's bait. Hey, the devil is fishing again. You're not going to bite, are you?

PHILIPPIANS 1:3 *"I thank my God upon every remembrance of you."*

January 30

Wouldn't it be foolish?

For some unknown reason, he has really taken a liking to you and wants to be your friend. You find that quite strange, especially knowing that he's a millionaire. He has offered to pay all your debts. He wants everything you owe transferred to his name. And, he wants you to put everything you buy in the future on his account. You will never have another debt, as all charges will be on his account from now on.

As time passes, you realize that he's not up to anything. He really, genuinely cares about you and just wants to be your friend. Knowing this, you would be foolish to turn down his generous offer. It would be dumb to struggle and worry over all your own debts when they could be transferred to someone who could easily take care of them.

Yes, it would be foolish to turn down such an offer. However, there is something infinitely more foolish than this.....the folly of paying your own sin debt. The Bible says, "*For the wages of sin is death.*" *Romans 6:23* There is a payment for sin. There is a debt that every living, breathing soul will have to pay. That payment, that debt, is eternal death or separation from God forever.

But, what if someone came along and paid that debt for you? Well, that is exactly what the Lord Jesus Christ did! When He died on the cross, he took upon Himself the sins of the whole world. He paid for every sin from the beginning of time to the last one that will ever be committed. He paid the debt for these sins Himself. The Bible says, "*Blotting out the handwriting of ordinances that was against us, which was contrary to us, and took it out of the way, nailing it to His cross.*" *Colossians 2:14* Just think: every sin you have ever committed or ever will commit can be transferred to Jesus. None of them can ever be charged to your account when they are placed on His account.

Wouldn't you be foolish to reject such an offer? How dumb and tragic it would be to say no to Jesus' offer. How foolish it would be to pay your own sin debt when He so willingly paid it for you. But, how do you make this offer a reality in your life? You come to Jesus just as you are. Confess to Him that you are a sinner. Realize that the wages of sin is death, but the gift of God is eternal life through Jesus Christ. Confess your need of Jesus as your Savior and Lord and ask Him to forgive and cleanse you from all sin. Ask Him to come into your heart. He will. Wouldn't it be foolish not to do this?

COLOSSIANS 2:14 "*Blotting out the handwriting of ordinances that was against us, which was contrary to us, and took it out of the way, nailing it to His cross.*"

January 31

Disconnected water faucet

Something is wrong with this water faucet. When I turn it on, no water comes out of it. It's a brand new faucet, so it's probably not defective. It looks good. It has been properly placed on the wall. It appears that everything is in perfect working order. Yet, when I turn it on, expecting water to come out of it, nothing happens!

Oh, I have found the problem. The water faucet was never connected to the pipes in the wall. It was never hooked up to the source. There's nothing to draw from. What looked good to the outward appearance wasn't all right inwardly, behind the walls. Appearances can be very deceiving.

Perhaps you are like that water faucet. You look good outwardly. You're a respectable person. You are a good, moral, upstanding member of your church and your community. You pay all your bills. You tithe faithfully. You have a stable, orderly life. And, you have really learned to talk the talk, giving the outward appearance of being a disciple of Christ. You know your Bible fairly well. In fact, you've even taught Sunday School and have been a leader in your church.

However, appearances can be very deceiving. In all actuality, you are not connected to the Source. You spend only a few minutes in the Word during the week, because of your hectic schedule. You pray briefly each night, but you do so very sleepily and half-heartedly, more or less out of duty. You never set aside time for extended prayer and fasting, seeking the mind and will of God. You are not heavily burdened for the lost. You never win a soul to Christ. You never reproduce yourself spiritually in the lives of others, having practically no impact on anyone's life. In reality, you just do not have a close, intimate, personal relationship with Jesus Christ and no deep, abiding peace within. It's all in your head, not in your heart. You are a disconnected water faucet. You look good outwardly, but you've never been connected to the Source of Living Water.

Well, friend, there is good news for you. The Master Plumber is on His way today. He's more than ready to connect you up to the Source of Living Water, Jesus Christ Himself...if you'll let Him!

I SAMUEL 16:7 *"for man looketh on the outward appearance, but the Lord looketh on the heart."*

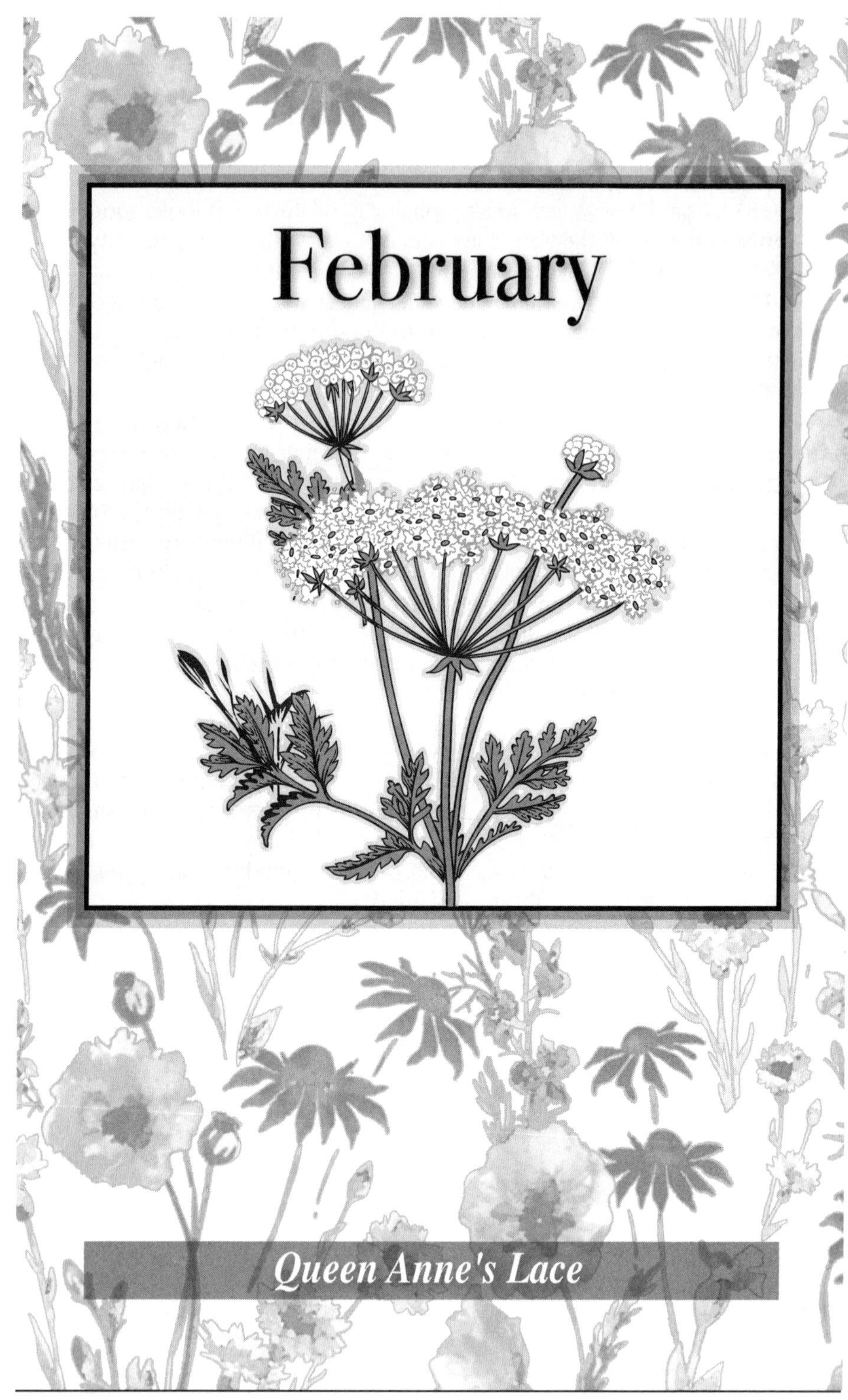
February
Queen Anne's Lace

February 1

What goes in is what comes out!

"Insanlari tek kez olmek, ardindan da yargiya gelmek bekliyor." (Ibraniler 9:27) You're probably wondering what in the world these words say. No matter how hard you try, you cannot figure them out. The reason you can't is because they have never been programmed into your mind. You cannot expect Turkish to come out if English is all that has been programmed in. What goes in is what comes out!

Now, if someone from Turkey were to read this, he would easily know that it says, "*It is appointed unto man once to die, but after this the judgment.*" *(Hebrews 9:27)* Turkish has been put into his mind; therefore, he thinks in Turkish terms. He has a Turkish mindset.

This concept of a certain mindset is very simple for us to grasp in relation to languages. However, we have not seemed to learn it in the spiritual realm. We sit in front of a TV set, watching secular programs for hours on end. Then we expect to make spiritual decisions and act in a spiritual manner. Instead of reading God's Word, we read the newspaper from cover to cover, read worldly magazines, and read secular books. Then we wonder why we have a difficult time with spiritual things. We fill ourselves full of worldliness, yet expect Godliness to come out. We want the mind of Christ; however, we fill our minds with the things of the world rather than with Him and with His Word. Remember: what goes in is what comes out!

The Bible tells us, "*Be not conformed to this world, but be ye transformed by the renewing of your mind.*" *Romans 12:2* In order to have a spiritual mindset, you must fill your mind with the Word of God. You are only going to have the mind of Christ and to act and think as Christ does by putting His mind and His thoughts into yours. The Bible is His mind and His thoughts. So, program your mind with His Word.

You can decide today whether you will have the mindset of the world or the mindset of Christ. It all depends upon what you program into it. You are your own computer programmer, so it is entirely your choice from here on out! But, remember: what goes in is what comes out!

ROMANS 12:2 *"be ye transformed by the renewing of your mind..."*

February 2

Bigger than any giant!

There were giants in the land, making the children of Israel look like mere grasshoppers. Why, there was absolutely no way they could conquer anything that big!Maybe God had not really looked over into that land. He certainly must not have been aware of the giants or He wouldn't have told them to go in and take over. Or perhaps God didn't really mean what He said. He had told them that the battle was His, not theirs; but He obviously hadn't removed the giants. If He had really intended on giving them the land, surely He would have already taken care of the giants before they got there.

So, the children of Israel turned back, but they made one very grave mistake in doing so. They were looking at the giants instead of at the God who was bigger than the giants. They were thinking of their natural abilities instead of God's supernatural ones. The bottom line was unbelief. They did not take God at His Word. If they had, they would have gone on in, disregarding the giants that were there.

Poor souls did not realize that God had left the giants in the land to force them to walk by faith. Had He removed the giants, they would have missed some very important lessons on faith! Faith is acting like God's Word is so, even before it's so, in order that it may be so. Faith is human response to divine revelation. Faith is standing up to the giants, knowing that they will fall before your God, because God has already promised that the battle is His. Faith acts upon God's Word when everything else tells you otherwise.

Today, child of God, there is a giant in your life. He's keeping you out of the promised land, the abundant Christian life. God has assured you of victory, but you don't really believe Him, so you keep wandering around in the wilderness, filled with doubts and fears and frustration. You have wanted God to remove the giant for you so you could just walk right on into the promised land. But, dear one, God is not going to remove that giant! He has left that big old obstacle there to force you to walk by faith. He wants you to quit looking at the giant, but rather look at the God who is greater than any giant!

Today, why don't you get up and do what God has told you to do? He has already promised victory! So, walk right up to that threatening giant, look him in the face, and tell him that you **can** and you **will** go in! God says so! And He's greater than any giant!

NUMBERS 13:33 *"And there we saw the giants...and we were in our own sight as grasshoppers."*

February 3

A cage of unforgiveness

He controls your life to some extent. You don't necessarily like him controlling your life, but then you're the one who put him in the cage. That cage puts certain controls upon him and upon you. You must feed him or the bird will starve to death. You must give him water or he will die of thirst. You must clean the cage and its surroundings or you will have an unsightly mess on your hands. As long as you keep that bird in a cage, he will never be free and neither will you. To be free yourself, you must set him free!

Perhaps this situation describes you perfectly.....not with a bird, but with another person. Maybe there is someone in your life whom you have put into a cage of unforgiveness. If so, then that person controls your life to some extent. The last thing in the world you probably want is that person controlling your life, but then you are the one who put him in the cage. That cage of unforgiveness puts certain controls upon him and upon you. You watch everything he does, trying to catch him in something to further justify your accusations. You listen to everything he says, picking up added fuel for the mental fire that burns continuously within you. You have a cerebral VCR that plays his wrongs against you day and night like a broken record. And you are constantly attempting to change this caged one. You'd like to force him to see things your way. You'd like to make him sorry for his words and actions against you. Therefore, this one you have in a cage of unforgiveness basically controls much of your thoughts, your mindset, your attitude, your emotions, and your time.

Wouldn't you like to be free from this mental torture? Well, to be free yourself, you must first set the captive one free. Picture the one whom you've never forgiven as being in a cage. Now, open the door and let him out. That means you totally forgive him of everything and anything he has ever done to you. That means he is clear of all responsibility for past actions. That means you are letting loose all those deeds, all those words, all those things for which you have held him accountable. And in the future, you will have absolutely no expectations of him. You are giving those to God!

Set him free! Let him go! Once you do, you will find that you are finally free yourself. Then, throw that cage of unforgiveness away. You will never need it again!

LUKE 6:37 *"forgive, and you shall be forgiven."*

February 4

Euclidean or non-Euclidean

San Francisco and Tokyo are 5,225 miles apart. San Francisco and Tokyo are 4,853 miles apart. Wait a minute! Both of these statements cannot be true. This is a contradiction! However, in spite of your opinion, both these statements are equally true. It all depends upon which geometric system of measurement you are using. In Euclidean geometry, the shortest distance between two points is a straight line. Using this system of measurement, the straight line would run through the earth, making the distance from San Francisco to Tokyo 4,853 miles. In non-Euclidian geometry, the shortest distance between two points may be an arc. Using this system of measurement, the distance would be 5,225 miles. In either case, the distance didn't change. Our geometric perspective changed instead. What appeared to be a contradiction was actually just two different perspectives!

When someone tells you there are contradictions in the Word of God, they are only seeing one side of it. They are trying to figure out the Bible using only the human ephemeral perspective, instead of also seeing it from God's eternal perspective. They may see Euclidean geometry when God also uses non-Euclidean geometry.

We humans are finite creatures. We operate in this world according to four dimensions: time, space, matter, and energy. However, physicists tell us that there are at least eleven dimensions in all. God operates in all of them and beyond all of them. He records them in His Holy Word, as the Bible speaks of such things as resurrection from the dead, incarnation, supernatural healings, walking on water, etc. We are unfamiliar with these things, because they are outside the dimensions we live and operate in. Therefore, we finite creatures try to figure out a book written by an infinite God. We cannot always figure it out.....we must faith it out. By faith, we can get beyond these four dimensions in which we dwell, get into a holy God's presence, and get His perspective on everything. Since He understands it all, then we need to find out everything from Him. Then, there will be no contradictions! We can then see Euclidean and non-Euclidean and know how they are both equally true!

PHILIPPIANS 2:5 *"Let this mind be in you, which was also in Christ Jesus."*

February 5

When.....then!

When all these troubles die down.....then I can really serve the Lord!

When I get these bills paid.....then I can do what God wants me to do!

When my husband gets saved.....then I can be free to obey the Lord!

When my physical body gets better.....then it will be possible to do things for God!

When my children get older.....then I'll have the time to follow Jesus!

When God revives my heart and sets me on fire.....then I can fervently serve Him!

When my church is what it's supposed to be.....then I can be a better servant!

When God shows me what to do.....then I'll be able to walk with Him!

Perhaps you've made some of these statements before, or at least you've thought them. Maybe one of these is a reason why you are not presently doing what God wants you to do. If you are a Christian and you're not actively and passionately serving the Lord, you have a reason. You probably have a when.....then!

It is time you learned a little secret. If you are using any of these as an excuse for not serving the Lord like you should, then you will never serve Him! There will always be a when.....then in your life! The devil will make sure of that!

Today God has a when.....then for you. He says, "When you believe Me and follow Me.....then I will be free to move mountains for you." He wants you to drop all your when.....thens and just follow Him! You will find that you have been waiting on some thing in the future, while all the time God has been waiting on you! When you.....then God!

ACTS 24:25 *"Go thy way for this time: when I have a convenient season, I will call for thee."*

February 6

Will you wholly follow the Lord?

As the twelve of us returned from searching out the land, I could hardly wait to share what I saw there! Flowing with milk and honey, it was a beautiful land that our God had promised us. I was ready to go on in and take it. However, ten of my colleagues were not in agreement with me. They were afraid, as they had been intimidated by the walled cities and the giants in the land.

As the people listened to this report of the impossibilities, they were persuaded that we were unable to conquer the land. I wanted to shake them and say, "But what about God? You just saw him part the Red Sea, didn't you? And yet you don't believe He can handle these walls and these giants and give us this land He promised us by His Word!"

Despite the discouragement, the doubts, and the fears around me, I believed God anyway. I determined in my heart to wholly follow the Lord. I believed that, what God had promised, He would provide! I held on to that promise for forty years, as we wandered in the barren wilderness due to the unbelief of the people. I could not afford unbelief, because my children and grandchildren were at stake. Their inheritance depended upon my belief in and obedience to God.

Now, I am so glad I wholly followed the Lord. It paid off! All those who did not believe Him died in the wilderness. However, He brought me into the land after all these years and has given me the mountain I chose so long ago. Now, I have an inheritance for future generations, because I wholly followed the Lord.

Christian, you also can be a Caleb. Don't faint! Don't give up! Just believe God in spite of the doubts, in spite of the discouragement, in spite of the fears. Listen to Him instead of to people, most of whom will never wholly follow the Lord and will never enter the land of Canaan. If you will wholly follow the Lord, He will give you your mountain one day. The future of your children and grandchildren hinges upon your belief in and obedience to God. Will you wholly follow the Lord?

JOSHUA 14:8 *"But I wholly followed the Lord, my God."*

February 7

Great white throne

Surely this was a nightmare! Directly in front of me was a great white throne, on which sat One from whose face the earth and heaven fled away. All around me were millions of people who were as shocked as I was! No one was talking. No one was smiling. Everyone looked entirely sober, as all seemed to know that this was Judgment Day!

As we all gazed on, the sea gave up the dead that were in it. All the souls that had perished at sea without Christ were called from their watery graves to stand before the Holy One. Hell also delivered up its dead...all those who had been held in that fiery jail, awaiting their trial and sentence before the Judge of the universe.

One by one each person stood before the Holy One seated on that Great White Throne. A big book, called the Lamb's Book of Life, was opened. The Holy One showed them that their names had never been recorded in this book! They were found guilty.....guilty of rejecting Jesus Christ, the Lamb of God. They were sentenced to imprisonment for eternity in the Lake of Fire!

Finally, it was my turn! As I stood before Almighty God, fear gripped my heart. Suddenly, everything became crystal clear. I had broken the laws of God. I was guilty, as charged. God had tried many times while I was on earth to intervene in my life. He had pricked my heart on several occasions, sending a message through others that Jesus Christ had made payment for my sins. He had let me know that, although I was guilty, He would take my guilt upon Himself and give me His righteousness instead. I had refused His gracious offer more than once.

So, here I stood face to face with God! Judgment was passed.....guilty! My sentence was given.....the Lake of Fire! The length of my imprisonment was set..... eternity! My fate was sealed forever. My nightmare was only beginning!

Friend, you are still alive today, because you are reading this. You still have a chance! Please accept Jesus Christ as your Lord and Savior. He's pleading with you through these words of warning. If you don't repent, then this story will one day be yours.

REVELATION 20:11 *"And I saw a great white throne..."*

February 8

He road to Bochim

Of all the places on earth to be, the children of Israel certainly didn't want to be here. They had never planned this. Filled with sorrow and remorse, they wept bitterly before the Lord. Appropriately, they decided to name the place "Bochim," which meant "weepers."

These sorrowful souls did not realize that the road to Bochim had started long before this day. God had given them definite instructions about the land of Canaan before they had ever entered it. He had even told them what to do with all the inhabitants of the land. "*Thou shalt not bow down to their gods, nor serve them, nor do after their works; but thou shalt utterly overthrow them, and quite break down their images. They shall not dwell in the land, lest they make thee sin against Me; for if thou serve their gods, it will surely be a snare unto thee." Exodus 23: 24, 33*

However, instead of following these instructions fully, the children of Israel only partially obeyed. They only drove out part of the inhabitants of the land. They figured there would be no harm in allowing a few Canaanites, a few Perizzites, a few Amorites, etc. to dwell among them. Surely, God would not be too upset if they failed to drive out every single one of the inhabitants. He would probably overlook this, since they had accomplished part of what He had told them.

But, the children of Israel were dead wrong! As a result, here they were at Bochim, a place of weeping. Because of their failure to do all that God had said, they were delivered into the hands of spoilers, sold to their enemies, and greatly distressed! Their children intermarried with these foreigners…and were lost to the strange gods that these foreigners served. The Israelites lost their children!

Oh what a price to pay for partial obedience! Christian, are you willing to pay that same price? You will if you don't do all that God tells you to do! You had better drive out all the sin in your life. Do not compromise in any form, for your children, your freedom, your mental wholeness, etc. are all at stake. Partial obedience is the road to Bochim.....and you don't want to go there!

JUDGES 2:5 *"And they called the name of that place Bochim..."*

February 9

Tomorrow's supply

As you awaken, you are strangely aware that something is different. Rubbing your eyes and sitting up, you get the greatest shock you have ever received in your life! Your house, which was beautiful when you went to bed the night before, has now become a rundown shack. There are holes in the floors and walls, the furniture is broken, the windows are cracked, and all the doors are hanging off their hinges. The bed you have been sleeping on is composed of several rough boards placed side by side. There is no mattress, no covers, and no pillows.

Hoping that this is just a bad dream, you make your way into the kitchen for a cup of wake-up coffee! However, the coffee pot is broken. Opening the refrigerator for something else to drink, you find it completely empty. Looking in the cabinets, you find them as bare as Old Mother Hubbard's. In exasperation, you decide to get a quick shower and go to the office, hoping to somehow sort all this out. But, there's no soap in the shower, no water in the faucet, and no clothes in your closet. What in the world is going on?

As you stand in utter despair, a bright light suddenly shines into the room. An angel appears, bringing quite a startling explanation of your circumstances. He tells you that the Lord has decided to switch things around a bit. Instead of supplying all your needs and most of your wants freely, He has decided to supply them in direct proportion to your thankfulness each day. So, your supply today is a result of your thankfulness yesterday.

The angel disappears, leaving you to your own thoughts. Summing up your life, you realize you are a chronic grumbler and complainer. What you see around you really is in direct proportion to how appreciative you have been to the Lord for His goodness!

What if this story came true in your life? If tomorrow's supply depended upon today's thanksgiving, how much would you have tomorrow? Why don't you start living each day practicing this principle? God certainly won't mind.....and others won't either!

EPHESIANS 5:20 *"Giving thanks always for all things unto God and the Father..."*

February 10

Right in his own eyes

"Well, I may smoke, but at least I don't drink."

"Well, I may drink a little, but at least I don't get drunk."

"Well, I may get drunk occasionally, but at least I don't do drugs."

"Well, I may smoke a little pot sometimes, but at least I don't do hard drugs."

"Well, I may do drugs, but at least I don't rob or harm others."

"Well, I may rob someone to get money, but at least I'm not a murderer."

"Well, I may murder an adult, but at least I don't molest children."

These statements are all symptoms of the "right in his own eyes" syndrome. This condition started when man was created and is still prevalent today. We rationalize and justify our actions. We work out a lifestyle that is comfortable to us, like a pair of shoes that we have broken in. We determine the level on which we want to live and we feel justified as long as we don't go beyond this level. We live what is right in our own eyes.

If we ever stood in the presence of Almighty God, we would immediately be cured of our "right in his own eyes" syndrome. Isaiah was a mighty prophet of God, who was living closer to the Lord than most are nowadays. Yet, when Isaiah had a vision of the Lord high and lifted up upon His throne, he cried, "W*oe is me, for I am a man of unclean lips and I dwell in the midst of a people of unclean lips, for mine eyes have seen the King, the Lord of hosts." Isaiah 6:5* When he found himself in the presence of such awesome holiness, Isaiah's own righteous lifestyle melted. He then saw his utter sinfulness. When he saw God, then he saw his own sin!

What about you today? Have you been rationalizing and justifying your lifestyle?Have you been afflicted with the "right in his own eyes" syndrome? You need to be cured today of this malady. Come to the cross and spend some time in the presence of the Lord. Let Him put that hot coal from His altar upon you and purge away all the sin. You'll no longer want to do what is right in your own eyes, but you'll want to live, not by bread alone, but by every word that is found in God's precious, holy Word!

JUDGES 21:25 *"Every man did that which was right in his own eyes."*

February 11

Not a caterpillar anymore

He was once a caterpillar, grubbing around in the dirt, having no power to lift himself out of the conditions around him. His existence was limited to the endless mounds of earth, leaves, sticks, and weeds encompassing his life. His circumstances controlled his life!

But, now he is a butterfly! He has been gloriously transformed. He is a new creature, no longer limited or held to the conditions around him. He has a new power to ascend, to soar above the circumstances that he once crawled around in. He is free from this old world. He doesn't have to live like a caterpillar anymore. Old things have passed away and all things have become new.

Have you ever grasped this concept spiritually? You were once a condemned sinner. You grubbed around in the world, having no power to lift yourself out of the circumstances surrounding you. You were bound to them, held by invisible cords of bondage that you could not break.

But one glorious day, you came face to face with the Lord Jesus Christ. As you became aware of your sinful condition, you turned to Him in repentance, and He saved you! At the same time, He marvelously transformed you into a new creation, from a spiritual caterpillar into a spiritual butterfly.

Now, you are no longer limited to the conditions around you. You are free from this old world of sin. You have the power to live a different life, the power to ascend above your former lifestyle. According to God's Holy Word, you are now "*seated in heavenly places in Christ Jesus.*"

So, why are you living such a defeated, helpless, dreary life? Wake up! You have been transformed! Old things have passed away. All things have become new. You're not a caterpillar anymore. You're a spiritual butterfly.... so get up out of the mulligrubs and fly!

II CORINTHIANS 5:17 *"Therefore, if any man be in Christ, he is a new creation; old things are passed away; Behold, all things are become new.."*

February 12

Life is great when you die!

Oh, woe is me! I am nothing but a seed. Just look at me.....one little old bitty seed encased in this hard shell. I am good for nothing. I cannot help anyone, change anyone, or be a blessing to anyone. Nothing I do makes any difference. Really, I'm quite worthless like this. Surely, there must be more to life than this!

Oh, wait a minute. What's going on? Where are you taking me? Oh, no! You're digging a hole in the ground. You're not planning to put me in that hole, are you? Glub... sputter...ach! Dirt! There's dirt all around me. I cannot see. It's dark. Oh, man, I have hit rock bottom. This is the end of the line.

Ah-h-h-h! I feel cool, refreshing water. It feels so good. And, something is happening inside me. Something is moving. I feel life within, pushing to get out. Now that I'm buried, this life inside me is trying to break forth through this old hard casing.

This is really unbelievable! I'm not just one little old bitty seed any more. The life inside me has burst forth, pushed up through the soil, and erupted into the light. I am now a bushy, flowering plant, absolutely beautiful to behold. But, the best part is that there is fruit hanging all over me. I can provide nourishment to so many people. I can also now furnish hundreds of seeds that can each grow new plants. Life is great when you die!

Christian, do you ever wonder if this is all there is to life? Are you feeling quite worthless and defeated? Well, like that seed, you are not much good to anyone in that shape. You need to be buried. You need to die to your flesh, your desires, and your plans. Bury everything of self down deep in the soil of forgetfulness. Allow the water of His Word to soften that hard outer shell. Then, the life of Christ will burst through, bringing forth a beautiful new plant filled with fruit. Your one little bitty seed will become a blessing to others. Life is great when you die!

Today, Christian, you have a choice. You can hold onto your life and live it just the way you want. Or, you can die to your flesh and allow God to live through you. You have a choice.....to die or not to die. What will your decision be?

I CORINTHIANS 15:36 *"That which thou sowest is not made alive, except it die.*

February 13

One little Christian

10 little Christians
All feeling fine.
One got a stomach-ache.
And then there were 9.

9 little Christians,
None filled with hate.
But, one got mad.
And then there were 8.

8 little Christians,
Talking about heaven.
One loved the world.
And then there were 7.

7 little Christians, Trimming
their wicks.
One got low on oil.
And then there were 6.

6 little Christians,
None liked to strive.
But, one began complaining.
And then there were 5.

5 little Christians,
Helping others through the Door.
But, one got tired.
And then there were 4.

4 little Christians,
All on bended knee.
One went to sleep.
And then there were 3.

3 little Christians,
None feeling blue.
But, one got depressed.
And then there were 2.

2 little Christians,
Standing by the gun.
One got afraid.
And then there was 1.

1 little Christian,
Standing all alone.
Standing firm for Jesus
Till God called him home!

Christian, be careful. There are many falling away today for various reasons: sickness, anger, love of the world, failure to stay filled with the Holy Spirit, complaining, burn out, failure to pray, depression, and fear. But, you can be that one little Christian who stands till Jesus comes!

LUKE 8:13 *"who for a while believe, and in time of testing fall away."*

February 14

Better use the manual

How would you like the pilot of an airplane, on which you were a passenger, to fly the big bird by his feelings? "I feel like we're going in the right direction." "I feel like we're at the proper height now to level off." "I feel like it's time to lower the landing gear." "I feel like the runway is there, even though it's so foggy I cannot see it." Certainly no one in his right mind would ever even consider getting on a plane if the pilot flew by his feelings. Fortunately, however, pilots don't fly by feelings…..they fly by facts. They spend countless hours studying manuals and learning everything about airplanes. They are trained thoroughly in all aspects of the plane they will be flying. They know every instrument and every gauge inside and out. Then, when they get in the cockpit, they rely completely on the facts, the data, the gauges, the instruments, etc. Their feelings don't count when it comes to flying a plane.

Friend, you would not dare get on a plane flown by feelings; yet, you are doing something far more dangerous than this. You are running your spiritual life by your feelings. "I feel like I'm going in the right direction." "I don't feel like praying or reading my Bible. The Lord knows that I really just don't have much time any more to spend with Him." "I feel like I can lower my standards; after all, everybody else is doing it and they're getting by just fine." "I feel like the Lord will bless me. He understands how hard it is nowadays to live a Christian life, and He will forgive and overlook the sin I am involved in."

Dear one, you are inevitably headed for a crash! You cannot run your life by feelings any more than a pilot could fly a plane by them. It will not work! You had better get out the manual, God's Holy Word, and spend much time in it learning how to fly your plane of life. It will tell you everything you need to know. It has training for every aspect of life. It will help you avert many a crisis and will guide you safely to those eternal shores. It never makes a mistake. It cannot lie. It is the truth, the facts.

So, Christian pilot, how do you want to fly? Had you rather trust your feelings…. or trust the facts of God's Holy Word? Which do you think is the most reliable? You are in the cockpit of life. Your hands are on the controls. It's completely left up to you as to how your life will be run! Will it be your feelings or the manual of God's Word from now on?

PSALMS 110:105 *"Thy Word is a lamp unto my feet, and a light unto my path."*

February 15

The faith killer

The faith killer has struck! It has nearly wiped out what little faith you had, leaving you defeated and discouraged. You are on the verge of giving up. That thing in your life for which you have prayed so long has not happened. In fact, it's further away now than when you started praying. It is impossible!

There was one in God's Word who experienced this same thing. Her name was Sarai. God had promised a seed, through which all nations would be blessed. Sarai had been filled with excitement at such a great promise. However, the faith killer struck, that one who stalks and kills faith. His name is time. When time passed and the promise had not been fulfilled, Sarai's faith waned. As her body aged, the promise became continually more impossible. Finally, she gave up all hopes of seeing the promise fulfilled.

Instead of patiently waiting in faith for God to fulfill the promise in His own way and in His own time, Sarai took matters into her own hands. She used carnal tactics, resulting in a grand mess. Finally, at age ninety, when the promise was humanly impossible, God stepped in! That's when God always comes through!

Friend, you are standing on the banks of impossibility today. The faith killer, time, has almost done you in. He has shot you through and through with arrows of unbelief. You have a decision to make. You can just quit praying and believing God, since He hasn't done anything yet about this situation. Or, you can take matters into your own hands, trying to figure out ways God can help you. Or, you can set your face like a flint, letting nothing deter you from praying and holding on until God gives the victory. You can rest in the fact that man's impossibility is always God's opportunity.

What will you do today? The faith killer is stalking you. He's a professional hitman and you are his target! Don't let him get you!

ROMANS 4:20 *"He staggered not at the promise of God through unbelief, but was strong in faith, giving glory to God."*

February 16

Better put that stone down!

"The service is just too long." "The preacher preaches too much on doctrine." "We sing too many choruses." "I don't like the way the church spends my tithes." "The invitation is too long and drawn out." "There's a bunch of hypocrites all around." "The preacher is always preaching on money."

Stone-throwing! That's what you're doing! What gives you the right, oh Christian, to be so critical? Have you been appointed as the Sherlock Holmes of the church? Do you have your life all together? How many lives have you brought to the Lord Jesus Christ? If you know so well how to run a church, then how come nobody is getting saved through the way you are doing things right now? You can criticize the preacher and others all day long; yet, you're not turning the world upside down either.

The Pharisees were stone-throwers too. With their little self-righteous attitudes, they accused the woman taken in adultery. Why, they would never stoop as low as she!They wanted to sweep her doorstep clean, yet completely ignoring the mess that was lying on theirs. Jesus just simply said to them, "*He that is without sin among you, let him first cast a stone at her." John 8:7* Boy did that dry up the stone-throwing quickly!

Before you cast another stone, maybe you'd better check out your own life. If it is pure and holy, leading multitudes of others to the Savior, then you might have something to say. If it's not, then you need to clean up your own life first before you ever throw that stone at someone else. You're not a Sherlock Holmes for the church....so put that stone down and start praying instead.

JOHN 8:7 *"He that is without sin among you, let him first cast a stone at her."*

February 17

The great physician makes house calls

"Oh, I am so sick! I must be dying, because nobody could feel this bad and still live. Everyone keeps telling me to go to the doctor, but I'm not about to do that. Doctors are just a crutch. They are for weak people. Everyone is crazy if they think I'm going to turn to a doctor when I'm down and out. That's what everybody else does! Hypocrites!They will live like they please all the time, but show up in a doctor's office when they are sick. Jail-house sickness! That's what that is! Hey, that's not for me!"

"Oh, my life is a wreck! My whole world is falling apart around me. They say when it rains it pours. Well, it is flooding at my house! There is absolutely no where else to turn. Everyone keeps telling me to turn to the Lord, but I'm not about to do that. Religion is just a crutch. It's for weak people. I'd be crazy to turn to the Lord when I'm down and out. That's what everyone else does. Hypocrites! They live like they want all the time, but get religion when the hard times come. Jail-house religion. That's what that is! Hey, it's not for me!"

Both the above philosophies are completely wrong! Of course, no one would ever think this way about their physical lives. They know that a sick person needs the doctor. That's exactly where a sick person needs to run. He goes to someone who can determine what's wrong with him and can offer the remedy for his condition. No one would ever think it hypocritical or weak to go to a physical doctor for help.

However, some of these same people who go to doctors when they are sick will never go to the Great Physician for the sickness of their souls. They somehow have the mistaken idea that they can doctor their own souls and survive eternally. They would not dare turn to Doctor Jesus for His help in straightening out their messed up lives. How tragic that they will perish eternally when they could dial heaven's emergency room and receive help any time day or night! The Great Physician makes house calls twenty-four hours a day!

LUKE 5:31 *"They that are well need not a physician, but they that are sick."*

February 18

I think I see God coming

They were trapped! In front of them was the Red Sea, with absolutely no way to get across. Behind them came the Egyptian army, bent on taking them back into captivity. As far as they could determine, they were standing on the brink of disaster! Either way they would lose!

In this terrible predicament, the children of Israel did what most of us would do. They worried and complained! Their spiritual vision was blurred. They only looked at the problem, seeing the impossibility and the hopelessness of their situation. Humanly, there just was no way of escape! They looked ahead at the Red Sea in despair and looked behind at the Egyptian Army with fear. They began to blame Moses for getting them into such a mess! It's always easier to blame someone else for bad circumstances rather than to trust God.

If they had only looked beyond the circumstances instead of worrying and complaining, the children of Israel would have seen God coming. God always shows up when His children are in hopeless situations! He loves parting the waters of the Red Sea, turning the impossible into the possible.

Today, Christian, is there a Red Sea in front of you and an Egyptian army behind you? Do you feel there is no way of escape? Are you on the brink of disaster? Have you resorted to worrying and complaining, blaming others instead of trusting God? Well, get your eyes off the Red Sea of impossibilities ahead of you. Quit looking at the Egyptian army behind you. Instead, look out over the Red Sea of your life. I think I see God coming. Don't you?

EXODUS 14:13 *"And Moses said unto the people, Fear not, stand still, and see the salvation of the Lord which He will show to you today."*

February 19

Where are the nine?

The anxious little group huddled closely to one another, hoping to see Jesus when He passed by. He was their last thread of hope. With bodies full of sores and emaciated limbs resulting from leprosy, they stood afar off. They were not allowed to come close to anyone. As Jesus passed by, they all lifted their voices from a distance and said, "*Jesus, Master, have mercy on us.*" Jesus responded by telling them to go show themselves unto the priests.

Acting in faith on Jesus' words, they all headed out for the priests. As they walked, they were cleansed. It was too good to be true! There was no cure for leprosy. They had been doomed, accepting a fate of separation from their loved ones, of decaying bodies, and of eventual lonely deaths. But now, their fates were changed in just one instant by this Man from Galilee, this One they called Jesus!

Stopping dead in their tracks, they wiggled fingers and toes that had once been nubs. They rubbed their hands across new skin that only seconds ago was decaying. As they were absorbed in examining their clean bodies, one of them turned back. He fell down at Jesus'feet and began glorifying Him with a loud voice. He was overflowing with love and gratitude. Jesus asked, *"Were there not ten cleansed? But where are the nine?" Luke 17:17*

Yes, where were the nine? Perhaps they were so excited over their good fortunes that they wanted to run home to share the good news with their families. They couldn't wait to get to their houses, where they had received warmth and comfort for years. They couldn't wait to put on the clothes that they used to wear. They couldn't wait to sleep in their nice, comfortable beds. They couldn't wait to get a warm shower and a good, home cooked meal! Their families, their possessions, and their fleshly desires were more of a priority to them than Jesus was!

Which of these are you? The one.....or the nine? Do you often fall at Jesus' feet? Do you glorify and praise Him? Is your heart overflowing with love and gratitude to Him?Or, are you too busy with your family, your possessions, and your fleshly desires to have time for the Lord? Has He asked, speaking of you, *"But where are the nine?*

LUKE 17:17 *"Were there not ten cleansed? But where are the nine?"*

And straightway it will

As He came to the house of the ruler of the synagogue, Jesus saw quite a tumult taking place. There were many people gathered about the house, weeping and wailing greatly. It was a sight to see and hear. Jairus' twelve-year old daughter had just died! Oh, if Jesus had only arrived sooner, He could possibly have prevented her death! But, now it was too late! The people were mourning and wailing as if this were some ordinary man standing in their midst. Jesus said to them, "*Why make you this ado, and weep? The child is not dead, but sleepeth." Mark 5:39* At hearing this, the people laughed Him to scorn. After all, they had seen the girl. She was dead! The breath was gone from her body. She had no pulse. There was no doubt to anyone in that crowd that the young girl was dead.

Going to the girl's room, Jesus put everyone out, except for the father and mother of the child and the disciples who were with Him. He didn't want anyone in that room that did not believe, because unbelief is all that can stop Him. Taking the child by the hand, He told her to arise. And straightway, she arose and walked! She responded immediately. When the King of glory speaks, every molecule in the universe instantly obeys.

How tragic that those people who were gathered at Jairus' house that day did not believe! Jesus had spoken directly to them, telling them that the girl was only sleeping. They had the very words of God. They didn't have to muster up a great belief.....or work themselves up into a fevered pitch to beg the Lord to raise her up. All they had to do was to take Him at His Word. If Jesus said she wasn't dead, then she wasn't dead. It didn't matter whether she had a heartbeat or not. It didn't even matter if rigor mortis had set in. What Jesus says overrides all physical laws. Even death obeys Him!

You are like those people gathered around that day. You are filled with unbelief. God gave you a promise long ago, but your promise is dead and can no longer be fulfilled. You have given up hope of ever getting an answer. Well, friend, if Jesus gave you His Word, then you should "*Be not afraid, only believe.*" It doesn't matter what the circumstances are. It doesn't matter how impossible your situation is. What Jesus says overrides everything else. And one day, hopefully soon, He will take you into that room where that promise lies dead and tell it to arise. And straightway it will!

MARK 5:36 *"Be not afraid, only believe."*

February 21

Spiritual molecules

Everything you see around you is composed of millions of molecules. It takes multitudes of all these invisible particles to form something visible. Now, each molecule is real and each one is vital. However, you cannot see each individual one. All you can see is the finished product - the tree, the flower, the cloud, the ocean, the person. Every created thing is visible only because of all the invisible.

The same thing is equally as true spiritually. You can think of each prayer that you offer up to God as a single molecule. A single prayer is real and it is vital. However, your physical eyes cannot see the results of it. It may take multitudes of prayers before there are enough spiritual prayer molecules to show up in the visible realm.

Exactly how many prayers will it take to see results? Well, how many molecules does it take for a flower to become visible? You don't know, do you? Neither do you know how many prayers you will have to send up for your prayer to become a visible reality either. You just keep praying. You just keep adding spiritual molecules. Then, one day, the last molecule will be put into place and you will see the finished product.

Christian, do not get discouraged in your prayer life. What if, in the creation of a flower, just one more molecule was needed? What if that one more was not added? A flower would be stopped short of becoming visible. Likewise, what if one more prayer is needed? What if one more spiritual molecule would bring the answer into visibility? You cannot afford to stop praying and believing. Too much is at stake! Perhaps only one more spiritual prayer molecule will bring the finished product into visibility!

ROMANS 1:20 *"For the invisible things...of the world are clearly seen, being understood by the things that are made..."*

February 22

Case dismissed

"Miss Lukewarm, please come forward. You stand in this courtroom today accused of being a Christian. We will examine all the evidence presented to decide whether you are guilty as charged."

"Mr. Pastor, did Miss Lukewarm attend church?"

"Well sir, your honor, Miss Lukewarm did attend church some. She came sporadically on Sunday mornings and occasionally on Sunday or Wednesday nights. And generally, she showed up for special services like on Easter and Christmas. However, I got the idea that she came mostly when it was convenient for her."

"Mr. Husband, did Miss Lukewarm read the Bible and pray at home?"

"Well, your honor, to tell you the truth, I only saw her reading her Bible a few times. She never read it regularly. She had too much to do, sir. There was always cooking and sewing and shopping at the mall. She worked out in the yard a lot, too. Besides that, she had to run the kids to dance lessons and ball practice and school activities. You see, sir, she just didn't have time. And, prayer.....well, I don't remember hearing her pray but a few times. I think she said the blessing once or twice when the Pastor came over for dinner. I never saw her down on her knees, though. She was just too busy!"

"Miss Friend, did Miss Lukewarm ever try to influence you for Christ?"

"Your honor, Miss Lukewarm and I never discussed Jesus. She did invite me to church a couple of times, but she had cut the Pastor to ribbons with her tongue. I didn't really have any desire to hear him preach after everything she had said about him. No, sir, she never gave me the impression that she was a Christian."

"Mr. Co-Worker, what did you see in Miss Lukewarm?"

"Sir, I am quite shocked that Miss Lukewarm has been accused of being a Christian. She looks and talks just like the rest of us at work. She laughs at our jokes and even tells some herself. She is just one of the gang, sir. There is no way under the sun that she can be accused of being a Christian."

"Miss Lukewarm, please step forward. After examining all the evidence, I find you, 'Not guilty.' The charges against you are proven false and your case is dismissed. You're free to go."

REVELATION 3:16 *"So then, because thou art lukewarm.....*
I will spew thee out of My mouth."

February 23

The fountain of freshness

Spread before you is a table filled with just about everything you can imagine. Your taste buds are in high gear as you sit down to partake of such mouth-watering delicacies. As you being eating, you receive one of the greatest shocks of your life. Everything is stale! The bread is so stale it has mold on it. The vegetables taste like they were cooked two weeks ago. The meat tastes like an old rubber tire. The drink is lukewarm, with a metallic taste to it. It doesn't take long to get all you want. And you certainly don't come back for more!

You would never invite someone over to your house to eat such a meal as this. Yet, you are doing something far worse than that. You are a Christian, but you are stale!You are supposed to be offering the lost folks around you a spiritual meal. There are multitudes of hungry, thirsty, dying souls out there that need to be fed. You are giving out the Bread of Life, as you claim to know the Word of God. However, you are cankered with mold from the world. You are stale bread! Yuk! It doesn't make the recipient want to come back for more.

The meat of the Word that you offer is like an old rubber tire. It is not even chewable. All you can tell people is what happened to you twenty years ago. There's nothing fresh happening now. You're a lukewarm drink of water, claiming to be saved, but living just like the rest of the world. You are stale...stale...stale! No wonder the lost world isn't beating down the church doors, begging to get in and sit down at that spiritual table! What they see certainly doesn't make their spiritual taste buds water!

Today, get before God and stay there until He cleans you up and fires you up! There's nothing like a fresh drink of water, fresh air, a fresh coat of paint, fresh strawberries, fresh-cut flowers, and a fresh child of God! You can be a fresh breath of air everywhere you go. You can be a fresh drink of water to the thirsty. You can be fresh new life to the dying. Come today to the Fountain of Freshness. You've been stale far too long!

PSALMS 92:10 *"I shall be anointed with fresh oil."*

February 24

Cover or confess

What we do with our sin determines what our sin will do with us. There are only two things we can do with sin. We can either cover it…or confess and forsake it. Each time we sin, we must do one of these two things with it.

The first option is to cover it. This started back in the Garden of Eden after Eve ate the forbidden fruit and gave to Adam to eat. They immediately saw their nakedness and made fig leaves with which to cover themselves. We call this "fig leaf" religion. It is simply man dealing with his own sin, making his own way out, covering up what he did. It would be like sweeping a dead rat under a rug, thus covering him up. He may be hidden, but some day he will start to stink. Covered up sin will do the same. Spiritual maggots will set in and its stench will eventually seep out and corrupt.

Our second option is to confess and forsake our sin. To confess means that we agree with God about our sin. We see it as awful, wretched, and deserving of hell. We realize how it has hurt a holy God. We are brought to a Godly sorrow for what we have done. With a repentant heart, we beg His forgiveness. Then we get up with full intentions never to commit the sin again. This clears the air, cleans us up, revitalizes our spiritual lives, and prepares us for usefulness to God. It's like removing the rat and burying him in the sea!

What will you do with your sin? You can either cover it and stink. Or, you can confess it, forsake it, and be a clean vessel for God to use. The choice is yours. What are you going to do?

PROVERBS 28:13 *"He that covereth his sins shall not prosper, but whoso confesses and forsakes them shall have mercy."*

February 25

Drive them or they'll drive you

Apparently, they only heard what they wanted to hear from the Lord. They liked the part where he said, *"I have given you the land to possess." Numbers 33:53* That sounded really good to them, especially since they had been wandering in the wilderness for forty long, hard, barren, monotonous years. It sure was nice to know that the land of Canaan was theirs...and all they had to do was to walk in and take it.

However, that wasn't all that God had said to them. He also told them that, although He was giving them the land, He was not driving out the inhabitants of it. That was their responsibility. And He said that they were not only to drive out the inhabitants, but they were also to destroy all the stone idols and the melted images and demolish all the high places in the land. If they failed in this responsibility, God had told them that those things they refused to drive out would then become barbs in their eyes, thorns in their sides, and a continual vexation to them.

Many times, we are just like the children of Israel. We hear what we want to hear from the Lord and ignore the rest. We like the part where God says, "*I have given you the land to possess.*" We want to go into the spiritual land of Canaan, the victorious Christian life. We want to live in that land where the love, the joy, the peace, and all the spiritual blessings of God flow like milk and honey. We want to enjoy the abundant fruit that's found in the land, especially after we have wandered in the barren wilderness of life for a while.

Oh, for sure, we want to possess the abundant land…but driving out the inhabitants is another story. We would like to go in and possess Canaan without having to drive out the things of the world that we have so long enjoyed and become comfortable with. We want to keep many of our same idols. We want to have our melted images. We want to still enjoy our high places. In other words, we still want to live like the world and live for Christ at the same time. But, it cannot be done!

Friend, perhaps you are not living the abundant Christian life today, because you won't drive out the world. Well, God has given you the land…but He's not going to run out the inhabitants. That's your responsibility. So, either you drive out the inhabitants…or they'll become barbs in your eyes, thorns in your sides, and a continual vexation to you. And, they will eventually drive you out of the land instead!

NUMBERS 33:52, 53 *" Then ye shall drive out all the inhabitants of the land…"*
"I have given you the land to possess."

February 26

Thank god for the whetting stone

"What are you doing to me? Why do you keep pulling me out of this drawer and rubbing me across that old whetting stone time after time? It hurts! I'm tired of the whetting stone! Every time I get comfortable and start to rest, you pull me out of the drawer again and we go through the same process. Meanwhile, all the other knives just lie there content, satisfied, and happy. You don't ever put them on the whetting stone!"

"Well, dear knife, you just happen to be my favorite knife. I know there are lots of other knives in the drawer, but you always seem to suit my purpose better. You're just the right size for the jobs I need to do. You always do a good job, too. I can count on you. And besides, your blade yields more to the sharpening process and you stay sharper longer than the others. I like to use you!

However, my special knife, every time I get you out of the drawer and plunge you into your surroundings, it dulls your blade somewhat. A knife with a dull blade is of very little use. That's why I put you on the whetting stone. It knocks off all those rough edges you get as you cut meats and vegetables. It smoothes and polishes your surface. It sharpens you for further usefulness. If you don't want the whetting stone, then I must put you in the drawer and never use you again. You should thank God for the whetting stone."

Christian, you are the knife God has chosen. He wants to use you! Now, you can stay in the drawer all your life, never allowing Him to use you for His kingdom. He won't forcefully pull you out of that drawer. However, if you want to be used to bless others, then He will take you out of the drawer and plunge you into the world. Your cutting edge will start to get dull and spiritual things will begin to grow dim. Then, you'll become comfortable and satisfied with your dullness. That's when He will put you on the whetting stone, knocking off all those rough edges, smoothing and polishing your attitude, and sharpening you for further use. But, it will hurt so good! Thank God for the whetting stone!

ISAIAH 41:15 *"Behold, I will make thee a new sharp threshing instrument..."*

February 27

You cannot legislate morality...or can you?

You cannot legislate morality," the liberals say as they stand in opposition to certain legislation being passed. They usually say it with arrogance, treating those they are informing as uneducated, backwoods country hicks. They say one must be "enlightened" in this modern age.....that it's old-fashioned to think you can still legislate morality.

Well, according to Webster's Dictionary, legislate means to make or enact a law. Morality is the means of evaluating human conduct. Therefore, to legislate morality would be to enact laws regarding human conduct. So, how would we go about this business of not legislating morality?

We could start by eliminating all laws regarding murder. That's human conduct. So, if we cannot legislate morality, then we cannot make any laws regarding murder. Everyone would be free to kill if they took a notion with no fear of any retribution. That means, Mr. Liberal, that someone could kill any member of your family and you couldn't do one thing about it. You cannot legislate morality, you know.

Next, we'd have to eliminate all laws regarding theft. That's human conduct. Mr. Liberal, someone could steal your car, your money, or any of your possessions and you could do nothing about it. You couldn't call the police. In fact, there would be no use of even turning this action in, because there would be no laws regarding theft. You cannot legislate morality, you know.

And, we'd have to eliminate all laws regarding drugs, D.U.I.'s, treason, rape, adultery, pornography, child molestation, stalking, spousal abuse, malpractice, fraud, embezzlement, forgery, and on and on. All these are human conduct. And, you cannot legislate morality, you know.

Then, where does all this leave us? If we cannot legislate morality, then what CAN we legislate? Everything we legislate involves human conduct, or morality, in some form. All legislation is morality.....somebody's morality. And we will either legislate it or have anarchy. So, Mr. Liberal, why don't you quit speaking out of both sides of your mouth? If you don't want morality legislated, then quit trying to pass any laws at all. You have legislated abortion, which is human conduct. You are working feverishly to legitimize gay marriages, adoption by gays, euthanasia, etc... all of which are human conduct. Thought you said we couldn't legislate morality. Is that the real problem, Mr. Liberal, or is it that you just want your morality legislated instead of ours? If you don't believe in legislating morality, then please shut up and quit trying!

I TIMOTHY 1:9 *"the law is...for the lawless and disobedient, for the ungodly and sinners."*

February 28

Peace in the midst of the storm

Your horizon is filled with ominous black clouds. Hurricane force winds are blowing in your life. Tidal waves are drowning all hopes and all expectations of an answer. You are completely overwhelmed. You cry out to God for deliverance, begging Him to get you out of this situation. You plead with Him to remove the black clouds and to calm the winds and the waves. However, it seems that God is a million miles away. He isn't doing anything. Satan whispers in your ear that God doesn't care. You just don't know what to do next.

Child of God, there is something you need to consider. There are times when God calms the storm for the child, and there are other times when He calms the child in the storm. Maybe God is trying to do something IN you rather than trying to do something FOR you! It could be that you are resisting a work of God in your heart. You could be holding onto every shred of self-sufficiency within you. You know how you want this circumstance to turn out; therefore, you're doing everything you can to assure you of the desired end.

Maybe God has sent this storm into your life to get your attention. You want out of the storm, but that is not God's plan. He has been dealing with you for quite some time about control. You always want to control everything in your life. So, God has sent this storm, something beyond your control, and you are balking!

Today, why don't you just give up your struggle? Had you rather be in the storm with God or be out of the storm without Him? Just let go and let God! Lay down all your plans, your desires, and your designs for your life at His feet. Give Him control, total control. Lose your life to Him. Give it up. When you do, you will actually find your life. The storm won't matter anymore. The waves won't overcome you. The winds won't blow you away. You will have gotten lost in the One who has overcome the world. Oh, the storm may still be there, but you'll now have peace in the midst of the storm.

LUKE 9:24 *"For whosoever would save his life shall lose it, but whosoever will lose his life for My sake, the same shall save it."*

February 29

So close, yet so far away!

What a tragic sight to behold! There, floating in the water, is a minnow bucket. It's tied to the dock, bobbing up and down with the gentle waves. The bucket is filled with dead minnows. They used up all the oxygen in their little watery world, thereby perishing. The tragedy is that there was a whole lake around them, filled with fresh, oxygenated water. Oh, so close, yet so far away! How tragic to perish when only a thin minnow bucket wall separated them from the life surrounding them!

There is something far more tragic than this. There are multitudes of people who will perish eternally in their sinful state, while all around them is a sea of God's mercy and grace. They are living in their own little worlds, having erected walls around themselves against intruders. Since they want to be in complete control of their own lives, they don't allow anyone, including God, access to the control panel in their hearts. They keep tight security locks on their hearts'doors. They are really dwelling in a minnow bucket of their own making in the midst of the ocean of God's grace.

Many of these people even attend church. Some teach Sunday School classes. Some are deacons in their churches. Some are big helpers in their community. They are depending upon their works in this world to get them to heaven. They are breathing worldly air. However, one day they will use up all the world's oxygen and they will die. All around them is the sea of God's grace, filled with heavenly, eternal oxygen. But, the minnow-bucket walls they have built keep them separated from that never-ending supply.

How about you today? Are you absolutely sure you're saved? Have you allowed your minnow bucket to be submerged into God's sea of grace, thereby setting you free?How tragic it would be to be so close, yet so far away!

MATTHEW 7:21 *"Not every one that saith unto Me, 'Lord, Lord,' shall enter into the kingdom of heaven, but he that doeth the will of My Father, who is in heaven."*

March

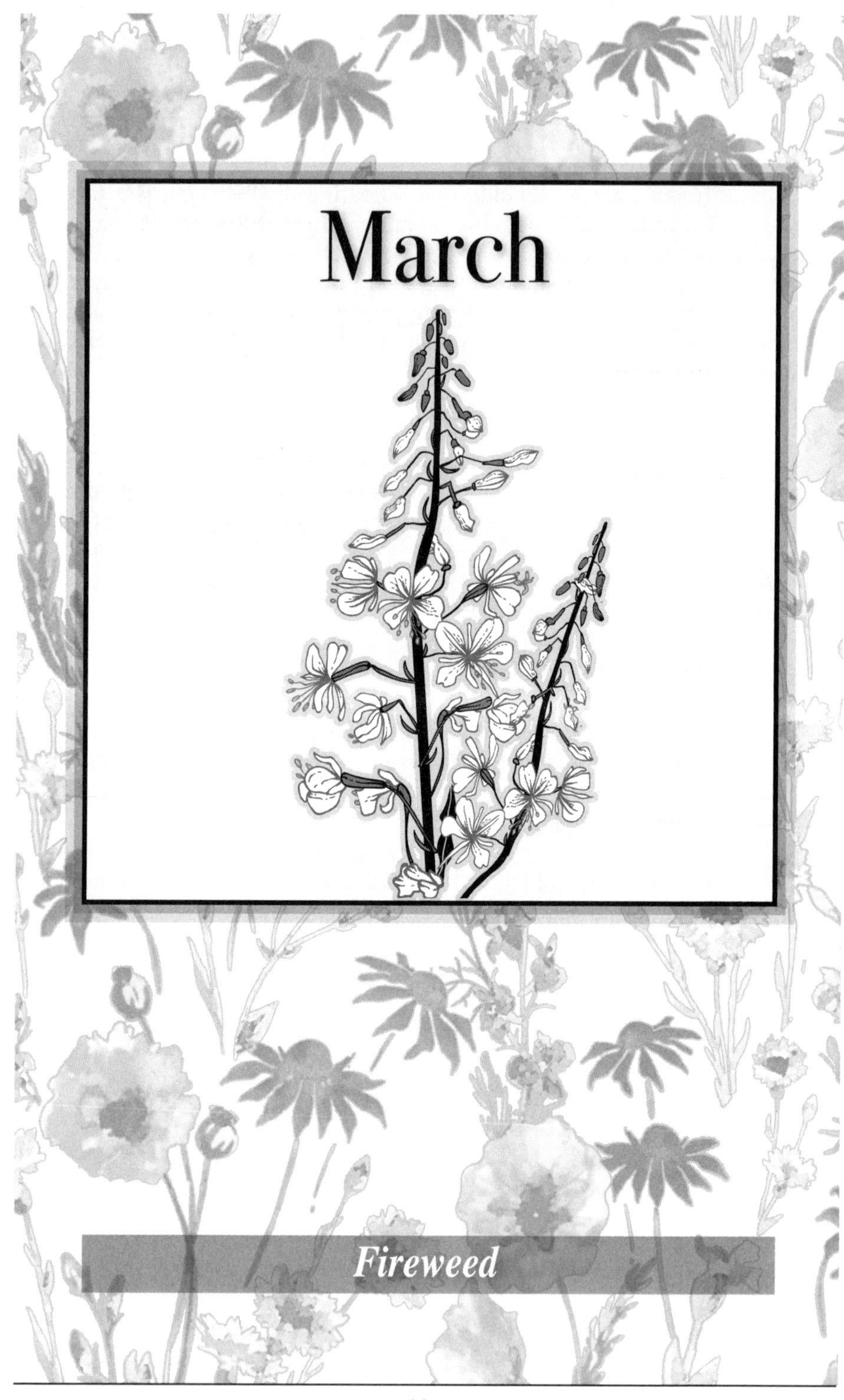

Fireweed

March 1

Mental mosquitoes

Those mental mosquitoes! They are buzzing around in your brain again and are about to drive you crazy! As long as you're involved in activity, it's tolerable. But, when you lie down at night, or when you're all alone, those mental "skeeters" come in hordes to bite and suck the blood out of your spiritual life. You swat at them with every weapon you can think of, but to no avail. Sometimes, they scatter for a short while, but they always return again with just as much vexation and annoyance as ever.

These mental "skeeters" are the negative thoughts that invade your mind. Some of the "skeeters" are critical, faultfinding ones. They buzz around your brain with all the bad stuff imaginable about another person or a certain situation. They will implant that poisonous venom into your brain and extract anything that's good or positive!

The "skeeters" also often inject high dosages of worry venom into your mind, affecting your emotions, your attitude, your faith, and even your physical condition. Or they drone around you, poisoning you with anger, fear, doubt, hurt, and bitterness. And all these mental "skeeters" have the same purpose. They are destructive spiritual pests that will rob you of your fervent, vital Christian walk with the Lord.

How do you get rid of "skeeters?" First, you need a "skeeter swatter." The Word of God is the only thing that will kill "skeeters." As you read and study the Word, you are able to "*bring into captivity every thought to the obedience of Christ.*" *II Corinthians 10:5* By staying in the Word, you also are able to "*set your affections on things above, not on things on the earth.*" *Colossians 3:2* Soon, you'll find the "skeeters" retreating and peace will return to your mind. "T*hou wilt keep him in perfect peace, whose mind is stayed upon Thee.*" *Isaiah 26:3*

Besides being a "skeeter swatter," the Word also provides a Heavenly Repellent for mental "skeeters. The Holy Spirit is that repellent. The Bible says, "*Walk in the Spirit and you shall not fulfill the lust of the flesh.*" *Galatians 5:16* As you soak your spirit in the Word, God soaks you in the Holy Spirit; thereby repelling the mental "skeeters" and sending them on their way.

So, today, get out your "skeeter squatter" and fill your mind with it rather than with the poison from the "skeeters." Pray to be filled with the Holy Spirit, which is the Heavenly Repellent for "skeeters".....cause you cannot walk in the flesh and in the Spirit simultaneously. Friend, you don't have to be plagued with mental "skeeters" any more if you'll only take the action necessary to get rid of them! It's up to you! There IS something you can do about mental "skeeters" just like there's something you can do about physical ones!

II CORINTHIANS 10:5 *"and bringing into captivity every thought to the obedience of Christ."*

March 2

Spring's coming soon!

Look at that tree! It is so barren. There's not even one single leaf on it, much less any fruit. It is just a trunk with a bunch of dead-looking limbs reaching toward the sky. "Tree, you're no good for anything. You are finished! You should be cut down!"

"Wait a minute. You don't understand. I know I don't look like much right now. I know you don't see anything going on when you look at me. But, that does not mean I am dead. Oh, if only you knew what I have been through! Fierce winds have blown, stripping off every leaf I had. Cold, icy rains have fallen on me, coating my branches so heavily that many of them even broke off. That's why I stand here alone, barren, and stripped on the outside.

However, if you could look on the inside, you would see differently. There is a steady stream of life-giving sap flowing within me to every branch. This sap is coming from my roots, which are buried deep beneath the soil, away from all the cold, fierce winds and the icy rains. Oh, things may not look too good on the outside right now, but you must realize that it is winter. When the winter comes in my life, it is a time of rest. It is a time to draw nourishment from my roots. It is a time when all activity ceases and inward renewal occurs. After the winds and the rains, I must be still and allow time for the precious sap to do its work.

You just wait. Spring's coming soon! And then I will have so many leaves that you cannot find my branches. And there will be fruit hanging in abundance. I am waiting patiently, not rushing into anything right now and not making any changes for the present time. I am waiting, because spring's coming soon. Yes, spring's coming soon!"

Friend, perhaps you're in a winter in your life right now. Fierce winds of adversity have blown and cold, icy, troublesome rains have fallen on your life, leaving you stripped and barren and alone. You know the life of Christ flows within you, yet outward circumstances look so grim right now. Well, just be patient! Spend much time alone with the Lord Jesus Christ. Let your roots go down deep into His Word and receive your nourishment from Him. Stay with Him and allow His precious, vital life to saturate you thoroughly. Stop all your hectic, busy, rushed activities and wait on the Lord. Hey, it may be winter, but spring's coming soon! Yes, spring's coming soon!

SONG OF SOLOMON 2:11, 12 *"For lo, the winter is past, the rain is over and gone. The flowers appear on the earth; the time of the singing of birds has come.."*

March 3

The most magnificent army

If you were responsible for organizing a magnificent army, what kind of recruits would you choose? You would probably pick strong, intelligent, brave, young men. You would be highly selective in your choices. You would want the cream of the crop. To marshal this great army, you would want a banner. You would need a symbol of your army, a slogan of strength and fortitude, an inspiring banner.

Today, the most magnificent army in the universe is being organized. It is the army of the Lord. But in this army, the recruits are not what you think. Often, they are the blind, the lame, the dumb, the feeble, the old, the brokenhearted, the poor, the unfortunate, and the rejected. They are anyone who will respond, as this army is totally voluntary.

This army also has a banner. However, it is quite an unusual one, one that most would not want to follow. It is a cross. How strange to use a cross, the symbol of suffering and death, to marshal a great army! That is like saying, "Come join this army and die." Who in his right mind would want to serve in an army like this?

However, in this army, it's not the recruits or the size of the army that makes it so magnificent. It's the Captain! He is a Mighty Warrior! He is the King of kings and the Lord of lords! He is invincible, eternal, indestructible, and incorruptible! He has never lost a battle and He never will. He even conquered death, hell, and the grave. There is no force that can stop Him, no power that can conquer Him, no chains that can bind Him, no enemy that can defeat Him, and no weapons that can wound Him. He has already fought the battle and won! He is the Victorious Warrior!

Today, this Mighty Warrior is calling for recruits, even though He has already won the war. The enemy keeps on fighting in spite of the fact that he has lost and the Mighty Warrior needs soldiers to stand up and run the enemy off the conquered territory. Wouldn't you like to be a soldier in this magnificent army, a soldier that gets to go in and reclaim territory that once belonged to the enemy, but now belongs to the Victorious Warrior? Well, you might as well enlist today, friend, because the whole thing will be over soon!The trumpet will sound and the Victorious Warrior will lead His army off the battlefield and take them home… to Heaven. And, those who didn't join the army will be left behind down here on earth with the army of the enemy, who'll be licking their wounds and pouring out a fury like the world has never seen!

II TIMOTHY 2:4 *"...that he may please Him who has chosen him to be a soldier."*

March 4

Only two roads

Suddenly, I was jolted into reality, as I stumbled over something in the road. It was a little black book. I picked it up and began to read. Instantly, things became crystal clear, like a dense fog being lifted from my eyes. I looked around, literally astounded at what I saw. There were millions of people, of which I had been a part, all going down this broad road. Everyone was laughing and joking and having a grand old time. They all seemed content to continue on down this road, which obviously was quite well traveled. It was evident that they were deceived, just as I had been. They all thought this was the road to Heaven. As I questioned them, I received many similar answers. "Oh, yes, I'm saved." "I joined the church when I was young." "I'm a good person." "I said a sinner's prayer one time and got baptized." "I've been confirmed." "I've always known the Lord."

Then, my eyes fell on some words written in the book, "*For wide is the gate and broad is the road that leads to destruction, and many enter through it." Matthew 7:13* Immediately, I knew that this was the broad road the little book was speaking of. I flipped through the little book for more information. It said, "*No one who is born of God will continue to sin, because God's seed remains in him; he cannot go on sinning, because he has been born of God. This is how we know who the children of God are and who the children of the devil are: Anyone who does not do what is right is not a child of God." I John 3:9, 10* I turned back a page to read some more. It said, "*The man who says, 'I know Him,' but does not do what He commands is a liar, and the truth is not in him." I John 2:4*

Overwhelmed with this information, I realized that all these folks were on their way to hell, yet believing they were going to Heaven. They were trusting in lies. They did not believe this little black book. Neither had I. So, I decided to turn around.

As soon as I turned, I found myself going against the stream of humanity that was traveling down this broad road. Up ahead, I saw an old rugged cross, standing at the entrance to another road. It was a small, narrow road with only a few travelers on it. It looked lonely and rocky and hard. The little black book said, "*But small is the gate and narrow the road that leads to life, and only a few find it." Matthew 7:14*

Now, I had a choice…I could see both roads, but could not go down both, because they led in opposite directions. I knew I could continue on down the wide and broad road with everyone else or I could go down the narrow one that was almost deserted. But, I knew already which choice I needed to make. I saw the end of both roads and that made the decision as easy as eating a piece of cake. I knelt at that cross, accepted Jesus as my Savior and Lord, and started down the narrow road. And I'll travel it till it takes me home!

There are only two roads, friend: the broad one and the narrow one. You cannot travel both! Either you will follow the broad road, which leads to hell, or you will follow the narrow road of the cross, which leads to Heaven! Which one are you traveling today?

MATTHEW 7:13, 14 *"broad is the road that leads to destruction…
narrow is the road that leads to life."*

March 5

Armchair Christians

They're a dime a dozen.....armchair quarterbacks. They sit in their comfortable chairs, scrutinizing the entire game. They can tell you exactly what is wrong with every play. They can tell you what plays would have worked better. They even yell at individual players for messing up, telling them what they should have done instead. Hey, with all that expertise, why are they sitting in that armchair instead of being the one out there on that field? Wouldn't it be funny if a hand reached through the TV, put them on the field, and exposed them to the millions of others watching them from their armchairs? Things wouldn't be so easy if the shoe were on the other foot!

Well, there are not only armchair quarterbacks, but there are armchair Christians as well. They sit comfortably in their little pews, watching the few out on the field of labor, without ever dirtying their own hands. They scrutinize every play. They can tell you exactly what is wrong with everything the church does and what would have worked better. They are quite proficient at finger-pointing and pinning the blame on the Pastor and other workers in the field. And, if the game doesn't go exactly as they want, they will just switch channels. So, they go to another church....and become armchair Christians there, too!

Wouldn't it be funny if God suddenly yanked these armchair Christians up and put them in charge? Since they are experts at knowing what to do, they should immediately begin seeing results. Obviously, if they are so knowledgeable about how to run the affairs of the church, they would certainly be running their affairs at home with great expertise. Also, they could bring their list of folks they've led to Christ...which should be very lengthy, since they know so much about how to be successful in spiritual matters. Hopefully, they would have the walk to back up their talk...else, they should keep their mouths shut!

Are you an armchair Christian? If so, get out of that chair and get on the field. You will never score a touchdown, never tackle the enemy and bring him down, and never help your fellow players win the battle from your armchair. Get out of it and chop it up for firewood! You don't need an armchair in this game we're in!

I TIMOTHY 5:13 *"...they learn to be idle, wandering about from house to house; and not only idle but tattlers also, and busybodies, speaking things which they ought not."*

March 6

Half a dress won't do!

Laying the pattern of top of the fabric, she hurriedly cut out the material for her new dress. Then, she sat down at her sewing machine to sew the dress together. However, she discovered that she had only cut out the front of the dress. There was no back to it. Laughingly, she joked about wearing only half a dress. This mistake made her realize how important it is to have the whole thing. The front of the dress was very important. It was a real part of the dress. But, the back was equally as important and was just as much a part as the front was. Both were separate parts, but it took each to make a complete dress.

There are many Christians today with just half a dress. Some Christians believe in the Word, the Word, the Word. They study for hours, attend seminars, read much Christian literature, and listen to many spiritual tapes. They are well grounded in the Word. They can tell you what the Bible says on many topics.

Then, there are other Christians who believe in the Spirit-filled life. Most of their talk is about the Holy Spirit. They depend heavily upon their experiences. They go from one experience to another, always looking for the next great emotional high. They determine the direction for their lives from past experiences, being ruled by what they have felt.

Now, in order to have a complete, whole Christian life, one must have the Word and the Spirit. Focusing mostly on the Word, with little of the Spirit, brings deadness. The Word tells us, "*The letter killeth, but the Spirit giveth life.*" *II Corinthians 3:6* Focusing mostly on the Spirit, with little of the Word, brings departure from the straight and narrow path. The Bible says, "*Thy Word is a lamp unto my feet and a light unto my path.*" *Psalm 119:105*

Solomon was the wisest man who ever lived. He wrote over 3000 proverbs, yet ended up a decrepit, anguished idolater. He had the Word without the Spirit. Saul went after experiences, even consulting a medium, which was strictly forbidden in the Word. His kingdom was torn away and he died a loser. He followed the Spirit without heeding the Word.

Christian, make sure you don't put on half a dress! You will look mighty strange if you do. Make sure you know and obey the Word. But also be continually filled with the Holy Spirit, who gives life to that Word!

I THESSALONIANS 1:5 *"For our gospel came not unto you in word only, but also in power, and in the Holy Spirit..."*

March 7

Speaking the truth in silence

We Americans have been blessed with an abundance of them. We have them in our homes, in stores, in hospitals, in office buildings…just about everywhere! And we use them on a regular basis. Men use them when they're shaving. Women use them when they're putting on makeup. Most people use them when they are fixing their hair, brushing their teeth, and judging how their clothes look on them. We'd find it harder to take care of our personal needs without them. Mirrors show us what we really look like on the outside, thus enabling us to make corrections, to cover up blemishes, or to change things that aren't right. Mirrors speak the truth in silence.

Yes, mirrors are great, but they have their limitations. First, they only reveal what you look like. They cannot make the essential changes. They can show you where the dirt is, but they cannot remove it. Secondly, mirrors are useless in the dark. You could look into one, but could not see a thing without the light. And thirdly, mirrors will not pursue you and make you look into them. You must avail yourself of them if they are to be helpful.

Just as mirrors show what we look like on the outside, there is a spiritual mirror that shows what we look like on the inside. It is the Word of God. Like a physical mirror, the Bible reveals the truth, but it cannot make the essential changes. Just knowing the Truth does not change you. The Truth, God's mirror, can show you where the dirt (or sin) is, but it cannot remove the dirt. You must do that by confession and repentance. You must act on the Truth for changes to occur. You are to be, not just a hearer of the Word, but a doer as well. You are to turn fact into act.

Secondly, the Word of God is no good in the dark. If you are lost, you are in spiritual darkness and cannot see spiritual truths. You can look into the Bible all you want, but it will really be meaningless and uninteresting to you. And thirdly, the Word of God will not pursue you and make you read it. You must avail yourself of it. You must get in it, read it daily, and apply it to your life. Without doing so, you have nothing to reveal what you look like on the inside. There could be a lot of dirt there that you don't see.

Friend, you need that spiritual mirror. It speaks the truth in silence. You will one day face God with how you look on the inside. So, why don't you get the mirror, God's Word, look into it often, and allow it to show you the changes that need to be made. You need to get all cleaned up internally and dressed up.....for you DO have somewhere to go!

PSALM 51:6 *"Behold, Thou desireth truth in the inward parts..."*

March 8

To stand or not to stand

Oh Lord, I'm tired.....so very tired.
I sure wish I could quit.
Or at least lay all my armor down
And rest a little bit.

The battle's so relentless,
So furious and strong.
I wouldn't mind it for a while,
But Lord, it lasts so long!

I just don't think I can go on.
I've been wounded in my heart.
And it wasn't from the enemy,
But from a fellow soldier's dart.

I'm tired of being ridiculed.
I'm tired of being alone.
It just "ain't" worth it, Lord.
Once more, I'll be my own.

But, wait! I hear a sound.
It's an agonizing wail.
Oh, no. It was my lost neighbor
Who died and went to hell.

I was gonna tell him about You, Lord.
But oh, God, now it's too late!
I've been wrapped up in my own life,
Unconcerned about his fate.

I've been licking wounds and resting,
And listening to Satan's lies;
So comfortable in my own little world,
It has drowned out lost men's cries.

Oh, God, please God, open up my eyes
And turn them from within,
To see a world around me
That's perishing in its sin.

I can lay my armor down one day And
rest forever in Your light.
But until then, forgetting myself,
I'm gonna stand and fight!

EPHESIANS 6:13 *"..and having done all, to stand."*

March 9

Do you possess what you own?

It was all his…the land, the stocks, the bonds, the possessions, the money…because he was the heir. It was all his, but only on paper, since he never probated the will and never claimed what was rightfully his. He owned it without possessing it. He had it in writing, but not in reality. And, he lived a meager, humdrum life, just barely making it from pay day to pay day, when instead he could have had everything he wanted. He lived as a pauper when he could have lived as a prince.

Now, it would seem pretty dumb to us for someone to be an heir and never claim his inheritance. However, we may be doing the exact same thing spiritually without even realizing it. According to the Word of God, those who are saved are heirs of God and joint heirs with Christ. All that is God's is also ours. *II Peter 1:3* tells us that God *"According to his divine power hath given unto us all things that pertain unto life and godliness, through the knowledge of Him that hath called us to glory and virtue; By which are given unto us exceedingly great and precious promises, that by these, ye might be partakers of the divine nature, having escaped the corruption that is in the world through lust."*

The Bible doesn't say that God "will" give us all things that pertain unto life and godliness, but that God "hath" already given them to us. It doesn't say He "will" give us great and precious promises, through which we can be partakers of the divine nature, but that He already "hath" given them to us. Therefore, we already own everything that is included in our inheritance. It's already ours! But, it's up to us to possess it!

Today, dear one, if you are truly saved, then you have a glorious inheritance. It's all on paper…it's all written down in Jesus' Last Will and Testament, the New Testament. It is all legally yours by the death of the Testator, Jesus Christ. You own it all…but, do you possess it? Perhaps you've been living a meager, humdrum spiritual life, just barely making it from day to day. You have practically no joy or peace. You're just going through the motions. You've been living as a spiritual pauper.

It's time, friend, for you to get out the Will, the Holy Bible, get in it, find out what all is yours, and start claiming it and living like it. Don't live like a pauper when you're a prince. Don't live like a slave when you're the King's child. You're an heir of God and a joint-heir with Christ…so why don't you start possessing what you already own?

II Peter 1:3 *"According to His divine power hath given unto us all things that pertain unto life and godliness."*

March 10

Read the directions

Ever wonder why the children of Israel wandered in the wilderness for forty years? As someone once said jokingly, "The men wouldn't ask for directions!" It seems that men are allergic to directions. There's just something about the makeup of a man that makes him think he can go places without asking for directions and can put stuff together without reading the directions. However, many times, a do-it-yourselfer winds up frustrated and upset after he has made a grand mess. And, at that point, as a last resort, he finally gets out the directions and follows them, even if he has to take the mess apart and redo it properly.

Now, that's only a minor problem when we're dealing with material things, because the mess can usually be corrected. However, it's another story when we're dealing with our lives, because the mess cannot always be straightened out. It would be tragically foolish to put a life together on our own, without consulting directions from the One who made us!

Now, you may be wondering where the directions are for our lives. You know that manufacturers always send along directions with their products, because the manufacturer knows how it is supposed to be put together and how it is to be run. Well, God sent along directions with His product, too. His directions are the Word of God. These directions contain all that we will ever need to know about life. There are directions for salvation, daily living, raising a family, marital relationships, friendships, attitudes, possessions, usage of money, warfare, blessings, etc. There is not one thing that can ever touch our lives that is not covered in God's all encompassing directions.

Looking around our society, we see that most are not following the directions. They've tried to run their lives their own way, without following the Manufacturer's directions. That's why their lives are in such a mess. They are nervous, discouraged, depressed, discontented, restless, fearful, and without hope. They have to go to psychiatrists and counselors, or resort to medication, just to help them cope. Their homes are breaking up. Their children are rebellious, on drugs, going nowhere in life. They've tried it all…and made a mess!

Well, when all else fails, read the directions! So, today, if you've tried to run your life your way, then get out God's Word and start lining your life up with it. Set aside some time each day to read and study the Bible. Spend time alone with the Lord in prayer. Fill your mind with Godly things, stay around dedicated Christians, and be faithful in church. Remember: read and follow the Directions. They have been tested and tried on thousands of other lives.....and they have never failed one time!

PSALM 119:105 *"Thy Word is a lamp unto my feet and a light unto my path."*

March 11

Run, bully, run!

There were knots in his stomach. His knees were shaking, as he was overcome with fear and doubt. He wanted so badly to turn and run. The neighborhood bully stood confronting him, taunting and teasing him, thus adding to his growing fear. The bully never let up until he provoked a fight. This time would be no different!

Suddenly, however, his fears melted into the dust, as his father came walking up. Holding his father's hand, he thought how small the bully looked now. All those threats and intimidations were meaningless and powerless. His father was big and strong. The bully was nothing in comparison with his father. Confidently, he commanded the bully to leave him alone. He could do this with the power and authority beside him, backing him up. He could do this without fear now, as "*perfect love casts out fear." I John 4:18* It worked, too! The bully ran!

Christian, you face the bully every day. He confronts you, taunting and teasing you. He puts doubts into your mind. Fear builds up as you listen to his never-ending tirades. But, if you'll look around, you'll see your Father coming. He will take you by the hand and you can confidently face the bully. Your Father is big and strong. The bully is nothing in comparison with your Father. So, you can command the bully to leave you alone. You can do this with the power and authority beside you, backing you up, as your Father is the highest authority in the whole universe. You also can do this without fear, as "*perfect love casts out fear.*" It will work. The bully is afraid of your Heavenly Father.

Today, Christian, aren't you sick and tired of all the lies and harassment and deception? You have been sitting back and permitting the bully, that old dragon, the devil, to frighten and intimidate you. You have allowed fear and discouragement and depression to overwhelm you and cripple you in the Lord's work. Well, the bully has intimidated you long enough. Take up the sword of the Spirit, the Word of God, and with your hand in your Father's hand, tell that old bully, "Run, bully, run!"

I JOHN 4:18 *"...perfect love casteth out fear."*

March 12

Umbrellas and faith

Open an umbrella and hold it out in front of you, as if you were holding it over a small child. You can see only one side of it, the side that is facing you. Now, rotate the umbrella clockwise and you can see the other side. You can always see the side that is facing you, but you cannot see both sides at one time. That's because you are looking at the umbrella from only one perspective.....lengthwise. Now, with the umbrella still in front of you, pivot it with the tip toward you and the handle away from you. Now, you are looking at it from the top down, and you can see the outside of the whole umbrella at one time. You're looking at it from a different perspective...depth.

This is easy for us to understand, because we operate in the dimensions of length and depth. However, we have much difficulty understanding other dimensions that we don't normally operate in. One of these areas is eternity. We are born in and live in time, which is one dimensional. It can only go forward. It cannot go backwards; it cannot go up and down; it cannot go in and out. Time always goes in the same direction.

However, God is outside of time. He is eternal. He views things from that dimension of eternity, kind of like rotating the umbrella from length to depth. He sees it all simultaneously. He can see the entire dimension of time, from beginning to end. He knows what happened hundreds of years ago, what will happen tomorrow, what will happen one thousand years from now, and what will happen through all of eternity.

This is where the life of faith comes in for us. We are limited to four dimensions: time, space, matter, and energy. If we walk by sight, we can only operate in these four dimensions. However, by faith we are seated in heavenly places in Christ Jesus. Faith allows us to see Him, who is invisible. Faith lets us see things that are afar off. By faith, we enter God's presence and He shows us things from His perspective. He makes known to us some things that He is going to do. Then, we can take those things back with us into our dimension of time. And, we can act on what we saw while in His presence.

Are you ready to go on a faith walk today? It will take you out of the four dimensions that you normally operate in and carry you into the far reaches of the universe. Why walk by sight when you can walk by faith? There's no comparison!

HEBREWS 10:22 *"Let us draw near with a true heart in full assurance of faith..."*

March 13

I can't wait to see how God is going to handle this

"Oh, Daniel. What in the world are you so excited about? Man, it must really be something great for you to be rejoicing like you are."

"It is great! King Darius has commanded that I be thrown into a den of starving lions. I can't wait to see how God is going to handle this. There are a lot of people who need to see that the Lord, He is God! What an opportunity for my God to work!"

"Oh, Shadrach, Meshach, and Abednego, what are you guys singing and shouting about? You certainly are overjoyed about something!"

"Yes, we are. King Nebuchadnezzar has ordered us to be thrown into the fiery furnace. We can't wait to see how God is going to handle this. Old King Neb and all these people sure do need to see that our Lord is the true God. Boy, this is exciting!"

"Oh, Moses, what are you so happy about? Why, there is a Red Sea in front of you and an Egyptian army behind you. It looks like there's no way out for you and your people. You have led all these people out here to see them die...and you're rejoicing?"

"Well, sure! I can't wait to see how God is going to handle this. Man, this is so exciting! I know that, when we get to the back end of ourselves, we are on the verge of finding the front end of God!"

"Oh, Paul and Silas! Have you guys lost your minds? Here you are in prison, in stocks, having been beaten almost unto unconsciousness. You are in a mess; yet you are singing and praying. What has gotten into you?"

"This is great! We have a great God and He has allowed us to be here for some reason. He never makes mistakes! So, we can't wait to see how He is going to handle this. Man's impossibility is always God's opportunity!"

Perhaps you're in a den of lions or in a fiery furnace today! Maybe there's a Red Sea in your life or a dark prison of circumstances. Well, Christian, rejoice as you say, "I can't wait to see how God is going to handle this!" Perhaps He is simply trying to get you to the back end of yourself so you'll find the front end of Him… so you'll quit trying and allow Him to handle it for you. What an opportunity for God to work and for everyone around to see that the Lord, He is God!

JAMES 1:2 *"My brethren, count it all joy when you fall into various trials."*

March 14

Taste and see

How would you describe a beautiful sunset over the ocean to someone who had been blind from birth? How would you describe heart-stirring music to someone who had never heard a single note? How would you describe the taste of an orange to someone whose taste buds had never functioned? You could probably come up with some descriptive words for these things and even some illustrations, but they would be inadequate. They could only serve to make the person want to see, want to hear, or want to taste. They could not actually provide him with the real experience.

All truth must be experienced to be known. You can have all the facts about something and have all the information you need stored in your brain. However, you cannot really know about that thing until you personally experience it for yourself. Experience brings reality to truth! It transfers truth from your head to your heart. Truth is the light, but experience turns the light on!

The same thing is true of God's Word. You can read the truths of this precious Book. You can memorize them and even quote them to others. But, they are just mere words, only knowledge for the head until you actually experience them. Then, they become a reality! That's why God is allowing you to go through all these things in your life right now. He wants you to taste of every word that is in His blessed Book, words such as, "*But my God shall supply all your need according to His riches in glory in Christ Jesus." Philippians 4:19* Up until now, these were just nice words that made you feel good. But, you are in dire need right now and, if God doesn't come through, you are sunk. You're about to literally taste that God will supply all your need. You are about to get some first-hand experience. You are about to see reality, to have truth transferred from your head to your heart. "*But my God shall supply all your need according to His riches in glory in Christ Jesus*" is Truth and Light…and experience is about to turn the light on!

So, friend, quit doubting and resisting God's work in your life. Get you a healthy spiritual appetite. Just zealously plunge into His Holy Word and begin delighting yourself in experiencing it and savoring every truth-packed morsel as you taste it for yourself!

PSALM 34:8 *"Oh, taste and see that the Lord is good..."*

March 15

Complete control

As you awakened this morning, did you worry about whether the earth would stay on course or fly off into space? Did you worry about whether the sun would remain at just the right distance so that the earth would not burn up or freeze? Did you worry about whether you would run out of air to breathe today? Did you worry about whether the oceans would stay in their bounds or overflow the earth? Chances are, you never even considered any of these things as you awoke this morning.

However, as you awakened this morning, you did worry about some things that are much smaller in magnitude than these things. You worried about some things that are going on in your life right now. You worried about people and circumstances in your life. You never gave those big things any thought, because you can't change them anyway. These things are totally up to God and all your worrying and fretting will not make one bit of difference with them. You have absolutely no control over these things!

So, what is the basis for worry then? Is it not control? Obviously, it must be. You don't worry at all about things over which you have absolutely no control. However, you do worry about things that you feel you have some control over, especially if you think you can change them in some way. You spend much time thinking, planning, and figuring out how to make things turn out exactly as you want them to.

Has it ever dawned on you that God wants complete control? Could it be that He is trying to rattle your cage, to get your attention, to get you to let go so He can work?How long has He been speaking to you to give everything to Him? How long has He been prompting you to quit trying and start trusting Him? The sun doesn't need your help. The earth doesn't need your efforts. And neither do your circumstances! Give God complete control today! He might not do things the way you would like them done…but, He will always do things the way that is best! If you can trust Him to keep a universe in working order, don't you think you can trust Him with your little circumstances?

MATTHEW 11:28 *"Come unto Me, all ye that labor and are heavy laden, and I will give you rest.."*

March 16

Scents are their road maps

The scout ant leaves his colony. Behind him, he leaves a trail of tiny drops, which contain a scent common to the entire ant colony. All the other ants just follow this scent. That way, they can leave their colony and find it again with no trouble. After all, they don't have road maps or landmarks to use! Scents, left by the scout ant, are their road maps!

What an awesome responsibility it is to be a scout ant! He can never forget to leave the droplets or it would be disastrous! He can never cross his own path either. The ants following him would go around in circles until they died if he did so. He is responsible for the whole colony finding their way home.

This is a valuable lesson for us as Christians, too. Each of us is a scout Christian to somebody. We are each leaving a scent for someone else to follow. There are only two scents a Christian can leave.....either that of Christ or of the world. If he leaves a scent of Christ, some in his field will pick up on this sweet aroma and follow. They will want what they see in this Christian. They will know he has something different. They will follow, because they recognize that he knows the way home. However, if he leaves a scent of the world, many of those in his field will pick up on that scent and will go around in circles all their lives. This scent does not lead home, so they will never find the trail to the Savior.

What kind of scent are you leaving today? You are a scout Christian and you ARE leaving some kind of scent, either that of the world or of Christ. It is vitally important that you leave, not so much as a droplet of the world, lest another who is watching you be led astray. Scout Christian, get busy and do your job. There is a lost world out there that needs to know the way home. You can be the one who leaves a heavenly scent everywhere you go so they can follow and find their way to the Savior.

HEBREWS 13:7 *"Remember them who have the rule over you, who have spoken unto you the Word of God, whose faith follow, considering the end of their manner of life."*

March 17

Take your hurt to the cross

You have been hurt.....very deeply and intensely hurt. It feels like someone is ripping your heart out of your chest. It would not hurt any worse if someone were sticking fifty knives into your heart right now. In fact, this is worse than any physical hurt you could ever receive. And, on top of all this, the devil is playing mind games with you. He's calling all the shots, and, according to all appearances, he's winning. He has you fully convinced that, if you were a mature Christian like you should be, you wouldn't be feeling this way.You should be shouting glory, walking around up in the clouds, and living in victory. Yet, you're having heart pains that are crippling. It's hard to go on when you're hurting like this!

Dear one, remember that the devil is a liar, wanting to blind you from the truth so you'll walk in defeat. The truth is that you're hurting, but you're not the only Christian who has ever felt this way. Just listen to the psalmist, *"Reproach has broken my heart; and I am full of heaviness; and I looked for some to take pity, but there was none; and for comforters, but I found none." Psalm 69:20*

Experiencing hurt is an inescapable part of life. The fact that you hurt is not a sin; it's what you do with that hurt that could become sin. You can do several things with hurt. You can respond inwardly by a decision to never allow anyone else to hurt you again...to do so, you must erect walls, or barriers, that will keep everybody out. You can respond inwardly by holding bitterness or anger or unforgiveness in your heart for how you were treated. You can respond outwardly with vengeance or retaliation, either verbally or physically or both. However, these are all incorrect human responses to hurt and they accomplish absolutely nothing for the glory of God.

The Lord wants you to respond to the hurt by running to Him, because He fully understands and wants to comfort you and help you. He's been there! In fact, He experienced greater hurt than you could ever think of experiencing. He was spit upon, mocked, scourged, and nailed to a cross by those He loved with His whole heart and soul. He endured the most horrible physical suffering known to man, that of crucifixion. He also endured the most horrible emotional suffering known to man, that of a broken heart. Jesus knows hurt.....great big hurt, because the more you love, the bigger is your hurt.

So, friend, take your man-sized hurt to the One who has experienced God-sized hurt, magnified millions of times beyond yours. Let Him teach you of Himself. Join in the fellowship of His sufferings. You can come to know Him through this hurt in a deeper way than ever before.....it will allow you to catch a glimpse of what He went through and how He felt when He was betrayed. It will give you a greater love and compassion and appreciation for Him. So, take your hurt to the cross today. Jesus will meet you there!

PSALM 69:20 *"Reproach has broken my heart; and I am full of heaviness..."*

March 18

Destined to be a diamond

There's absolutely no reprieve! Day after day, week after week, month after month, year after year, there hasn't been a letup, not even for a single second. The heat is just unbearable. And the relentless pressure that is pushing in from all sides grows more intolerable every day. But, there's no escape! Here he lies, buried deep beneath the surface of the earth, with no way out! And he just cannot understand why he must suffer so much in his life. After all, he's just an ordinary old lump of black coal...out of sight, doing nobody any harm, just minding his own business. He cannot understand any reason for all the heat and all the pressure. He just doesn't understand!

The little piece of coal does not know he's destined to be a diamond. He sits alone... helpless and afraid and hurting! Things have been this way for so long that he has very little hope any more. He just wishes he could die and get out of all this suffering!

But one day, the earth begins to shake and move, as many shovels are plunged into it time and time again. For some strange reason, men are digging up the earth all around the little lump of coal. Finally, all the dirt around him is removed and daylight shines upon him for the first time. Quite unexpectedly, a hand reaches down, picks him up, and tenderly brushes all the dirt off. Thankfully, he lets out a big sigh of relief that he has been delivered from the miry clay, from the world of darkness into the glorious light.

The relief soon turns into sighs of despair, however, as the little lump finds himself in the hands of someone called a master jeweler. The jeweler begins cutting and chipping and polishing. Just when it appears he is finished, he starts again. He is relentless. All this hurts so badly. The little lump just can't figure out what is happening.

Finally, the master jeweler is finished. He sets the little lump out for everyone to see. People begin raving over him, commenting on his brilliance, his shine, and his luster. Everyone is wanting him. Suddenly, he realizes that he used to be a lump of coal, but now he's a diamond. And now, he finally understands and realizes that it has been worth it all. All the pain, all the hurt, all the disappointments, and all the trials have helped to shape him into a beautiful diamond.

What about you? You, too, are destined to be a diamond. So, when the heat becomes almost unbearable; when the pressures all around are crushing the life out of you; when you feel you cannot go on any longer, just remember: you're just an ordinary life that God is shaping into a beautiful diamond! So, just yield to the heat, the pressure, and the work of the Master Jeweler's cutting tools! You are destined to be a diamond!

MALACHI 3:17 *"And they shall be Mine, saith the Lord of Hosts, in that day when I make up My jewels."*

March 19

Want to hug Jesus?

With the grass beneath me, the trees around me, and the blue sky above me, I was enjoying spending time alone with the Lord. This was His handiwork, His creation, His world. Overwhelmed with love for Him, I began pouring out my heart of gratitude for Who He is and for all He does for me. Suddenly, I was filled with this intense desire to see Jesus…to hug Him and to kiss Him all over His face. Looking up into the blue sky that He spoke into existence, I said, "Lord, I just wish that I could hug You right now. And I'd give anything if I could kiss your face, too. I believe I would kiss it a hundred thousand times without stopping!"

Very softly and tenderly, this loving answer came back in my heart, "You can, My child. Every time you hug a Christian, you're hugging Me, because that Christian's body is My temple, My habitation. Every time you kiss the face of a Christian, you're kissing Me. And not only that, little one, every time a Christian hugs you, that's Me hugging you. And every time a Christian kisses your face, that's Me kissing you!"

Stunned by such a simple but profound revelation, I sat for a while in awe of my Lord. Why, I had never looked at it in this way. I had casually hugged people and kissed them on the cheek, usually without really thinking of what I was doing. Sometimes, it had been just simply a duty, something expected, done without my heart really in it. Most of the time, I looked at people as just being people…not thinking about them in the light of the fact that their bodies are the temple of the Holy Spirit…that Jesus actually lives in them!

This was a brand new way of looking at my Christian brothers and sisters and it has changed my view of them. It has given me a desire to cherish every moment spent with them, as time being spent with the Lord. It has taught me to guard my tongue, making sure my words are full of grace, seasoned with salt, because they are going in the ears of Jesus. It has increased my desire for ministering to brothers and sisters: feeding them, clothing them, taking them into my home, or whatever else is needed. Knowing that giving even a cup of cold water in Jesus' name is the same as doing it unto Him sure makes me want to minister to my Lord by ministering to others.

Friend, do you want to hug Jesus today? Want to kiss Him on the cheek, show Him how much you love Him, and minister to Him? Well, you know where He lives, where His temple is…so why don't you hug Jesus today?

I CORINTHIANS 6:19 *"What? Know ye not that your body is the temple of the Holy Spirit who is in you, whom you have of God, and you are not your own?"*

March 20

Plunge into the water brook

Gaining ground with each step, the enemy was rapidly closing in on him. Fear gripped his heart, as he knew his life was in imminent danger. He was getting so tired that he could not last much longer. Every muscle in his body ached. His throat was parched and dry. Oh, how he longed for the water brook! If only he could get there, he would be safe.

Suddenly, there it was! The deer plunged into the water brook without hesitation. How cool and refreshing it felt, as his hot, tired body was immersed in the life-preserving waters! Soon, the enemy gave up his pursuit, as the scent of the deer was lost in the swift water.

Perhaps you are like that deer today! The enemy is relentlessly tracking your soul. Day and night, there is no relief. Your survival as a Christian is in danger, as the enemy is gaining ground with each attack. You are wearing down. You're so tired that you don't feel you can go another step. Your soul is parched and dry. Spiritual things don't thrill you as they once did. Your prayers get no higher than the ceiling. You are on the verge of giving up.

Then, you remember the water brook. You get out the Word of God and plunge in! Your tired, worn-out soul finally finds the refuge it has been seeking. What peace, what comfort, what security, and what refreshment you find in the water of the Word! The enemy soon loses your trail and you are at rest. Oh, blessed rest! You wonder now why you ever strayed so far away from the water brook. And you realize that you must continue daily in the water brook, for your survival depends upon it!

PSALM 42:1 *"As the deer panteth after the water brooks, so panteth my soul after Thee, O God.."*

March 21

Holy of Holies

Behind a heavy veil was the Holy of Holies. Only the high priest could enter this holy spot and even he could do so only once a year. He sprinkled the blood of the sacrifice seven times before the mercy seat for the sins of the people and for himself. If he did not do this properly, he would be smitten of God. He would then be dragged out by the rope, which was tied around his leg, as no one else was allowed to go into this holy place. This is how seriously God takes the worship of Himself!

No one would have dared go into this holy place and pour beer or wine on the mercy seat. No one would have dared commit sexual immorality here. In fact, no one would even have murmured and complained and gossiped in this place. This place was serious business to God. If He would kill a priest for not administering blood properly on the mercy seat, what might He do to someone for doing other things?

Today, God's presence no longer dwells in a manmade temple. His Holy of Holies in this day is the heart of those who are born again. "*What? Know you not that your body is the temple of the Holy Spirit, who is in you, whom you have of God, and you are not your own?" I Corinthians 6:19* Therefore, when you are in the presence of a Christian, you are standing at the temple of God.

Since God never changes, He still takes the worship of Himself as seriously today as He did years ago. He is very particular about His Holy of Holies. That's why you must be very careful about how you treat other believers. You would never give strong drink to them any more than you would pour beer on the mercy seat. You would not expose them to sexual immorality any more than you would do so in the Holy of Holies. You would not murmur or complain or gossip about others around this one in whom God dwells.

Also, Christian, you are God's temple. You should "*sanctify now yourselves and sanctify the house of the Lord (you)...and carry forth the filthiness out of the holy place (your heart)." II Chronicles 29:5* God is holy. He commands you to be holy! You had better watch how you treat the Holy of Holies.....in your own life and in the lives of others...or somebody may be dragging you out with a rope.

II CORINTHIANS 7:1 *"...let us cleanse ourselves from all filthiness of the flesh and spirit, perfecting holiness in the fear of God.*

March 22

Bought off the slave block

The bidding had started! Hanging his head in utter shame and disgrace and hopelessness, he stood naked on the slave block. He was being auctioned off to the highest bidder, as though he weren't even a human being. Being a slave from birth meant that he had no possessions, no freedoms, and no rights. Even his family did not belong to him. As he stood in humiliation, however, a tiny spark of hope stirred within him. Maybe this time a kind and gentle master would buy him and his whole family. Having belonged to a cruel, merciless master, he was grateful for even this slim chance to be released from such an evil one's control.

As the bidding continued, his eyes fastened upon one in that disorderly crowd that he had never seen before. This man was different! His eyes were filled with mercy. His whole countenance radiated peace and holiness. Love poured forth from him like a river. He made his way through the crowd, stopping at the slave block. Silence fell across the crowd as this stranger spoke. "I'll buy this one, no matter what the cost!"

Completing the transaction, this stranger turned to him and asked him to follow. Arriving at their destination, he was shocked to see his family, a new home, transportation, food, and clothing. His master spoke, "I have paid a dear price for you. You are mine forever. No one else can ever buy you again. However, I am setting you free. You do not have to serve me. I will provide all your needs, take care of you, protect you, and guide you if you will let me. I will be your loving master and will give you a blessed, fulfilled, fruitful life if you will only continue to follow me. But, if you choose to be your own master, I will step aside and allow you do to so. You can take all the things I have provided freely for you and use them as though they were your own. However, I warn you! You cannot serve two masters. I will either be complete master, or I will not be master at all. Follow me with your whole heart, no matter what path I take you. If you do, you'll never be sorry."

Christian, you are that slave! Jesus bought you off the slave block of sin by paying for you with His own blood. However, He then set you free. He has given you a choice: to follow Him and allow Him to be your new Master, or to go your own way and be your own master. He won't force you to love Him and serve Him. So, how are you treating this One who purchased you at such a dear price and has so gracefully and liberally provided for you? Does your life show your appreciation and love for Him? Is He your complete Master...or is not Master at all?

I CORINTHIANS 7:22 *"For he that is called in the Lord, being a servant, is the Lord's freeman; likewise also he that is called, being free, is Christ's servant."*

March 23

Recnac

Concerned over your constant tiredness and your weight loss, you decide to go to the doctor. He runs many tests, feeds the information into a computer, and then informs you of the results. He says you have "recnac." He tells you it's a strange new virus he knows little about. It will just have to wear down on its own with rest and a proper diet.

As several months pass and your condition continues to worsen, you return to the doctor. He repeats the tests, feeds the information into the computer, and gives you some shocking news. The computer had spelled your disease backwards, showing that you had "recnac," when you really had "cancer." The cancer has now grown to the point of being inoperable. You are overwhelmed with grief and unbelief, as you realize how one little mistake, simply calling something by another name, can be disastrous!

In America today, liberal doctors are examining our land, feeding the information into their computer brains, and renaming the sin that is deteriorating our land. Alcoholism is a disease. Abortion is getting rid of fetal tissue. Homosexuality is an alternate lifestyle. Whoredom is living together. And rebellion is doing what I please with my body.

If the devil can deceive people into calling sin by other names, the people will become comfortable in that sin, having no fear of judgment or of consequences. They will also seek the wrong cure: the cure for disease is varied, depending upon the disease, but the only cure for sin is the cross! When a person comes to the cross with a repentant heart, confesses the sin, and turns from it, instant spiritual removal of the sin occurs! However, if he doesn't see it as sin, it will never be removed and will ultimately result in his death and separation from God forever in hell.

How the devil loves to rename sin! He especially loves to rename a lost person's condition. He will tell them they are backslidden; they are a good person; they are a church member; they have been sprinkled, baptized, or confirmed. This will keep them from seeing themselves as lost sinners in need of God!

Today, examine your life. Have you renamed some sin in your life? Have you been deceived about your soul? Feed everything into God's computer, the Bible, and let God tell you what your condition is. He never makes mistakes! How sad it would be to go to hell because you were deceived about sin, calling it by some other name!

JAMES 1:15 *"..and sin, when it is finished, bringeth forth death."*

March 24

Sowing for tomorrow

Crouched in the ditch, hiding from their stepfather, the two sisters cried silently in fear. Their stepfather had become enraged with the mule for balking at the end of every row. So, he had tied the poor mule to a tree and beat him mercilessly with a chain, stripping all his skin off and finally killing him. Afraid to move, the girls were begging God to stop this awful act!

Twenty years later, one of the sisters was on her knees, praying for her stepfather. He had undergone surgery and could have no pain medication due to the location of the surgery. He was suffering in excruciating pain in the hospital. As Brenda earnestly prayed, the Lord spoke strongly to her heart. "Get up. There is no use praying. Do you remember what your stepfather did to the mule twenty years ago? Well, he's reaping what he sowed, and I will let him up when I finish with him."

This true story is an apt description of God's Words, *"Be not deceived. God is not mocked, for whatever a man sows, that shall he reap. For he that sows to the flesh shall of the flesh reap corruption." Galatians 6:7, 8* God is not ignoring sin! He is holy and His wrath is against sin. He will not tolerate it, because it destroys and ravages lives. He tells you in His Word what sin is, what to do with it, and how to live a life pleasing to Him. You can disregard Him if you like, go on living as you please, and perhaps continue on for years like this. But, don't be deceived! God is NOT mocked! You will reap what you sow…that's a given!

Sowing and reaping are unchangeable laws in God's universe, both physically and spiritually. You always reap what you sow…more than you sow…and later than you sow. If you sow corn, you will reap corn; if you sow to the flesh, you will reap corruption of the flesh. If you sow one seed, you will reap a vine; if you sow one sin, you will reap a vine of problems. And, if you sow today, you will reap sometime later. It may be several days or months or years before you reap. But, you WILL reap!

Today, you are sowing a crop. You are sowing either sinful or righteous seeds and you will reap a crop from these. Whatever you would like to reap is what you must sow. Therefore, today, begin sowing for tomorrow. The crop you reap will be the one you have sown.

GALATIANS 6:7,8 *"Be not deceived, God is not mocked, for whatever a man soweth, that shall he reap. For he that soweth to the flesh shall of the flesh reap corruption."*

March 25

Get out of the basement!

Your prayer life is the pits. You pray and pray, but rarely see any answers. God has promised that you can have the desires of your heart, but He's not giving you any of those things you want. You might as well throw in the towel on prayer. It doesn't work!

Friend, you are missing something vital about prayer.You think prayer is a means of getting things from God instead of a means of getting to know God. You are looking for God's hand instead of looking for His heart. To you, prayer is a vehicle to carry you to the goal you desire. You have failed to realize that prayer IS the goal. Prayer IS the end!

Prayer is communication with your Heavenly Father...and communication is a two-way street. You tell Him all that is on your heart: all your hurts and disappointments; all your joys and delights; all your hopes; all your sin and failure; and everything that is going on in your little world. He also tells you everything that is on His heart: His joys and His sorrows; His burdens; His love for His creation; His plans for you; His desires for you: His expectations of you; and everything that concerns His purposes and His heart.

If you still consider prayer as just asking God for a list of things you want, your prayers are still on a very elementary level. You see only a small part of the whole. You are hanging around in an unfinished basement when there is the whole house. An unfinished basement cannot satisfy all your needs. You need a kitchen when you're hungry, a bedroom when you're tired, a bathroom when bodily toxins need to be expelled, a den when you need to relax, and a game-room when you need to laugh and play.

Today, God loves you and desires an intimate relationship with you. This is only developed through the Word and prayer. He wants you to get out of the basement and live in the whole house. He wants you to look for His heart, not just His hand. He wants you to learn that prayer is not a means to an answer: prayer IS the answer!

PSALM 63:1 *"O God, Thou art my God, early will I seek Thee; my soul thirsteth for Thee, my flesh longeth for Thee, in a dry and thirsty land, where no water is."*

March 26

Get off the rug and onto the rock

Your company didn't give you the raise you deserve. Your co-worker complained to the boss about you. Your husband won't come to church with you. Your children are out of God's will, living in the world. Your trusted friend betrayed you. Your family members are having more problems than you can count. You had extra bills this month and not enough money to pay them. None of your friends came to see you in the hospital.

Disappointments! Disappointments! Disappointments! Life is filled with them. You get your hopes up, only to have the rug jerked out from under you every time. Each time it gets jerked out, you fall flat on your face.

Well, no wonder! You are putting your hopes and expectations and desires in a company, or a person, or finances, or your circumstances. You are putting yourself into things that can change in a split second. You are building your house on sinking sand. If your purpose in life is any of these things and your joy is derived from them, then prepare yourself for the rug to be jerked out!

Why don't you get off the rug and onto the Rock? A rock cannot be jerked out from under you. A rock is solid. A rock is strong. Jesus is that spiritual Rock! It is time you begin building everything upon Him. Build all your hopes, all your expectations, all your desires, all your life upon Him! If He is your heart, your breath, and your life, then there will not be anything to jerk out from under you except Him...and He can't be moved!

What are you standing on today? Is there anything that could trip you, shake you, or bring you down? If so, you are standing on a rug, just waiting for it to be jerked out from under you. It is simply a matter of time. So, why don't you get off that rug and onto the Rock? You'll be eternally glad you did!

I CORINTHIANS 10:4 *"... for they drank of that spiritual Rock that followed them, and that Rock was Christ."*

March 27

All that glitters is not gold!

My hopes have just been shattered! I thought I was rich. After searching for years, I finally struck what I thought was gold! It was everywhere! Oh, I could just imagine buying all those things I had wanted all my life but could never afford. I was so excited!

However, my excitement was short-lived, as I was told that this was fool's gold. It looked exactly like the real thing but was worthless. I had given my whole life for nothing. Everything had revolved around finding the big one. Upon finding it, I now discovered that I had been a fool. I had gone after something that did not profit me, something that left me completely empty and defeated.

Maybe this describes you. You are on a search in this life. You are looking for happiness, prosperity, and stability. You have been searching for years. You thought your spouse could bring you what you wanted. You thought more money could do it. You thought a new house would change things. You thought a change of jobs would help. So, you have gone from one thing to another. You are restless. Your soul is like the troubled sea, whose waters cast up mire and dirt.

Are you tired of looking, especially since everything you have touched has turned to fool's gold? Well, the real thing has been there all the time, but you have overlooked it. The real thing is Jesus Christ. He is what you are looking for, although you have never realized that. Things, people, jobs, money, nor all the world has to offer can ever satisfy you. They always leave you dry, barren, and thirsty.

Today, why don't you turn to Jesus? Beware of fool's gold. The devil will dangle many good things in front of your face to entice you. They will look exactly like what you need to help you and solve your problems. But, just remember: All that glitters is not gold. Real gold is Jesus. Everything else is only fool's gold.

PHILIPPIANS 3:7 *"But what things were gain to me, those I counted loss for Christ."*

March 28

What about my rights?

How can this be? This One, whose celestial home is more glorious than anything eyes have ever seen, has no place to lay His head. This One, who fashioned man from the dust of the earth, is washing the feet of those He created. This One, whom myriads of angels surround in praise and adoration, has been deserted by all His friends. This One, who spoke rivers and oceans into existence, is crying, "I thirst." This One, who planned and created the earth and all that's on it, is hanging suspended on a tree He made Himself. This One, who is life itself, has tasted death.

How can this be? This One, who has all legal rights to the universe, has given them up! He has laid them aside to completely give Himself for others. The Highest has become the lowest. The Creator has become a servant. The Exalted One has humbled Himself.

In this modern age, the age of rights, people everywhere are clamoring for their rights. Minority groups are screaming for their rights. Women are proclaiming the right to do what they choose with their unborn children. Children are standing for their rights against their parents. Welfare recipients are asserting rights. Accident victims are suing for their rights. Even in churches, people are claiming rights to run things their way.

This is madness! This is backwards! The creature has the soft pillow while the Creator has a stone. The creature is being served, demanding that the Creator give him what he asks for. The creature is being praised and exalted, some being paid millions of dollars to run a ball up and down a field or to strum a guitar, while the Creator is being ignored. The creature is insisting on his rights, while his very existence depends upon the One who laid down all His rights for others.

Where do you fit in this picture? If your great Creator gave up His rights for you, then why are you holding onto yours? If He came to minister, not to be ministered unto, then why are you expecting everyone to minister to you? Give up your rights. They are not yours anyway.You have but one right.....the right to serve God and others with all your heart!

PHILIPPIANS 2:8 *"He humbled Himself and became obedient unto death."*

March 29

Try or trust

Stepping aboard the huge jet, you find your seat and sit down. You have committed yourself to the airplane to take you to your destination. You have entrusted your life into the hands of a pilot whom you don't even know. Having confidence in the airlines, you figure the pilot has been thoroughly trained and is entirely able to fly this big bird safely. You don't run up to the cockpit, telling him how to fly the plane. You don't panic when he makes a sudden turn. You don't tell him to change directions when the plane hits turbulence. You don't even ask the pilot if he knows what he is doing. You just sit there and trust him. After all, you can't fly a plane. It would crash! It is either try or trust!

As you step aboard the plane of life, you find your seat and sit down. You are headed for a destination, but you cannot get yourself there. So, you must commit yourself to One who can take you. You must totally put your life into the hands of the One who is the Master Pilot. He knows much more than you do. He created life, so He certainly ought to know how to run one. If you can't trust Him, then whom would you trust? He has run millions of lives before yours, so you can just put it all in His hands.

Don't try to help Him run your life. Don't panic when your life takes a sudden turn. Don't tell Him to change directions when your life hits turbulence. In fact, don't even ask Him if He knows what He is doing. After all, you can't fly the plane. It would crash...and your life would end up one big, crumpled, ruined wreckage. It's either try or trust.

Today, won't you commit yourself to Jesus? Quit trying and start trusting! He will take you safely to your destination. Get on board, find your place, and put everything in the Master Pilot's hands. Enjoy your journey!

PROVERBS 3:5 *"Trust in the Lord with all thine heart and lean not unto thine own understanding. In all thy ways acknowledge Him and He shall direct thy paths.*

March 30

Webs and water

Early in the morning, after the dew has fallen upon the earth, spider webs will often appear all over your lawn and shrubs. These webs were invisible in the night to the eye. They are also invisible after the sun rises and dries the dew from the grass. It is only as the dew falls and each little bead of water cups itself around a strand of the web that the web becomes visible to the human eye.

Spiritually, this is also true. There are many spider webs of sin in each of our lives. Thousands of strands have been woven by the master deceiver, Satan. We can go along through our lives perfectly fine, never even taking notice of all these hidden webs. They are invisible to the spiritual eye. They are invisible, that is, until the dew falls! The spiritual dew is the precious Word of God. God says of His church that "*He might sanctify and cleanse it with the washing of water by the Word." Ephesians 5:26*

As you spend time in the Word, quietly allowing God to speak to your heart, the precious dew will begin to cup itself around each strand of sin in your life. These webs will be exposed and can be seen by your spiritual eyes. You will recognize, for the first time, sins in your life that you didn't know were there. You must get still and settled, however, for this dew to fall. Busyness, activity, or too much wind will keep the dew from falling. The Bible says, "*Be still and know that I am God." Psalm 46:10*

Once a spider web is exposed, that is the time to get rid of it. If you wait until later in the day, the dew will be gone and you can no longer see the web. The same thing is true when God's Word exposes your sin. Deal with it immediately. Confess it , agree with God that you have wronged Him, turn from it, and God will forgive and cleanse you of that sin. The web will be gone forever!

Christian, there are many webs of sin in your life that cannot be readily seen. Even you don't know all the sins that are there! They need to be removed so your life can be more effective for God. But, webs need water to be exposed. Therefore, get in the dew of God's Word and let its waters do their work!

EPHESIANS 5:26 *"That he might sanctify and cleanse it with the washing of water by the Word."*

March 31

Syrophenician faith

It was too good to be true! Jesus, the Man of miracles, had come into the borders of Tyre and Sidon where she lived. She had heard much about this One they called Jesus and knew that He was her only hope. She had tried everything else and no one could even come close to solving her problem. In desperation, she cried out to Him, believing that he could and would help her. "*Have mercy on me, Thou Son of David; my daughter is grievously vexed with a demon.*" *Matthew 15:22*

Jesus answered her not a word. At this point, most of us would have been picking up the pieces of our shattered faith and leaving this time of prayer in defeat and discouragement. Just a little silence from the Lord would stop our feeble prayer wheels from turning. But it didn't stop this Syrophenician woman! Her faith could not be turned into doubt that easily. Even the attitude of the disciples did not stop her. As the Jews had little use for the Gentiles, the disciples must have been aggravated and put out by this persistent Gentile woman. They came to Jesus, saying, "*Send her away; for she crieth after us.*" *Matthew 15:23*

However, in spite of Jesus' silence and the rejection by the disciples, the woman came back to the Lord again and even worshiped Him. Still believing He would meet her need, she said, "*Lord, help me.*" *Matthew 15:25* This time, He answered her, but with a seemingly harsh and inconsiderate answer, "*It is not right to take the children's bread, and to cast it to dogs.*" *Matthew 15:26* By now, most of us, without hesitation, would have thrown in the towel! And, we'd probably have joined into partnership with "bad attitude," "pity party," "blame," "unbelief," or one of the other intruders that always show up at times like these, offering their logical, but deceptive advice.

Ah, but not the Syrophenician woman! Completely ignoring these intruders, she still believed the Lord in spite of all odds. She responded, "*Truth, Lord; yet the dogs eat of the crumbs which fall from their master's table.*"*Matthew 15:27* Realizing that she was undeserving and unworthy did not stop her. She knew that Jesus didn't answer prayers based on one's worth or merit, but rather based on one's faith. Therefore, as she kept on knocking, Jesus responded, "*O woman, great is thy faith; be it unto you even as you will.*" *Matthew 15:28* and He granted her the petition she desired of Him.

How's your faith today? Have you thrown in the towel? Has your prayer life just about dried up in unbelief? If so, perhaps you need to visit the Syrophenician woman today and take some lessons from her! All you need is some Syrophenician faith!

MATTHEW 15;28 *"O woman, great is thy faith; be it unto thee even as thou wilt."*

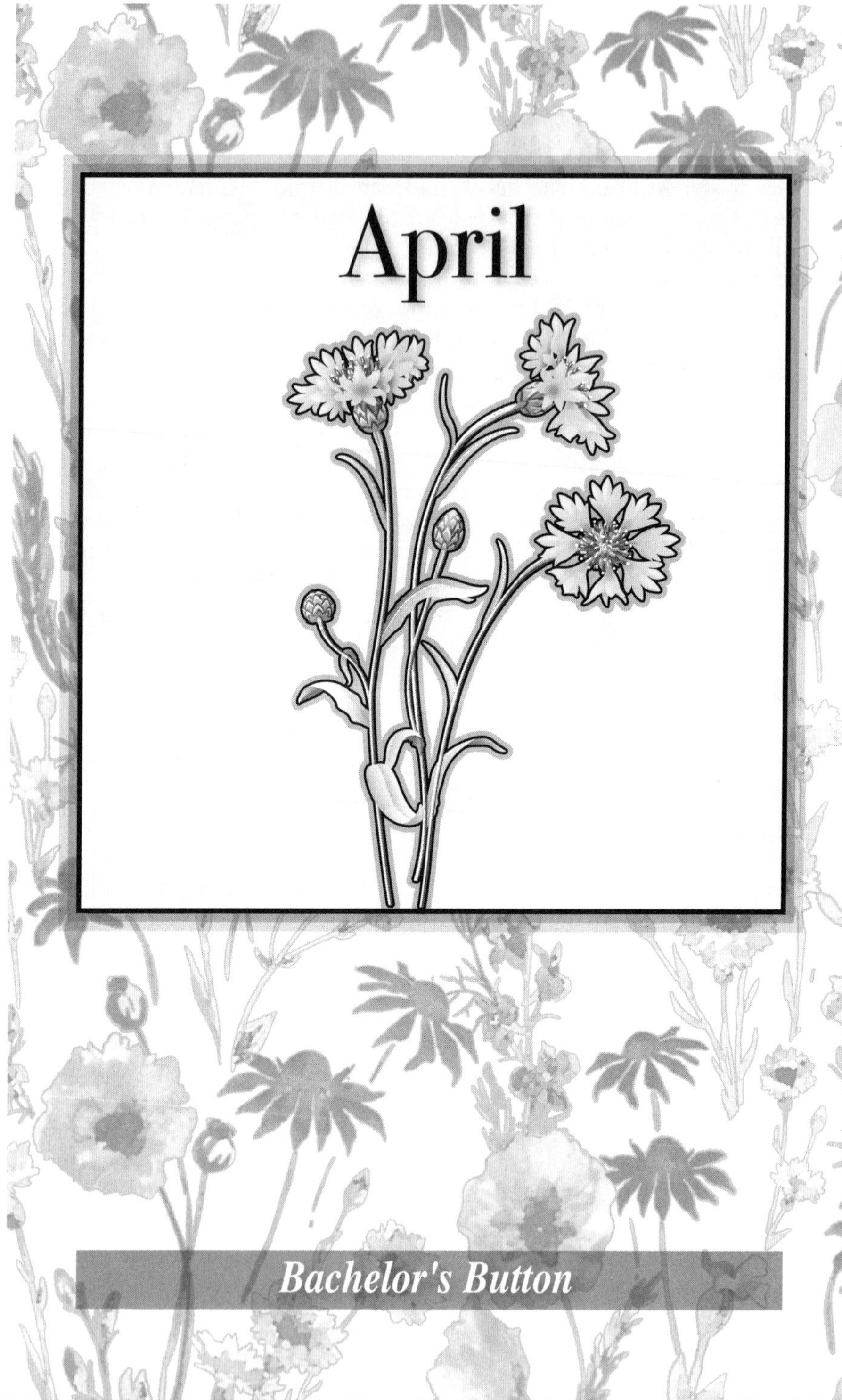
April
Bachelor's Button

April 1

Do you have bloody hands?

Never before had he experienced anything even remotely similar to this! He had been working in this same slaughter-house for years, just doing his job like he was supposed to do. It was Joe's responsibility to kill the cows as they passed down the assembly line. With one hand, he would pull the cow's head back. With the other hand, he would draw the knife across the throat of the cow as she passed by on the line. And, immediately upon slitting the cow's throat, she would fall over dead.

But, this was totally different! This wasn't a cow…and didn't respond like a cow. No one had bothered to tell Joe that the slaughter-house had added lambs to their inventory. Joe had never killed a lamb before. But, because it was his job, he proceeded in much the same way as he had with the cows. He pulled the little lamb's head back with one hand and drew the knife across its throat with the other hand. However, unlike the cows, the little lamb did not fall over dead immediately. Instead, with blood gushing forth and covering Joe's hands, the lamb continued to stand on its feet. Without making a sound, it looked over at him with the most pitiful, loving eyes he had ever seen…and licked the blood off his hands before falling over dead!

What a picture of our precious Lord this is! *Isaiah 53:7 says, "He was oppressed, and He was afflicted, yet He opened not His mouth. He is brought as a lamb to the slaughter, and as a sheep before her shearers is dumb, so He openeth not His mouth."* As the perfect "Lamb of God" was being slaughtered for sins He did not commit, He looked with loving eyes on those who had nailed Him to the cross and said, *"Father, forgive them; for they know not what they do."Luke 23:34*

When I look back on this scene, I realize that it was my sins that put Jesus on the cross. It was not just the sins of the Roman soldiers; it was not just the sins of the government of that day; it was not just the sins of those shouting, "*Crucify Him*" that nailed Him to that cross. Oh, no! It was also my sins that nailed Him there. *Isaiah 53:5 says, "But He was wounded for* ***our*** *transgressions, He was bruised for* ***our*** *iniquities…"* So, it was my sin, my wickedness, my disobedience, and my pride that put Jesus on that cross. I am guilty! However, just as the little lamb took the blood off Joe's hands, so the precious Lamb of God is calling to whosoever will…"*Come unto Me and I will wash the blood from your hands.*"

Have you ever been to Him, the One whom you have wronged, to ask forgiveness? He was wounded for your transgressions. He was bruised for your iniquities. He died on the cross, not just for the sins of others, but for your sins as well. And, He is pleading with you to come today…just as you are. He wants to take His blood off your hands…but He cannot do so until you come! May today be the day of your salvation!

JOHN 14:6 *"Jesus said unto him, I am the way, the truth, and the life…"*

April 2

One-sixth or five-sixths?

They had never seen anything like it! It was a beautiful land, a fruitful land, a land flowing with milk and honey. The grapes that were growing in the land were so large that one cluster had to be carried on a pole over the shoulders of two men. Joshua and Caleb couldn't wait to tell Moses what they saw in the land. They figured that Moses and all the children of Israel would be ready to go in and take the land, especially since God had already told them the land was theirs. So, Joshua and Caleb, after spying out the land, came back with a positive report, ready to step out on the Word of God!

But, the other ten spies who went with them didn't agree. They came back with a negative report. They told Moses and the Israelites that there were giants in the land…big, strong giants. They also told them that the cities all had big, huge walls surrounding them, making them impossible to conquer. Therefore, they reported, in no uncertain terms, that they could not go in and take this land that God had promised them!

To whom would you listen in a case like this? If five-sixths of the people agreed on a certain course of action and only one-sixth agreed on another course, it would only seem logical to go with the majority. And, of course, that's exactly what the children of Israel did. They went with the five-sixths. They judged their course of action by looking at the circumstances which the ten spies reported, believing that they could not overcome giants nor bring down walls. They ignored God's Word in favor of sight. They refused to go into Canaan and take it. The abundant land of Canaan, which God had said was theirs, was only eleven miles away. Yet, because of unbelief, they wandered in the wilderness for forty years, one year for each day they searched out the land. They settled for thorns when they could have had roses.

However, Joshua and Caleb, the one-sixth, survived the wilderness wanderings. And, because of their belief in God despite the giants and the walls, they got to go into the land of Canaan after all. They saw a God who was bigger than any obstacle they could ever face and they believed Him. They believed…they stepped out on His Word…and they conquered!

Today, Christian, you are either part of the five-sixths or part of the one-sixth. You are either going with the majority or with the remnant. It's up to you where you want to dwell while here on earth…in the wilderness or in the spiritual land of Canaan. You can choose, by unbelief, to wander in the wilderness of Christian experience, like the majority are. Or, you can believe God, step out on His Word, and conquer the giants and walls that you come up against. Like Caleb and Joshua, you can be that one-sixth who go in and possess the land!

NUMBERS 14:30 *"Doubtless, you shall not come into the land, concerning which I swore to make you dwell therein, except Caleb… and Joshua…"*

April 3

The tongue: Prosecutor, Jury, and Judge

The courtroom is in session! In fact, it's in session most of your waking hours. Numerous trials take place in this courtroom every day. Multitudes of people are on its docket during the course of a lifetime. Many assassinations occur here. Many are put in chains here. Many are ruined for life here. Many are tried repeatedly and sentenced to strange and unusual penalties here. This unusual courtroom is your mouth. And, inside its doors, sit a prosecutor, a jury, and a judge…each of which is your tongue!

Pretty soon after waking up in the morning, the prosecutor (your tongue) starts his job. First, he hears evidence against someone from another party. And, as he begins to question witnesses, he picks up even more evidence. Then, upon considering this evidence, the prosecutor presents his opening statement to the jury. He enumerates many negative things about the accused….and, of course, he has a list a mile long. No matter how many good things there are about the accused, the prosecutor won't mention any of them. He presents his biased, negative, judgmental information to the jury and to anyone else in the courtroom who will listen in an effort to convince them of the accused one's guilt. And, since most folks like a stink, the prosecutor usually has no problem persuading others to see things his way.

Next, after the prosecutor has finished his job, the jury…which is also your tongue… takes over. It weighs all the evidence presented by the prosecutor and decides on a verdict. Of course, all the evidence is one-sided, as there is no defense attorney on the case. Therefore, with nothing but negative, critical, judgmental evidence whatsoever in the accused one's favor, the verdict is always the same.....guilty!

And finally, your tongue sits as judge. After the prosecutor has presented his airtight case and the jury has rendered a verdict of guilty, the judge has no choice but to pronounce the accused one guilty, as charged. Then, the judge proceeds with the sentence, which is always derogatory and punitive instead of corrective.

How's the courtroom of your mouth today, Christian? Perhaps your courtroom needs some major changes. It could easily be altered if the prosecutor became a defense attorney instead. Rather than looking for incriminating evidence against another person, try looking for good things about them. Present the jury with every good quality, every strong point, every positive thing you can name about the accused. The jury will pronounce the accused one not guilty, if it receives such overwhelming evidence in favor of the accused. And the judge, after hearing the verdict of not guilty, will dismiss the case.

Today, friend, your mouth is a courtroom. Your tongue holds a strategic position. It's either prosecutor or defense attorney. It can bring death or life to others. What position does your tongue hold?

JAMES 3:6 *"And the tongue is a fire, a world of iniquity; so is the tongue among our members that it defileth the whole body, and setteth on fire the course of nature."*

April 4

Is your soul in a drought?

The things I always want to do
I cannot seem to do.
Instead I do the other things
I never want to do.

I plan each day to meet with God
To read the Word and pray,
But it seems that something else
Is always getting in my way.

Each morning is a mad rush…Getting
dressed and clothed and fed. And at
night, I'm just so tired
That I fall right into bed.

No wonder I stay worried,
And filled with fear and doubt.
I'm not drinking Living Water,
So my soul is in a drought.

Well, today I have decided
Life's too short to live this way.
Instead of letting "self" control,
It's Christ I'll now obey.

I'll rise early every morning
While my household's still in bed,
And spend some time alone with God,
Drinking Water and eating Bread.

I'll start and end each day with Christ
To Him, I'll give my best,
And then, I know He'll fill my soul
With peace and joy and rest.

Then that parched and barren desert
Which once described my soul
Will become a watered garden
And at last will be made whole.

There are many American Christians who have such a hectic lifestyle that they have very little time for God. They feed, water, and exercise their bodies, but neglect their souls. This results in barren, dry, parched, malnourished, weak, sickly souls…filled with fear, doubts, discouragement, depression, etc. The answer to this dilemma is Jesus Christ…spending time alone with Him in the Word and in prayer. Nothing else will work! Only Jesus can satisfy the soul!

PSALM 63:1 *"O God, Thou art my God, early will I seek Thee; my soul thirsteth for Thee, my flesh longeth for Thee, in a dry and thirsty land, where no water is.*

April 5

Grace, Grit, and Glory!

For years, I had been struggling with it! It was on my mind all day long, off and on. I just couldn't ever seem to get victory over it. At times, I would think I had victory and would do pretty good for a little while…but then, the stronghold would come back just as bad as before or even worse. I knew the Lord wanted complete control over this area of my life, but I had never surrendered it to Him completely. I wanted to eat what I wanted, when I wanted, and how much I wanted. I really didn't want to turn my eating habits over to the Lord and eat exactly what He said, when He said, and how much He said. I was reserving the right to make the final decision myself in this important part of my everyday life.

Oh, I would tell folks I wanted victory over it, because I felt guilty. I even had people pray over me for deliverance…but to no avail. I tried a lot of different things, none of which worked for long. Finally, I came to the conclusion that I just couldn't do it. I couldn't get victory over my eating habits. I decided that God would just have to do it for me. What I really wanted, however, was the easy way out. I didn't want it to cost me anything. I didn't want to say no to my flesh. I didn't want to suffer!

Then one day, I came to a rude awakening. I was listening to someone who was overweight condemning someone else who smoked…and I was agreeing. It just slapped me in the face. It's as if God said to me, "Who do you think you are? How in the world can you help others with their strongholds when you don't have victory over yours?"

Suddenly, I realized that I had not believed God! I had actually called Him a liar when I said I couldn't, because He said in His Word that I can do all things through Christ who strengthens me. The bottom line wasn't that I couldn't…it was that I wouldn't! I was too soft and lazy. It dawned on me that, if lost folks training for the Olympics can get victory over their eating habits with their own will power, then I certainly should be able to do so with God's power. He already won the victory on Calvary and imparted His power to me at my spiritual birth. So, I didn't need prayer for deliverance…I needed grit! I needed to stand in His victory by the sheer determination of my will. He saved me by His grace (justification)… with nothing on my part! One day, He will take me to glory (glorification)…with nothing on my part. But, between grace and glory, there's grit (sanctification)….with me daily learning to die to my flesh and live unto Christ. That's my part! It's not easy, but then God hasn't called me to a picnic. He has called me to a battle. I'm to be a good soldier, not entangling myself with the affairs of this life.

So, I have made up my mind. I am standing in His victory! I refuse to be a wimp for my Lord! I refuse to let the world do, by their own power, what I should be able to do with God's power! I surrender my eating habits to the Lord and I can and will eat what He says, when He says, and how much He says! "*I can do all things through Christ, who strengthens me.*"

PHILIPPIANS 4:13 *"I can do all things through Christ, who strengtheneth me."*

April 6

The Battlefield, the Enemy, and the Weapons

"For we wrestle not against flesh and blood..." Ephesians 6:12 If we could ever learn this, we would have learned a most valuable lesson in our spiritual walk. We waste so much time on the wrong battlefield, fighting the wrong enemy, using the wrong weapons. No wonder the war still rages and people around us remain unchanged! We are busy attacking decoys while the real enemy goes unopposed! So, let's learn how to fight effectively.

First, get on the right battlefield. The battlefield is not your circumstances or your problems, so quit setting up camp and dwelling there. The battlefield is your mind. Your adversary, who has been around for over six thousand years and is much smarter and more experienced than you are, launches his attacks in your mind. So, to defeat him, you must bring your Captain to the battlefield. Fill your mind with thoughts of Him. Learn to take every thought captive to the obedience of Christ. Allow Christ to take control of your mind. Stay on your knees until your have prayed through to victory.

Second, make sure you are fighting the right enemy. That person in your life or that situation is NOT your enemy…so quit attacking them with your words. You'll never win the battle that way. Satan is your real enemy. He's the one you should be going after. He is behind all those attacks. So, gird up your loins with Truth, put on the breastplate of righteousness, shod your feet with the preparation of the gospel of peace, take the shield of faith, put on the helmet of salvation, take the sword of the Spirit, and use it all against the right enemy…the devil!

Third, make sure you use the right weapons. The only weapon you have against Satan is the Word! That's the weapon Jesus used against him! It is not your words, your works, your prodding, or your efforts. It is God's Word that defeats the wicked one! God's Word is your sword!

Friend, are you constantly fighting but never seeing anything changed? If so, perhaps you are fighting on the wrong battlefield, focusing on your situation or your circumstances. Or you may be using the wrong weapon…your tongue… against the wrong enemy…another person. It's time to get on the right battlefield, attack the right enemy, and use the right weapon. This is war…fight it God's way!

EPHESIANS 6:12 *"For we wrestle not against flesh and blood, but against principalities and powers, against the rulers of the darkness of this world..."*

April 7

Kibrothhattaavah

Dead bodies were everywhere! It appeared that something awful had happened, killing all the people simultaneously. But something was very strange about it all. Every one of the dead had something in their mouths and something coming out their nostrils. It looked as though they were killed, perhaps poisoned, by this stuff, which actually was some kind of meat.

The few folks that were left alive were digging graves and burying all the dead. They knew exactly what had killed the multitudes. They knew…and, with a fear of God, they named the place, Kibrothhattaavah, which means graves of lust. They knew that it wasn't poisonous meat or some strange disease that killed everyone. It was lust. Lust dug those graves!

Going back to this particular time in Israel's history, we find the circumstances leading to this tragedy. God had miraculously parted the Red Sea, delivering the children of Israel from Egypt. He led them with a cloud by day and a pillar of fire by night. And, the Lord fed them supernaturally with manna, which literally fell from heaven each night. All they had to do was gather and prepare it. God delivered them, led them, and fed them.

Yet, in spite of such awesome miracles, and in spite of God's wonderful provision and protection, the Israelites were dissatisfied. They began murmuring and complaining. They remembered the worldly things in Egypt…the onions, the leeks, and the garlic…and they longed after those things. They whined about the manna, begging God for meat instead. They kept on begging and kept on begging and kept on begging until God finally relented. He told them they could have what they insisted on, but they wouldn't want it after they got it. He told them it would come out their nostrils, which it did!

Today, God has led you out of your Egypt into salvation. He is leading you daily by His Word and providing for you along the way. Don't make the same mistake the Israelites did. Don't be whining and murmuring and complaining about things during your spiritual journey. Don't be lusting after things you used to have in the world. God may let you have those worldly things if you keep pushing Him..... but they will come out your nostrils! Lust for worldly things will only kill your spiritual life and you will end in a spiritual grave! You will, like the Israelites, end up in Kibrothhattaavah!

NUMBERS 11:34 *"...there they buried the people that lusted."*

April 8

Going on a dead rat hunt

It was a lesson she would never forget! She had always thought, "Out of sight, out of mind," but it certainly wasn't true in this case. It might have been out of sight, but the smell was a dead give away! She had been in a big hurry when she found the dead rat in her outbuilding that day. She didn't have time to remove him then, so she just swept him under the rug temporarily...and planned on removing him later. However, she forgot about him…until company showed up. Taking them to her outbuilding to show them where she stored things she didn't use all the time, she discovered that you cannot simply cover dead things! You must remove them!

There are many folks today who deal with their sin as this woman dealt with the rat. They cover it up. They sweep it under the rug rather than remove it. They go about their business as usual, as though everything is fine. And, their sin will go unnoticed for a time. However, covered sin will do the same thing as that dead rat. It will eventually start stinking. Out of sight does not mean out of mind. You may bury your sin down in the depths of your heart, but the filth and stench of it will inevitably seep into all other areas of your life.

Today would be a good day to go on a dead rat hunt. Maybe you have some buried rats that you have forgotten about. Get out your sin detector, the Word of God. It will prick your heart every time it passes over a buried rat. Perhaps there is some bitterness that you have carried against your parents since childhood. Perhaps you have been dishonest with someone or have hurt someone in the past and have never made it right. Maybe there is an unresolved rift between you and someone else. Maybe you have judged, gossiped, or harbored unforgiveness. Maybe you have been critical, impatient, deceptive, proud, foolish, covetous, jealous, or envious.

If you are really serious about finding dead rats, God will help you. Make some time to get alone with Him. Find a quiet, undisturbed place. Allow enough time to do heart business with the Lord. Take your Bible, some paper, and a pen. As you read the Word, meditate on it, and pray over it, ask the Lord to reveal every dead rat in your life. Write them down as He brings them to your memory. Then go back and confess each sin individually before God, claiming *I John 1:9*. As you confess, God will remove the sin. It won't be just swept under the rug. It will be gone forever!

Friend, you don't want to stink spiritually, do you? If not, then deal with the sin in your life today...and keep short accounts with God. Remember: You cannot cover dead things. You must remove them!

LUKE 12:2 *"For there is nothing covered, that shall not be revealed..."*

April 9

Get in the wheelbarrow

Looking out across the mountain on which you are standing to the neighboring mountain, you spot a tight rope stretched between the two mountains. Between the mountains, lying thousands of feet below, is a valley. A man pushing a wheelbarrow rolls right up in front of you and asks, "Do you believe I can roll this wheelbarrow over the tight rope, across to the other mountain, and then back to you again?" You quickly shake your head "No" in unbelief. You know that it would be highly unlikely for someone to do something so foolish. However, the man proceeds to go across. He walks as straight as an arrow, with not even the slightest bobble. He goes across to the neighboring mountain and then back again quite easily. Then, rolling the wheelbarrow back up to you again, he asks a second time, "Do you believe I can roll this wheelbarrow over the tight rope, across to the other mountain, and back to you again?" You quickly respond, "Yes." Then, the man says, "Well, get in!"

This is where the rubber meets the road. It is very easy to say you believe about something, but to "get in" is another story. If you really truly believe, you will have no problem getting in. Otherwise, you still have doubts, indicating unbelief.

Today, you are sitting on the mountaintop of the present. Across from you is the mountaintop of eternity, with a great gulf between. Jesus comes up to you, telling you He will carry you across. You have a decision to make. You can sit there, saying you believe in Him. You can talk about it. You can even watch others get in. But, your belief about Him will not get you across the gulf. You must get in yourself. That is, you must fully commit your life to the Lord Jesus Christ. You must turn the complete control of your life over to Him. You must let go of the world, leave all the worldly things behind, get in the wheelbarrow of God's love, and let Jesus carry you across.

"For God so loved the world that He gave His only begotten Son, that whosoever believeth IN Him should not perish, but have everlasting life." It is not enough that you believe about Him. The devils believe and they tremble! You must believe IN Him, getting into His wheelbarrow and allowing Him to carry you across time into eternity. Why don't you get in the wheelbarrow today, if you haven't already done so?

JOHN 3:16 *"For God so loved the world that He gave His only begotten Son, that whosoever believeth in Him should not perish, but have everlasting life."*

April 10

Come

Peter stepped out of the boat with confidence. Jesus had said to him, "*Come*," and that was all Peter needed.....just one word from his Lord. He knew he could step out on what Jesus said. Peter knew he was not stepping out on the water.... he was stepping out on the Word, the one little word, "Come!" He never even thought about the circumstances. He didn't consider the high winds and huge waves. He was not thinking about the impossibility. All he was thinking about was that his master had said, "*Come*"...and he did exactly that!

However, once he stepped out of his comfort zone, out of the security of the vessel, he began to look around. At that point, he realized what a nut he was. He must be out of his mind! Anyone with good sense would not get out of a secure boat into an ocean, especially in the fourth watch of the night, between three and six A. M. It was dark! And besides, the wind was turbulent and the waves were enormous. No one could make it under these conditions. Recognizing the utter impossibility of his situation brought doubts and fears and Peter started to sink. It was not the winds and the waves that sank him. Oh, no! He had been walking on top of them just a minute before. It was unbelief that sank him. He had taken his eyes off Jesus. He had forgotten Jesus' Word to him, "*Come*." He had instead looked at his circumstances and had quit believing....and he began to sink!

Perhaps it's dark in your life right now. Fierce winds of adversity are blowing. There is much turbulence. You want Jesus to calm the winds and still the waves, so you can stay in your comfortable little boat. However, He is not speaking to the storm. He is speaking to you! He wants to see how much you really believe Him. He wants you to, "Come." So, are you going to look around at your situation and sum up how hopeless and impossible it is? Will you sit there in fear as you look at the winds and the waves? Or, are you going to fully set your eyes upon Jesus, looking to Him rather than the impossibilities, and step out in your storm? Will you trust Him today? He has said, "*Come.*" What are you going to do?

MATTHEW 14:29 *"And He said, "Come."*

April 11

What are you preparing for?

He was a very wealthy man. He had the finest of clothing, dressing in royal purple and fine linen. He always had the choicest and most appetizing food and drink at his table. Everything he needed and wanted was at his disposal. He was proud of his accomplishments, because he had worked hard to get where he was. He disdained the poor, looking down on all those who had not made anything of their lives.

Daily at his gate was a certain poor beggar, named Lazarus. Lazarus was unsightly, with his body full of sores, which the dogs came and licked every day. Lazarus was hungry. He begged for even the crumbs from the rich man's table. But, the rich man had no use for Lazarus, no time for this beggar, no sympathy for this low class individual.

However, death came knocking one day. The rich man had spent his entire life preparing to live. He had invested his time and efforts into making money and looking after his own needs. He had not made time for others. Lazarus, on the other hand, had spent his life preparing to die. He had given his heart to God. Instead of having the things of the world, he had the things of eternity.

Unprepared, the rich man slipped through the fingers of time into eternity. In a split second, he closed his eyes to the finer things of life and opened them to the eternal torments of hell. He was in an everlasting abyss of flames…forever! Lazarus closed his eyes to the tragedies and trials of poverty and opened them to the riches of glory…forever!

One day you will also slip through the fingers of time into eternity. You are preparing now for where you will be at that time. Are you busy preparing for life, caught up in the world with all its pleasures and attractions and entertainment? Are you concerned only for you and yours? Are you passing by the Lazaruses at your gate? Or, are you busy preparing for death, laying up treasures in heaven rather than on earth? Are you giving a drink of cold water in His name, visiting the sick, helping the widows and orphans, taking care of the needy…in other words, are you ministering to the Lazaruses around you?

Friend, you only have one life, one short life, and an unending eternity. Which one are you preparing for?

LUKE 16:23 *"...and in hell he lifted up his eyes, being in torments..."*

April 12

Diamonds aren't made on sofas

Diamonds aren't made on sofas. Neither can they be produced by opening a packet, pouring it into a glass, stirring…..and presto…..instant diamond! They cannot be ormed in an hour, a day, a year, or in any length of time you might wait. You cannot go through a drive-through window, a fast-diamond store, or even a manufacturing plant to produce them. They are made in solitude, alone in the heart of the earth. There, as intense heat and pressure from the earth are exerted over a period of time on a lump of coal, a marvelous transformation takes place. A black, dirty looking piece of coal becomes a sparkling, shining diamond. A single, worthless, common, ordinary lump becomes something of great beauty, value, and worth.

The trouble with us Christians is that we want to be diamonds for God, but we aren't willing to go through the diamond producing process. Somehow, in America, we've come to the conclusion that diamonds are made on sofas. We have the mistaken idea that we can lie in front of a TV set for hours on end and still be a diamond for God. We think we can half-heartedly serve God and yet become a jewel for Him. Our Americanized Christianity, the revised version, says that we can say a little prayer asking Jesus to save us, go out and live like we always have, and go to heaven when we die. Not so! Our imitation salvation today is like a drive-through window. "I'll take one Jesus to go; but hold the suffering and persecution. I'll take a side order of pleasing self and a big glass of carnality. Oh, and by the way, charge that to Jesus."

Friend, diamonds aren't made on sofas, and neither are valuable Christians. There's no such thing as an instant, drive-through Christian. A diamond Christian cannot be produced in an hour, a day, or even in a year. It takes a lifetime of heat and pressure, a lifetime of taking up the cross and following Christ. The cross is not comfortable or fun. It's suffering! Yet, it is the cross which puts the flesh to death, resulting in that black, dirty looking soul being transformed into a sparkling, shining diamond for God. That one ordinary, common, worthless life becomes something of great beauty and value and worth to the kingdom of God. So, yield gladly to the suffering, Christian. Yield to the persecution. Welcome the heat and pressure with thanksgiving. Remember: diamonds aren't made on sofas.

MALACHI 3:17 *"And they shall be Mine, saith the Lord of hosts, in that day when I make up My jewels"*

April 13

You can fly!

He could stay in the nest no longer. It had been lined with rabbit and squirrel fur and was soft and comfortable. However, his mother had removed all the lining and now there was nothing but sticks left. Since his nest was so uncomfortable, the baby eaglet wandered out to the edge of the cliff. He looked out at the strange new world that was all around him.

Moving in right beside him, the mother eagle beckoned her young one to get on her back. Not knowing what was in store, the eaglet complied. His mama soared off the cliff, right out over the deep valley below them. He held on for dear life. Gradually, he began to grow accustomed to this new way of life and even found it enjoyable. However, his joy was short lived. His mama suddenly began flying upside down. He dug his claws into her back and held on as long as he could. Finally, he lost his grip and plummeted downward, screeching and crying frantically as he fell. What he didn't know was that his mama could fly faster than he could fall. She swooped under him and caught him on her back before he hit the ground.

This process was repeated several times. Eventually, the eaglet began flapping his wings. Much to his surprise, he discovered that he, too, could fly. He had wings all along, but he just didn't know how to use them. He had to be dropped off into circumstances that forced him to use the wings God had granted him at conception.

Do you feel like that little eaglet? Has God removed all the comfortable lining from your nest, forcing you out into the world? Has God dropped you off a cliff of circumstances and you're plummeting downward at incredible speed? Friend, just remember: God won't let you hit bottom! He is there to catch you! He's just simply trying to teach you. He is putting you into circumstances to force you to use the spiritual wings He gave you at your new birth. You already have them, but have just never learned to use them yet. Little Christian, you can fly above the circumstances. So, spread your spiritual wings. Quit squawking and start flapping! You can fly, little Christian! You can fly!

JOB 12:7 *"But ask, now, the beasts, and they shall teach thee; and the fowls of the air, and they shall tell thee."*

April 14

Boot camp of your child's future

There's a lot more to it than you think there is! It consists of much more than just carrying him to church, reading the Bible with him, praying with him, and teaching him about the Lord. That's part of it…but it's only part. The Bible says, "*Train up a child in the way he should go, and when he is old, he will not depart from it." Proverbs 22:6* Likewise, the converse is also true. Train up a child in the way he shouldn't go, and when he is old, he will not depart from it either.

Train up a child to eat whatever he wants, whenever he wants, and however much he wants…and when he is old, he will not depart from it. Train up a child to stay home when he feels a little "under the weather," even though he has no fever, is not throwing up, and isn't terribly sick…and when he is old, he will not depart from it. Train up a child to run to the medicine cabinet to take something for every little bitty ache and pain, to depend upon something else to help him cope with whatever bothers him…and when he is old, he will not depart from it. Train up a child to be soft, always looking for ways to make life easier for himself…and when he is old, he will not depart from it. Train up a child to quit something when he doesn't like it, when it becomes too hard and too demanding…and when he is old, he will not depart from it. Train up a child to talk back to authority (his parents), to pitch a fit in order to get what he wants, and to always have his way… and when he is old, he will not depart from it. Train up a child to have no self-discipline and no self-control…and when he is old, he will not depart from it. Train up a child to sit for hours in front of a TV set, letting it do the thinking for him…and when he is old, he will not depart from it. And the list goes on and on!

Parent, your home is the "boot camp" of your child's future, the training grounds where he is being prepared for the battles of life. You are the commander in charge of the camp and are presently training your child up in some way. You are either training him to be self-disciplined or undisciplined; God-centered or self-centered; responsible or irresponsible; an achiever or a quitter; a warrior or a wimp.

So, how are you doing, commander? How's the training coming along? Are you training up your child in the "way" he should go…or in the "way" he shouldn't go? Boot camp will soon be over…and he will take what he has learned into the real world!

PROVERBS 22:6 *"Train up a child in the way he should go, and when he is old, he will not depart from it."*

April 15

Something's missing

All morning long, you have been anticipating this glorious moment! With your mouth watering and your eyes closed in expectation, you take that first big bite of your freshly baked, scrumptious, chocolate cake. However, your taste buds immediately rebel in shock, as they discover that something's missing in the cake. In a matter of seconds, you figure out that you failed to put one very vital ingredient…sugar…into the cake. The cake looks all right on the outside, but something's missing on the inside.

Perhaps your life is like this chocolate cake. Something's missing and you just aren't satisfied. Things may seem good on the outside. You have a good job, a comfortable living, a good home, and all that you really need and want in life. Everyone thinks you have it all together, because your life appears whole and complete. Yet, there is a void deep within you. And, when all the lights go out at night, this void grows louder and louder in the dark stillness. It pierces your being with the terrible feeling that "something's missing."

Determined to rid yourself of this void in your life, you have tried to fill it with a variety of things. You saturate your life with activity, noise, amusements, pleasures, relationships, etc. You have even tried Christian work, becoming involved in numerous church activities, socials, plans, and programs. But, so far, nothing has succeeded in filling the void! Nothing has satisfied that "something's missing" syndrome that you are afflicted with.

Friend, aren't you tired of this charade? If you are, then today just stop all the running, stop all the activity, and turn off all the noise around you. Take a long, thorough look into the interior of your heart. Is Jesus Christ at the hub? Does everything in your life revolve around Him? Do you spend sweet, uninterrupted, intimate time with Him, getting the fresh, early morning dew from His Word? Do you allow Him time to melt you, to mold you, to fill you, to speak His thoughts for the day into your heart, to share with you the burden of His great heart? Is He the very center and core of your being? Is Christ really your life?

If Christ is not the center of your life, then that is exactly what you're missing. You have left out the most important ingredient of your life. No wonder you're not satisfied! No wonder you have the "something's missing" syndrome. Only Jesus can satisfy your soul, dear one. He's much more vital to your life than sugar is to a cake.

Today, just take a look at yourself. You have known for a long time that something's missing, and now you know what it is…the Lord Jesus Christ! Won't you invite Him into your heart today and make Him the most important ingredient in your life?

ISAIAH 29:8 *"…his soul is empty."*

April 16

Sticketh closer than a brother

Defeating you is my game.
Controlling you is my aim.
Capturing you is my fame.
And worry is my name.

"I am your constant companion, your bedfellow, and your "enemy" that sticketh closer than a brother. You have never caught onto my tactics. I always come in unannounced and you fall for me every time. You love carrying me around with you, even though I am physically devastating to you. I can cause ulcers, heart attacks, high blood pressure, upset stomachs, and numerous other ailments. I can even shorten your life span. I also can cause mental, emotional, and spiritual problems, too.

However, in spite of all the damage I do to you, you have somehow accepted me as normal. You think everyone has me, so you passively tolerate me. You allow me to travel with you daily without ever even raising an eyebrow at me. I am a perpetual part of your life."

Friend, worry is NOT acceptable for a Christian! Worry is a sin! It is an affront to our holy God. Worry is saying, "God, I don't trust You. I cannot depend upon You. You are not reliable." Worry is putting myself into my own hands instead of into God's. It is placing myself in control, thinking I can do a better job than God can. Worry belittles God, reducing Him to a human level, making Him no bigger than I am. Worry is a horrible, horrible sin. Worry is calling God a liar....and that is definitely serious!

Wonder how God feels when He promises to supply all our needs according to His riches in glory by Christ Jesus and we just plain don't believe Him? Wonder how God feels when He tells us that if we abide in Him and His Words abide in us, we can ask what we will and it shall be done unto us…and we spend very little time in His Word or in prayer? Wonder how God feels when He tells us to trust in Him with all our hearts and lean not to our own understanding and He shall direct our paths…and we don't trust Him, we try to figure everything out, and we direct our own path? Wonder what God thinks when He tells us we are more than conquerors through Christ…and we walk around defeated and discouraged, with our faces dragging the ground? Wonder how God feels when He has promised to love us, to take care of us, to provide for us, to never leave us or forsake us… and we worry?

Well, today, friend, it's time to take your enemy that sticketh closer than a brother to the cross. He needs to be crucified and buried.....and not resurrected! It is high time you quit calling God a liar by your worry. Recognize it as a sin against God, confess it, and forsake it! There's no place for worry in the life of a born-again child of God! God either meant what He said, or He lied. And, since He cannot lie, then all His promises are true and a child of God is foolish for worrying!

PHILIPPIANS 4:6 *"Be anxious for nothing.."*

April 17

Only a law can overcome a law

It's a law. It works the same all the time, whether in China or America or England. You can throw something into the air, but this law will pull it back to the earth. You can jump as high as you want, but this law will bring you down again. It's the law of gravity. This law, as all other laws, is constant and consistent. It cannot be overcome by will power, except temporarily. Your will power can briefly hold a book out in front of you, but eventually the law of gravity will cause your arm to fall. You cannot continue holding the book. Will power cannot overcome the law of gravity.

Only a law can overcome a law. The law of aerodynamics can overcome gravity. Get in an airplane and the law of aerodynamics will take over. As long as you stay in the plane, you are an overcomer of gravity, but step out of the plane and gravity will prevail. Another law which overcomes gravity is the law of buoyancy. The less dense molecules are, the less effect gravity has upon them. That's why you can fill a balloon with helium and it will rise. The law of buoyancy overcomes the law of gravity.....with no effort.

Paul teaches us a similar lesson in Romans 7 and 8. He finds that there is a law within him, the law of sin. Like the law of gravity, it is constant and consistent. It's always pulling down. The harder he tries to overcome it, the worse he gets. He ends in frustration over all his attempts to overcome the law of sin in his flesh. With his mind, he serves the law of God, but with his flesh, the law of sin. He finds that his will power cannot overcome the law of sin.

Seeing the futility of his struggle, Paul makes another startling discovery. He finds it will take a law to overcome a law. The law of sin can only be overcome, not by will power, but by a stronger law. He concludes, "*For the law of the Spirit of life in Christ Jesus has made me free from the law of sin and death." Romans 8:2* The law of the Spirit is all that can overcome the law of sin. Paul knows that he must be filled with the Spirit. Then, like the law of buoyancy, without effort, this law will overcome the law of sin in him. It won't be his will power or his effort. It will be the Spirit of Christ in him. "*Walk in the Spirit and you shall not fulfill the lusts of the flesh." Galatians 5:16*

ROMANS 8:2 *"for the law of the Spirit of life in Christ Jesus has made me free from the law of sin and death.."*

April 18

You can't change Arsenic to powdered sugar

Contrary to the beliefs of our enlightened society, there are still absolutes. Arsenic is absolutely poisonous and will absolutely kill you if ingested. Now, you can change the label on the arsenic bottle if you want to. You can call it powdered sugar if that would make you feel better. But changing the label has absolutely no effect whatsoever on the contents. Arsenic is still in the bottle and it's still poisonous regardless of what it's called, regardless of what one's opinion is, and regardless of what one feels about it. The truth is always the absolute truth and cannot be changed by labels, opinions, beliefs, or feelings. The only thing that changing the label alters is one's response to the truth. One might use the bottle of arsenic in a cake if it had the label "powdered sugar" on it. When a person's perception of truth changes, so does his response to that truth.

America was founded on the absolute truth, the Word of God. She was brought up with the right labels on the right bottles. Sin was called sin - black was black and white was white. America wasn't interested in opinions or beliefs or feelings. She was concerned with "*Thus saith the Lord.*"

However, somewhere along the way, she discarded the absolute Truth, saying that it had become too old-fashioned and out of date, no longer suitable for our modern technological age. With no absolute Truth as a standard any more, America could now change labels on all the arsenic bottles to "powdered sugar." This sounded much better in a cultured society and also evoked an entirely different response...acceptance rather than avoidance, reception rather than repentance, tolerance rather than termination. Alcoholism became a disease. Homosexuality became an alternate lifestyle. Abortion became the mother's rights. Adultery and fornication became living together. Serving Satan became straddling the fence.

Oh, friend, the labels may have changed but the Truth hasn't! How sad it will be when all those broad-minded folks take their last breath and find themselves in the eternal Lake of Fire. They will finally know then that changing the labels didn't change the arsenic into powdered sugar after all. What God called sin remained sin...and all those who kept sampling it were poisoned eternally. And that's the absolute truth!

ISAIAH 30:1 *"Woe to the rebellious children...who cover with a covering... that they may add sin to sin.."*

April 19

House of prayer or Den of thieves?

What a shock they received! From all the reports they had heard, Jesus was a meek and gentle man, always helping and loving and healing everywhere He went. So, they certainly never expected anything like this. They had been exercising their greed in the temple, becoming wealthy from their greatly inflated money exchange rates and from their exorbitant prices for the sacrificial animals. Up to this time, they had been free to do this without any interference. But, with the appearance of Jesus, everything suddenly came to an abrupt halt. Jesus drove them out with a scourge of small cords, poured out their money, and turned over their tables. After thoroughly cleansing the temple, He said, "*My house shall be called of all nations the house of prayer. But you have made it a den of thieves." Mark 11:17*

Obviously, desecration of the temple was a very grave matter to our Lord! He was filled with righteous anger over the impurity, the greed, the selfishness, and the flippant attitude toward holy things that was prevalent in His temple. He would stand for it no longer.

Today, the temple of the Lord is the body of born-again believers. "*What, know ye not that your body is the temple of the Holy Spirit, who is in you, whom ye have of God, and ye are not your own?" I Corinthians 6:19* Jesus is just as concerned and just as protective over this temple today as He was over the temple that stood in His day. It is still His house! As He bought it with His own blood, He expects it to be pure, holy, and righteous.

Christian, your body is His temple! Have you made it a house of prayer or a den of thieves? "Oh," you say, "I would never allow thieves to carry on business in this temple!" Well, could it be that there are some thieves, but you have never recognized them?Are there any thieves robbing you of your moral purity? Are there any thieves of your time, robbing you of intimacy with Christ? Are there any greedy thieves, causing you to use your body for your own convenience and pleasure and entertainment? Are there any thieves offering you enticing things of the world, thereby stealing your affections and causing you to love the world and the things in the world more than God? Are there any thieves burglarizing your holiness through self-pity, compromise, lust, harmful habits, pride, gossip, judgmental attitudes, lack of compassion, etc.?

Well, Jesus said He won't strive with man forever...and that includes you! Who knows...He may be on His way right now with His scourge of small cords! If you've found any thieves, it's time to run them off before the Lord has to do so. Make your temple today a house of prayer...not a den of thieves!

MARK 11:17 *"My house shall be called of all nations the house of prayer. But you have made it a den of thieves."*

April 20

Here comes the bride!

Everyone is standing. All eyes are focused on the doorway, as the organist begins playing, "Here Comes the Bride." The bridegroom is anxiously waiting, anticipating the moment he will be united with the beautiful, radiant love of his life.

But, something is wrong! The bride is not arrayed in a beautiful white wedding dress. Instead, she has on short shorts, a halter top, and is barefoot. She is walking down the aisle, but she is flirting with every man she sees on the way down. She is even stopping to kiss some of them. She is making a complete mockery of the sacredness of marriage. Obviously, her mind is not on her bridegroom! She is killing the bridegroom.....you can tell by his face. You can see the hurt, the grief, the anguish he feels as she tramples his heart under her feet. Her love and passion are being thrown to the world even as she is on her way down the aisle to be united with him in marriage.

Today, you may be that bride and your bridegroom is the Lord Jesus Christ. He courted you, wooed you, and lavished you with His love until one day you said "yes" to Him. You became a born-again believer at that time. You were betrothed to Him.....and to Him alone! From the day that you said "yes" to Jesus, you have been traveling down the aisle of life. You are headed for the Marriage Supper of the Lamb, where you will be united with your Bridegroom forever. He is waiting on you.

As you walk down that aisle of life, where is your mind and your focus…on the Bridegroom or on other lovers? Are you flirting with the world, having an affair with the things it has to offer? Do those things mean more to you than Christ… things like money, materialism, power, your job, another relationship, greed, or lust? Are you spending a lot more time with another lover, like the TV set or magazines, than you are with your Bridegroom? Are you scantily clad spiritually, because you spend very little time in feeding and nurturing your spirit? Are you making a mockery of everything that is sacred to our Lord Jesus Christ by your lifestyle, thereby hurting and grieving Him terribly?

Or, do you think about your Bridegroom all the time and talk with Him often? Do you spend much time alone with Him, praising and adoring and worshiping Him? Are you so devoted to your Bridegroom that no one or nothing else can sway your heart? Are you keeping your eyes on Him as you walk down that aisle of life?

Friend, you are heading down the aisle of life! The music is already playing, "Here Comes the Bride." The Bridegroom is in place, eagerly waiting and watching you as you travel down that aisle to meet Him. All of heaven's eyes are upon you… especially His! Don't let your Bridegroom down!

REVELATION 19:7 *"Let us be glad and rejoice...for the marriage of the Lamb is come."*

April 21

He came to us

Watching the tiny ant crawl through the maze of dried leaves, dead pine straw, and sticks, I thought about how small his little world was. He could probably see only an inch or two ahead of himself. Yet, I could see way back where he had come from and I could see where he was going. I was sitting so far above him that his view of things could not even begin to compare with mine.

Crawling right up to me and onto my leg, the little ant was totally unaware of me. I was so much bigger than the ant that he could not even see me. His tiny eyes could not take in anything of my magnitude. He crawled across my leg as if it were just another limb or stick. I thought, "If I wanted to get a message to this little ant, how would I do it?" I could make no sound or no gesture that could get an ant's attention. The only way I could get a message to the ant would be to become an ant myself and go down where he dwelt. The ant could relate only to another ant.

Friend, this is what our God did for us. He loved us with an everlasting love and desired with all His heart to make this message known to us. However, He knew that we, in our limited and finite capabilities, could never comprehend an infinite, all-powerful, supernatural God. His thoughts are so much higher than our thoughts and His ways are so much higher than our ways that our minds could never fathom such a God!

So, our God came down to earth as a man. He took on flesh and blood just as we are. He walked here on earth in a human body, in the person of Jesus Christ. Our God came down to dwell with us. He experienced everything we can ever experience humanly. He felt every feeling we could ever feel. He was tempted with the things we're tempted with, yet without sin. He even tasted death for every man. He became sin for us and paid the penalty for them as though they were His sins. He was crucified, buried, and resurrected for us.

It is absolutely unbelievable that our God would leave the splendors of heaven and walk here with us as a man, showing us personally the message of His everlasting love. He came to us so that we might one day go to Him.

JOHN 1:1, 14 *"the Word was God.....the Word was made flesh, and dwelt among us."*

April 22

Until "I will" becomes "I have!"

As I knelt down to pray at the altar, I had a particular burden that weighed heavily upon my heart. But before I could even begin praying about it, a most wonderful thing happened. It was as though the Lord Jesus Christ Himself knelt down right beside me and put His arm around me. I had goose bumps from my head to my feet. The peace and security I felt were indescribable. Without thinking, I just looked over at Jesus and asked Him if He would handle this burden for me…and I knew beyond a shadow of a doubt that He would! His presence assured me of that.

Shortly afterwards, *I John 5:14, 15 became alive to me. "And this is the confidence that we have in Him, that if we ask anything according to His will, He hears us; and if we know that He hears us, whatever we ask, we know that we* **have** *the petitions that we desired of Him."*

Oh, at that moment, I knew! I knew! I knew! I had prayed and prayed about this particular thing for years, but had never had the confidence that it was answered. I always felt like Jesus was telling me, "I will." However, on this particular day, He was no longer saying, "I will," but "I have." In that moment, my hope, which was based on a future tense verb, became a certainty, based on a past tense verb. It was done…finished!

Then, as I was reading in the book of Genesis, I discovered a similar occurrence in the life of Abram. God had called Abram out of his homeland, promising to take him to a new land. God said, "*I will make of thee a great nation, and I will bless thee…Unto thy seed I will give this land…For all the land which thou seest, to thee I will give it, and to thy seed forever." Genesis 12:2, 7, and 13:15* In Chapters 12 and 13, the Lord kept telling Abram, "*I will.*" But, in Chapter 15, things changed! God made a covenant with Abram, assuring him of His promise. Then God's Word tells us, *"In the same day the Lord made a covenant with Abram, saying 'Unto thy seed I have given this land, from the river of Egypt unto the great river, the river Euphrates." Genesis 15:18* God's Word had now changed from, "I will" to "I have"…from future tense to past tense! Abram's hope became a certainty!

Perhaps you've been praying for years about a certain matter, Christian! Well, keep praying until you have the confidence that God has heard and you know you have the petition you desired of Him. Pray until God's "*I will*" becomes "*I have,*" when future tense becomes past tense, when hope becomes certainty.

GENESIS 12:7; 15:18 *"Unto thy seed I will"… "Unto thy seed I have"… "given this land.."*

April 23

Left alone

"I want to be left alone. I just want to live my life, be a good person, work hard, and pay my bills. I get so angry when these folks talk to me about going to church or about God. I don't see that it's any of their business. Why, I have my own thing with God and it's very private. I don't need anyone prying into my personal life. I don't try to tell them how to live their lives…and I resent them telling me how to live mine."

Friend, you have made a fatal mistake. You say you do not want to be disturbed. Your motto could be, "Live and let live." You have hung a "Do Not Disturb" sign on the doorknob of your life and you're perfectly comfortable just like you are. You have your life planned and ordered. You are in control and you like it that way. Therefore, you don't want anyone, including God, telling you that you need to change. You'd rather be left alone.

Maybe you think you'd like to be left alone. But, perhaps you'd better rethink that philosophy of life. If God left you completely alone, then He would have to withdraw Himself from you. In doing so, several things would occur. First, God is light and His withdrawal would leave total, complete, black darkness. Second, God is love and His withdrawal would leave only hate, bitterness, coldness, and hardness. Third, God is joy and peace and His withdrawal would leave you with a raging war in your soul, with never another moment of rest, never even the slightest hint of tranquillity. Fourth, God is hope and His withdrawal would leave absolute despair and desperation. You would be left with the utter, endless reaches of hopelessness engulfing your soul. Fifth, God is everything good, just, holy, and pure. His withdrawal would leave nothing but evil, impurity, ungodliness, and no justice.

Perhaps today you need to take a second look at this "I want to be left alone" lifestyle of yours. It may be all right for now, but it will end in tragedy. One day, if you keep pushing God and the people of God away, wanting to be left alone, the Lord will finally give you your desires. He will give you, at long last, what you wanted during your earthly life…..to be left alone. He will withdraw Himself from you forever. And since hell is the only place in the universe where God isn't, then you will find yourself in hell…left alone eternally, never to be bothered by people, never to be bothered by God, never to be bothered by anyone prying into your personal life, never to be bothered by anyone reaching out, and never to be bothered by even another smile or a hug. You can then completely have the privacy you wanted and you can have it forever, because you will be eternally "left alone!"

HOSEA 4:17 *"Ephraim is joined to his idols; let him alone."*

April 24

Spiritual salt shaker

"You can lead a horse to water, but you cannot make him drink." You've probably heard that statement numerous times in your life, and it's absolutely true! You cannot make a horse drink, but there is something that you CAN do instead. You can put a bunch of salt on the horse's food and, since salt creates thirst, there's a good possibility the horse will drink afterwards. The salt will do its job. And, it doesn't even have to exert any effort in the process. It doesn't have to beg or plead. It doesn't have to worry or fret. Salt just simply has to be salt and it will create thirst. Therefore, if you give a horse enough salt and he gets thirsty enough, he'll desperately want something to drink. Then, you can lead him to water and you won't have to make him drink. In fact, you can't keep him from drinking!

We Christians face this same problem in dealing with people. We use the excuse, "Well, I can't make people get saved." Or, "I can't make people go to church." That's true!We can't! However, there is something we CAN do. We can be spiritual salt shakers, sprinkling salt everywhere we go. We can be such salty Christians that, when the lost are around us, they will begin to thirst. We won't have to exert any effort. We won't have to beg or plead. We won't have to worry and fret. We can just simply be salty and those around us will get thirsty. Then, we can lead them to the Water of Life and they'll drink then.

Well, just exactly what does it mean to be a salty Christian? Jesus told us that we are to be the salt of the earth…so what does salt do? First, it creates thirst. Second, it endures heat. Whereas water boils at 212 degrees F., salt boils at 2575 degrees F. Third, it preserves. It binds water particles together so bacteria cannot get in and spoil. Fourth, it heals….we often gargle with it or soak sores in it. Fifth, it flavors. It makes food so much better. Sixth, it is useful and necessary for life, as our very blood is a saline solution and our tears and sweat are salty. And last of all, salt sticks together. Salt licks for animals will hold together to the last few grains.

So, Christian, how salty are you? Do you make folks thirsty for Jesus? How much heat can you endure, keeping a sweet and humble spirit? Do you help bind people together in unity, so the bacteria of sin cannot penetrate and destroy? Do you bring healing to damaged emotions, sicknesses of the soul, and wounded spirits? Do you bring peace where there is dissension? Are you loyal, sticking to the other members of the body to the last few grains?

Oh, little spiritual salt shaker, are you sprinkling salt everywhere? If not, perhaps you need to unclog your dispenser today. The world desperately needs salt!

MATTHEW 5:13 *"Ye are the salt of the earth.."*

April 25

The Solomon syndrome

It's as old as dirt. Lots of people have said it and many more have thought it. A few find the answer to it. But, the majority reach the end of their earthly journey, still searching for the elusive answer to this age old dilemma. "There's got to be more to life than this."

Even King Solomon was baffled by it. He was the wisest man who ever lived. He also was blessed by God with great riches, good health, and a kingdom. He had the money to buy everything he wanted and try anything his heart desired. Nothing the world had to offer was withheld from him. Yet, after having it all and trying it all, he was left with frustration and defeat. He wrote the book of Ecclesiastes, in which we plainly see the results of man's efforts. Solomon said, "*Vanity of vanities...all is vanity,*" *Ecclesiastes 1:2* meaning empty, without permanent value, and that which leads to frustration. In other words, Solomon concluded, after trying all that the world has to offer, "There's got to be more to life than this."

Perhaps you have the Solomon syndrome. You have discovered that the new house, the new car, the nice clothes, the condo on the beach, the vacations, the money, and all the pleasures of life did not make you happy for long. So, you went from one thing to the next, searching for a deep, inner peace and satisfaction, all of which left you empty and dry. You even tried religion, but the modern day pabulum from the pulpits did not feed your starving soul. You finally concluded that life is filled with oppressions and inequalities. Nothing is fair. You work, work, work.....and then you die, only to leave what you worked for to someone else who might squander it away. The Solomon syndrome left you with this unanswered, age-old, perplexing thought, "There's got to be more to life than this."

Yes, there IS more to life than this. But, you will never find it in earthly things. You'll never find it in relationships. You'll never find it in the natural, manmade, temporal realm. You will find real lasting peace and joy only in one place.... and that place is in Jesus Christ! A life totally surrendered to and captivated by Him is the "more to life" that everyone is looking for. You'll conclude, as did Solomon, "*Fear God, and keep His commandments; for this is the whole duty of man.*" *Ecclesiastes 12:13* That's the only cure for the Solomon syndrome!

ECCLESIASTES 1:14 *"all the works that are done under the sun.....
all is vanity and vexation of spirit"*

The McChurch theology is for the CDO's

It's a dilemma! There are more of them today than ever before. Something is terribly wrong in our society when the HSDO's, the "High School Drop-Outs" are increasing in number every year. The school system must be sowing improperly for there to be such a reaping of "HSDO's." Therefore, we need to make some much needed corrections in our schools. Perhaps we should go to the dropouts and ask them what they want in a school. If we took all their interests into consideration and tried to develop a school system that would suit them, maybe they would all come back to school and graduate. Maybe then we wouldn't have so many HSDO's!

Obviously, it would be absurd to develop a school system based on what the "HSDO's" want. They have already proven by their lives that education is not their top priority. Their ideas of a "student friendly" school would be one with all reminders of school removed. They would want no books, no principal, no homework, no studying, no classrooms, etc. They would have a McSchool, offering drive-through McNuggets of knowledge, loaded with fat grams of entertainment and fun.

We would consider it totally outlandish to build such a school! However, many churches are using this approach. They are going out to the lost community, to the CDO's, the "Church Drop-Outs" and asking them what they would like in a church. They feel that building an "outsider friendly" church will draw these "CDO's" back into church again. How absurd to consult "CDO's" about church development. They have already proven by their lives that church is not high on their list of priorities. Their ideas of an "outsider friendly" church would be one with all reminders of church removed. There would be no cross, no talk about the blood, no hymn books, no altars, etc. They would build a McChurch, offering drive-through McNuggets of spiritual food, highly spiced with entertainment and fun.

These "outsider friendly" churches are springing up all across America. However, there's one thing that cannot be found on their menus.....Jesus! Providing salvation for us was not a fun, easy, entertaining, cheap undertaking for Him. It cost Him His life. That's why you won't find Him at any of the modern McChurches. You'll find Him where the cross and the blood are preached and taught…and where disciples, who really want to follow Him, are praying, fasting, and crying out to Him to come on their churches. So, let's leave today's McChurches to the CDO's…and let's go back to the old-fashioned, Holy Ghost anointed, hell-preaching, God fearing, sin hating, narrow walking churches where Jesus is the one and only attraction!

PHILIPPIANS 3:18 *"...they are the enemies of the cross of Christ."*

April 27

Love and power stand knocking at your door!

If you want to see the glory of God, look to the heavens! If you want to see the handiwork of God, look to the firmament! If you want to see the love of God, look to the cross! And if you want to see the power of God, look to the empty tomb!

Have you ever thought about love and power? What if God had love without power? If that were true, He could not have paid for our sins. All the love and tears and broken-heartedness could not help us when we come to death's door any more than we can help our loved ones at that point. Love is wonderful in life but helpless at death.

And what if God had power without love? In that case, He could pay for our sins, but He would not want to. Love is the most compelling force there is. It moves us beyond ourselves. It moves us to pay any cost for the object of our love, even suffering and death. So, without love, power could be awful. It could even be used in the opposite direction, against us rather than for us.

How thankful and grateful we should be that our God is a God both of love and of power. Love brought Him to this earth to live as a man, to suffer and endure everything we would ever face in life. Love carried Him to the cross, causing Him to take upon Himself all the sins of the entire human race. Love carried Him to death's door, as He paid the wages for sin, which is physical and spiritual death. And, after love poured itself out in totality, power stepped in, rolled away the stone, and raised love from the tomb. Power overcame death, hell, and the grave!

Today, love and power stand knocking at your door! Love beckons you to come. Love has already paid the price for you..."*For God so loved the world that he gave His only begotten Son...*" And then, power assures you of its overcoming, conquering ability if you will yield to it. "*...that whosoever believeth in Him should not perish, but have everlasting life.*" *John 3:16* God, the One who is extending this promise to you, is the only One able to make such a promise. God is the only One who has both the love and the power to carry through with such a promise! Will you surrender today to love and power?

I CORINTHIANS 6:14 *"And God has both raised up the Lord, and will also raise up us by His own power."*

April 28

Wild oats make bitter bread

He stood speechless as Nathan, the prophet, nailed him to the wall with this stern rebuke, "*Thou art the man." II Samuel 12:7* As Nathan uncovered and exposed his hidden deeds, David realized that his sin had truly found him out. The prognosis from the Lord was not one that David wanted to hear. "*Now, therefore, the sword shall never depart from thine house, because thou hast despised Me, and hast taken the wife of Uriah...to be thy wife." II Samuel 12:10*

Overcome with sorrow over what he had done, David repented and was completely forgiven by the Lord. Nathan said, "*The Lord also has put away thy sin." II Samuel 12:13* However, repentance does not remove consequences nor alter the law of sowing and reaping. David was soon to find out that "*whatever a man sows, that shall he also reap." Galatians 6:7* He discovered that this is a law, just as certain and sure and unchanging as the law of gravity.

Much to David's chagrin, the crop of wild oats he sowed came up later and greater than he originally sowed. He lost his baby son; his daughter, Tamar, was raped; his son, Amnon, was killed; his son, Absalom, revolted against him; Absalom lay with ten of his father's concubines and also was later killed; his son, Adonijah, was killed; and his son, Solomon, fell into idolatry because of so many wives. David sorrowfully discovered that wild oats are quite easy to sow, but they are extremely hard to reap. The price is far too great!

If David lived today, in all probability there would be no Nathan coming on the scene and confronting him. He would more than likely receive quite a different prognosis about his sin. Dr. Deceit would attribute it to a dysfunctional family. Nurse New-Age would attribute it to his need to "find himself." Coddling Co-Worker would attribute it to stress from his job. And, instead of a stern rebuke from Pastor Passive, David would hear only about God's love and forgiveness. Therefore, he would never realize that the sickness, the rape, the death, and the idolatry were all wild oats coming up from his sowing days. He would never know to repent, allow God to walk him through the bitter reaping, and start sowing to the Spirit instead of to the flesh, so that he could begin reaping a crop of good oats.

If you are presently sowing some wild oats instead of living in obedience to God, then don't expect anything but wild oats to come up! If you sow to the flesh, you WILL of the flesh reap corruption! You can "*Be sure your sin will find you out." Numbers 32:23* Whatever you sow in your garden of life will come up for you and your children to reap. So, you'd better be careful about what you sow. Wild oats make bitter bread!

GALATIANS 6:7 *"Be not deceived, God is not mocked; for whatever a man sows, that shall he also reap."*

April 29

"I" trouble

He was extremely nearsighted, being able only to see his little world right around him. He had very severe "I" trouble. You can find him in Luke 12. His thoughts were recorded here in this passage. He spoke sixty-five words within himself, eleven of which were either "I" or "my." Now, eleven out of sixty-five adds up to be one-sixth. One-sixth of his thoughts were "I." You can see from his words what the focus of his life was!

First, he questioned, "*What shall I do, because I have no place to bestow my crops?" Luke 12:17* He did not consult the Word of God. He did not pray or seek the will of God. He was looking to his own self for the answer, because he was really his own god. Whatever or whoever controls one's life is, in actuality, that one's god.

Second, he said, "*This will I do." Luke 12:18* He then proceeded to name what he would do. Since he had always taken things into his own hands and controlled his own life, that is exactly what he decided to do this time. As usual, he could figure out a logical way to solve his problems. He always had before.

Third, he planned his own future. He analyzed how it would all turn out once he put his plans into action. He could retire, take it easy, and enjoy the fruits of his labor. He felt secure within himself. He had done a pretty good job so far with his life, so he felt that his future was in good hands.....his own!

We are not given this man's name. Oh, but wait! There, in verse twenty, God does give him a name. He says, "*Thou fool." Luke 12:20* How ironic! Here was a man who was wealthy and apparently had it all together. He had made it pretty big in life, was probably respected by others for his success, and had his life and future secure in the world's eyes. However, God calls him a fool! He had "I" trouble. His vision was on himself rather than on God and it resulted in the loss of his very own soul that same night!

What about you today? What consumes most of your thoughts...God or yourself?Do you have "I" trouble? If so, then commit your whole life to the Lord Jesus Christ. Change your vision! If you have "I" trouble, God calls you a "fool," and you, too, will lose your soul when your allotted time on earth is up.

LUKE 12:17 *"...What shall I do..."*

April 30

Facts, faith, feeling

That will never work! It doesn't matter how much smoke is bellowing up. It doesn't matter how much the engine is revved up, ready to go. It doesn't matter how good the conductor is. The train cannot go anywhere with the cars reversed. With the caboose in front and the engine at the end, the train may make a lot of sounds, but it won't go forward at all!

Likewise, our spiritual lives will not go forward either without the proper hookup…facts, then faith, and then feelings. However, we often reverse these. We put the caboose of our feelings up front and the engine of the facts on the end. We want to feel first before we do anything or say anything. We base everything on our feelings. We want to feel like praying, feel like witnessing, feel like going to church, and feel like giving. We start with the caboose of our feelings and then, if we feel it, we will exercise our faith, based on those feelings. And finally, if we feel it and faith it, then we will plug it into God's Word and make them all fit together like a nice little choo-choo train.

However, running a life by feelings will get us no further than running a train by the caboose. There may be a lot of smoke and a lot of noise, but when all that clears, nothing has moved. There will only be defeat and frustration over an unproductive spiritual life.

Today, it is time to disconnect the cars and put them in proper order. Put the engine of God's Word first. Get in the Bible: read it, meditate upon it, memorize it, pray over it, and allow God to speak to you through it. It is the facts! Allow the engine to pull the rest of the train. As God speaks to you through His Word, then step out in faith upon what He says! Ignore your feelings.....remember, they are the caboose. Just let your faith follow the engine of God's Word instead of following the caboose of your feelings!

And, as you obey the Word of God, your feelings will trail along. You'll find that they are the end, not the beginning; the carried and not the carrier; the effect and not the cause; the result and not the reason. They are the caboose!

Putting facts, faith, and feeling in their proper order will bring results. Your spiritual life will begin to move forward. Your spiritual train will keep a steady, consistent, faithful course all the way to its final destination!

PSALMS 119:169 *"Oh, Lord, give me understanding, according to Thy Word."*

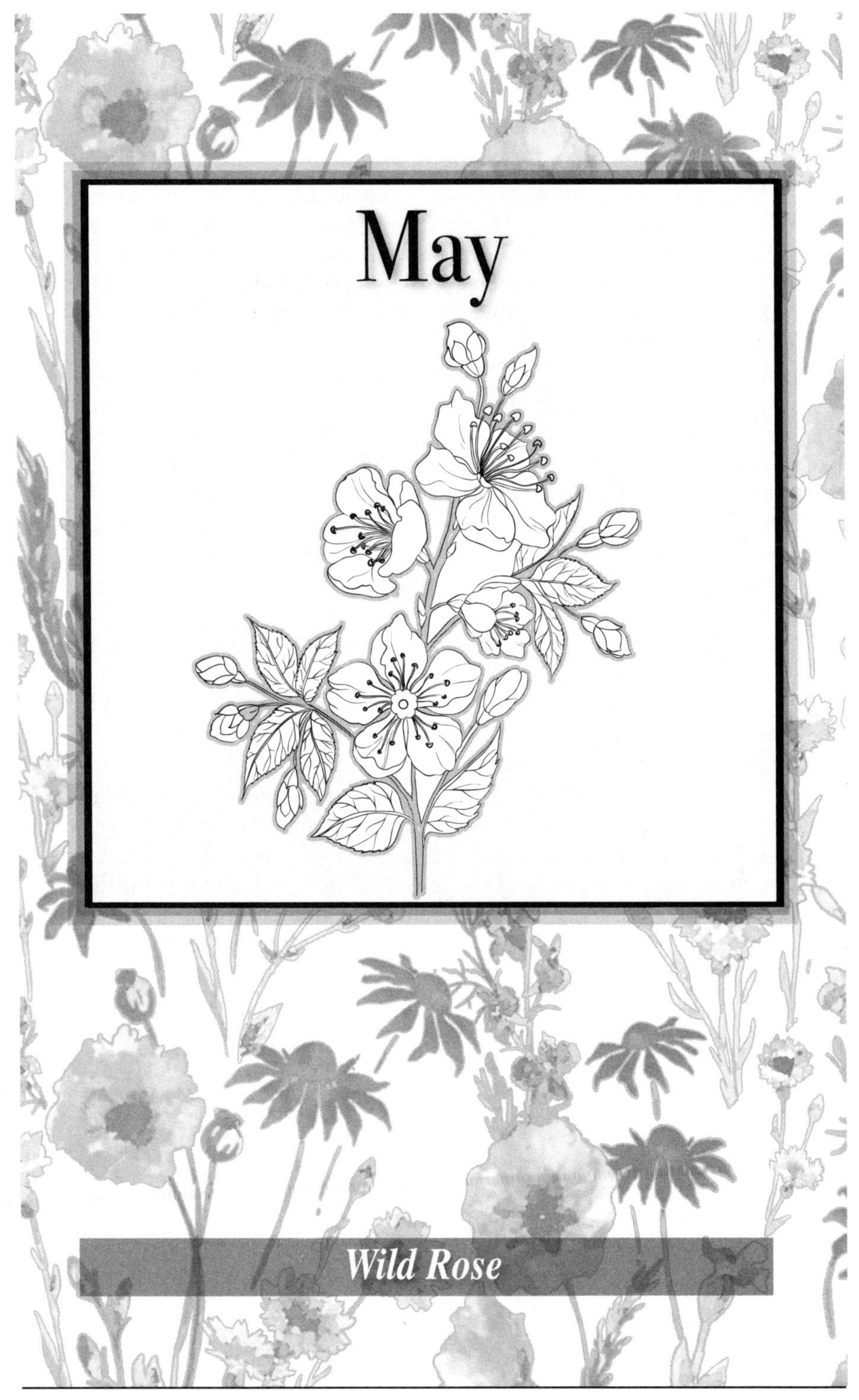
May
Wild Rose

May 1

Three are pointing back at you

Hold your hand up as though it were a gun aimed at someone in front of you. There is only one finger pointing forward, but three are pointing back at you. The next time you want to blame someone or aim your venomous thoughts toward them, remember that there are more aimed at you than at them. It might just be that YOU are the one to blame! You're looking for the speck in your brother's eye, yet failing to see the beam in your own.

This finger pointing has resulted in restlessness. Although your Pastor is faithfully and diligently preaching the Word, you say he is not feeding you anymore. You say his sermons are boring. You feel he is the reason your church is not on fire like it used to be. Your finger is pointed straight at the Pastor, but you never see the three pointed back at you. Are YOU getting up early every single morning to spend much time alone with the Lord? Are YOU fasting and praying with a broken heart for extended periods of time for your Pastor and for your church? Are YOU laying prostrate before God, beseeching Him to come upon your services with His mighty power?

No, you haven't been doing these things. You're too busy pointing that one finger. You have even gotten so discouraged that you are planning to change churches. Well, go ahead! However, in two or three years, your gun will be back up, aimed at the new Pastor.You will spend the rest of your life aiming at targets when YOU are the main problem of your own life!

Today, why don't you put your gun up? You have no right to say anything about someone else when you aren't even willing to pay the cost yourself! You are so spiritually lazy that you don't even want to exert your own flesh. You want the Pastor to do all the feeding rather than getting in the Word and studying diligently for yourself. You want the Pastor to do all the fasting and praying and weeping over lost souls. You want the Pastor to do all the visiting, all the encouraging, all the motivating, and all the work. Oh, you'd like to be on fire for the Lord, but you'd rather blame the Pastor for not being on fire than to get that way yourself!

So, go ahead! Point that finger! Blame someone else for the rest of your life. Be a church hopping, thumb sucking, Pastor blaming, pew-warming spiritual brat the rest of your life. You can point that finger.....but just remember: there are three pointing back at you!

LUKE 6:41 *"And why beholdest thou the mote that is in thy brother's eye, but perceivest not the beam that is in thine own eye"*

May 2

Harboring Barabbas

You are harboring a Barabbas in your home. He's guilty of just about anything you can name, yet you are allowing him free run of your house. And what's worse than that is that you are protecting and nurturing and pampering him. You treat him as though he hasn't done one thing. You get extremely angry and even defensive when someone suggests that he is less than perfect. It's as though you are trying to make everyone think he is really good and sweet and nice instead of facing the truth.

That Barabbas is your "self," your old man apart from Jesus Christ. He is rotten to the core. The Apostle Paul, one of the greatest Christians who ever lived, recognized this. He said, "*For I know that in me (that is, in my flesh) dwelleth no good thing.*" *Romans 7:18* The mighty prophet, Isaiah, recognized this. He said, "*But we are all as an unclean thing, and all our righteousnesses are as filthy rags.*" *Isaiah 64:6* If Paul and Isaiah said this about themselves, admitting that they were rotten sinners, then why would we ever try to appear otherwise?

The trouble with us today is that we're harboring Barabbas. We are allowing our old man free run of our lives and all our affairs. We seldom ever tell him no. We protect and nurture and pamper him, as though he deserves the best of everything. Then we get very upset and quite defensive if anyone says anything bad about him. We try to make others think we are good, nice, kind, spiritual people. We want to look good in the eyes of others, so we hide Barabbas and pretend he isn't there.

Christian, stop defending Barabbas! Quit protecting him and just admit the truth. Your heart is desperately wicked. You often have evil thoughts. You battle with anger, depression, jealousy, bitterness, anxiety, unforgiveness, coldness, apathy, vengeance, pride, and a host of other things too numerous to even list. Barabbas has stuffed all these things into a closet in your heart, has locked the door, and has thrown away the key.

Today is a good day for cleaning out closets! Just be real and truthful to God and to others about yourself. Confession opens the door and clears out all the junk that Barabbas has locked away. Confession puts Barabbas back on the cross where he belongs and sets the Lord Jesus Christ free to live in you and through you. Don't allow Barabbas free run of your heart any more. Crucify him and release Jesus today!

ISAIAH 64:6 *"But we are all as an unclean thing...our righteousnesses are as filthy rags."*

May 3

Get out your fishing gear and go

You've never caught a fish. But then, you've only been fishing a couple of times in your life. There's really no way to catch fish without going fishing. You certainly don't catch them haphazardly, just by walking down a street. And they don't jump in your car as you ride along the highway. You must purpose to catch fish, get all the necessary equipment, go out to where the fish are, and cast in. If you are persistent, you will eventually catch some fish. The only people who never catch fish are those who never go fishing.

As Jesus walked by the Sea of Galilee, He came upon Peter and Andrew casting their nets into the sea, for they were fishers. He said to them, "*Follow Me, and I will make you fishers of men." Matthew 4:19* Jesus is extending that same call today to all who will follow. There's a sea of lost people all over the world and the Lord needs some fishermen to catch them.

Jesus is calling you today! Maybe you've never won anyone to Christ in your entire life. Is it because there are no lost people out there? Is it because there is no one in whose heart Jesus is working? Is it because the Lord has no power to save anyone? Or is it because you've just never been fishing? Perhaps you have just expected to catch them haphazardly as you go about your daily tasks. Or perhaps you expect them to run up to you, asking how to be saved. However, that rarely ever happens! Remember: the only people who never catch fish are those who never go fishing. Persistent fishermen are the ones who bring in the big ones.

Today, there's a fishy smell on the ocean of life, so get out your fishing gear and go. All you'll need are two legs, a mouth, and the Word of God. You cannot make the fish bite, but you can sure throw the bait out! Tell people about Christ. Tell them what God is doing in your life. Give out tracts everywhere you go. Invite people to church. Be excited about the Lord, full of joy and enthusiasm, so the fish will want what you cast out. And just remember: you're not going to catch every fish that you go after. There are multitudes of fish swimming around in a lake, but they don't all bite the bait. However, if you fish long enough, you'll run across a hungry fish one day that you can reel into God's kingdom. So, get busy. Get out your fishing gear and go! It looks like good fishing weather!

PROVERBS 11:30 *"he that winneth souls is wise."*

May 4

Chosen

As he stood there holding his breath, that familiar feeling of rejection crept over him once again. They were choosing sides for a baseball game. He generally struck out, so no one wanted him on their team. He shuffled his feet nervously, as one by one all the other children were chosen. Now, he was the only one left. With his hands in his pockets and his eyes on the ground, he quietly walked away to sit and watch as he usually did. Once again, he had not been chosen!

Friend, perhaps this describes you. You have been rejected all your life. You were always the last one picked when the kids were choosing sides. You were never chosen for anything in school, not even for cleaning the chalkboard. You were never chosen at home either, but were always pushed aside and ignored. You know the awful, soul-wrenching feeling of rejection that results from not being chosen.

Well, get your hands out of your pockets and your eyes off the ground, because the King of all the universe has called your name. He has looked out over the billions of people on earth and has chosen you. Yes, you! You have not chosen Him, but He has chosen you! The God of glory has picked you for His own, calling you His friend. You have been chosen.

Will you ignore this call today? Will you walk away from this One who has chosen you, deciding not to be on His team? Do you realize that this wonderful Captain paid a dear cost for you so that you could be on His team? He gave His life's blood on Calvary for you. He has chosen you! He has called your name and is waiting for you to respond.

Why don't you run to Him today? Get on His team and be the best player you can be. Give one hundred percent to this dear One who gave His all for you. You no longer have to be on the sidelines. He wants you on first string. Maybe you have never been chosen on earth, but you've been chosen in heaven! So why spend your life giving yourself to a world that doesn't want you? Why not instead serve a Savior who loves you with all His heart?

The game of life is underway. The Captain is choosing His team. He has called your name. You have been chosen....now what will you do?

JOHN 15:16 *"You have not chosen Me, but I have chosen you..."*

May 5

He could.....but he's not!

God is the Almighty, all powerful, sovereign Lord of the universe. He could do anything He chooses, any time He chooses, and in any manner He chooses. He could.....but He's not! He could just speak and cause crops of corn and wheat and potatoes to grow up out of the ground. He could.....but He's not! God has chosen to allow man the privilege of being a co-worker with Him. God is the Author, originating the very life within each seed. God is the finisher, bringing forth that life out of the seed, up through the soil, and into the light. And man is in the middle, sandwiched between the beginning and the end - preparing the soil, sowing and tilling, fertilizing and reaping. Man cannot start it and man cannot finish it, but he can cooperate with God in the middle to produce a crop. Or he can refuse to cooperate, thus hindering or preventing any crop at all.

Prayer is like that crop. God is sovereign and He could do anything He choosesany time He chooses, and in any manner He chooses. He could.....but He's not! He could just speak and save sinners, change circumstances, break strongholds, etc. He could.....but He's not! God has chosen to allow man the great privilege of being a co-worker with Him in spiritual matters through prayer.

God is the Author of prayer, depositing His God-breathed seeds of desire within the heart of man. God is the Finisher of prayer, bringing forth the answer from the spiritual realm into the physical realm. And man is in the middle, sandwiched between the beginning and the end. Through prayer, man must prepare the spiritual soil, sow the spiritual seed, till the spiritual ground, and fertilize and gather the spiritual crop. Man cannot start anything and man cannot finish it, but he can cooperate with God to accomplish it or refuse to cooperate with God, thus hindering or preventing the work of the Lord from being done.

Maybe you have taken prayer very lightly in the past, never realizing that "*you have not because you ask not.*" *James 4:2* If you don't plant, you don't reap.....if you don't ask, you don't receive. God could do anything He chooses. He could.....but He's not! He has put you in the middle to carry out through prayer what He has started and what He wants to finish. So, get on your knees! There's lots of work to do!

JAMES 4:2 *"yet you have not, because you ask not."*

May 6

An audience with the king

The ruthless king was seated on his throne. One by one, the people came to make their petitions to this one who ruled over them. One poor soul besought the king with great earnestness, with tears and sobs of anguish. He thought he might be heard because of his deep sincerity. Another entreated the king with eloquent speech, thinking to impress his master with his ability and knowledge. Still another presented the king with all the things he had accomplished in life, hoping to gain the king's favor by his works.

The calloused, hardened king brushed each of these aside without so much as a blink of an eye. But then, to everyone's amazement, a young man came through the crowd and was greeted with open arms by the king. It was obvious that he had stolen the king's heart. Questions rumbled through the crowd! Was it the young man's sincerity? Was it his knowledge? Was it his works? What gained him such immediate favor?

Then the answer was made quite clear. The young man was the king's son! The blood of the king, passed down to his son, was the one thing that guaranteed him this open and instant audience with the sovereign ruler of the land.

Today, there is a sovereign King, who rules the entire universe. He is a holy, righteous, Almighty ruler. Many come to Him, seeking an audience with Him that they may receive the answers to their petitions. Some think they can be heard for their deep sincerity. Others think He will hear them on the basis of their great ability and knowledge. Still others think they can gain an audience with Him by the works they do in His name. However, there is only one thing, and one thing alone, that secures an audience with the King of kings and Lord of lords! One must be His child, born again by the precious blood of Jesus and adopted into the royal family. Every person on earth, whether a Moses, an Abraham, a Paul, or a Billy Graham has access to God only one way. That is by the blood!

Examine your life today! Do you pray based on your sincerity, your ability, your knowledge, or your works, thinking that these things gain an audience with the King? Or do you pray based solely on the fact that you are a blood-bought child of the King, thereby giving you access into His throne room? If you want an audience with the King, then there is only one way…it's through the blood!

EPHESIANS 2:13 *"But now in Christ Jesus you who once were far off are made near by the blood of Christ."*

May 7

Get on your own field

Calling your three sons at the beginning of the day, you assign each his duties. There is much work to be done on the farm. You assign one to a certain field, where he is to go and plant seeds. You assign the second to another field, where he is to plow. And you assign the third to yet another field, where he is to pick the already ripened fruit.

At the close of the day, you call your three sons back to your side to reward them. Which should get the greatest reward? Should it be the third one, since he has the most to show for his work? Why, of course not! Each is rewarded, not for the results, but for his obedience. Each was responsible only to do what his father told him to do!

Christian, perhaps you are discouraged in your life right now because you don't have a big basket of fruit. Really, there are no lasting results in your life to speak of. As you look at others' lives, you feel like crawling under a rug somewhere. You would love to sing like that one who has the voice of an angel, who always touches many lives through song. You would love to play the piano or a musical instrument so all would be blessed. You would love to be able to teach like that one who just opens his mouth and out pours a river of life. You would love to be like that one who has such a sweet, compassionate spirit that everyone just loves her. But, look at you! You are so plain and ordinary. Surely, God could not be pleased with you! You just do not have much to show for your service for Christ.

Dear one, God had a plan for your life even before He put you here on earth. He equipped you and prepared you for this plan before you were ever born. At the beginning of each day, He calls you to His side to give you your duties. All you are responsible for is obeying what He tells you to do. Quit looking around at all the other laborers and wishing you were on their fields. God hasn't called you to be like them! So, just get on your own field and be the best you can be on it. Then, at the close of the day, you will give an account only for the work done on your field. If you've been faithful to what your Father asked of you, He will say, "*Well done, thou good and faithful servant.*" You will not be judged for results.....but for your obedience instead!

MATTHEW 25:21 *"Well done, thou good and faithful servant."*

May 8

Digging in all the wrong places

How ironic that He who created every lake, river, and ocean in the word was thirsty! He could have called any spring He desired up out of the ground and right to His mouth. He could have had His own water fountain just by speaking the word. And, if He ever wanted water, it was now! His mouth was dry.....so dry, in fact, that his tongue stuck to the roof of His mouth. Most of His bodily fluids had drained out during the process of crucifixion, leaving Jesus agonizingly thirsty.

However, Jesus was not on that cross to be delivered from suffering and death. He was hanging on it to be the Deliverer instead. And even though His physical thirst was awful, He had a far greater thirst in His soul. He was thirsting for the multitudes of lost people, which He loved with an everlasting love. He also was thirsting for you...yes, you!He suffered this excruciating thirst of body and soul that he might become the Living Water to you, and to all those who come to Him with parched, dry, thirsty souls throughout the ages.

Perhaps today your soul is parched and dry. You have been digging around in the world's wells to find some cool, refreshing water that can quench your thirsty soul. You've run across some good-looking wells along the way and you drank deep and long from them. But you later discovered that they contained either stale or polluted water. Every drink from these wells left you empty, dry, and spiritually sick....with no peace, no joy, and no lasting happiness.

Aren't you tired of digging in all the wrong places and drinking from the wrong fountains? Well, throw away your secular shovel and your carnal containers. You won't need anything of the world when you come to the Fountain of Living Water. All you need is a soul that is thirsty, a soul that cannot make it any longer without an eternal drink from that Fountain that never shall run dry, that Fountain that was opened at Calvary.

The Fountain is flowing today. So, thirsty one, why don't you open the mouth of your soul to the Lord Jesus Christ and allow Him to fill you with the Living Water? Just take a drink from this Fountain and you'll never thirst again. And you will, at long last, find what your soul has been searching for since birth!

JOHN 4:14 *"But whosoever drinks of the water that I shall give him shall never thirst..."*

May 9

How are you planning on getting there?

"Everyone tells me you are going to London, England. You seem very excited about it, as though you can hardly wait for the trip. Guess you're making all your plans, huh? So, how are you planning on getting there?"

"That's simple. I'm going to start hanging around the airport. I will help everyone that I come in contact with. I will follow the Ten Commandments and the Golden Rule. I will be such a good person and do so many good deeds that I will be assured of getting to London. My good works will get me on a plane headed for that city!

"Oh, friend, you're deceived. All those things you plan to do are wonderful. However, they are NOT the way to London! You must first purchase a ticket, reserving you a place on a flight bound for London. Then, on the appointed day, you board the plane, commit yourself totally to the care of the pilot, and allow the plane to take you to your destination. You cannot get to London by your works or by your own efforts!"

No one in his right mind would try to get to London by being good. However, multitudes of people plan on going to heaven like this. They hang around the church, helping people and doing many good deeds. They follow the Ten Commandments and the Golden Rule as closely as they can. They think if they can be good enough, it will assure them a place in heaven. They are deceived into thinking heaven is earned by goodness. They have failed to realize that their works or their efforts cannot get them to heaven any more than they can get them to London.

Being good is not the way to heaven! John 14:6 tells us that Jesus is the way!First, you must have a ticket, reserving you a place in heaven. That ticket was bought and paid for by the blood of Jesus Christ, the only ticket that God will accept. When you commit your whole life to the Lord, your name is recorded in the Lamb's Book of Life. This is your reservation. This places you *"in Christ."* He is your pilot and will carry you to your final destination when this life is over.

Have you accepted Jesus as your Savior yet? Have you gotten on board? Have you totally committed your life the Christ? Are you allowing Him to take you to heaven?If someone asked you today, "How are you planning on getting there," what would your response be?

EPHESIANS 2:18 *"For through (Jesus) we both have access by one Spirit unto the Father."*

May 10

The victory thief

Pulling up to the drive-through window of the bank, he reluctantly made his deposit and drove off. However, he had not even pulled out onto the highway before he started worrying. He just didn't trust the bank. Mr. Wur Ree felt safer with the money in his own hands. So, he turned around, went back to the bank, and withdrew the money he had just deposited. Temporarily relieved, he headed home. On the way, he stopped at a convenience store for some milk and bread. As he stepped up to the counter to pay for them, a masked man with a gun told him to empty his pockets. Mr. Wur Ree ultimately lost all the money he was holding onto himself. Oh, if only he had left it in the bank!

Perhaps you're Mr. Wur Ree. There is a very heavy, worrisome burden in your life that you desperately need to deposit with the Lord. Time and again, you have gotten down on your knees, carrying this burden to God's throne of grace. You have given it to Him with your mouth on numerous occasions, because you just felt you couldn't handle it any more. However, each time you gave the burden to the Lord in word only. You never gave it to Him with your heart. You never really let go of it. You never got out of the drivethrough window without taking back the deposit you tried to make.

Friend, you really don't trust God! You don't literally believe He can handle this for you...or at least you don't think He will handle it like you want Him to. You are being held up by the silent stalker, the "victory thief." He is robbing you of the victory that is in Christ Jesus. He is convincing you to hold onto your burdens and problems, thereby robbing you of all your peace and joy and freedom.

Mr. Wur Ree, it's high time you learned something about making heavenly deposits. Heaven's bank is the highest in the universe. It will never go bankrupt. It is backed, not by the FDIC, but by God Himself! He will never let one of His depositors down. Whatever is lost to Him is kept. Whatever is kept from Him is lost. So today, get on your knees and give everything to God. Then get up, leave it there, trust Him completely with it, and show the deposit slip to the "victory thief" every time he comes around!

PSALM 4:5 *"Put your trust in the Lord."*

May 11

The courtroom of eternity

Trembling inside with an intense feeling of dread, he stood before the judge. A sick feeling crept over him as the judge said, "I find you guilty, as charged. You are sentenced to a $10,000 fine or one year in jail."

Realizing his utter helplessness, the guilty one stood in silence. He was not prepared for what followed. The judge stood up, took off his robe, and laid it on the back of his chair. Then, he came down from the bench and stood beside the accused. Pulling out his wallet, the judge removed a wad of money and began counting it. After carefully counting out $10,000 and placing it on the bench, the judge ascended back to his chair. He put his robe back on and resumed his position as presiding judge. He said, "I find you guilty, as charged. You are sentenced to a $10,000 fine or one year in jail. However, I see that your fine has already been paid. You are free to go. Case dismissed!"

Over two-thousand years ago, the sovereign Judge of the universe looked out over the courtroom of all mankind, declaring him guilty.....guilty of sin. The Judge pulled out His Law Book, which stated, "*The wages of sin is death.*" *Romans 6:23* Declaring man guilty and sentencing him to death, the Judge closed His Book. Then, He stood up, laid aside His robes of royalty, and came down to earth to walk with the accused.

For thirty-three years, He lived with the guilty, not as Judge, but as Friend. He never committed one sin. He lived a perfect life. Then, at age thirty-three, He got up on a cross, took all the sins of all mankind upon Himself, and died. He paid the wages for man's sin, which is death. Three days later, He rose from the grave and ascended back to glory.

One day, your life will be over and you will stand before Him. He will have His robe back on then. He will sit as Judge. If you accepted His payment for your sins during your earthly life, your record will be clear. He will say, "You are guilty, as charged, but I see that your fine has already been paid. You are free to go. Case dismissed!" However, if you didn't accept His payment, then you must pay yourself!

The courtroom will soon be in session. The Judge has put on His robe and is taking His seat. How you respond right now will determine what He says to you on that day. What will you do about this courtroom of eternity?

COLOSSIANS 2:14 *"Blotting out the handwriting of ordinances which was against us...nailing it to His cross."*

May 12

Jump out before it's too late!

It would happen gradually, so he would never even notice it at all. He would boil to death; yet never feel a single thing. That's because a frog is cold-blooded and his temperature is regulated by his surroundings. Therefore, if you put the frog into a pan of lukewarm water and begin to heat it slowly, his body temperature would rise in exact proportion to the rise in temperature of the water. The frog would sit contentedly in the pan as he boiled to death.

The church must also be a cold-blooded organism. Its temperature is regulated by its surroundings, by what goes on in the world. As the world's temperature gets more wicked every day, accepting things that it would not tolerate at one time, so does the church! The church today is in the same place the world was years ago. The church accepts as normal the things that our Godly forefathers would have been highly offended and grieved by. Our forefathers would turn over in their graves to look at the things we allow in the church today.

We have replaced agonizing in prayer over lost folks with activities to draw them. We have replaced a broken heart over our own spiritual conditions with backbiting over the condition of others. We have replaced dying to self with deliverance from anything that might be too hard on us. We have replaced faith in God with faith in our own faith. We have replaced holiness with harmony. We have replaced our influence on the world with influence by the world. We have replaced Jesus'nail-pierced hands with our nail-polished ones. We have replaced love of God with love of pleasure. We have replaced eating spiritual food with eating physical food. We have replaced quiet time with the Lord with quest for entertainment. We have replaced repentance with rehabilitation. We have replaced Spirit-filled living with sensual living. We have replaced thirst for the Scriptures with thirst for TV. We have replaced worship of God with worship of things.

The devil has put us into his worldly pan, has turned the burner of deception on, and has slowly brought us to the point of destruction. We are like that frog.....cooked, but still cool! Oh, Christian, wake up and jump out before it's too late!

EZEKIEL 16:49 *"Behold, this was the iniquity of thy sister, Sodom: pride, fullness of bread, and abundance of idleness."*

May 13

Spiritual spinach

Somehow he always waited until the situation was totally desperate and hopeless and he was absolutely exhausted from all his efforts before he would pull out his old reliable, proven, surefire solution. Just about the time Bluto was whipping him soundly, Popeye would say, "I've had all I can stands. I can't stands no more!" Then, he would reach into his pocket, pull out his spinach, and gulp it down! And, presto! Instantaneously, he grew big old muscles and brutally beat the daylights out of Bluto.

Christian, perhaps today you are in a Popeye predicament. Your situation is completely hopeless. You feel desperate, exhausted, worn out, and unable to go on any further. You've done everything you possibly can to change your circumstances, but they keep getting worse instead of getting better. Bluto has been whipping up on you…he's winning the battle right now and you feel like you're down for the last count! Just like Popeye, you've finally reached the point where you're saying, "I've had all I can stands. I can't stands no more!"

Well, get out the old reliable, proven, surefire solution…your spiritual spinach…the Word of God! It says that you are "*more than conquerors through Him that loved us." Romans 8:37* It says, "*Now thanks be unto God, who always causeth us to triumph in Christ." II Corinthians 2:14* It says, "*and this is the victory that overcometh the world, even our faith." I John 5:4 It says, "greater is He that is in you, than he that is in the world." I John 4:4* And these are just a few of the many bites of spiritual spinach found in the Word of God. So, friend, just swallow down these nuggets and digest them…take them into your heart, not just into your head. Believe them, rest on them, stand on them, depend on them, and act on them. And, presto! Instantly, you'll grow big old spiritual muscles and you'll be able to beat the daylights out of Bluto!

It's high time you put Bluto…that deceiver, that thief, that robber, that murderer, that big old bag of hot air…on the run! He has deceived you long enough. He has kept you from your spiritual spinach too many times. He has had you cowering and jellyfishing around like a discouraged, defeated victim when, in actuality, you should be a determined, dogged, dominant victor! You have some spiritual spinach available at all times, friend, and it's far, far greater than that green stuff Popeye had! This spiritual spinach is the most powerful stuff in the universe. So, why don't you get it out, swallow it down, and whip up on Bluto for a change?

PSALM 119:107 *"I am afflicted very much; revive me, O Lord, according unto Thy Word."*

May 14

Others may…I cannot!

When asked if she wanted a banana split, she replied, "Others may. I cannot." While others slept soundly in their beds during the early morning hours, she was "up and at 'em." As her feet pounded the pavement and every bone in her body screamed out to just back off a little, she kept telling herself, "Others may. I cannot." At night, when others were lounging comfortably in front of their TV sets, she was enduring very rigorous training. When her muscles ached until she felt she couldn't take any more and she wanted to rest like everyone else, she would simply tell herself, "Others may. I cannot."

You see, she was in training for the Olympics and couldn't afford to be sidetracked, diverted, or hindered in any way. She wanted to win the gold medal more than she had ever wanted anything else in her whole life, a goal which required total dedication and commitment to attain. Therefore, she must give up many things that were "good" in order to have the "best," always telling herself, "Others may. I cannot."

Christian, we are also in training, but for something far greater than any earthly Olympics. We are in training to rule and reign with Christ during the Millennium. And we are striving, not for a gold medal, but for crowns, which we can lay at the feet of our precious Lord and Savior when the race is over. I Corinthians 9 tells us "*Run in such a way as to get the prize. Everyone who competes in the games goes into strict training. They do it to get a crown that will not last; but we do it to get a crown that will last forever. Therefore, I do not run like a man running aimlessly; I do not fight like a man beating the air. No, I beat my body and make it my slave so that after I have preached to others, I myself will not be disqualified for the prize.*"

If you have been truly saved, then you are in this race whether you want to be or not, and you are running! Perhaps today you have weights in your life that are hindering you from running effectively. These weights may be things that are not necessarily sinful, but will sidetrack and divert you from the race. Well, friend, if you really love the Lord, then you need to "*lay aside every weight and the sin which does so easily beset you and run with patience the race that is set before you.*" *Hebrews 12:1* You must lay aside even the good in order to have the very best. It's time you learn to say, "Others may. I cannot. I am in a race and I am running to win!

HEBREWS 12:1 *"…let us lay aside every weight and the sin which does so easily beset us and run with patience the race that is set before us."*

May 15

Returned: Insufficient funds

Returned: Insufficient Funds! Those are two words in the English language that you do not want to hear, because it means you have had a check to bounce. You were careless and failed to follow the proper procedures of the bank, thereby resulting in a great cost to you and in a great deal of frustration.

Well, perhaps you have had the same problem at the Bank of Heaven. You have sent up prayer after prayer, but many of them have bounced. Therefore, you have concluded that God just doesn't care about you at all. You have decided that He will answer other people's prayers but not yours. Having become frustrated and defeated in your Christian walk, you are praying less and less and you are getting very lax in your Bible reading. You have almost quit doing any business at all with the Bank of Heaven.

Friend, perhaps it is time today to check out your heavenly account. There is a reason why your prayers keep bouncing! Maybe you are not following the proper procedures. In the first place, you must be a joint-heir with Christ, thereby placing you on His account in heaven…which, by the way, is the only account in that Heavenly Bank. You must have committed your life to Christ, resulting in your name being written down in the Lamb's Book of Life. If not, all your requests from the Bank of Heaven will be denied…Returned: Insufficient Funds.

In the second place, there can be no known, unconfessed sin in your life. The Heavenly Bank Manual, God's Holy Word, says, *"If I regard iniquity in my heart, the Lord will not hear me." Psalm 66:18* Therefore, if you continue in sin willfully, being unwilling to confess and forsake it, then none of your requests made to the Bank of Heaven will be heard. The Heavenly Bank doesn't do business with accounts that are never purged.

And finally, in order to make withdrawals from the Bank of Heaven, you must also make some deposits, some investments, in that Heavenly account. You must spend some time alone with the Lord Jesus Christ, developing a sweet, intimate, personal relationship with Him, depositing yourself and all that is yours in Him. If you never deposit anything, then how in the world can you ever expect to make any withdrawals?

Friend, there is no need for your prayers to be denied, marked, "Returned: Insufficient Funds." Just follow the guidelines in the Heavenly Manual and your prayers will not be bouncing any longer!

PSALM 66:18 *"If I regard iniquity in my heart, the Lord will not hear me."*

May 16

Martha, Martha

As He was passing through the town of Bethany, He came to her house. Filled with excitement over His visit, she gladly welcomed Jesus into her home. It was quite an honor and privilege to have Him as her guest. However, she had no time to spend with Him, as she was busy preparing the meal and serving her guests. As she rushed around, Martha suddenly felt anger rising up within her. Her sister, Mary, was sitting at the feet of Jesus while she was doing all the work!

Finally, in her frustration, Martha went to Jesus with her complaint. "*Lord, do You not care that my sister has left me to serve alone? Bid her, therefore, that she help me." Luke 10:40* To this, Jesus replied, "*Martha, Martha, you are anxious and troubled about many things. But one thing is needful, and Mary has chosen that good part, which shall not be taken away from her." Luke 10:41, 42*

Perhaps you are a Martha. One day Jesus passed by your heart and you invited Him in. It was quite an honor and privilege to have Jesus residing within you. However, you quickly got busy serving Him. You took various jobs at church. You saw multitudes of needs around you and immediately began trying to meet them. Finally, you became so busy and so cumbered with serving that you had practically no time alone with Jesus anymore. Bible reading and prayer became secondary to your service.

As you looked around the church, you noticed that you were busy doing much of the work. Resentment of the other members set in. You got bitter at many of them who had been there much longer than you and were sitting comfortably, watching you work. You began expressing your frustration, grumbling and complaining audibly about them.

Well, why don't you come to Jesus? Tell Him your complaint. He will call you by name, as He very gently tells you, "You are anxious and troubled about many things. Come and sit at My feet awhile. You have gotten so busy serving Me that you have neglected Me completely. Put all your service here at My feet and just spend some time with Me. I came here to have a relationship with you, to enjoy your fellowship. I want YOU.....not what you can do for Me."

Martha, Martha, stop all your busyness. Quit your worrying and fretting and just get at the feet of Jesus. He is too valuable a guest to ignore!

LUKE 10:41 *"Martha, Martha, thou art anxious and troubled about many things."*

May 17

Are come up for a memorial

It certainly would be quite an honor to have one on earth! Usually, however, only people who attain a very high position of prominence ever have one, people like Abraham Lincoln. Because of Lincoln's fame and earthly recognition, there is one built in Washington, D. C. in his honor. It's called the Lincoln Memorial. Everything in it is a reminder of Abe, keeping alive down through the years the memory (memorial) of who he was and what he accomplished.

Now, it would be great to have a memorial on earth! But, there's something far greater than that! There is something we can do, according to the Word of God, that will come up for a memorial before God. Acts 10 tells us that there was a man named Cornelius, who was *"devout, feared God with all his house, gave much alms to the people, and prayed to God always."* In a vision, he saw an angel of God coming to him and saying, "*Thy prayers and thine alms are come up for a memorial before God.*"

Imagine that! Our prayers and alms must be pretty important in God's sight if they could come up for a memorial before Him. God puts such a high priority on them that they are the only two things listed in the whole Bible that we can do that will be a memorial before God. Now, man, unlike God, puts a high priority on other things, such as on works, on talents, on abilities, on education, on spiritual gifts, etc. Man praises and lauds the great preachers and teachers, those who can sing like a nightingale, those who are very accomplished on musical instruments, those who win multitudes to Christ, those who are strong leaders, etc. Man recognizes and memorializes those things that are outward. God recognizes and memorializes the prayers of a devout, God-fearing, alms-giving, praying man or woman.

Christian, perhaps you are very discouraged. You're unable to do great things for God because…you're sick a lot…you're getting too old…you have no talents or abilities…you are uneducated…you have no money…or you have various other handicaps that hold you back. You feel like a hopeless failure to God's kingdom.

Well, fret not, dear one. The greatest thing you can ever do is pray! You can touch the entire world on your knees. And while you are doing so, your prayers could very well be coming up for a memorial before God. You might not ever have a memorial here on earth, but you can certainly have one in heaven. So, pray, Christian, pray!

ACTS 10:4 *"Thy prayers and thine alms are come up for a memorial before God."*

May 18

Changing names, but not natures

How do you know if an animal is a dog or not? Well, if it's a dog, it looks like a dog, barks like a dog, and smells like a dog. It does dog things. It has the heart and mind of a dog. You could take a cat, put dog fur on it, put a dog collar around it, and call it a dog all day long. However, it would not start barking frantically at the garbage man. It would not jump up on you and start licking you in the face. You could call it a dog, but it would not be interested in dog things. In order for it to act like a dog, it would have to be given a new nature. The cat nature would have to be removed and a dog nature put in its place.

How can you tell if a person is a Christian or not? Well, if he's a Christian, he will look like a Christian, talk like a Christian, and act like a Christian. He will do Christian things, because he has the heart and mind of a Christian. When a person gets saved, he gets a new nature, making him a new creation. He does not have the same desires any longer. He wants to do Christian things instead. He wants to go to church, read God's Word, pray without ceasing, and be around fellow believers. These are the things that thrill his new nature, which is that of Christ.

Today, many people call themselves Christians. Many of them have changed names but not natures. They have taken their old nature and put new clothing on it, new talk on it, and new actions on it. However, that old nature has not been changed. Outwardly, they may look and sound like a Christian, but inwardly they are still the same. They still like to do "world" things, being attracted to the world and all it has to offer, because they have simply changed names but not natures.

Where do you stand today? Have you been radically changed inwardly? Do the things of the world still interest you? Examine yourself. How tragic it would be to think you are a Christian, only to find out too late that you have been fatally deceived. How sad it would be to change names without changing natures.....and end up eternally in hell!

JAMES 4:4 *"Whosoever, therefore, will be a friend of the world, is the enemy of God."*

May 19

One lone, isolated Ark

The people gathered around. Word had quickly spread throughout the land about the crazy old man. Everyone wanted to come and see for themselves if it were true. Sure enough, the old man was building a huge boat, right there on dry ground, just like everybody said. Why, there wasn't even a water hole in sight. He kept saying something about water falling from the sky. Boy was that a joke! Water had never fallen from the sky before. The earth was watered by a mist coming up from the ground. Water had never come down from the sky.

As they watched inquisitively from the sidelines, some began to mock. After all, the crazy old man had been saying for years now that God would soon send the rains and floods and destroy the sinful race from the face of the earth. And, nothing had happened yet. As they mocked and jeered, Noah begged them to repent. He repeatedly told them that God's Word would not fail and that judgment was coming.

Then one day, as a thief in the night, judgment fell! The heavens above were opened, as a dam breaking, unleashing torrents of water. When the fury of the winds and waters ceased and the whole world lay covered underneath those waters, there remained one lone, isolated figure floating on top....an ark, with Noah and his family inside.

There is coming another day that God's Word calls the day of the Lord. It "*will come as a thief in the night, in which the heavens shall pass away with a great noise, and the elements shall melt with fervent heat; the earth also and the works that are in it, shall be burned up.*" *II Peter 3:10* The first judgment upon earth was by water; the second one shall be by fire. All God will have to do is speak and unleash the elements all around us. Our air is composed of oxygen, hydrogen, and nitrogen, all of which are flammable. Water is composed of hydrogen and oxygen, which are flammable. God is holding them in store, reserved unto the day of judgment. When He lets them go, every molecule in every body of water in the world and every molecule in the air around us will burst into a blaze of unquenchable fire!

As in Noah's day, you can mock if you choose. But, friend, you should be looking instead for that Ark of safety that God has provided, which is the Lord Jesus Christ. Christians all around are warning you. Preachers are telling you. And, you still refuse to listen. But one day, the fire will fall and it will be too late for you then. All that will remain after the fire has fallen will be one lone, isolated Ark. That Ark is Christ! Will you be inside that Ark when the fire falls?

II PETER 3:10 *"But the day of the Lord will come as a thief in the night..."*

May 20

Forget about those cobwebs and kill that spider!

Every Sunday, it was the exact same routine. He would always go to the altar at the end of the service, get down on his knees, and pray loudly, "Oh, Lord, please get the cobwebs out of my life." After several months of this, one of the spiritual sisters in the church got tired of this weekly rerun. So, one Sunday, as the old man filed down to the altar for a cobweb removal, the sister just stepped out in the aisle behind him and followed him to the altar. Waiting patiently for him to finish his usual prayer, she then chimed in and said, "Lord, forget about those cobwebs and kill that spider!"

Christian friend, perhaps like the old man, you are always asking God to remove the cobwebs from your life, too. You've tried everything you know to get rid of them. At times, it seems like they are gone and you think you have the victory. But, as usual, they reappear, just as bad as ever, and maybe even a little worse.

Well, it's time to quit praying about the cobwebs and kill that spider! Perhaps you have a spider of rebellion in your life, an area that you've never totally submitted to the Lordship of Christ. You do not want to give the Lord total control of it, for fear that He might not run things the way you want. You might have to give up something in your life that you love. You might have to crucify your flesh...and that's painful! So, you have reserved the right to make the final decision in your life in this area. You have a spider of rebellion that keeps spinning webs of strongholds in your life. And, you always deal with the webs rather than with the spider.

Or, perhaps you have a spider of unbelief in your life. You see the giants of impossibility and the walls of impenetrable circumstances in your situation..... and you don't believe the Lord will take care of them for you. You have never completely abandoned yourself to God to either sink or swim, to do or die, to conquer or be conquered. You're hanging on a limb and you will not let go. You just don't believe God will catch you. The spider of unbelief keeps weaving his webs of doubt in your life.

Friend, do you have any recurring cobwebs in your life? If so, you can rest assured there's a spider somewhere...either a spider of rebellion or a spider of unbelief that's causing all your problems. You've fooled with the webs long enough. It's time to forget about them and kill that spider instead!

JOB 19:28 *"seeing the root of the matter is found in me?"*

May 21

Though now for a season

My world was crumbling right before my eyes. Everyone I talked to was falling apart. Everywhere I looked there were more problems than I could even number. I felt like a million-pound weight was resting on my shoulders. I wished I could just run away. However, knowing my only hope in times of distress is my Savior, I took my Bible, went outside, and sat under the trees. Opening God's Word, my eyes fell upon these words from *I Peter 1:6 "though now for a season."*

"Though now for a season," I thought, "then this set of trials will be over. They won't last forever. Soon, this will all be just a vague memory." But meanwhile, reality was knocking on my door. My feelings were right here in the present, because my season wasn't over yet; a season, as I Peter said, of "*heaviness through manifold trials.*" So meanwhile, what was I to do until my season was over? Since my feelings had crash-landed on the bedrock of despair, I saw absolutely no way for them to take wings and soar out of this valley. I thought seriously about just setting up camp here, going to bed, pulling up the covers, and waiting until the season passed!

But then, I saw the first part of the verse, "*In this you greatly rejoice.*" How in the world could I possibly rejoice in such darkness, especially when I felt anything besides jubilant! However, examining the verse more closely, I found that the "in this" referred me back to the previous verses. And then the light came on! I suddenly realized that I was focusing on my circumstances, my problems, my trials instead of on what God's Word said to focus on. The Lord, through His Word, showed me what to focus on…the fact that He had begotten me into a living hope by the "*resurrection of Jesus Christ from the dead, to an inheritance incorruptible and undefiled, and that fades not away, reserved in heaven for me.*" He also showed me that He keeps me by the power of God through faith unto salvation, ready to be revealed in the last time.

Therefore, I decided to greatly rejoice in these things. I chose, by an act of my will, to praise the Lord and rejoice in such a great Savior! I decided that I would not allow my feelings to control me anymore. I determined to start shouting, 'Glory,'and kicking up my heels, regardless of whether I felt like it or not. I made my plans that day to rejoice by choice from that day forward, especially when those "*Though now for a season*" times show up.

As I practiced by faith what I could not see by sight, I discovered a little secret! I found that rejoicing gives birth to wings, wings that will lift one out of the valley of despair and into the Sonlight again!

If you find yourself today in a "*Though now for a season*" period, then just get up, start praising God, start shouting "Glory," and rejoice, rejoice, rejoice! You, too, will find that it works!

I PETER 1:6 *"In this you greatly rejoice, though now for a season, if need be, you are in heaviness through manifold trials."*

May 22

A spiritual millionaire

Upon receiving the news of a distant relative's death, you are told that he left everything to you, making you an instant millionaire. It will take about six months to settle the estate. Knowing that you have this inheritance makes quite a change in your life!

First, your attitude is affected. You are completely set free from worry over finances. You know that the money is coming, so, even if you couldn't pay all your bills right now, you would not worry in the least. You know they will get paid and you can rest completely in that assurance.

Second, your emotions are affected. You live with more joy and enthusiasm. Your depression and "just making it by" lifestyle are replaced with an excitement. You begin living in anticipation of your new treasure. Even on bad days, you know you can endure anything for a short time. Soon, the inheritance will be yours; therefore, there's no way to remain sad for very long.

Third, your focus is affected. No longer is your mind preoccupied with your present circumstances. Instead, you find yourself daydreaming about your inheritance. You begin planning all the ways you are going to spend your money. Your focus is now on the goal, not on what it takes day by day to get there.

Friend, you have something far greater than this. At salvation, you became an heir of God and a joint-heir with Christ. All that Jesus has is yours! It has been title deeded to you through His Word. Everything that is yours is listed in this precious document. Now, knowing all this, shouldn't you live without worry? After all, He promises that He will provide! Shouldn't you live with more joy and enthusiasm? After all, you are just passing through, soon to partake of the most glorious inheritance possible! And shouldn't you have a different focus? After all, you are a spiritual millionaire, oh child of God. So, why don't you get up and start living like it?

ROMANS 8:17 *"And if children, then heirs - heirs of God and joint heirs with Christ..."*

May 23

Where are you anchored?

The ship was in the middle of a storm. Fierce winds were blowing, tossing the big ship about like a toy. Turbulent waves rocked it back and forth, up and down. It sure looked like the old ship would be battered into a million pieces. There was no use to anchor. It would not hold! Finally, however, the ship made its way to shore. When it had come in as close as possible, a small boat took the big ship's anchor, carried it to shore, and firmly secured it to solid ground. Now, the ship could be tossed about but remain anchored to something that would not move.

Today, your soul is floating around on life's ocean. Sometimes, fierce winds of adversity blow and toss your soul around like a toy. Turbulent waves of doubt, fear, and anxiety will roll your soul back and forth, up and down, and will threaten to capsize your old vessel. At times, it seems that the storm will never cease. Sometimes, there is a temporary calm, but it isn't long until another unexpected, sudden storm arises and throws your soul back into turbulence again.

Life is filled with these sudden, unexpected storms. There is no way to escape them as long as you are sailing life's ocean. Maybe you have just about had all you can take. You feel that there is no way to go on. You have tried to anchor repeatedly, but your anchor never holds. You anchored to money, but it would not buy your way out of some of life's storms and could not give you the peace and comfort you were looking for. You anchored to material possessions, to your job, to a relationship, to alcohol, to drugs, to sex, etc. You anchored to everything you could possibly try. Now, you have exhausted everything you can think of that might bring peace, comfort, joy, and hope to your old battered soul!

Oh, friend, you have tried to anchor to shifting sand when you need to anchor to the Solid Rock. That Rock is Jesus Christ! Today, come to Him, bringing your old storm-tossed soul. Put your anchor, your trust, your security, your hope, and your all in Him. Once you anchor your soul in Jesus, your vessel will be safe. It can be tossed and blown and battered, but your anchor will hold eternally. You will be anchored up instead of down. The storms of life, with all the winds and waves, can never shake you loose.

Today, where is your hope? Where are you anchored? Are you anchored down.....to the things of the world, to the things around you? Or, are you anchored up.....to Jesus Christ? Your eternal destiny is determined by where your anchor is!

HEBREWS 6:19 *"Which hope we have as an anchor of the soul, both sure and steadfast..."*

May 24

A healing or a resurrection?

Lazarus was sick, even to the point of death. His sisters, Martha and Mary, were greatly concerned. They had sent for Jesus, because they knew He could heal their brother. With this hope in their hearts, they confidently anticipated Jesus' arrival. Both sisters kept looking out the window, expecting Jesus at any moment. However, as moments turned into hours and Jesus still had not come, their hopes grew dim. And, alas, their brother died.

It had been four days now since Lazarus had died. Four days now....and Jesus still had not shown up. All hope had vanished at Lazarus' death. As Martha and Mary were in mourning, someone came excitedly to their house to tell them that Jesus was on His way. Both women said exactly the same thing at seeing Jesus. "*Lord, if Thou hadst been here, my brother had not died.*" *Luke 11:21* Their faith was limited to what they wanted...their brother to be healed. They had faith in Jesus, but faith only to do what they thought was best. In their little feeble faith, they wanted a healing. But, Jesus wanted a resurrection instead. Why settle for a healing when you can have a resurrection?

Perhaps today your hopes are growing dim. You have been praying for something for a long time and Jesus hasn't shown up yet. You have kept looking for Him and waiting patiently and nothing has happened. And now, your hopes have grown so weak that you do not pray and believe with fervency anymore. In fact, you rarely even pray about this at all now.

Well, dear one, do not worry about the Lord's delays. His delays sometimes mean that He has something much better in mind than you have thought of. Your little faith is limited to what you want and to what you think is best. You cannot see afar off as He can.

So, you need to learn to put your trust in Him, period...not in what He can do, but in Him. Learn to trust Him for what is best, when it is best, and how it is best. Do not limit Him to what you want. Expand your faith to believe and accept whatever He chooses!

Oh, you of little faith! Quit whining and doubting and grow up! Put your total trust in Him today. Wait upon him. Who knows? You may want a healing, but He may want a resurrection!

JOHN 11:25 *"...I am the resurrection, and the life...."*

May 25

Putting wood on the fire

It was a cold winter's night. They stood around the huge campfire, as the wood crackled and the flames licked the air. The fire made the night seem almost like day with its bright light. What comfort and security the light and warmth from the flames brought to all who were near! As sleep overtook each camper, they retired one by one to their tents. And gradually, the fire went out, leaving no light or heat for anyone in the darkness. *"Where no wood is, there the fire goeth out."*

It is a cold dark world all around us. It is midnight, as dark as dark can be. People everywhere are groping in the darkness and shivering in the cold. They do not know where to turn. They are depressed, discouraged, and disillusioned. They have tried everything to find happiness and peace, only to watch it slip through their fingers like sand. They are left in the darkness all alone. Oh, if they could only find a fire! Where, oh where, is a fire?

You used to be a fire! You lit up the darkness all around you. The flames of the Holy Spirit, that fire within you, burned day and night. You had a holy passion and a fervent zeal for the Lord Jesus Christ. Everywhere you went, that fire brought light and heat to poor souls out in the midnight of life. But, sleep overtook you. You got lazy and tired and laid down for a while. You quit putting wood on the fire and it went out! And now, you are cold.

Friend, it is high time you got your fire started back up again. You need to put some wood on your fire. A fire cannot continue to burn without wood. Wood does not put itself on a fire; neither does it burn forever. So, you are the one who must continually be putting wood on your own fire to keep it going. You cannot lie down and sleep.

Exactly how do you put wood on? Well, you must feed the fire within you with spiritual wood, which is the Word of God. You must attend every church service so more wood can be added. Every time you miss, your fire does not get the spiritual wood it needs to keep its intensity. It dies down just a little. And, you must get in the Word of God daily yourself, allowing that spiritual wood to keep your blaze burning brightly. If you do not add wood every single day, your fire will eventually go out.

Wake up, oh sleeping one. Your fire is almost extinguished and it's growing darker all around. Get out the Word and stay in it until that flame is once again burning brightly.

PROVERBS 26:20 *"Where no wood is, there the fire goeth out."*

May 26

Matches in their mouths

I've never seen anything like it! It happened so fast that it was absolutely unbelievable! Somebody had walked to the back door and had just happened to look out when it first started. They began screaming, "There's a fire! Out there in the back yard by the fence, there's a fire! Of course, we all jumped to our feet and ran outside as quickly as we could. We all just stood in silence and watched helplessly as a wildfire jumped from bush to bush alongside the fence. In a matter of a few minutes, the fire had consumed everything in its path, including all the growth alongside the fence and the scrub brush and grass in the field behind the house. As I stood looking out over the field, I saw the blackened ground…I saw destruction! Immediately, the thought came to my mind, "Nothing will grow in this soil again for a while." It just seemed uncanny that years of growth and productivity could be destroyed in just a few minutes!

Well, somebody needs to look around the church today and start screaming, "Wildfire! Wildfire!" There are some spiritual arsonists loose in the church, carrying around matches and starting a bunch of fires. Those matches are in their mouths. They're called tongues! James 3:6 says, "*And the tongue is a fire, a world of iniquity; so is the tongue among our members, that it defiles the whole body, and sets on fire the course of nature, and is set on fire of hell.*" One of the most wicked things in the church today is a loose tongue. It tears down, rapes character, criticizes, maligns, accuses, and often destroys lives. In just a few minutes, it can destroy growth and productivity that took years to build.

Oh, you probably know a couple of spiritual arsonists. They'll call you up and say, "I need to share this with you. I am so concerned and so burdened. We need to be aware of this matter so we can pray." And they might even pray with you about it! But then, that seemingly sweet and caring "spiritual arsonist" will turn around and call somebody else and tell them the same thing. They'll set a bunch of fires with those matches in their mouths and will even get several other folks in on their spiritual arson as well.

According to Proverbs 18:21, "*Death and life are in the power of the tongue.*" So, why not use your tongue for life rather than for death? Instead of setting wildfires, why don't you start setting Holy Ghost fires? And stay away from the spiritual arsonists. They'll burn you with those matches in their mouths!

PROVERBS 18:21 *"Death and life are in the power of the tongue."*

May 27

A spiritual atomic bomb

Everything looked so peaceful and quiet. There was no activity whatsoever on the mound. But that quickly changed, as I began plunging a big stick right down into the soft dirt. Everywhere I stuck a hole, ants began pouring out by the dozens. They were falling all over each other in a frantic frenzy. I was disturbing their nest, tearing down some places where they had gotten comfortable, and just wrecking havoc in their little world.

As I watched the ants in their mad craze, I thought, "God, that's what I would like to do to the devil's kingdom. I'd like to shake it up, stick some holes in it, disturb some comfortable places, and break up some strongholds. I'd love to stir up the kingdom of darkness so much that demons would be falling all over each other in a frantic frenzy. There is nothing that would delight me more than to mess up the devil's nest, which he thinks he has cleverly camouflaged and hidden from sight."

Suddenly, I realized that I have a secret weapon, one the devil fears more than any other thing in the universe. It's a spiritual atomic bomb, with the capabilities of doing massive damage to Satan's kingdom. No matter how cleverly he has things disguised, this weapon will penetrate to the very heart of his nest. It will dislodge him and his demonic hosts, regardless of how long they've been entrenched. It will scatter, shake them loose, and set them to running from the beachheads where they've set up camp. It's a weapon they tremble at, a weapon all of hell wants to render inoperable. That's why the demonic hosts spend more time and effort disarming this weapon than they do on anything else.

This spiritual atomic bomb is prayer! The devil and his forces don't care how much you work for the Lord as long as you don't get in your Father's presence and earnestly, sincerely pray, staying before God until He answers. All of hell will try to stop you from genuine prayer. But, don't let them! Get on your knees, Christian. Start blasting away at Satan's kingdom of darkness with your spiritual atomic bomb, and watch those demons scatter in a frantic frenzy. All of hell trembles when you hit your knees!

JAMES 5:16 *"The effectual, fervent prayer of a righteous man availeth much..."*

May 28

Have you been through the door?

Arriving at the family reunion, you receive the shock of your life. The doors into the big community room are locked. You can see all your loved ones inside, laughing and talking and having a joyful time. However, they cannot hear you. You try and try to get in, but finally have to give up. What an awful, sunk feeling to be on the outside looking in. How tragic it is to be excluded from being with those you know and love!

It would be extremely frustrating to be in a similar situation here on earth. But, that would be nothing in comparison with being excluded from your family in heaven throughout all eternity. It would be ever so tragic to find the door to heaven closed and locked forever.

Maybe you are thinking that there is no such thing as a door to heaven. Well, according to *John 10:9*, Jesus said, "*I am the door; by Me, if any man enter in, he shall be saved...*" There is not another way to heaven except through the door, Jesus Christ. The Bible never says that your works are a door, that your goodness is a door, or that your religion or your denomination is a door. It does not even say that Jesus is a door. It says that Jesus is THE door!

Now, when you come through a closed door, you must put your hand on the knob, turn it, and push open the door. In other words, you must touch the door to come through it. Likewise, when you are ready to come through "the door" to heaven, you will touch Jesus. And, when you touch Him, who is the awesome Creator, you will know it. You will never be the same again.

It is wonderful to know today that "the door" to heaven is unlocked and anyone who chooses can enter in. We are living in the age of grace, in which God is extending freely to everyone his invitation to the eternal reunion. The invitation has been sent out to you. God has done His part. Now, the response is entirely up to you. You can put off coming through "the door," but be careful. One day soon, "the door" will be closed eternally. Then, from hell, you will see all the people inside heaven, laughing, talking, singing, and praising, but you cannot get in! You will realize, at that instant, that "the door" was open to you for years and years, but you never chose to go inside.

Today, why don't you give your life to Jesus Christ? Enter in through "the door." Tomorrow, it may be closed and locked forever.

JOHN 10:9 *"I am the door; by Me, if any man enter in, he shall be saved..."*

May 29

Too busy!

"My child, you are breaking My heart! You are hurting Me and grieving Me so deeply that it feels like My heart is bleeding. Although you are unaware of it, I am crying because of you. I have loved you with an everlasting love. I have been there for you through every heartache, every burden, every tear. I have comforted you, encouraged you, helped you, and loved you. I have shared My heart with you…My joys, My sorrows, My burdens, and My desires. I have enjoyed the closeness with you, the sweet fellowship we have had together, and the precious times we have spent with each other. Our relationship has been a joy to My heart!

But, things have changed, My child…not with Me, cause they'll never change with Me…but with you! You are anxious and troubled about many things. Your life has become so busy and hectic that you feel you don't have time for Me any more. But, I know differently, little one. I know you would make time if you really wanted to, cause you make the time for everything else. You'd come and talk to Me, even if it were just a few minutes here and there; and you'd lay aside some of those other things and make time for us to spend together if you really, really wanted to. So, I know all your excuses, but I know the real truth, too. The bottom line is that you don't really love Me any more. It's yourself that you love. You don't want to spend the time and effort it takes to have a relationship with Me. It's too hard…and you'd rather hurt Me than yourself!

And you know, My child, the sad thing about it is that you don't even see that you're hurting Me, because you are lost in your own little world. Oh, you go on as if things are OK. You try to talk to Me occasionally and even tell Me that you love Me. But, you're not fooling Me or others…just yourself, little one. You have treated our relationship very flippantly, very lightly, as if you can act any way you want, smooth it over, and never deal with the wrong you've done to me. But, you cannot come back to Me without repentance…which comes, not from realizing your attitude, but from realizing how your attitude has hurt Me.

My child, we can never be close again until you want our relationship restored!There's nothing I can do! My heart is hurt and you're the only one who can fix it. Oh, how I long for you to come back to Me with a broken heart, longing to have our close relationship back again, and wanting to spend time with Me once more! I love you with all My heart! I miss you so much! Please, please, please come back!"

Luke 21:34 *"And take heed to yourselves lest at any time your heart be overcharged with…the cares of this life."*

May 30

No tend-likers in heaven

We called it "tend-like" when I was a child. That's Southern for "pretend like." Oh, we would tend-like we were a family, going through all the motions, just as if we were real mommies and daddies. We would put everything we had into what we were doing. We would work just as hard as we could work for hours, planting our tend-like crops, cooking our tend-like food, and cleaning our tend-like houses. Sometimes, we would even go so far as spending days on a tend-like project, such as digging a tend-like swimming pool. We would get so absorbed in this tend-like life that it would actually become, not just make believe any more, but a reality to us!

This tend-like life is OK for kids…that's just what kids do! But, sad to say, there are multitudes of adults in America who practice it in the church their entire lives. They tend-like they are Christians, doing many of the things that real Christians do. They come to church on a pretty regular basis. They tithe. They do a lot of good deeds in the community. They even get involved in the church…teaching Sunday School, ministering as deacons, serving on various committees, singing in the choir, and even pastoring churches. Outwardly, it appears that they are doing all the right things, but in actuality, it's only tend-like.

They have carried on this tend-like lifestyle for so many years that it has become to them, not just make believe any more, but a reality! They really do believe they are saved and are on their way to heaven, because they are good people. However, if you somehow got inside their hearts, you'd discover the real truth. You'd find they have no personal, intimate relationship with the Lord Jesus Christ. The Bible doesn't hold as much interest for them as the daily newspaper. The things of God are not what they love and think on all the time. Prayer is a shopping list of wants and needs rather than sweet communion with their Father. In fact, as you look around inside their hearts, you don't even see Jesus there at all. For you see, Jesus is only in their heads. He never made it eighteen inches down to their hearts. Therefore, they've had to tend-like for all these years.

Friend, have you been playing tend-like with God? If so, you might get by with it on this earth! But one day, when you stand before the Great White Throne of God, He will say to you, *"I never knew you; depart from Me."* There'll be no tend likers in heaven!

MATTHEW 7:22, 23 *"Many will say to Me in that day, Lord, Lord…And then will I profess unto them, I never knew you; depart from Me, ye that work iniquity."*

May 31

Will the real servant of god please stand up?

When is the last time you saw a real, genuine miracle? Have you ever seen a leper cleansed, the lame made to walk, blinded eyes made to see, or the dead raised to life again? Or have you ever seen food that never ran out, fire coming down from heaven, or lions having lockjaw? Have you ever witnessed anything similar to any of these?

Maybe God does not work miracles in these days, do you think? In Old Testament times, miracles often accompanied God's people and the heathen world looked on in amazement at such an awesome God. Many believed in this God after witnessing His miraculous power. And, even in the early church, miracles were common. They authenticated the servants of God and resulted in many believing in God.

But, that was way back then. Maybe God does not work that way today. Well, ask yourself this. Are there any lost people around who need to see the true and living God?Do the servants of God need to be authenticated in this age? Is there a need for people, even Christians, to be shaken and stirred to reality to see the awesomeness of the God we love and serve?

The answer to all three of these questions is a definite "YES!" There are hundreds of false cults and thousands of false prophets. We are bombarded by the news media with religions too numerous to count, all claiming to serve God. Now, what in the world are lost people to believe? How are they going to know what and whom to believe in this wacky world of today? How can they know who the real God is? Will the real servant of God please stand up?

When the lost world looks at you, what do they see? What do they know of God by looking at your life? Does your life make them want to know the God you serve? Well, maybe, just maybe, God is looking for some servant somewhere who is willing to step out and believe Him. Maybe He is looking for a servant whose life cannot be explained; a servant who will not compromise with the world, but will dare to believe God for the impossible.

Maybe YOU are that servant! It is time to get out of your lukewarm condition and get in God's Word and in prayer. It is time you start living a life every day in which God must come through with a miracle or you are sunk! God still works miracles today. He still wants to authenticate His true servants as He always has. He is looking for someone. How about you? Will the real servant of God please stand up?

JUDGES 6:13 *"...and where are all His miracles, which our fathers told us of..."*

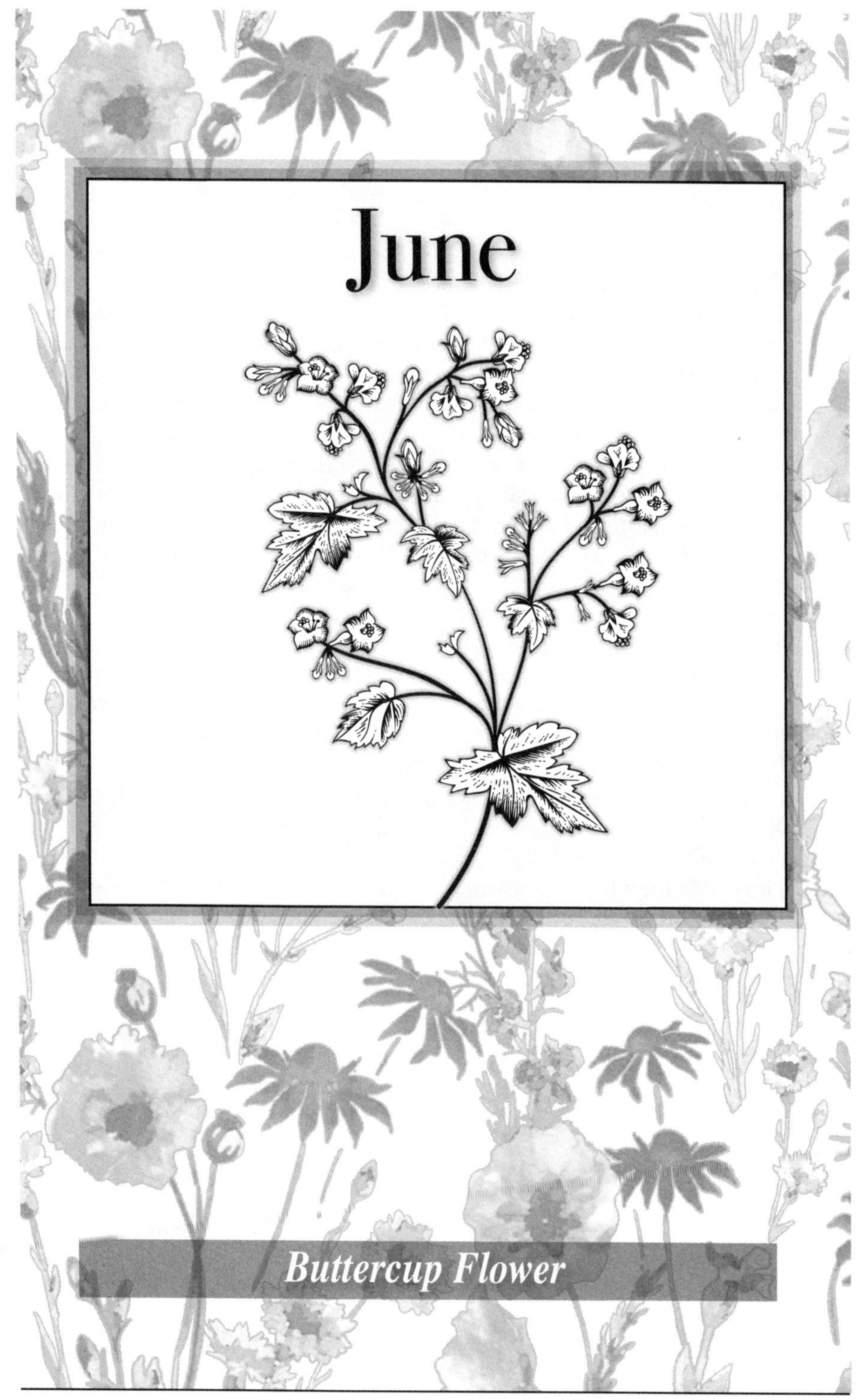
June
Buttercup Flower

June 1

Goodbye, flesh, goodbye

I want what I want when I want it. I am greedy, determined, and persistent! I have an insatiable appetite. I will not take "no" for an answer. I do not like to be denied and I will push and shove until I get my way. I do not want any restraints placed upon me. You may try for awhile, but I will eventually burst out of those restraints. I never give up either. Just when you think you have me conquered, I will rise again. I want my way. I want to be unbridled, undisciplined, unrestrained, unhindered, and uninhibited. I WILL control you! I will resist your control over me to my death...and I can hold out longer than you can. I will win, or die trying! Know what I am? I am your flesh.

Wait just a minute, flesh! You are barking up the wrong tree. You will NOT control me! I have been gloriously saved and washed in the blood of the Lamb of God. Jesus Christ Himself has come to live within me in the person of the Holy Spirit. He has come in and has given me all power over you. I no longer have to submit to you. I submit only to Him. I have the power to say no to you, flesh! And the answer is "No, no, no, no, no!"

You are right about one thing, though. You WILL die trying! Come here, flesh!There is no use trying to hide. I see you! Come here. Oh, you can wiggle and squirm and resist all you want, but I am nailing you to this cross. There...how does that feel? Are you enjoying those nails? Crucifixion is painful, isn't it? You can yell and kick and threaten all you want, but I am leaving you on this cross.

Flesh, I owe you nothing. In fact, I owe Him everything. I have decided to walk with Him and you are my biggest hindrance. So, I am getting you out of the way. All you have ever done is get me in trouble, mess up my life, and hurt those I love. It is high time I put you to death and followed my precious Savior. I cannot afford to let you be in control because your rotten, stinking ways will frighten inquiring souls away. I choose today to crucify you, flesh, and to walk in the Spirit. Goodbye, flesh, goodbye!

GALATIANS 5:16 *"...walk in the Spirit, and ye shall not fulfill the lust of the flesh."*

June 2

It couldn't just happen

"Isn't this watch a magnificent piece of workmanship? Know where I got it? Well, one day, there were some pieces of glass, metal, springs, and batteries lying on a table. Suddenly, the table began to spin. At first, it didn't spin very fast, but it gradually began to pick up speed. As it spun faster and faster, a most miraculous thing occurred. All those materials on the table just came together and this watch was the result!"

Now, no one in the world would ever believe such a ridiculous story. Anyone with half a brain would know that something as complicated as a watch did not just come together. It could NOT just happen! Order never comes out of chaos! And, if something as insignificant as a watch could not be created by a table turning and objects spinning and coming together in perfect order, then how in the world could anyone believe an orderly universe started spinning and just came together?

Our universe is in such astounding order and minute precision that it can all be calculated and figured out mathematically. The surface of our earth at the equator rotates at about 1,000 miles per hour. Our earth is orbiting the sun at about 67,000 miles per hour. Our solar system whirls around the center of our galaxy, the Milky Way Galaxy, at about 490,000 miles per hour. And our Milky Way Galaxy is hurtling through space at about 1.3 million miles per hour. How awesome that we are standing on this little old ball, called earth, moving at all these incredible speeds, and we can't even feel that we're moving at all! Wow!!!!!

Do you think for one second that this kind of order just happened? No, a thousand times, no! Just look around you! There is a mastermind behind all of this. Any time you have a design, there must always be a Designer. The Designer of our universe is Jehovah God. He also designed and created you and has written a book just for you, called the Bible. He spoke through human instruments to give you all the instructions you would need for living. And since He is the Author and Creator of all this, don't you think it would be wise to follow His instructions?

Today, why don't you quit doubting and start trusting? Since He keeps an entire universe working smoothly and efficiently, He certainly can run your little affairs a whole lot better than you can. Every time you look at your watch, remember that someone made it and it works without your help. It didn't just happen. Your life is like that watch...it didn't just happen. God started it, He will keep it working, and He will finish it...if you'll let Him!

GENESIS 1:1 *"In the beginning God created the heaven and the earth."*

June 3

Little is much when god is in it

We are all fascinated by Ripley's Believe It or Not. We are dumbfounded to the point of disbelief at some of the things in the Guinness Book of World Records. But, these things have absolutely nothing over some of the things in God's Word.

Would you believe that insomnia saved a whole race of people? Did you know that one little stone defeated an entire army? Would you believe that five-thousand men plus women and children were fed with just five loaves of bread and two fish? Can you possibly believe that three young men were thrown into a fiery furnace and not even one hair of their heads was singed? Or can you picture three armies surrounding one little group of people and all three armies being destroyed down to the last man by the little group singing and praising? Have you ever heard of someone's tax money being in a fish's mouth? Can you picture the waters of a swollen, rushing river being rolled back as the feet of some priests stepped in? Or have you ever heard of hungry lions having lockjaw? Can you believe that the walls of a city, walls which were twenty-five feet high and twenty feet thick in some places, could come crumbling down at the sound of a trumpet and a shout?Have you ever seen someone who has been in a grave for four days come walking out when his name was called? And what about casting a stick into a river and watching an ax-head rise to the surface?

Listen, do not ever underestimate God! He delights in using the foolish things of the world to confound the wise. He will take the smallest, most insignificant things and absolutely blow your mind with them. God is not looking for the intelligent, the most likely to succeed, the proper, or the good-looking. He is instead looking for one single person who believes that little is much when God is in it.

Today, do you feel like a little insignificant person? Do you feel you have about as much capability as a rock? Have you been defeated and pushed down so much that you have to reach up to touch bottom? Well, my friend, God's eyes are upon you. You are a perfect candidate for Him to use to confound this old world. After all, it is not the rock, or the stick, or the fish that gets the job done. It is God! Remember: little is much when God is in it!

I CORINTHIANS 1:27 *"But God has chosen the foolish things of the world to confound the wise..."*

June 4

A plumb line

"I just made a mess. I have put up a whole room of wallpaper and it is so crooked. What in the world did I do wrong? It looked straight. Why, I even stood back after hanging each strip to make sure it was level."

"Well, friend, let me tell you what you did wrong. You failed to use a plumb line. Instead, you were just going by what it looked like. Looks are deceiving, you know. You MUST have a standard of measurement to go by, or you are really just guessing. And when you are guessing, you can get by all right for a while, but things will end in a mess in the final analysis. The only way to tell if wallpaper is being hung correctly is to put it beside a plumb line and adjust the paper to the plumb line. Let the plumb line, not your opinion, be the guide you follow."

In our journey here on earth, God has given us a plumb line. It is the Word of God. It is the only correct measuring stick for our lives. We must lay out the Word and then lay our lives beside it. We must make any necessary adjustments and corrections based on the Word. If we try to adjust the Word to our lives instead of our lives to the Word, we will end with a crooked, tangled, confused mess.

In our day, people are doing just as they did in the days of the Judges: "*...every man did that which was right in his own eyes." Judges 21:25* In Solomon's day, people were still following their own ways, as we are told twice in Proverbs, "*There is a way which seemeth right unto a man, but the end thereof are the ways of death." Proverbs 14:12* and 16:25 We are also told "*The way of a fool is right in his own eyes, but he that hearkeneth to counsel is wise." Proverbs 12:15*

If you are building your life today by what you think or by how you feel, then you are building on the wrong thing. You are building on something that looks all right and will stand for a while. But, it will not stand up under the test of time. In the final analysis, it will be a mess. Look, if it takes a plumb line to do something as simple as hanging wallpaper, then how in the world do you think you can run a complicated life without the plumb line of God's Word? Don't guess......don't make a mess......use the plumb line instead!

AMOS 7:8 *"Then said the Lord, Behold, I will set a plumb line in the midst of my people."*

June 5

Falling asleep

Have you ever thought about what happens when you fall asleep? Usually, the first thing you do is lie down. You get comfortable, close your eyes, and gradually drift off to sleep. You do not know at what moment you go to sleep. Neither do you realize that you are asleep until you wake up.

Likewise, a Christian can fall asleep spiritually. First, he must lie down in his spirit. He gets tired of the battle, tired of the struggle, and tired of always being alienated and attacked. So, he retires from the front lines, deciding that it will be much easier to just go with the flow. That way, he will not face the opposition and discouragement anymore. It's easier to retreat than to fight!

After he retreats for a while, he begins to get very comfortable. It feels good in the "comfort zone." He doesn't have to witness any more. Instead, he can just carry on normal conversations with people without having to be concerned about their souls. He can live like he wants, sleep as much as he wants, and eat what he wants, because he doesn't have to check in with God any more about his daily decisions. He has more money, because he doesn't have to be concerned with tithing anymore. And, he doesn't have to spend much time with the Lord now, so he has more free time to do whatever he wants.

Soon after getting settled into his "comfort zone" and getting all relaxed and cozy, he closes his spiritual eyes. He is no longer excited about hearing and learning spiritual truths. He becomes disinterested in God's Word and what it has to say to him. He does not care to be around Christians that are full of Jesus any more, because they disturb his comfort. His prayer life becomes dry, routine, dull, and infrequent. He just half-heartedly goes through the motions of being a Christian. And, gradually and unknowingly, he drifts off to sleep!

Now, this Christian is totally unaware that he is asleep. Just as when one is physically asleep, he gets nothing done. He does not accomplish anything for the cause of Christ. Oh, he's alive. He's breathing and going through the motions, but he's not making any impact for eternity. And, he will probably remain asleep until a spiritual alarm clock, which is often some sort of tragedy, goes off and jolts him into reality and wakes him up again!

What is your condition today? If you've fallen asleep, then wake up! Wake up, Christian! Hell is raging, souls are dying, and time is running out. It is high time to awake out of sleep!

ROMANS 13:11 *"And that, knowing the time, that now it is high time to awake out of sleep..."*

June 6

Behold Him!

Behold His hands: the hands that created the universe; the hands that measured out heaven with the span; the hands that formed man from the dust of the earth. How can it be that such precious hands are now pierced with nails?

Behold His body: the body He created; the body He inhabited, He who has all power and all authority and can turn the hearts of all men. How can it be that this body has been so beaten and mutilated that it is not even recognizable?

Behold His clothing: He whose robe in glory was one of righteousness and was wholly pure and sinlessly clean. How can it be that He, who was so majestically and royally attired, has been stripped of all His garments to hang ashamedly before the world?

Behold the place: He whose home was celestial; He whose home was a royal habitation, indescribable in beauty and glory. How can it be that He is now fixed to a cross in a despicable, unclean place, a place of suffering, degradation, and death?

Behold His desire: He, from whose throne flows a crystal river; He who measured the waters in the hollow of His hand; He who is the Living Water. How can it be that He is now crying, *"I thirst?"*

Behold His death: He who is the author and creator of life; He who controls life and death; He who is eternal. How can it be that He is crying, *"It is finished," John 19:30* and is bowing His head in death?

Behold His burial: He who owns the cattle on a thousand hills; He who said, *"The earth is mine and the fullness thereof." Psalm 24:1* How can it be that He is being buried in a borrowed tomb?

Oh, but what is this? The stone has been rolled away from the tomb and someone is coming out! Why, it is He! He is holding something in those precious, nail-scarred hands. It is the keys to death, hell, and the grave!

Behold the Savior of the world!

JOHN 1:29 *"Behold the Lamb of God, who taketh away the sin of the world."*

June 7

Feet on your prayers

As a Christian, you often hear people say, "You've got to put feet on your prayers." By that, people are actually saying that you can get down and pray, but then you need to get up and do something about it. This is the prevailing philosophy in our churches today and it really boils down to what man can do.

Well, exactly what can man do? Oh, he can come up with newer and better programs. He can think of gimmicks to draw people in. He can build bigger and more beautiful facilities. He can have more activities and more ministries. He can go out knocking on doors and inviting people. He can study about church growth and do all the things the books say on the subject. But, what is all man's activity accomplishing? It is accomplishing only what man can do. It is NOT changing our society! It is NOT making a dent in the corruption and evil around us! It is NOT causing the lost world to take notice! It is NOT stopping the advance of crime and ungodliness!

Something is desperately wrong in this picture. Could it be that the church has followed the world and its ways? The church plays at prayer, but then adopts the world's philosophy, "Pull yourself up by the bootstraps." In other words, "Put feet on your prayers." YOU do something!

Do you know what is wrong with this way of thinking? It is really a cop-out for intense, prolonged, agonizing, burdened, seeking, prevailing prayer. It is a quick fix. You just run in and pray a little; then get up and do something. Whatever happened to real prayer? Whatever happened to the saints who got a hold of the horns of the altar and stayed there until God answered? Whatever happened to those who so prayed in the presence of Almighty God that, whenever they got up, GOD put feet on their prayers? Then, everywhere they went, there were supernatural results! With the power of God upon them, even lost people were convicted just by being in their presence. When God puts feet on prayers, they are supernatural feet, unlike anything this world has ever seen!

What is your prayer life like? Do you just play at prayer? Do you lightheartedly pray, but then get up and put feet on your own prayers? Or, have you learned to pray with maturity, seeking the face of God until He answers? Have you learned how to pray until God Himself puts feet on your prayers, feet which are supernatural and accomplish more unknowingly than natural feet do with years of effort? Who is putting the feet on your prayers?

JAMES 5:16 *"The effectual, fervent prayer of a righteous man availeth much."*

June 8

Head for the son

Eagles are fascinating creatures. There is something mysterious and majestic about an eagle as he gracefully soars through the air. Far above the ground, he glides on airlifted wings, appearing to have not an enemy in the world.

However, the eagle does have enemies, as do all of God's creatures. But, the eagle has a very unusual way of dealing with them. An eagle is equipped with an extra set of eyelids that come from the sides of his eyes. When an enemy comes toward him, he rolls that set of eyelids over his eyes and heads toward the sun. The eyelids are a shield against the bright, blinding rays of the sun, similar to a pair of thick sunglasses. The enemy is not blessed with this extra set of eyelids and cannot stand the blinding rays. He soon has to turn back. The eagle does not have to focus on or fight his enemy. Instead, he simply heads for the sun.

Spiritually, you can defeat your enemy the same way the eagle defeats his. When the enemy comes after you, you don't have to fight either. After all, God says in His Word, "*The battle is not yours, but God's.*" *II Chronicles 20:15* So, like the eagle, rather than focusing on your enemy or on what he is doing, you just turn your back on him and head for the Son!

You do this by getting in God's Word and by praying. You spend your time alone with the Lord of Glory rather than by wasting it with the enemy, worrying and fretting and wringing your hands over what he is doing. He is not worth even a first thought, much less a second one. He was defeated two-thousand years ago on Calvary by the Son, so there's absolutely no need for you to acknowledge him or his doings in any way. Just spend your time praising and worshipping the Victor, the Son…not the defeated foe!

At first, the enemy will stay in hot pursuit, trying to frighten and harass you by his persistent, relentless attack. He will do everything he can to keep you out of the Word and off of your knees…because he knows he cannot follow you there. If you head for the Son, the enemy will have to turn back!

So, today, why don't you take a lesson from the eagle? Quit focusing on and fighting your enemy. Quit worrying and fretting and grumbling and murmuring. Instead, get in the Word of God, pray, and praise the Lord of Glory! Just turn your back on the enemy and head for the Son!

II CHRONICLES 20:15 *"The battle is not yours, but God's."*

June 9

Don't depend on it

I have this lump that has appeared under my skin. It keeps growing and is too sore to even touch. My family is quite upset over it, but they have no right to tell me there is something wrong with me. Why, I know they think I have cancer, but I'm all right! I KNOW I am all right, because I am a good person. I cook for the sick, I visit the hospitals, and I am always helping people. Therefore, I just know I could not possibly have cancer.

This type of reasoning would be very foolish, as being good is totally unrelated to cancer. Now, you can see the absurdity of this way of thinking, but you may never have realized that many people think this way spiritually. They believe that they could not possibly go to hell, because they are good. They may cook, visit, help, and even pour out their lives for others. But what they fail to realize, however, is that being good doesn't keep one out of hell any more than it keeps one from getting cancer.

According to God's holy Word, each of us has a big, cancerous lump in our souls. It is called sin. You may have some family members who are very concerned about you. You wonder what gives them the right to think there is anything wrong with you. Why, you are a good person, so you must be all right. But, my friend, these people who love you know that, unless the lump of sin is removed, you will die and spend eternity in hell.

God is holy and the Bible says that sin will NEVER enter His presence! When you die, unless your sin has been removed by the Great Physician, you will not spend eternity in His presence. Good works can NEVER do away with sin! There is only one thing that can take away sin. *I John 1:7 says, "...and the blood of Jesus Christ, His Son, cleanses us from all sin."*

Today, why don't you come to the Great Physician? Get on your knees and confess to Him that you are a sinner. Surrender your heart to Him, asking Him to come into your heart, forgive you, and cleanse you. Let His precious blood wash away that old cancerous lump of sin and give eternal life to you.

Do you think your good works will keep you from getting cancer? Don't depend on it! Do you think your good works will keep you out of hell? Don't depend on it!

I JOHN 1:7 *"...and the blood of Jesus Christ, His Son, cleanses us from all sin."*

June 10

You can go....but

When Moses went before Pharaoh to persuade him to let the Israelites go, Pharaoh offered four compromises. First, he told Moses that they could go and sacrifice to their God...but "*in the land.*" In other words, he told them they could sacrifice to God, but they could not go out of Egypt to do so. Pharoah will tell you the same thing today, too. He will try to persuade you that you can serve your God, but you must stay in the world at the same time. He wants you to think that you do NOT have to *"come out from among them and be ye separate,"* as *II Corinthians 6:17* tells us.

Moses did not fall for that deception, so Pharaoh came up with another plan. He told Moses they could sacrifice to the Lord in the wilderness as they wanted...but, they could not go very far away. Pharoah will tell you that, too. He will tell you that you can serve your God, only do not go too far with it. Do not go off the deep end. Do not be one of those religious fanatics. He will convince you that you can go to church some and serve God some, but just don't go to the extremes with it.

Well, Moses said no to this deception also, so Pharaoh offered a more subtle compromise. He told them they were free to go and sacrifice any way they wanted...but the children must remain in the land. After all, they were just children. Pharoah will tell you that, too. He will tell you that children do not really understand about sacrifice. They need to stay where it is comfortable, where they can participate in all the worldly activities and continue their education. They need to play and be entertained and have a carefree life. Now, it is all right for you to live such a narrow life, but give your children the opportunity for prosperity and fun and worldly success.

And, finally, when that did not work, Pharaoh offered one more compromise. He told Moses they could go and even take their little ones...but they must leave their flocks and herds behind. In other words, he told them they could serve God all they wanted; they could even train up their young ones for Him, but they must leave some of their possessions in the world. Pharaoh will say the same to you. He will tell you that you should not forsake all and follow Christ... that you will need some stakes put here if you are going to have a stable and steady life for yourself and your family. He will fool you into believing you will starve if you forsake all...that you cannot possibly survive if you do.

Perhaps today, Satan is offering you these same compromises. He will tell you that you can "*Go, serve the Lord your God.......but...*" If the enemy is trying to persuade you with any of these "buts," then you should do just what Moses did! Don't budge, don't compromise, don't be deterred! Take the "but" off and "*Go, serve the Lord your God.......period!*"

EXODUS 10:8 *"Go, serve the Lord your God; but..."*

June 11

A labor drought

Something is wrong, America! You have more money than any nation has ever had; yet look how you are struggling just to make ends meet. You have more modern conveniences and more ways to make life easier than anyone in history has ever had; yet life is harder and more complicated than ever. You have more pleasure, more vacations, and more entertainment than any people have ever known; yet your people are depressed, discouraged, disillusioned, and dependent upon drugs and psychiatrists for help. Oh, America, land of plenty, land of the free and home of the brave, you are losing your heart. What is wrong with you?

Maybe you should listen to the prophet Haggai as he speaks to the Jews. It sounds like he's speaking directly to you, too, America. "*Consider your ways. You have sown much, and bring in little...and he that earneth wages earneth wages to put it into a bag with holes." Haggai 1:5, 6* "*You looked for much and, lo, it came to little; and when you brought it home, I did blow upon it...And I called for a drought upon...all the labor of the hands." Haggai 1:9, 11* Look around, America! The same thing is happening to you that was happening to the people of Haggai's day. There is even a drought upon all the labor of your hands now, with all the downsizing and job losses that occur frequently. You cannot even get any kind of job and depend on it any more.

What was the problem in Haggai's day that caused God's judgment? Listen to Haggai again, "*Why, saith the Lord of Hosts? Because of My house that is waste, and you run every man to his own house." Haggai 1:9* "*...you dwell in your paneled houses, and My house lies waste." Haggai 1:4* America, how tragic that you spend more per year on dog food than on propagating the gospel. You spend more on entertainment and recreation than on God's holy work. Knowing how God has richly blessed you and how you are returning that blessing by spending it upon yourselves, is it any wonder that there's a drought upon all the labor of your hands?

Oh, land of milk and honey, you have forgotten what brought you here and made you great in the first place! You came to seek first God's kingdom and His righteousness. You did not come here for more money, more entertainment, or more ease. You came here to worship God! When you seek Him first, then all the other things you need are added. And when you quit seeking Him first and put yourself first instead, then all the other things you need are removed.......and you're left with a drought!

HAGGAI 1:11 *"And I called for a drought upon...all the labor of the hands."*

June 12

Two, three, four, five

Would you like a change in your life? Maybe you are sick of yourself and wish your whole life could be different. You worry a lot, you get depressed easily, you feel defeated, and you are so discouraged. You are looking for something big to come along and make a drastic change in you.

Friend, there are four little, bitty words in the Bible that can absolutely revolutionize you. It is usually not the big, but the little, that God uses. One of these words has two letters, one three, one four, and one five. Just remember: two, three, four, five. This could change your life forever!

Jesus Christ spoke these four life-changing words, *"Have faith in God." Mark 11:22* To put it as two, three, four, five, it would be *"In God have faith."* Jesus did not say, "Have faith in money or material gain." If that is where your faith is, then you will be shaken by financial losses and upset by anything that affects your financial situation either now or in the future. If you have faith in God, then anything monetary will have no effect upon you, because your faith is in God, who owns it all. Since He is not affected by the world's monetary system, then faith in Him is likewise not affected by it.

Jesus did not say, "Have faith in a relationship. If that is where your faith is, then you will be influenced by the relationship and it will affect your service for the Lord. If you have faith in God, then no relationship will control your life, affect your joy, interfere with your peace, or affect your security. Since God is not affected by relationships, then you won't be either if your faith is in Him.

Jesus did not say, "Have faith in circumstances." If that is where your faith is and your circumstances control your faith, then you will live a roller coaster life. You will be high when circumstances are good and low when they're bad. If you have faith in God, then your circumstances cannot control your joy, your enthusiasm, or any aspect of your life. God is NOT affected by circumstances and you won't be either if your faith is in Him.

Today, where is your faith? If there is anything that controls your life, consumes your thoughts, and affects everything you do, then that thing is where your faith is. And it will lead to much frustration, discouragement, and ineffectiveness. You need to pluck up that seed of faith out of the wrong soil and and bury it in God instead. Remember, it's two, three, four, five…or *"In God have faith."*

MARK 11:22 *"Have faith in God."*

June 13

Your way won't work

He was captain of the host of the king of Syria. He was an important and a great man, a mighty man of valor, leading Syria into many victories. But, he had a serious problem, one for which there was no human help or answer. Naaman had leprosy. All his authority, all his power, and all his riches were incapable of helping him. He had tried everything possible...every plan, every idea, and every resource...but nothing worked.

Upon this scene stepped a little maid, a little Israeli servant girl, who had been taken captive during one of Naaman's raids on Israel. She was brought into Naaman's house as servant to his wife. She would have been the last one he consulted for an answer, as she was insignificant in comparison with him and with others he knew. Yet, she knew the answer. She served an Almighty, supernatural God, the God who spoke the universe into existence from nothing. She knew that leprosy was no big deal to Him. He was Naaman's only hope.

So, the little servant girl suggested that Naaman go to the prophet Elisha in Israel, a holy man of God whom God used mightily. Since Naaman had nothing to lose, he took the servant girl's advice and made the trip to Israel.

When he arrived at the prophet's house, Naaman expected some big fanfare... after all, he was a very important man. However, Elisha made no big deal over this great captain. In fact, he did not even come to the door, but sent a messenger to tell Naaman what to do. (God is no respecter of persons.) The message was that Naaman should go and wash seven times in the Jordan River and he would be healed. Naaman was infuriated! The Jordan River was dirty and it wasn't even in his own country. This was absolutely foolish, he thought, when the Abana and Pharpar Rivers in his country were so much cleaner and better than the Jordan. No one of his prominence should be subjected to something as lowly as washing in a dirty river.

At first, Naaman wasn't going to heed the advice of God's prophet. However, due to the promptings of his servants and since he had nothing to lose by it other than his pride, he finally yielded to Elisha's advice. And, much to his surprise, it worked! He was totally healed! He was so impressed with the God of Israel that he publicly acknowledged that there was no God in all the earth but in Israel. This humbling experience changed Naaman's life.

Perhaps today you are discouraged, dear one. You have a serious problem, for which you have tried everything imaginable and nothing has worked. All your plans, all your resources, all your money, and all your power have failed. So, why don't you go to God and do what He says to do? You probably won't like His answer. It will look foolish. It won't be anything that will puff up your flesh... rather, it will probably be very humbling. The devil will tell you it won't work..... and you may even get mad. But, friend, nothing else has worked up to this point, so why don't you just try God's way this time?Your way won't work. Give it up and obey God instead. What do you have to lose, other than your pride?

II KINGS 5:15 *"Behold, now I know that there is no God in all the earth, but in Israel.."*

June 14

Born again

The birth of a baby into the world is quite a miraculous and remarkable event. It begins when the seed of a man is planted within a woman. Now, many, many seeds can be planted but never come to anything. But one day, that one seed is planted at just the right time, penetrates the egg, and lodges within the woman's womb. For nine months, it grows in the darkness and protection of the womb. And then one day, labor begins. The labor worsens as the time of delivery draws nearer. Finally, after much travail and agony, the child is translated from the world of darkness into the light of the physical world. We say it has been born. Immediately, it becomes aware of and starts to learn about its new dwelling place. It can see, hear, smell, taste, and feel, the five channels through which it will learn all about its new environment.

Spiritual birth has many similarities. It, too, is a most miraculous and remarkable event. It begins when the seed of the Word of God is planted within a person's heart. Now, thousands of seeds could have been planted through the preaching and teaching of God's Word, yet never found a lodging place. However, one day, just the right seed is planted at just the right time, penetrates the human will, and lodges within the heart. There, it begins to grow. It may grow for months or even years, until one day, labor begins. The person's soul enters into a battle. It worsens as the time of deliverance draws nearer. However, after much travail and agony, which varies with the person, deliverance comes. The heart fully accepts Jesus as Savior and Lord and the person is immediately translated from the spiritual kingdom of darkness into the kingdom of God's dear Son, the kingdom of light. We say he has been born again, or saved.

Immediately, the person becomes aware of and starts to learn about his new spiritual environment. His spiritual eyes are opened to the spiritual light, which is the Word of God. He begins his new life of faith, walking by the Word of God instead of by his feelings.

Today, dear one, you have been born once, translated from physical darkness to physical light. You know you have, because you are here. That's proof enough! But, have you ever been born again?

JOHN 3:7 *"You must be born again."*

June 15

At a crossroads

You have just received some devastating news. Immediately, a black cloud of doom settles upon you, as all looks rather hopeless on your horizon. Your first thought is, "God, why did You let this happen to me? I have been faithful to You, serving you with all my heart and soul and mind. But, since I made the decision to follow You, one bad thing after another has happened to me. It is just too hard serving You. Things were better for me and easier before I made this total commitment to You."

Oh, friend, sure things were easier before you turned your life over to the Lord. The devil had you in his clutches, right where he wanted you. You were his prisoner and did not even know it. Why would he bother you if you were not trying to escape the chains of bondage with which he held you? He now wants you back in that prison again, so your life will be totally ineffective for the Lord Jesus Christ. And, what would be the best way to shake you loose from following Jesus and capture you for his own again? Exactly what has just happened - that is what will do it!

Well, what are you going to do? You are at a crossroads! There are two roads you can take. You CAN just wimp out! Hey, the devil knows how to get to you. He knows you don't have much backbone, much determination, or much fight in you. You are easy prey!So just go ahead and have your big old pity party. Just give up on serving God and let Satan control the rest of your life. It will be so much easier to just go with the flow than to fight. Just let Satan win! That is really smart to fall for the lies of a murderer, a woman abuser, a rapist, a pornographer, a child molester, a thief, and a liar. Oh yes, that really makes a lot of sense!

Or, you could take the other road and follow Christ! Just plant your feet firmly on the rock of determination and serve God more than ever. Start praising Him in your situation. He says that all things work together for good for those who love Him…..and, since He cannot lie, then all this is working for your good, regardless of how it looks to you. Your Father is in control. He didn't look down and say, "Oops!" He already knew about this before it ever happened…and He already knows the outcome! So, are you going to believe Him, who cannot lie, or believe him who is the father of all lies?

Today, you have been devastated and are ready to throw in the towel. You are at a crossroads in your life. What a wonderful opportunity to prove to God, to Satan, and to the world where your love, devotion, and allegiance lie! What an awesome time to prove God's faithfulness in your life, just as Job did when he adopted the philosophy, "*Though He slay me, yet will I trust in Him.*" It worked for him…and it will work for you!

JOB 13:15 *"Though He slay me, yet will I trust in Him..."*

June 16

Quit picking leaves and get to the root

There is a battle going on inside you. God has put His finger on one particular area in your life that is not pleasing to Him. You know this thing is a hindrance to your spiritual life; yet, you struggle with it endlessly. It bothers you almost all your waking hours. You make decisions to get it under control tomorrow, only to fail again when tomorrow comes. Then, you feel guilty because you promised God that you would do something about it, and you completely failed again to make good on your promise.

Why can't you conquer this area? Why does it defeat you over and over, leaving you frustrated, angry with yourself, and disappointed at failing God? What in the world is wrong with you?

This is one of Satan's most powerful and most effective strategies against Christians. He cannot get you to go out and get drunk, to commit adultery, or to kill, so he devises a scheme to keep you frustrated and ineffective in your Christian life. He attacks the weak area of your life and accuses you relentlessly with it. He always shows you the spotted, diseased leaves....but never lets you see the root! You continually pick off those leaves, focusing entirely on them. Yet, you never get to the root of the problem, so the leaves grow back. It is a vicious cycle.

Well, it's about time you get your mind and attention off the leaves and look at the root of the problem. As long as you focus on the outward manifestations of the problem, or the leaves, you will not be victorious. Do something about the root! The Bible says, "Walk in the Spirit, and you SHALL NOT fulfill the lust of the flesh." So, the root problem is that you are not walking in the Spirit. When you are walking in the Spirit, the Bible says you shall not...not maybe you won't...but shall not…fulfill the lust of the flesh.

So, Christian, get your focus off the problem and onto Jesus. Quit worrying and fretting over your failure and concentrate on loving and adoring Him. You CANNOT overcome the problem, so let Jesus overcome you! Quit picking leaves and get to the root!Walk IN the Spirit, not IN the flesh!

GALATIANS 5:16 *"Walk in the Spirit, and you shall not fulfill the lust of the flesh."*

June 17

To hear or not to hear

What chances would a child have of getting something from his father if he is living in disobedience and rebellion against his father? Would it do him any good to ask for a new bike when he is ignoring his father's word and living as he pleases? If the father gives the child what he asks for, even though he is living in disobedience, then the father is putting his stamp of approval and acceptance on rebellion. He is rewarding the child for a rebellious lifestyle.

Do you think for a second that God would ever reward any of His children for their rebellion or disobedience? Would He place His stamp of approval and acceptance on this kind of attitude? Of course He wouldn't! He says, "*But your iniquities have separated between you and your God and your sins have hidden His face from you that He will not hear." Isaiah 50:2* He also says, *"If I regard iniquity in my heart, the Lord will not hear me." Psalm 66:18*

So, God Himself is telling us that sin has drastic results. Not only will God not answer our prayers, but He will not even hear them, or acknowledge them. If we think we can live any old way, come to church as we please, read the Bible and pray when we feel like it, walk as the world walks, and then get down and pray and see God answer, then we have another thought coming!

Does God hear and answer your prayers? If not, then maybe you need a sin check. He says, "*To him that knoweth to do good and doeth it not, to him it is sin." James 4:17* Is there something you know you should do but aren't doing? Is there an area that God has put His finger on and you won't respond? If you know His Word says it and you won't do it, then you are living in disobedience and rebellion against His Word. To know to do good and not to do it is sin! It is conscious, deliberate disobedience of His Word!

Are you living by faith? The Bible says, "*Whatever is not of faith is sin." Romans 14:23* God promises to supply all your needs, if you seek Him first. He promises to guide and protect you. He promises to work all things together for your good if you love Him. But, you do not believe Him, do you? You keep trying to handle all these things yourself...trying to do it your way. You are living in disobedience to the walk of faith.

Today, seek His face. Ask Him to show you any rebellion and disobedience. Confess it and forsake it. Then, you can have your Father's ear again. To hear or not to hear....what will your Father do? That is really left up to you!

ISAIAH 59:2 *"But your iniquities have separated between you and your God, and your sins have hidden His face from you, that He will not hear.""*

June 18

Turn fact into act

You can know all about food, but die of starvation unless you eat. You can know all about high blood pressure, but die from heart problems related to it unless you take the proper medication. You can know all about high cholesterol, but get clogged arteries unless you maintain a proper diet. For, you see, it's not enough to just know "about" something. You must actually take the information that you know on any given matter and put that information to use. Fact without act can dig you a premature grave!

In the spiritual realm, fact without act can also dig you a grave. You can have all the facts "about" Jesus. You can know that He was God in the flesh. You can know that He died on an old rugged cross to pay for your sins. You can know that He is the Way, the Truth, and the Life, and that no one comes to the Father except by Him. You can know enough about Jesus that you could actually write a book about Him. However, you can know all these facts "about" Jesus...and still go to hell. For, you see, it's not enough that you know "about" Jesus. You must actually take the information that you know and act upon it. Fact without act can dig you a grave...only this grave is an eternal one!

Dear one, today would be a good day to examine your life to make sure there's no grave digging going on. Perhaps you feel there is something missing in your life. Maybe you've been thinking lately, "There just has to be more to life than this." You have no meaning, no satisfaction, no fulfillment in life. You are just existing, just going through the motions, and you don't understand why you feel like you do. Well, there is a great possibility that you have many of the facts, but have never acted upon them.

The fact is "*All have sinned and come short of the glory of God." Romans 3:23* The act is that you confess to God you are a sinner and have come short of His glory. The fact is "*The wages of sin is death." Romans 6:23* The act is that you realize you are destined for death and need a Savior. The fact is Jesus paid the wages for you and offers you the gift of eternal life. The act is that you accept Jesus' payment and receive His free gift by believing Him in your heart and confessing Him with your mouth; by turning the controls of your life over to Him.

Today, would you turn fact into act in your life? Don't play around with eternal things...there's too much at stake! Transfer that truth from your head to your heart, or you'll miss heaven by eighteen inches!

PSALM 51:6 *"Behold, Thou desirest truth in the inward parts, and in the hidden part Thou shalt make me know wisdom."*

June 19

Activity...or intimacy?

If you were given the job of judging the success of a marriage, you must have some criterion to base those judgments upon. You could base your judgments upon activity...by how much the couple worked; by how much money they jointly brought home; by how much they were involved in the community around them; by how many material possessions they had accumulated. Or, you could base your judgments upon intimacy...by the couple's closeness to each other; by their love for each other; by the time they set aside to spend together; by their being best friends.

Obviously, the best means of judging the success of any marriage would not be by activity, but rather by intimacy. There can be lots of activity in homes where couples have hardly any relationship at all or even in homes on the verge of collapse. Activity is no indication of success whatsoever.

This is very easy to see in the area of marriage. But, we have failed to see this vital component in the church of Jesus Christ today. As we look around at the church in America, we see lots of activity. People are busy for the Lord. They are planning all kinds of programs. They are involved in endless ministries, reaching out to the world around them. They are engrossed in church socials, in seminars, in Bible studies, in musicals, etc. They are busy...busy...busy. They have decided that the success of their church is determined by its size, by all its activities and programs, by all its fellowships, by all the monies it takes in.

However, is that an accurate gauge for the success of a church? Well, eleven men in the beginning of the New Testament church, who were filled with the Holy Spirit, turned the world upside down for God...without any programs, without any resources, without any money, and without all the busyness. Yet, we aren't even making a dent in our world today...and we have mega churches with every kind of resource imaginable. Sounds like something is rotten in Denmark in the church today!

Perhaps we have substituted activity for intimacy. It could be that our folks don't really have time to spend alone with the Lord Jesus Christ. It could be that we aren't madly in love with the Lord and are just going through the motions of serving Him. It could be that we aren't getting up at three or four each morning so that we can begin our day with our Father. It could be that we are spending more time in front of the TV than we are with our Savior.

The church today is busy...but she seems to have very little intimacy. She has substituted activity, because it can be measured. But...what about you, Christian? Hope you haven't done the same!

PSALM 18:1 *"I will love Thee, O Lord, my strength."*

June 20

Will you run to Him today?

You are standing on the seashore, watching the waves roll gently up on the shore and retreat again. There is a beautiful sunrise on the horizon and a soft breeze blowing across your face. The sound of the sea brings a sense of peace and calmness to your soul. At that moment, it is as though you have the whole world in your hands. All is well.

But, oh how quickly that can change! That same seashore that brought peace and calmness can bring fear and destruction. That breeze can turn into a hurricane, with fierce and powerful winds, wrecking and destroying everything in their path. Those gentle, lulling waves can turn into a boiling cauldron, overcoming the bounds of the seashore that once held them. That beautiful sunrise can turn into dark, threatening, ominous skies of despair and fear. At that moment, you realize that you are not in control. You realize how helpless you are and how totally unable you are to change your situation. You are at the mercy of God!

Now, in both these situations, you are the same. You have no more ability in the first situation than you do in the second one. You are equally as helpless and dependent in either case. You are NOT in control of the sea. However, your perception changes, your feelings change, and your response changes. The hurricane opens your eyes to your helplessness, driving you to seek refuge and safety from the storm. Only a fool would stand on the shore as though all is well.

You have been standing on the seashore of life, but suddenly a storm has arisen in your life. The skies are dark. The winds are fierce. The waves are boisterous. The "all is well" syndrome has melted into fear and uncertainty. You have realized how helpless you are. You see that you are NOT in control after all and that you are at the mercy of God! Do not be a fool and stand on the shore as though all is well. Just because you have always thought and acted like you were in control, do not try to prove that you are now. Oh, friend, run to safety! Run to Jesus! He is the shelter. He has sent this storm into your life to open your eyes, so you can see how helpless and dependent you really are. He wants you to run to Him. He is the One in control, not you. He wants to save your soul from the wrath that is to come. Will you run to Him today?

PSALM 18:6 *"In my distress I called upon the Lord..."*

June 21

Spiders don't bark and chase cats

Have you ever seen a dog spin a web.....or a whale climb a tree.....or a goat peck worms from the ground.....or a fish crawl through the grass on his belly? Or, have you ever heard a cow bark or a seal meow or a pelican baa? You are probably thinking how crazy this sounds, because none of these ever have been or ever will be possible!

God did not make everything alike. Everything He created is unique, having its own special purpose and plan for its existence. He has equipped all of His creation with the abilities to live according to His design for them.

Take, for instance, a spider. A spider is born equipped to spin a web. Its body parts are specifically and carefully designed for this. Spiders don't bark and chase cats. They are not designed to do either of these. God only expects a spider to be a spider.

Friend, you are unique, too. God has created you one of a kind. Never before since time began and never again throughout eternity will there ever be anyone else exactly like you. You are absolutely, uniquely you. God designed you with His plans and purposes in mind and He equipped you from birth to carry these out. Don't try to fly when God has equipped you to swim. Quit measuring yourself by others. That makes about as much sense as a grasshopper measuring himself by an elephant. It does not matter what others are doing. God did not call you or equip you to be them.

Today, maybe you have been trying to peck and God has equipped you to spin. That is why you lead a frustrated life. You are trying to be something God did not call you and equip you to be. Just get in God's Word and in prayer and spend time getting to know Jesus intimately. His main purpose for you is your personal, intimate relationship with Him. Maybe you are trying to substitute something else in the place of that. Maybe you have never seen that as His purpose and plan for your life. You have been worried and fretful over what you can "do" and you are failing just to "be." If you will just fall in love with Him and spend much time with Him, you cannot help carrying out His purposes any more than a spider can help spinning a web. You'll just do it! So, thank Him today for making you "you." Don't try to change what He has made. Instead, just be what He has created you, as a unique individual, to be!

II TIMOTHY 1:9 *"...called us with an holy calling, not according to our works, but according to His own purpose and grace, which was given us in Christ Jesus...."*

June 22

Feelings are like banana peels

God was a million miles away at the time! I prayed, but every prayer just vanished into thin air about as quickly as warm breath on a cold morning. I couldn't feel the Lord's presence. I couldn't sense His nearness. I couldn't hear His voice. I felt about as dead as a stump spiritually. In fact, I really didn't even feel saved.

Sitting down in the grass, I proceeded to have myself a pity party. I had served the Lord faithfully. I had given myself wholly to Him. I spent time every day in His Word and in prayer, earnestly seeking to know Him and to love Him more. Yet, I felt deserted, alone, and unloved. As I bathed in my little tub of self-pity, I even began questioning God. "Lord, you just don't love me any more, do You? It must not matter to You that I'm sad and alone. Do you even care about me at all, Lord?"

Casting my eyes to the ground, I saw a little patch of green beside me. Not really thinking about what I was doing, I picked some of the green stuff and looked at it. I immediately recognized it as clover; however, I had never paid very close attention to clover before. This particular kind of clover had three leaves to each stem, each leaf being shaped as a perfect heart. Very gently, the Lord spoke to my heart. "My child, I love you. Oh, you just don't know how much I love you. You see, I have even left messages of My love all around you, but you have failed to see them. I have given you this clover to remind you of My love. It has three heart-shaped leaves, showing that you are loved by God the Father, God the Son, and God the Holy Spirit. I love you perfectly."

Suddenly, I was overwhelmed with a sense of God's presence and His love. How awesome that He had created a world of sights, sounds, smells, tastes, and feels just for me! How comforting it was to realize that all of nature is a message of God's love and concern for the human race. With a heart of gratitude, I asked His forgiveness for doubting Him. I had learned a most valuable lesson. Feelings are like banana peels - they'll sure trip you up. It's very unwise to trust them. Conversely, God's message remains the same whether or not I can see it or feel it. God never stops loving and caring. And, He has a whole beautiful world out there to prove it!

PSALM 33:5 *"the earth is full of the goodness of the Lord."*

June 23

Look for him!

If you are in a valley of despair and discouragement;
If huge mountains of impossibility rise on all sides of you;
If you feel you cannot go on;
    Jesus is the Lily of the Valley. Look for Him!

If you are surrounded by darkness;
If it's the midnight hour of your life;
If there is not even the slightest ray of light on your horizon;
    Jesus is the Bright and Morning Star. Look for Him!

If your life is troubled and filled with turmoil;
If your soul feels like a raging sea inside;
If you feel you are going under for the last time;
    Jesus is the Prince of Peace. Look for Him!

If your soul is parched and dry;
If you feel like a dying man on a desert without water;
If you have tried everything to satisfy you;
    Jesus is the Living Water. Look for Him!

If the foundation of your life is crumbling;
If your world is falling apart right before your eyes;
If you feel like everything around you is shifting sand;
    Jesus is the Rock of Ages. Look for Him!

If the hounds of hell are after you;
If you feel alone and deserted;
If your protection and guidance and help are gone;
    Jesus is the Great Shepherd. Look for Him!

No matter what your circumstances are;
No matter what your problem or impossibility is;
No matter what else you have tried;
    Jesus is the Answer! Look for Him!

HEBREWS 12:2 *"Looking unto Jesus, the Author and Finisher of our faith..."*

June 24

Are you an Ali Hafed?

Years ago, there lived a man in Persia, named Ali Hafed. Upon hearing one day about some precious gems that would bring great wealth, he became consumed with the desire to find these gems, no matter where he had to go to get them. Eventually, he even sold his farm and left home in pursuit of the rare and precious jewels he had heard about, called diamonds. Over a period of years, Ali used up his money searching for diamonds and died a poor man on the shores of Barcelona. Meanwhile, back on the farm Ali had sold, the new owner found an unusual pebble one day in the brook, the very brook where Ali had often watered his cattle. This pebble turned out to be a diamond. Soon, many more diamonds were discovered on the property. In fact, this is the exact location of the world-famous Golconda mines…the mines from which many famous jewels were placed on the crowned heads of Europe. Ali had searched for diamonds all over the world when, in fact, he had acres of them right in his own yard all the time. He died a pauper because he did not look in the right place!

Spiritually, there are multitudes of Ali Hafeds all over the world. They are searching for some "precious gems" that will bring them love, joy, peace, happiness, and contentment. They are consumed with the desire to find these "gems" of life, no matter where they have to go or what they have to do to get them. Some search in materialism, thinking this new home, this new car, this new condo, this extra money will be the "gem" they are looking for to bring them happiness. Some search in their jobs; some in alcohol; some in drugs; some in entertainment; some in self-indulgence and pleasure; some in relationships; and some in many other things. Some search all their lives and eventually die as poor men on the shores of spiritual poverty, having never discovered the "precious gems" they longed for.

It is too bad for all those "Ali's" who never look in the "brook" in their own yard. For, if they did, they would discover what they have been searching for all along. This "brook" is the Word of God, the Living Water. It is loaded with acres of "precious gems and nuggets of truth," providing all the love, joy, peace, happiness, and contentment anyone could ever want for all eternity. There is no need for anyone to ever die a spiritual pauper when he has the famous mine of the Word of God right in his own possession, just waiting to be discovered and used.

Friend, today you are sitting on a precious treasure. You have it already in your possession. So, why don't you get it out and start digging in it daily and extracting all the "precious gems" you will ever need!

MATTHEW 13:44 *"…the kingdom of heaven is like treasure hidden in a field…"*

June 25

Are you a geyser or a deep stream Christian?

What a showy thing a geyser is! It draws attention to itself by the outward manifestation of unusual displays of ordinary water. People are strongly attracted to a geyser and will even drive hundreds of miles to see one. People are always attracted to showy things! A geyser is quite spectacular to behold; however, it does not provide life and sustenance to anyone.

While the geyser is showing off, there is another stream of water that lies buried beneath the earth's surface. It is an unnoticed, everflowing, steadfast stream of crystal clear water. If it could think, it would probably want to be like the geyser. It would be so much more appealing to have recognition and prominence and admiration of others than to flow out of sight and unappreciated. However, the little stream, unlike the geyser, has provided life-giving water and sustenance to many down through its years of existence.

In the spiritual realm, there are geysers and deep streams also. A geyser Christian is a showy one, drawing attention to himself by outward manifestations and unusual displays. He often has a "word from God" for others, making it seem as though he has some direct access to God that others don't have. He has spectacular visions and revelations, which he spouts out at intervals. People are strongly attracted to him, because he outwardly seems to "have" something.

While the geyser Christian is busy spouting off, there is an unnoticed, seemingly unappreciated Christian who, without many words, just remains steadfast and faithful. He has a calm, tranquil holiness that touches you without any words or outward manifestations. This Christian is not busy trying to "be." He just simply "is!" Down through the years, he will leave behind him countless numbers of lives who have been sustained and encouraged and helped by him. It won't be because he announced that he had something for them. It won't be because of his showy manifestations. It won't be because he intentionally planned or even knew he was helping. It will come instead from a consistent, lifelong, daily, steadfast, faithful walk with Jesus Christ.

What kind of Christian are you? A geyser or a deep stream Christian?

REVELATION 2:10 *"Be thou faithful unto death, and I will give thee a crown of life."*

June 26

God's throw up zone

Throwing up is one of life's obvious indications that something is wrong. None of us like even the thoughts of throwing up, as it is most unpleasant. It can result from sickness, from tainted food, or from a highly repulsive, disgusting, nauseating circumstance.

Did you know that there is something that nauseates God? There is one thing His Word speaks about that causes Him to spew something out of His mouth. Spew comes from the Greek word, "emeo," which means to vomit. Can you imagine what could be so sickening to God that He would vomit it out of His mouth? It must be something so awful that we could hardly comprehend it. Surely, it must be something like child abuse, rape, murder, pornography, or the like.

Dear friend, prepare yourself for a shock. It is none of these awful things that nauseate God. The people who commit such atrocities are lost, in darkness, and have no knowledge of the truth. God grieves over them and longs for them to be saved. He hates their sin, but His Word does not say He is nauseated by them. It is not the lost people, who know not God, who nauseate Him. It is the saved who know Him and are lukewarm. It is those who have experienced His love, His forgiveness, His power, and His glory; yet, they have settled into a comfort zone. It is those who have tasted of the heavenly manna, yet return to the earthly pleasures and live in them. It is those who play church, or don't even come at all, after having been granted eternal freedom. It is those who have received a supernatural life, even God Himself dwelling in them, yet live like everybody else around them. It is those who know what His Word promises, yet they still trust in their own money, their own jobs, their own abilities, and their own ways.

Do you make God sick? If you are lukewarm, you do! If you have settled into a comfort zone, you had better get out fast. That is God's throw up zone. You may think you are pleasing Him, but you have gotten comfortable and do not even realize how nauseating you are to your holy, heavenly Father. If you don't want to be spewed out of His mouth, then you'd better get out of the lukewarm, apathetic, unconcerned, throw-up zone that you have settled into!

REVELATION 3:16 *"So, then, because thou art lukewarm...*
I will spew thee out of My mouth."

June 27

The Master Glassblower

It was so fascinating to watch! I stood, probably with my mouth open, as I watched the glassblower form a beautiful glass bowl from just a plain, old, simple, ordinary chunk of glass. Time after time the glassblower plunged the glass into the oven, which was heated to 2000 degrees. When he withdrew the long, hollow tube to which the glass was attached, the glass would be red hot, pliable, moldable, and shapeable. He would immediately begin work on it, either blowing into the tube, or shaping some part of the bowl with other instruments. However, it would not be but a few minutes before the glass began to cool and would start to become brittle. At that point, he would plunge the glass back into the furnace again. He repeated this process too many times to count..but each time, the bowl began to take on more and more of its final shape.

During this plunging and blowing process, the glassblower occasionally dipped the hot glass into some red fragments and swirled them into the bowl. This required even more heat…but the bowl came out of the heat with a beautiful red color. As I observed this process, I realized that the glassblower knew exactly what he was doing. He didn't leave the glass in or out of the furnace too long. He knew exactly how much fire it could take and he knew exactly when the fire was needed. With such care, he formed the beautiful glass bowl. The final product was amazing. It even had a scalloped edge around the top of the bowl. To me, it was a masterpiece.

In God's kingdom, He is the Glassblower and I am the unformed, rough, chunk of glass. Time after time, He must plunge me into the heated, fiery trials of life, so I will become moldable, pliable, and shapeable. It is during those times that He really works on me, forming me into the vessel He has in mind. When I start to cool off and become a little hard and brittle, He plunges me back into the fiery trials. Sometimes, He wants to add a little more color to my life, so He dips me into some different colors of trials and back into the fire. However, He knows exactly how long to leave me in the fire. He knows how much I can take and when more fire is needed. He also knows how long to leave me out of the fire…not long enough to become too hard to mold any more. With such tender, gentle care, He is forming me into a beautiful vessel. I will be His masterpiece. I am so glad I am in the hands of the Master Glassblower. Just wait…you won't believe the final product!

JEREMIAH 18:4 *"And the vessel that He made of clay was marred in the hand of the Potter; so He made it again, another vessel, as seemed good to the Potter to make it."*

June 28

The army of God

Hark! Sound an alarm! There's a noise of battle in the land. Blow the trumpet!Assemble all the soldiers for war. The forces of darkness have overtaken our land. There is every evil imaginable, as God has given mankind up to uncleanness through the lusts of their own hearts. They have been turned over to reprobate minds. They are marching through our country as a cancer let loose, and America is about to succumb! She cannot survive much longer in the shape she's in.

But, where is God's army? Why aren't they stopping this flood tide of evil? There are multitudes claiming to be saved, making them a part of this vast army, so why aren't they doing something?

Well, just take one glance at the army of God and you will see why! It is the most slipshod outfit you have ever seen. It is in total disarray. It is the biggest bunch of wimps around. In the first place, they are in a twilight sleep. They hear all that is going on, but they just really don't care. They have been pampered and babied and had it easy for so long that they do not want to be aroused from their slumbering state. They do not want to pay any kind of cost. War is too hard! It might cost them their smooth knees, their fat bellies, their pleasure trips, and their Sundays in bed. It takes commitment to be a good soldier, and they do not want commitment. They had rather let America go down the drain than to stand up and be a powerful man or woman of God, paying whatever it costs and fighting for their precious freedoms that were bought with blood!

In the second place, they are so wrapped up in their own little bitty worlds that they cannot even see beyond their noses. One little puff of the winds of adversity is all it takes to blow them away. They are weaker than a newborn calf that cannot stand up on its wobbly legs at first. What a puny, wimpy, pitiful excuse of an army!

Oh, soldier of Christ, are you going to wimp around for the rest of your life like you have been doing? Or, will you determine in your heart to be a real warrior, enduring hardship as a good soldier of Jesus Christ, not entangling yourself in the affairs of this life? You have a mighty, victorious Captain! You have all the weapons you need to fight!You have a country worth fighting for! You have nothing to lose and everything to gain! So, what are you waiting on? Get in God's army and fight!

II TIMOTHY 2:3 *"Thou, therefore, endure hardness, as a good soldier of Jesus Christ."*

Has the Lord shut up your womb?

Every year, they went from their city of Ramah to Shiloh, to worship and to sacrifice unto the Lord. She had come year by year with her husband, Elkanah, to this house of the Lord. She came and she went, nothing ever changing, coming and going out the same. However, this year was different! Here they were once again at the house of the Lord, but she did not want to go home the same this time. She was barren! The Lord had shut up her womb. She had tried everything, but none of man's ideas or plans worked. Her barrenness had driven her now to a place of total desperation!

Hannah rose up and went to the temple. Only God could open her womb. She was in such a grief stricken state that she would not eat. She wept bitterly. She poured out her soul to God, speaking with her heart instead of with an audible voice. Hannah gave herself completely and totally to God. She held back nothing. She promised God that, if He would open her womb, she would dedicate entirely the fruit of her womb to Him. Hannah meant business with God...and God heard and answered her heart-cry. Unto her was born Samuel, one of Israel's greatest prophets and priests, who served God faithfully all his life.

Today, you feel like a Hannah. You are spiritually barren! The Lord has shut up your spiritual womb and there is nothing but dryness and deadness. There is no fruit whatsoever coming from your spiritual womb. You go to the house of the Lord week after week, but you always come home the same. You feel like an empty shell walking around. You have tried everything you can think of to change, but nothing works!

Well, friend, rise up and go to God! Only He can open your spiritual womb. Get before Him and pour out your soul to Him, giving yourself and the fruit of your womb completely to Him. He does not answer weak, halfhearted, insincere, painless, effortless prayers. God responds to the broken and contrite heart! Just go in desperation as Hannah did and stay there until He answers and opens up your womb once again!

I SAMUEL 1:6 *"...because the Lord had shut up her womb."*

June 30

Trust and obey

This is your first time ever to fly on an airplane. You stand looking at this huge jet, apprehensive and fearful of doing something you have never done before. You know that countless others have experienced this before you, but it must have been easier for them. In order to get to your destination, you will have to do two things...trust and obey. You must have enough trust, even if it is shaky, to enable you to make that first step. Then, you must obey, actually getting on and committing yourself to the plane. Now, you can stand here and allow your fears to defeat you; or you can trust and obey.

You are facing something in your Christian walk that you have never faced before. God has moved on your life in a new direction. You are filled with fear and apprehension, as you have not walked this way before. Others have been down this path, but it seemed so easy for them. Surely, they must not have faced the same struggles as you, which are raging within you like the rising tides, threatening to overcome you.

In order to reach the new destination, you will have to do two things...trust and obey. You must have enough trust in God, even if it is no more than a grain of a mustard seed, to enable you to make that first step. All you need to do is to step out, to trust God, and then obey Him! Just as you would step on an airplane, commit yourself to it, and let it take you to your destination, do the same spiritually.

Today, you are standing on the brink of an exciting new path. You can replay all those old fears repeatedly in your mind and allow them to defeat you. You can settle down into a comfort zone, where it is easier and requires nothing from you. You can be a weak, nauseating, noodle-backboned wimp. Or, you can trust and obey. You can dare to be an adventurer, an overcomer, and a conqueror through the Lord Jesus Christ. He has already walked every path before you, won every battle, and made all the crooked places straight. Don't you think you can trust and obey Him?

Doubt and disobey. Just do it your way.
You'll mess up your life if you doubt and disobey.
Trust and obey. Just do it God's way.
Your life will be blessed if you trust and obey.

PSALM 27:11 *"Teach me Thy way, O Lord, and lead me in a plain path.."*

July

Sneezeweed

July 1

A product of the cross

"Well, I just cannot help how I am. I am exactly like my dad. I am falling into the same pattern. It has been passed down for generations, so there is nothing I can do about it. It must be in the genes."

"Oh, I know now why I am like I am. It is the way I was raised. My childhood was terrible. My parents did not raise me right. They really messed me up for the rest of my life. It is all their fault."

Have you ever heard either of these statements? Guess where they came from?Why, they came straight from the pits of hell, right from the mouth of the father of lies. He would love for you to think this way, because it labels you for life and leaves absolutely no hope of change for you. It is an excuse to remain like you are and never have to change!

If you are a Christian, then you are no longer a product of your past. You are now a product of the cross. You no longer have to live out of what you were, how your parents raised you, or what your circumstances have been. You can now live out what God's Word says you are, because of what the shed blood of Jesus Christ on the cross of Calvary purchased for you.

Just think of it. You have been bought with royal blood, perfect blood, sinless blood. Genes have nothing to do with this blood. How you were raised has nothing to do with it. Your circumstances have nothing to do with it. It doesn't matter what anyone in your past was or what kind of patterns anyone has fallen into. The blood that was shed for you has washed you, made you clean, and made you a new creation. You are now an heir of God and a joint heir with Christ. All that God is and has is yours also! Why be dominated by your past when God says He makes all things new!

Quit blaming everything on your past. Get to the cross and let Jesus make you a new creation. Then, get up and live out what God says you are instead of living what your past says you will be. You are a product of the cross, not a product of your past. Hallelujah for the cross!

EPHESIANS 3:20 *"Now unto Him who is able to do exceedingly abundantly above all that we ask or think, according to the power that worketh in us."*

July 2

The pen in his hand

The writer has a message burning in his heart. He longs to get this message to others, as he feels it would help them tremendously. These thoughts are doing no one any good, as they are only in his head at this point. So, he sits down at his desk, gets out some paper, and picks up his pen. The words begin to flow from his mind, down through his arm, into his hand and fingers, and onto the piece of paper through the pen. Now, the pen is doing all the writing; however, it is simply a vessel or a channel for the writer to use. The pen has absolutely no power within itself. It can do nothing of its own accord. But, once it is yielded to the hand of the writer, it can become a miraculous instrument. Many can be touched and helped by these words that have come forth from this pen. Yet, the pen does not get the glory for the writing...the writer does! The writer is the mastermind and the power behind all of it and the pen is simply the channel he uses to work through.

God has a message burning in His heart. He longs to get this message of His love and forgiveness to others. He needs a vessel or a channel through which He can get the message from His heart to the hearts of the people. He looks around for such an instrument. He spots one, as He sees you. You are perfect for the job. You know that you are nothing on your own accord. You know that you have no power within yourself. You feel totally helpless. You have ceased trying to do things on your own and you have yielded totally to Him. You are just sitting there awaiting His mighty hand to pick you up and use you. You will not resist and pull your own way, nor will you try to help Him. You have learned to just let go and let Him have His way.

As He picks you up, His thoughts begin to flow from His mind, down through your mind, and out through your mouth and your life. You become a miraculous instrument in His hands, as He touches and helps people through you. He gets all the glory because it is Him doing it all. He is the mastermind and the power behind all of it. You are simply the pen in His hand.

II CORINTHIANS 3:3 *"Forasmuch as you are manifestly declared to be the epistle of Christ, ministered by us, written not with ink but with the spirit of the living God..."*

July 3

The greatest sin

What would you consider the greatest sin? Perhaps your guess would be murder, rape, child molestation, abortion, pornography, physical abuse, bestiality, or sodomy! Or maybe your guess would be something on a more massive scale, such as euthanasia, ethnic cleansing, or genocide. As your mind considers various sins, what do you think is the one more atrocious, most horrible, most abominable, most hideous sin any person could ever commit?

It might come as quite a shock to you to find out that the most appalling sin one could ever commit is actually none of the above things, even as formidable as they all are. In fact, the greatest sin is worse than all of these put together, because all these atrocious sins actually stem from this one itself. They are all various offshoots from the one main sin that is behind it all!

In order to find the one great sin of all times, we must find the one great commandment, or law, that has been laid down by God Himself. If we could find the one great commandment, then the greatest sin would be breaking this great commandment. Fortunately, God's Word has this answer for us, so that we never have to guess. Jesus Himself said, "*Thou shalt love the Lord, thy God, with all thy heart, and with all thy soul, and with all thy mind. This is the first and great commandment.*" *Matthew 22:37, 38* Therefore, thy greatest sin would be the breaking of this commandment…in other words, the greatest sin would be not loving the Lord, thy God, with all thy heart, and with all thy soul, and with all thy mind.

Uh-oh! I have been caught red-handed! I am guilty, guilty, guilty…guilty before You, God, of committing the greatest sin by breaking the greatest commandment. I don't always love You with all my heart. I am afraid that my heart is sometimes divided, trying to love You, but also loving the world with its pleasures and entertainments at the same time. I often find myself conforming to the world around me and just kind of blending in with it. I don't always set my affection on things above either, Lord, nor do I keep my mind upon You and upon Heavenly things like I should. Sometimes I get so busy with my little world that my mind is on everything else but You. I even find myself worrying over stuff when You have promised that You will take care of me. And, Lord, sometimes I even lay up treasures here on earth rather than laying them up in heaven. I invest my time, my energy, my abilities, and my substance on things of the world rather than in the souls all around me.

Oh, Jesus, please forgive me! Today, I repent of breaking the great commandment. I repent of committing the greatest sin. Please, Father, draw me near Your heart and teach me to love You with everything that is within me!

MATTHEW 22:37, 38 *"Thou shalt love the Lord, thy God, with all thy heart, and with all thy soul, and with all thy mind. This is the first and great commandment."*

July 4

Oh, church!

It is obvious as we look around our country that we are in a mess. We have watched the moral and spiritual decline of this once Godly nation. We have seen prayer removed from schools, abortions legalized, homosexuality protected, fornication flaunted, heinous crimes excused, and politics corrupted. It is easy to place the blame on the government, on the ungodly, or on the devil; therefore, we think the answer to our dilemma is new politicians, a stricter justice system, more education, more protests, or more giveaway programs.

Everyone seems to have answers to the problem, most of which seem legitimate and logical. However, these answers will not solve the problem any more than putting a Band-Aid on cancer will cure it. We MUST get to the root of the problem. The root is that the spring of life has dried up and stagnation has ensued. The salt that stops corruption has lost its savor. The light which overcomes darkness has become barely visible. The soldiers have started partying instead of fighting.

What are we talking about? We are talking about the church of the Lord Jesus Christ. There she stands today, with her carpeted aisles, plush seating, beautiful decor, elegant lighting, and rich attire! But, where are the sackcloth and ashes? Where are the battle garments? Are we in a war or at a picnic? There's no alarm being sounded. There's no fervent cry over the condition of our land. There's no brokenness over the millions of souls being held captive by the enemy. There's dust on the altars, dry eyes in the pulpits, and a smug satisfaction with our little programs and our few little souls being saved.

Oh, church! You are rich and increased with goods. You are not desperate for a move of God. You have settled on your lees and you are comfortable! Wake up, church, wake up! God offers a remedy for America, *"If My people, which are called by My name, shall humble themselves, and pray, and seek My face, and turn from their wicked ways, then will I hear from heaven, and will forgive their sin, and will heal their land." II Chronicles 7:14*

Do you think God means this statement? Do you think our land needs healing?Well, if you really think our land is in a mess and that God means what He says in His Word, then why aren't you taking Him up on what He says? Why aren't you humbling yourself, praying, seeking His face, and turning from your wicked ways? Is it because you had rather play than pray? Is it because you don't want to pay the cost…because you're too comfortable, too complacent, and too lazy? Is it because you'd rather just let somebody else do it? Oh, church! Wake up! Your country needs you!

REVELATION 3:17 *"Because thou sayest, I am rich, and increased with goods, and have need of nothing, and knowest not that thou art wretched, and miserable, and poor, and blind, and naked."*

July 5

Afar off

Afar off? How in the world could this be? He had watched as Jesus opened blinded eyes. He had watched this man from Galilee heal and cleanse the lepers. He had been there as his Lord took two fish and five loaves of bread and fed five thousand men plus women and children. He had stood in astonishment as Jesus called Lazarus, who had been dead for four days, to get up from the grave. And now, in the time of his Lord's need, Peter followed afar off!

Maybe Peter had never considered what all was involved in following Jesus. He may not have counted the cost at the onset. Oh, it was easy to follow the Lord as He caused the lame to leap, as He cooled fevered brows, as He taught the things of God, and as He went about healing and helping. But, this was different! Peter had not counted on suffering. He did not know there would be a cross involved. He had not fully realized until now that he must forsake all to follow his Friend. This was hard! Many others had already turned back and followed the Lord no more. But Peter just followed afar off instead.

What about you today? Have you been following afar off? Oh, you want to go to heaven. You want the free gift of salvation. You greatly desire the power of His resurrection and you revel in the blessings and miracles of the Savior. But, you do not want to follow Him to the cross. You have turned back and followed at a distance when it cost you persecution, tribulation, and suffering. You have not forsaken all in order to follow Him. Somewhere, you have drawn a line. You have said that you will follow Him so far, but there is a point which you will not go beyond. You want a crown without a cross, glory without the shame, acceptance without rejection, and the sweet without the bitter.

Friend, Jesus is calling you today. He wants you to be a disciple. He says you must forsake all, take up your cross daily, and follow Him. There is NO other way to be a disciple. What will you do with the rest of your life? Follow Him all the way? Or follow Him afar off?

LUKE 22:54 *"And Peter followed afar off."*

July 6

Knowing the author makes the difference

As you walk through the parking lot of the shopping center, you notice a letter lying by the curb. You pick it up and read it. It is a love letter, written to someone you have never heard of before. The letter does not mean anything to you, nor does it do anything for your emotions. You do not even understand some of the things the letter speaks of. As you finish reading it, you toss it into a nearby garbage can, never to pick it up again. You are not bothered in the least by tossing it aside, because you do not know the author.

Friend, as you walk through this life, you will sooner or later come across a letter written quite some time ago. You will pick it up and read parts of it. You will discover that it is a love letter, written by God to His people. This letter is called the Holy Bible. Perhaps this letter will not mean anything to you. It may not do one single thing for your emotions. You may not even understand the purpose of it or many of the things it is speaking of. You can easily put it aside and never pick it up again, because it really does not apply to you or interest you in the least. That is because you do not know the Author. Since you do not know Him, then the letter is not a personal love letter to you.

Oh, but friend, it is quite a different story if you know the Author. When you surrender your life to the Lord Jesus Christ and He becomes your Savior and Master, everything changes! You begin to have a personal, intimate relationship with Him that is sweeter than anything you have ever known. Suddenly, you find that He is in all your thoughts. He becomes the center of your life and everything concerning Him becomes of utmost importance to you. You pick up His love letter, the Bible, and it now comes alive with meaning to you. It thrills your emotions, as you read what this One who died for you has written to you personally. It explodes with excitement to your heart and soul and you find that it is hard to even put it down. Oh, what a difference it makes to know the Author!

Today, friend, what does the Bible mean to you? Do you love it? Is it an exciting book? Is it personal? If not, it could very well be that you do not really know the Author. Knowing the Author makes the difference!

HEBREWS 12:2 *"Looking unto Jesus, the author and finisher of our faith..."*

July 7

Putting out the welcome mat

He is alive and well. I thought I had him pretty much under control. In fact, I actually felt some degree of success in subduing him and restraining him from his activities. I wanted to do as God's Word said, "*put off the old man with his deeds,*" and "*put on the new man, that is renewed in knowledge after the image of Him that created him.*" *Colossians 3:9*, 10 However, my old man was so cleverly camouflaged that I didn't even see him lurking in the shadows. He was hiding, laying low, not making much noise, so that I wouldn't know he was there. He let me go on with my service for God, my daily activities, and my little routine, while he stayed quietly in the background.

But then, someone else stepped into the picture. He came right up and immediately pinpointed the old man. Wasting no time whatsoever, conviction pushed the old man out of the shadows and into the light. The old man stood bare, exposed, and uncovered, having absolutely nothing to say for himself. Conviction had once again shown up the old man for what he really was.

How clear it all was to me now! I was not dead to the world, dead to the thoughts and opinions of others, dead to the influences around me. No, I wasn't dead at all! The Lord had spoken to my heart about a matter. He had approached me about this same thing on other occasions, but the old man always intercepted the message and passed it off by justifying it to me. However, conviction pierced my heart like an arrow, dislodging my old man from his position. The Lord had asked me, "If I asked you to do something for My glory that would appear foolish to the world, would you do it? Would you obey Me anyway in spite of what everyone thought? Would you be willing to be a fool for My sake?"

In shame, I cried and prayed, for I actually was more concerned about what others thought than about what my Savior thought. I realized that I still wanted to be liked and approved by others. My old man was far from being dead; rather, he was very much alive. But, I thank God for conviction, for he exposed the old man and drove him from his hiding place. I am putting out the welcome mat for conviction. He is number one in the heart cleaning business, and I am desperately in need of his services!

COLOSSIANS 3:9 *"put off the old man with his deeds."*

July 8

Has your shout turned into a grumble?

They had been miraculously delivered from Egypt, forced out by Pharaoh, as God put pressure on him through ten successive plagues. Then, they had come to the Red Sea. They had watched as God rolled the waters back, allowing them to walk through on dry ground. And, as soon as all of them had passed to the other side of the sea, God then rolled the waters back together, thereby drowning the pursuing Egyptian army in the same waters He had delivered them through. It had only been three days since they watched in awe as God saved them by such an awesome miracle.

Now here they were three days later, facing another crisis. They had walked in the wilderness for these three days and their water supply had almost run out. As they came upon a stream of water, called Marah, they were quite excited at their discovery. However, the waters of Marah were bitter and undrinkable.

Instead of believing God in an impossible situation, they began to murmur and complain. They thought that, since God had miraculously delivered them, it would be smooth sailing from then on. They expected God to make their lives easy. So, when things did not happen as they expected, they began to grumble. Their shout, three days prior to this, had now turned into a grumble.

Has your shout turned into a grumble? God saved you and you were on cloud nine for a while. You never thought things could change! However, you came to some bitter waters unexpectedly and you got angry and upset with God. You expected God to make your life easy, but instead you are facing difficulties. Now, you are doubting God and you are filled with worry as you are facing this impossible situation.

At Marah, God told Moses to cast a tree into the waters and they would be made sweet and drinkable. In your situation, there is a tree, too. It is the cross of Calvary. It will make your bitter waters sweet and drinkable, too. God is teaching you to trust Him. He wants you to learn to apply the cross to all your situations, because the cross has already conquered! Today, do not let your shout become a grumble. Trust God, rejoice, believe Him, and watch those bitter waters become a helpful growth in your Christian walk.

EXODUS 15:23 *"And when they came to Marah, they could not drink... for they were bitter."*

July 9

Cafeteria lifestyle

It is great to go to a cafeteria. You do not have to prepare the food, serve it, or clean up afterwards. You can pick out what you like from the variety of foods already prepared, sit down and eat, and then go home full. It calls for no responsibility on your part.

America has become a "cafeteria" nation. We have "cafeteria" marriages, selecting carefully what we want and trading what we don't like in for something else. We have a "cafeteria" workplace, with both employers and employees choosing what they like without any commitment or loyalty to each other. We have a new generation of "cafeteria" kids, wanting only to enjoy life without any responsibilities or commitments. And, our entertainment industry has highly capitalized on our "cafeteria" lifestyle, becoming rich off the American public who pays for them to prepare, clean up, and do all the work.

This "cafeteria" lifestyle has carried over into our churches also. We now choose which church we want to attend, based on what we like. We look at the menu to decide where to attend - what programs are offered, what the music is like, and what kind of preacher it has. No longer do we seek God in fasting and prayer for His choice for us! It is no longer what God says, but what we want that fashions our decisions. We want to go to church "cafeteria" style. Let someone else prepare the food. Let someone else serve. Let someone else clean up. We will just come and enjoy, with no responsibility, no commitment, and no loyalty.

Aren't you glad that God is not a "cafeteria" style God? We would be in a mess today if He were! We might not be what He is looking for on the menu! Friend, our nation is in deep trouble because of this dangerous "cafeteria" philosophy. It is time we all realize that we are not in a cafeteria. We are in a battle, and there is no picking and choosing in war! It is time we take responsibility and commit to fight until the battle is over!

MATTHEW 20:28 *"Even as the Son of man came not to be ministered unto, but to minister..."*

July 10

FWD box

"Oh, ye of little faith," (Matthew 6:30) Jesus said to His disciples, as He was giving them the antidote for anxiety. He explained to them how He takes care of the fowls of the air, the lilies of the field, and all the grass…without them ever worrying or trying to help Him out. He then went on to explain how we, who are much more important to Him than any of His other creation, should realize and know that He will even more so take care of us. If we will only just put Him first, believe Him, and trust Him entirely, all our fears, our worries, and our doubts will be eliminated.

However, we today are just like the disciples were back then… "*of little faith.*" We have so many fears…fears about our families; fears about the future; fears about our jobs; fears about our retirement; fears about our health; and on and on. We worry and fret constantly. Oh, we trust God to handle the big things, like keeping enough oxygen on earth for us to breathe; making the sun rise and set each day; keeping the oceans within their bounds; sending the rain; etc. But, we just don't trust Him to take care of our lives.

Friend, are you of little faith? If you are, your fears, worries, and doubts are an affront to God. How would you like it if your children didn't believe you and doubted you all the time? Well, it's time today to do something about it. You have a choice, you know. Perhaps it might help if you will get an FWD box. Every time you have a fear, a worry, or a doubt, write it down on an index card, date it, and drop it into your FWD box. As you are dropping it in, say, "I don't have time to handle you right now, so I'm giving you to God. I'll let Him take care of you. I'm forgetting about you for the time being. I'll just deal with you later when I have time." Then, after you drop every fear (F), every worry (W), and every doubt (D) into the box, you can go fwd, or forward, with you life, trusting God with your FWD's rather than trusting yourself.

Some time later, go back through your FWD box and pull out all the fears, worries, and doubts that you placed there. Chances are, most of them can be thrown away at that time, because they will already have been handled…or somehow they will have lost their hold on you. You'll find that your fears have turned into faith, your worries have turned into worship, and your doubts have turned into dependence. You'll never go wrong by trusting God, my friend. He will never let you down!

I PETER 5:7 *"Casting all your care upon Him, for He careth for you."*

July 11

Death is swallowed up in victory

Sitting by her bedside, I watched her struggling for every breath. Cancer had taken its toll on her body, ravaging and destroying its vitality and wholeness. Only two years prior to this, my sister had been very much alive, healthy, and vibrant. How strange it seemed to me that this once healthy body was now totally incapacitated. No longer did she talk or even open her eyes, as the morphine was keeping her in an unconscious state.

With tears running down my face, I watched a most unusual battle. Charlotte's last enemy, death, had come to claim her. However, her body did not want to succumb to that final enemy, as it continued for several days wrestling for every breath. Watching this, I thought, "Truly, death is an enemy, a very feared and undignified and dishonorable enemy." Death comes to snatch away everything that is precious and dear. Death robs us of life. Death cheats us out of time with our loved ones. Death separates us from all our possessions. Death strips us of all our abilities. Death reduces us to the state in which we were born…bringing nothing into the world and carrying nothing out. Death is our final enemy!

As I watched death slowly wrapping its greedy fingers around my sister's life, a promise from God's Word suddenly came to my remembrance. "*Death is swallowed up in victory." I Corinthians 15:54* On the cross, Jesus overcame death, hell, and the grave. He won! He destroyed even the very last enemy that any of His children will ever face, that of death. So, Charlotte was on the brink of the most glorious experience of her life. She was standing on the edge of eternity. For her, death carried no sting. Its sting, which is sin, had been removed two years before this when she accepted Jesus as her Savior. For her, death would only be a shadow. For her, death would be a promotion.....from earth to glory!

All of a sudden, as death tightened its grip, heavenly visitors entered that hospital room and snatched Charlotte from death's clutches, carrying her to her heavenly home. The whole room became holy ground, kind of like a suspended area between earth and heaven, temporarily connecting the two by this awesome visitation. The ones present at this scene knew they had passed through a very unique experience, that of watching a saint of God being ushered by angels from this life into glory. Those of us who went to the room afterwards were still very aware that this was holy ground. It felt as though time stood still and we were in the presence of God. We didn't want to leave there. And, even when we walked out into the hall, some of the hospital staff said we were glowing. We knew why! We had just been in His presence, where Charlotte's last enemy on earth had been destroyed. We were standing on the spot where a miraculous occurrence had just taken place. Death had just been swallowed up in victory!

I CORINTHIANS 15:57 *"But thanks be to God, who gives us the victory through our Lord Jesus Christ."*

July 12

Satan's sifting

He could not believe his ears! Jesus had just told him, *"Simon, Simon, behold, Satan has desired to have you, that he may sift you as wheat." Luke 22:31* On the heels of this statement, Peter probably expected Jesus to say He would stop Satan. Or at least, He expected Jesus to say He would block or hinder Satan from working in his life. But, Jesus did not say He would even rebuke Satan, much less block or stop him. Instead, He looked at Simon Peter and said, *"I have prayed for thee, that thy faith fail not." Luke 22:32*

Peter was taken aback at this, for he did not see any possible way that his faith could fail. He felt so strongly about Jesus that he even told Him, *"Lord, I am ready to go with Thee, both into prison and to death." Luke 22:33* Little did Peter know about the power of his own flesh. He didn't realize that he was putting all his confidence in his flesh, which was as the chaff that needs separating from the wheat. He didn't know how badly he needed his Master's prayers. No one could ever have convinced him that he would follow Jesus afar off, sit down among his Lord's enemies, and even deny the One he loved so much!

Not realizing how he needed to be sifted, Peter could not appreciate his Lord's words, *"But I have prayed for thee, that thy faith fail not." Luke 22:32* Of all the words Jesus could say, these were the greatest; yet, Peter was totally unaware of their significance at the time.

Today, the devil desires to have you also, that he may sift you as wheat. Perhaps you want Jesus to stop Satan. Or, you would at least like for Him to block or hinder Satan from sifting you. You don't enjoy sifting! So, you beg God and cry out to Him continually to rebuke Satan and get you out of these terrible circumstances. Why don't you just hush and listen? Isn't that the Lord speaking? "My child, I have prayed for thee, that thy faith fail not." Oh, those are the greatest words you could ever hear. Jesus has said He will pray for you. So, quit begging and start believing. Although Jesus is allowing your faith to be sifted, He is praying fervently that your faith fails not. From now on, rejoice in Satan's sifting.....it always brings the High Priest's prayers!

LUKE 22"32 *"But I have prayed for thee, that thy faith fail not."*

July 13

Two sides

There are two sides to fire. One side is good and beneficial. We use fire in order to cook, warm ourselves, weld things together, melt steel and iron, and a multitude of other things. However, fire is also bad and destructive. In seconds, it can kill, destroy, and demolish what took years to build. We learn early in life not to play with fire!

There are two sides to wind. One side is good and beneficial. Wind can cool us in the hot summer time, carry a sailboat across the water, or generate electricity through a windmill. However, wind is also bad and destructive when it becomes a tornado or a hurricane. The same wind that brings blessing can also bring cursing.

There are two sides to God. One side is the God of love. He loves people. In fact, He loves us so much that He came to earth as a man, faced everything we will ever face, and died on a cruel cross in our place. He literally became our substitute, taking upon Himself all the sins of the human race, and paying the wages of our sin, which is death. God loves us so much that He wants us free from the destruction, the control, and the penalty of sin. He wants the very best for us. He is a God of love, kindness, compassion, and forgiveness.

But, God also has another side as well. He is a God of wrath. He hates sin, because sin separates, destroys, and kills. There is nothing good about sin. God's wrath is aimed at sin. He does not wink at it, overlook it, ignore it, or pass by it. Sin MUST be dealt with! God is a just and holy God and can never have any sin in His presence.

You will one day face God, either now or in eternity. As you stand before Him, the sin question WILL be dealt with! The choice as to how it will be handled is left completely up to you. Jesus Christ paid the sin debt in your place and the wrath of Almighty God was poured out upon Jesus on the cross, as He "*who knew no sin was made sin for us.*" *II Corinthians 5:21* If you accept Jesus' payment, then God's wrath has already fallen upon your sin and you are forgiven and cleansed. If you do not accept Jesus' payment for you, then you must pay for the sin yourself when you face God on that Judgment Day.

There are two sides to fire, to wind, and to God. Which side are you on? Which side will you face as you stand before Him on that final day?

I THESSALONIANS 5:9 *"For God has not appointed us to wrath but to obtain salvation by our Lord Jesus Christ."*

July 14

My will be done

The young child spots a toy in the department store that he wants so badly he can almost taste it. His mother tells him no. He lies down in the floor and begins screaming and kicking and pitching a temper tantrum. What he is really saying by his actions is that he wants his own way. He is telling his mother that he will not yield to her, but is determined to have the final say in the matter himself.

We call this rebellion. Simply put, rebellion is reserving the right to make the final decision. It is not something we have to sit our children down and teach them to do, saying, "Now today, son, we are going to learn how to be rebellious." Quite the contrary, we are born rebellious, beginning soon after birth practicing it. We spend much of our lives exercising our independence and doing it our own way. Our motto should be, "My will be done."

Now, we all hate to see rebellion in someone else and we are very quick in spotting it in others. However, we are not nearly as adept in spotting rebellion in our own lives, especially spiritual rebellion. One reason we fail to see it in our own lives is because the master deceiver, Satan, has fooled us into calling our rebellion by some other name. "I was born this way." "I have a right." "I do not have time." "I am too old (or too young or too scared or too uneducated, etc.)" "I will do it later." "I do not have the means or the ability." No matter what excuse we concoct, it is not legitimate - it is rebellion!

Once we give our lives to Jesus Christ in total surrender, we are no longer our own. We belong to Him, having been bought by His very blood. Thus, He becomes our new Master… and "My will be done" changes into "Thy will be done," as we submit and yield to Him in all areas.

Are you totally submitted to the Lord Jesus Christ today? Is He in complete control of your life? Or, are you reserving the right to make the final decision in some areas? If you are, you are in rebellion, and God says that rebellion is as the sin of witchcraft. He hates it - and He WILL deal with it! Where do you stand today? "My will (or Thine) be done?"

I SAMUEL 15:22, 23 *"Behold, to obey is better than sacrifice, and to hearken than the fat of rams. For rebellion is as the sin of witchcraft..."*

July 15

Who lives here?

What would you think if you saw on TV an old, unpainted, run down, forsaken-looking house with a big sign out front that said, "The President of the United States lives here?" Wouldn't you find it rather difficult to believe that the President would live in a place like this? No matter what they said on TV, you would have a hard time accepting the fact that this really is the President's home. If they finally convinced you that it was true, it would probably lower your respect for the President. You would expect his home to look like a President's home, not be dirty and dilapidated, with doors and windows falling off. After all, he's the President. And his home would be a representation of him, of his character, of his high standards, of his worth. His home should be the best!

Well, the moment you accept Jesus Christ as your Savior, He comes to dwell within you. He makes your body His home. So, you automatically put up a sign that says to the world, "Jesus lives here." As people watch your life, would they find it rather difficult to believe that Jesus could live in a place like this? No matter what you say, do others still have a hard time accepting the fact that you really are a Christian, with Jesus living inside you? If you do finally convince them that you are saved, would what they see in your life lower their respect for the Lord? After all, they expect the Lord's home to look like a King's home, not be sloppy, unkempt, undisciplined, slipshod, etc. He is the Lord of Glory and His home is a representation of Him. It speaks of His character, His high standards, and His worth. His home should be the very best!

Would you examine your home right now? Do you think God cares about His dwelling place? Do you think it matters to Him where you go, since you are taking Him, too? Do you think it matters to Him what you say, since He lives inside you and is hearing everything you say? Do you think it matters to Him how you act, since it is telling the world about Him? Do you think it matters to Him how you look, since you are His representative? If you are truly saved, then put up your sign, "Jesus lives here," and start living like it. Then, people will not have to ask, "Who lives here?" They can tell!

I CORINTHIANS 6:19 *"What, know ye not that your body is the temple of the Holy Spirit...."*

July 16

No imitations in heaven

It's the American way and we've become quite proficient at it. From purses to perfumes, from watches to rings, from apparel to accessories, we have produced imitations in almost every area of life. Folks who cannot afford the authentic version can purchase a much cheaper imitation, which often is so close to the genuine thing that the average person would never know the difference.

Now, there certainly isn't any harm in someone purchasing a cubic zirconium or imitation crab meat. But, when it comes to the affairs of the soul, it would be a cataclysmic tragedy to settle for an imitation. However, because Americans have become so accustomed to the instant, the easy, and the imitation, they have also settled for an easy, no-cost, imitation salvation. Our Americanized salvation has a "yard sale" mentality…we want the best deal for the least cost! Most folks are willing to say a little sinner's prayer, go to church a little, read their Bibles occasionally, and pray sporadically; but, they do not want to change. They think they can do a few religious things, keep on living as they please, and still receive eternal life, as though that were their pay for the tidbit of time they gave to God.

However, it just "ain't" that way. Genuine salvation is not some "yard sale" deal. It's not some kind of cheap imitation. It is not obtained by someone throwing a few good works God's way and hoping He will pay them well in return. Oh, no! Genuine salvation means a serious, definite, earnest committal of one's life to the Lord Jesus Christ. It occurs when a person realizes that he is a lost sinner on his way to hell; when he knows he is completely helpless and unable to save himself; when he finds out that he is a slave to sin and he desperately needs a Savior. Without Christ, he knows he is forever lost, forever without hope. And, he surrenders his whole heart, soul, and life to Christ.

Today, dear one, do you have genuine salvation? Or, have you bought into the imitation, Americanized replica that is carrying multitudes to hell? Jesus warned, "*Not every one that saith unto Me, Lord, Lord, shall enter into the kingdom of heaven, but he that does the will of My Father, who is in heaven. Many will say to Me in that day, Lord, Lord, have we not prophesied in Thy name? And in Thy name have cast out demons? And in Thy name have done many wonderful works? And then will I profess unto them, I never knew you; depart from Me, ye that work iniquity." Matthew 7:21, 22*

Friend, when you breathe your last breath and stand before God, what will He say to you? Hope you haven't settled for an imitation salvation…because there won't be any imitations in heaven!

MATTHEW 7:21 *"Not every one that saith unto Me, Lord, Lord, shall enter into the kingdom of heaven….."*

July 17

One hundred years from now

If you could come back to this earth one hundred years from now, wonder what you would find? What would the house you are living in right now look like one hundred years from now? Where would the car you are driving every day be at that time? And what about all your clothes and your shoes? Where would they be? Do you think there would be anything at all left to show that you had ever lived on this planet?

Just think what a difference one hundred years would make! Yet, one hundred years is such a short time when you think of eternity. For you see, one hundred years from now, you will not be living on this earth any more. You will be in eternity. You will be out there beyond this present world in either heaven or hell. And out there, what will it even have mattered what you had on earth? Will it matter what kind of house you lived in? Will it matter what kind of car you drove? Will it matter what clothes you wore, what job you had, how your yard looked, what vacations you had, what sports events you attended, and how much money you had?

Friend, one hundred years from now, all these things that you have will be gone forever. You will suddenly realize that all those things you put your time into, all those things you worked so hard for, and all those things that were so important to you did not even matter after all.

What WILL matter at that time is what you did with Jesus! Where you are throughout all eternity depends upon what you did with Jesus while on earth. If you totally committed your life to Him, to love Him and serve Him, and He was your Master and Lord on earth, then you will be in heaven with Him. But, if you lived your life the way you chose, making your own way, being in control of your life, and laying up treasures here on earth, then you will be in hell!

How about your life today? What are you doing with the Lord Jesus Christ? Are you living so that one hundred years from now you will have no regrets? Ask yourself this question, "One hundred years from now, what will really have mattered in my life?"

MATTHEW 16:26 *"For what is a man profited, if he shall gain the whole world and lose his own soul?"*

July 18

You play.....you pay!

How excited they all were! They were playing harps, psalteries, timbrels, cornets, and cymbals. What a joyous occasion this was! The ark of the covenant had been in the house of Abinadab for twenty years.....twenty long years they had been without their blessed ark. And now, they were bringing it home. As 30,000 Israelites had gathered for this great occasion, the earth must have resounded with their jubilant praises!

Their joy, however, was very abruptly snuffed out! Right in the middle of all their rejoicing, a terrible tragedy occurred! The oxen had stumbled, causing the new cart, on which the ark rested, to be jostled about. As it looked like the ark might fall off, Uzzah put forth his hand to steady it. God immediately struck him dead right there on the spot for his error.

As the fear of God fell on the congregation, King David and all those present learned a valuable lesson that day. They discovered that it is very unwise to take God's Word lightly. God is not playing a game with mankind. Unlike most parents today, God only speaks once. He doesn't change His mind; He doesn't relent; He doesn't give in. He says what He means and means what He says! And we can either heed or bleed.

Everyone in that great host of people that day, including King David, knew what the Word of God had said about moving the ark. God had given them explicit directions about this. In the first place, the ark was to be carried by staves, borne on the shoulders of the Levites. God had never told them to set the ark on a cart. That was the method the heathen Philistines had used in transporting the ark.....not God's way! In the second place, the ark was never to be touched. God had said, "*but they shall not touch any holy thing, lest they die.*" *Numbers 4:15*

Taking the Word of God lightly and doing things their own way resulted in tragedy, even though what they were doing looked right. God had said.....you touch, you die.....and He meant what He said! God didn't change His Word to fit the situation. He never does, and He never will! His Word is still true today. He still says what He means and means what He says. He has spoken once in His Word and He won't speak again. Play around with Him if you want, but you'll always be the loser. You play.....you pay!

II SAMUEL 6:6,7 *"Uzzah put forth his hand to the ark...and there he died by the ark of God."*

July 19

Spring house cleaning

Can you imagine what would happen if you lived in your house and never cleaned it at all? How long could you stay there without washing the dishes, or vacuuming, or washing clothes, or dusting? Why, you would not even think of living in your house without doing some kind of cleaning!

Daily, you do a certain amount of cleaning, even if it is just washing dishes or folding a load of clothes or putting something back in its place. Then, weekly, you either clean your house or have someone else come in and clean it. But even with all this, you still need to do some deep and thorough cleaning occasionally. Maybe once a year, you have a spring house cleaning, when you really clean it up good.

Well, friend, you have a spiritual house, too. It is your body, which is the temple of the Holy Spirit. Can you imagine what would happen if you never clean it at all? What kind of place would the Holy Spirit be living in if you just let it go? You need to take care of your spiritual house just the same as you do your physical one.

Daily, you must do some cleaning. As you walk in the world each day, your spirit is exposed to the dust and dirt of the world and some of it rubs off on you. That is why you should go to the Lord in prayer and confess the sins daily that He brings to your mind. If you confess, He is faithful and just to forgive you and to cleanse you. Don't let these things pile up in your life.

Then, occasionally, you need a good spring house cleaning. Set aside a definite time for this and get alone with God. Turn off or remove any distractions so you can concentrate on cleaning. Get out your Bible and some paper and a pen. Read awhile, so God can prepare your heart. Then, write down on your paper every sin that He reveals to you, no matter how seemingly insignificant. Continue this until there is nothing more that the Lord brings to your mind. Be prepared for several pages - there may be more dirt than you counted on. Finally, when you finish this, confess each sin one by one, claiming I John 1:9. Then, burn your paper, because these sins are gone forever. You have a clean house!

Today, Christian, has your spiritual house gotten dirty? If you are lukewarm, settled, and not excited about the Lord, it could very well be that your house needs cleaning. Why don't you set aside some time soon for a good spring house cleaning?

I JOHN 1:9 *"If we confess our sins, He is faithful and just to forgive, us our sins and to cleanse us from all unrighteousness."*

July 20

Looking for Him

You have been praying for something in your life for a long time and you have yet to get the answer you've been looking for. You feel great disappointment and frustration. You have even gotten discouraged, because it just does not seem that your prayers are doing any good. Why, the devil has even put doubts in your mind about your salvation! After all, how could you possibly be saved if God never hears and answers your prayers?

It could be that you have the wrong focus. Maybe in your prayers you have been looking for results instead of looking for God. If you pray looking for Him, you will never be disappointed or discouraged. You will realize that your greatest need is not results, but God. You don't need an answer. You need Him, for when you have Him, you have it all!

Maybe you have the wrong idea about prayer.You think that the purpose of prayer is to tell God what you want and to change His mind about things. That is not the purpose at all. The real purpose of prayer is for God to tell YOU what He wants and for you to get the mind of God, not change it. God wants to tell you His thoughts, His desires, His plans, and His mind. As He fills you with Himself, you will be transformed. Suddenly, you will begin to see things from His perspective. You will share His heart, His love for others, His burdens, and His plans. Your prayers will become His.

Your little world will miraculously open and expand to the limitless possibilities of the great "I Am." You will now be looking through a telescope instead of through a microscope. Prayer will no longer be a shopping list, focused on you and your little needs and wants. It will become a personal, intimate, sweet, precious time with the One you love with all your heart.

Why are you praying? Are you looking for results? Or are you looking for Him?

PSALMS 25:1 *"Unto Thee, O Lord, do I lift up my soul."*

July 21

One piece at a time

What is this on the table? It looks like a scrambled mess that could never be straightened out. Oh, I see! It is all the pieces of a puzzle, all one thousand pieces, that have been dumped out on the table for someone to put together. Here is the box, showing me how the puzzle should look when it is completed. But, how in the world can I get from all the jumbled mess here on the table to the finished picture? Guess I will have to do it one piece at a time!

Do you ever feel like your life is this puzzle? It is such a scrambled mess that it looks impossible to ever straighten out! It seems that all the pieces have been dumped out for someone to put together. You know what you want the finished picture to look like, but you cannot figure out how to get there. It is just too overwhelming! You have almost succumbed to despair.

Well take heart, dear one. There IS a way to put the pieces of this puzzle together. First, you must have a good foundation. Pieces will not be stable and will not stay together without the proper foundation. The only foundation for your life is Jesus Christ. Make Him your Savior and Lord. Give Him total control over your life, allowing Him to do with you as He pleases.

Now, He will guide you one step at a time, piece by piece. His Word is the picture that you go by. It shows the finished product. As you read it and pray, the Lord will show you which piece needs to fit next. Do not get discouraged, as this takes time. If it takes time to put a puzzle together and it must be done step by step, then what DO you think it will take with a life? Progress is slow and each piece seems insignificant. However, pretty soon a picture will begin to form and you will see what God is doing. Trust Him. He sees the completed picture and it is a masterpiece!

Today, put your life into His hands. You have made such a mess of it. It's about time you get out His blueprint and start to work on the puzzle of your life, one piece at a time.

PSALMS 37:23 *"The steps of a good man are ordered by the Lord..."*

July 22

Adding a fifth part more thereto

"I have an apology, a confession I'd like to make to you today. I know I got angry and that was wrong of me; but it was your harsh words that caused me to be angry. Please forgive me for my anger and I will forgive you for your harsh words." Perhaps you have apologized to someone this way before, thinking that you were practicing Biblical confession. However, this could be called "balancing accounts," for it certainly isn't Biblical confession. To compute how much I owe you and how much you owe me is really not a Christian practice at all. In fact, it is the world's way of handling things.

In order to understand the Biblical principle concerning "righting wrongs" where others are involved, we need to go back to Leviticus 6, which deals with the trespass offering. This offering, unlike the sin offering which dealt with the guilt of sin, instead dealt with the injury done by the sin. This injury could be, not just physical, but emotional or mental as well. In the Old Testament, when someone committed a trespass, God said, "*He shall even restore it in full, and shall add the fifth part more thereto: unto him to whom it appertaineth shall he give it, in the day of his being found guilty." Leviticus 6:5*

In God's economy, we see, first of all, that restoration should be made at the first opportunity (in the day of the guilt.) Procrastination would be like allowing a wound to continue festering without treatment. God also requires us to restore, not just in full, but to add a fifth part more. God doesn't want His children to do just barely enough to get by. He wants us to be generous in the things we do, always going the extra mile. In apologizing to others, the Lord wants us to take the full responsibility on ourselves, dismissing any wrong that they may have done to us. We are not to balance accounts; rather, we are to restore and add the fifth part more besides. This will be a strong reminder not to commit the same act again, since it is a losing proposition and costs us much more than we really want to pay. When we take five-fifths and have to restore six-fifths, we won't be quick to do the same thing again!

Have you been balancing accounts, dear one? Is there someone you need to go to today and make things right? Perhaps you need today to offer up a trespass offering God's way…by adding a fifth part more thereto.

LEVITICUS 6:5 *"He shall even restore it in full, and shall add the fifth part more thereto…"*

July 23

One week left

If you knew that Jesus was coming back one week from today, would it make any difference in your lifestyle? Are there some things in your life that you would change?Would you invest your money, your time, and your attention on the same things that you are presently investing in? The chances are good that your whole life would change.....it would probably be turned upside down.

First, all the earthly, temporal things would become insignificant. It would not really matter anymore whether you had a nice home, a new car, dishes that all match, designer clothes, or a big savings account. It would not matter if you had a vacation planned or not. It would not matter which football team won the Super Bowl. You see, all those things that consumed much of your time, money, and attention would suddenly fade into nothingness in the light of eternity.

Second, you would take a thorough inventory of your life, laying it beside the plumb line of God's Word. Since you would be standing before the Righteous Judge in one week's time, you would want to make sure that everything was fine between your soul and your Savior. You would want to tie up all loose ends, confessing and repenting over sins, making reconciliation where needed, and obeying everything that your Master laid upon your heart. You would want to be prepared for that breathtaking event, having a holy and righteous life with which to face the supreme Judge.

Third, you would attend to eternal things. You would probably go to every loved one to inquire of their soul's condition. With a broken heart and a fountain of tears, you would plead with your loved ones to come to Christ. You would suddenly have a holy boldness and a relentless resolve that you never had before.

Yes, things would probably change for you if you knew Jesus was coming back in one week. Every second would count for eternity. It's too bad you aren't living that way now, living each day as though it were you last. For, you see, it might be!

I PETER 3:11 *"Seeing, then, that all these things shall be dissolved, what manner of persons ought you to be in all holy living and Godliness..."*

July 24

One word or no word

They all stood in total amazement, as the walls around the city of Jericho crumbled to the ground before their eyes. To watch a wall that was twenty-five feet high and twenty feet thick in some places fall flat to the ground was enough to astound anyone!This was the same wall that had defeated them and discouraged them for forty years from entering the land of Canaan. But, what looked like a bona fide, genuine impossibility to the children of Israel was no more than a puff of smoke to the Lord. He had told them to go in and that was all they needed. One word from God is sufficient!

So, now that they had conquered Jericho, they faced another city, Ai. Since it was a small city with no walls around it, they assumed that it would be easy to capture. The appropriate thing to do, judging from the appearance of things, would be to send in a relatively small band of men and take the city. However, they tried this and were embarrassingly defeated. God had not told them to go in, because there was sin in the camp that had to be dealt with first. What looked easy to do in view of all the circumstances turned out to be disastrous! No word from God means don't move.

This just goes to prove that we should never base our decisions on how things appear. Neither should we base them on what people say, for the people were wrong in both these cases. Our decisions should be based completely on the Word of God, because our human tendency is almost always wrong. To fail to act when God says, "Go" results in wandering in the wilderness, missing the "milk and honey" of the Christian life. It robs us of God's blessings, leaving us a life of mediocrity and ineffectiveness. To act when God says, "No" results in defeat and disaster. It melts the heart of courage into retreat and often leads to anger at God, as He gets the blame for the conditions caused by our own presumption.

Today, oh child of God, get in God's Word and base all your decisions upon what He says. His Word alone should be the road map of your life. One word or no word - that is all you need to make your choice!

PSALMS 119:104 *"Through Thy precepts I get understanding; therefore, I hate every false way."*

July 25

You cannot survive without eating

The human body is the most amazing piece of equipment there is. We are still learning about it. It is so complex that, even with all our advanced technological knowledge, there is still a lot we don't know about it. We may not understand all the body's complex functions, but we do know the elementary things that are necessary for it to function properly.

One of these basic necessities is that of eating. The body CANNOT survive without food, and food is needed daily. The mouth is the channel through which food enters the body. Once food is in the mouth, it is chewed, swallowed, and the rest is history as far as our conscious mind is concerned. We go on to other things, totally unaware of the processes operating within us. That food goes through our digestive system and is dispersed throughout our entire bodies, being carried even to our toenails, our hair, and every part of us. The food literally becomes part of us. Now, we do not have to understand anything about the digestive process any more than a newborn baby does, nor do we have to be aware of what's going on within us. All we have to do is eat. Our choice is whether or not to eat, when to eat, and what to eat. Once we eat, then our bodies take over.

It is amazing that we see and take care of this necessity physically, yet we ignore it spiritually. One of the basic necessities for the spirit is that of eating also. The spirit CANNOT survive without spiritual food and that food is needed daily. Our spiritual food is the Word of God. The channels through which spiritual food enter the spirit are our eyes and ears. Once food is taken in, then our spirits chew and swallow it. We meditate on it, think upon it, study it, and break it down in our spiritual mouths. Then, this food is spiritually digested and literally becomes a part of us, bringing life, nourishment, and vitality to our spirits. Now, we do not have to understand all about spiritual things, nor do we have to be aware of all that is occurring within us spiritually. All we have to do is eat. Our choice is whether to eat, when to eat, what to eat, and how much to eat.

Christian, you are feeding your physical body well, because it shows! But, it looks like you might not be feeding your spirit as well. It shows, too! Don't you think it is about time you start eating right spiritually? You cannot survive without eating!

JOB 23:12 *"I have esteemed the words of His mouth more than my necessary food."*

July 26

What's dead is dead!

You could take a dead man out of his casket and do everything in the world to improve him, but he is still dead. You could take him to a hairdresser for a modern hairstyle, give him a manicure, and dress him up in the finest clothes, but he still stinks! You cannot improve him, fix him, or change him. What's dead is dead! And, the best thing to do with something dead is to bury it.

It would be utterly foolish and useless to prop up a dead man and try to get him to carry on with life. Now, all the life-things would still be going on around him. Light and sounds would be bombarding his body the same as they would be yours, but he would be unresponsive to them. He would be completely unaffected, entirely oblivious to everything, because he would be dead to his environment.

Christian, when you accepted Jesus as your Savior, you were supernaturally carried back to the cross and your old man was nailed there with Jesus. *"Knowing this, that our old man is crucified with Him, that the body of sin might be destroyed...For he that is dead is freed from sin." Romans 6:6,7* Now, why do you want to get that old man off the cross and dress him up? Why do you want to modernize him, to improve and fix him with self-help courses, or try to get him to fit in with the times? He is dead and he stinks! That is why there is such turmoil and confusion in your life. You are trying to prop up your old man. Why don't you just let him be crucified instead? Let Jesus live now. Let Him have control. Let Him get down off that cross and your old man stay on it.

Oh, Christian, it is time you learn that flesh is flesh and it will always be flesh. You cannot improve it. It will always stink no matter what you do. Now, it will still be bombarded by sin, because sin is not dead....your old man is! So, you reckon yourself dead to sin, dead to everything around you. You do not HAVE to respond to sin or be affected by it any more than a dead person has to be affected by his environment. Why don't you just bury your old man? He gets in the way and is a hindrance to the life of Christ. What's dead is dead! And, it's high time to bury the dead!

ROMANS 6:6 *"Knowing this, that our old man is crucified with Him..."*

July 27

Don't mess with the vineyard

As the king of Israel, he was accustomed to getting what he wanted. His palace in Jezreel was close to a vineyard, owned by a man called Naboth. Ahab really wanted this vineyard, but Naboth would not sell it to him, so Ahab pouted and became sullen. He even refused to eat. His wife, Jezebel, was a wicked, evil schemer and devised a plan to get Naboth's vineyard for her husband. She wrote letters to the elders and nobles of the city, telling them to hire false witnesses, who would testify against Naboth before all the people. This they did, and, because of the customs of the times, innocent Naboth was stoned to death. Jezebel's plan was successful…she got Naboth's vineyard and gave it to her greedy husband.

Did God wink at such a heinous act of bloodshed? No, it resulted some time later in total retribution. Ahab was killed in battle. His son, Joram, who reigned after him, was killed on that same plot of ground in Jezreel where Naboth's vineyard was located. All seventy of Ahab's descendants in Israel were killed and their heads were all brought to Jezreel in baskets. Even Ahab's grandson, Ahaziah, who reigned over Judah was killed, followed by the death of forty-two of his relatives. And, the wicked queen, Jezebel, did not escape either. She was thrown from a window and completely eaten by dogs, except her skull, the palms of her hands, and her feet. This all happened in Jezreel, avenging the innocent blood shed at Naboth's vineyard.

A vineyard in Scripture always represents Israel. God's vineyard, Israel, has been trampled down by Gentile nations. Millions of innocent Jews have been slaughtered. Much blood has been shed on God's vineyard. God did not wink at what happened at Naboth's vineyard, so do you think for a second that He will wink at what happens on His vineyard, Israel? No! One day, in the future, all the armies will gather and come against Israel at the Battle of Armageddon. However, God Himself will fight for Israel and all the mighty armies will be wiped out. In that day, so much blood will be shed on the plains of Jezreel that the blood will run to the horses'bridles for two-hundred miles. That same plot of ground that Ahab deceitfully took hundreds of years ago will once and for all be avenged with the blood of those who have dealt treacherously with Naboth's vineyard and with God's vineyard!

Do not trifle with God. He will NOT be mocked! His mill grinds slowly….but it grinds exceedingly fine!

ISAIAH 5:7 *"For the vineyard of the Lord of hosts is the house of Israel..."*

July 28

Angry at God?

Have you ever gotten upset or angry with God for something that was happening in the life of a lost or backslidden loved one? Perhaps you have prayed and prayed for that one you love and things haven't improved at all. In fact, once you started praying, things have gotten worse for them instead of better. With problems piling up on top of each other and life becoming harder by the day for your loved one, you are feeling sorry for them and have actually become highly upset at God, blaming Him for all that's happening.

Friend, if this ever happens to you, you can immediately know one very significant thing about yourself. You can know that there is someone in your life that you love more than the Lord. For you see, you are more concerned about what God is allowing to happen in your loved one's life than you are about what your loved one is doing to God! It is your loved one you should be upset with..... not God. God is extending mercy by the bushels to your loved ones. He has allowed them to live in America, where they are free. He has provided air for them to breathe, lungs that work, a body and a brain that function, food to eat, water to drink, a place to live, a car to drive, legs to walk with, eyes to see with, etc. And, how are they repaying Him? They are ignoring His laws, spurning His love, rejecting the blood of His Son, and slapping Him in the face by their haughty, self-centered, Christ-rejecting attitudes.

So, you are angry with God for what's happening to your loved one! Well, you had better get it straight as to whom is the most important in your life. God says that He will have NO other gods before Him! If you truly love Him with all your heart, then it will break your heart to see how He is treated, even by your closest loved one. It will grieve your heart that anyone could be so cruel and heartless to the Lord Jesus, who so freely poured out His blood for them. Your love for Him should be so much greater than for anyone else on earth that you cannot bear the thoughts of anyone, even your dear ones, living a life that doesn't bring honor, glory, and praise to Him.

Who is first in your life today? Do you love Jesus so much that your love for everyone else is dim in comparison? Make sure that you have no other gods, including yourself or someone very close to you, in His place!

LUKE 14:26 *"If any man come to Me, and hate not his father, and mother, and wife, and children, and brethren, and sister, yea, and his own life also, he cannot be My disciple."*

July 29

Your speech betrayeth you

They couldn't tell by looking at him, for he looked just like the rest of them. Twice already they had tried to identify him with Jesus, but he had denied it both times. And now, for the third time, they were again accusing Peter of being with Jesus. However, this time their method of measurement was not by his appearance. Instead they said, "*thy speech betrayeth thee.*" *Matthew 26:73*

Just as Peter's speech betrayed him, so also does ours! The mouth is a mirror to the heart, because what comes out of the mouth reflects the contents of a person's heart. By just simply speaking with someone for a few minutes, you can tell where his affections and devotions lie. You can tell who or what his idols are. If someone mentions his spouse or his children or another person repeatedly, you know he idolizes them. If someone speaks of his job repetitiously, you know he idolizes his work. If most of a person's conversation revolves around money, you know that money is that one's god. If someone speaks mostly of sports, of exercise, or of any other thing, you know those are the things he worships, the things that have captured his heart and soul.

Likewise, when a person speaks of the Lord Jesus Christ on a regular basis, then you know that's where his affections lie! The Bible says to "*Set your affections on things above, not on things on the earth.*" *Colossians 3:2* No one or no thing on the face of the earth should have our hearts like Jesus. He should be the subject of most of our conversations, the focus of our lives, the center of our attention, and the hub around which our lives revolve. He is a jealous God, saying that "*Thou shalt have no other gods before Me.*" *Exodus 20:3* No one else should capture our hearts besides Him. He should be our source, our course, and our force.

How about you, Christian? Your speech betrayeth you! Everyone around you knows exactly where your heart lies. Your mouth is a mirror to your heart. Every time you open it, the contents of your heart spill out. You may fool yourself into thinking that you love Jesus more than anything or anybody in the whole world, but you cannot fool others. They know by listening to you. You may be deceived into thinking you're a good Christian. But, just remember..... your speech betrayeth you!

MATTHEW 26:73 *"Surely thou art one of them; for thy speech betrayeth thee."*

July 30

What is truth?

From the day of your birth until this present time, you have been building belief systems. You have a belief system about your world and space and the universe. You have a belief system about food - what is good for you, what is harmful, and what is enjoyable. You have a belief system about people, about life, about work, about recreation, about the government, and on and on.

To believe something means that you have accepted it as the truth. Once you have accepted it, you begin to think something is the absolute gospel just because you believe it. However, this is not so. The truth is the truth and your belief has no effect on truth whatsoever. The world is round whether you believe it or not. Your belief changes nothing but your behavior. People at one time believed the world was flat, but that did not make the world flat. The truth is that it is round. Their belief did not change the truth; it changed their behavior. They would not sail very far out on the ocean for fear of falling off the earth.

So, your beliefs in every walk of life affect your behavior in that area. But, what if your beliefs are wrong? What if they are based on false information rather than on truth?That would lead you to behave or respond inappropriately, as people did about sailing out on the ocean.

It would be a good idea to examine some of your beliefs today, especially your spiritual beliefs, as they have eternal consequences. Put away the notion that it is true just because you believe it. You could be basing your beliefs on something that is not truth. So, the determining factor is, "What is truth?" and not "What do I believe?" Everybody believes something, but everybody is not right.

The Bible says that Jesus is The Truth. And, since the Bible is Jesus written down on paper, then God's Word is truth. So, you should first go to the Truth, then line up all your beliefs according to it. If they don't line up, throw them out! You have many beliefs now about your spiritual life, about going to heaven, about eternity. Are they based on the Truth....or on your own belief? The Bible says that straight is the gate and narrow is the way that leads to everlasting life and FEW there be that find it. Those few will ONLY be those whose lives have lined up with the Truth. Does yours?

JOHN 17:17 *"Sanctify them through Thy Truth; Thy Word is truth."*

July 31

Everything you need

Finally the day arrived, the day he had anticipated for such a long time. Proudly walking across stage, he received his diploma, confirming that he was now a college graduate. He could hardly wait until afterwards, as his dad had promised him a brand new car for his graduation. Upon arriving home, his dad presented him with a gift. With his heart pounding, he opened it, expecting to find the keys to a new car. But instead of keys, there was a Bible. His dad said to him, "Son, you'll find everything you need right here in the Word."

In anger, he stormed out of the house. How could his dad do such a thing to him?He got in the old car that he had been driving and took off. Filled with disappointment, hurt, and anger, he felt he could not face his dad again. So, he left home, having absolutely no contact with his family for several years. He did not see them again until the news of his dad's impending death reached him.

As he arrived back home, it was already too late. His dad had passed on the night before. Walking through the house, he discovered the Bible that his dad had given him at graduation, the Bible he had never even picked up, the Bible he had left behind. Sitting on the bed, he opened the Bible for the first time. There inside the cover was a check for the exact amount of the new car he had wanted. The check had been there all those years. If only he had opened the Bible, how different his life would have been. How foolish he had been!

Christian, perhaps you have gotten away from your Father, too. At one time, you loved the Lord and served Him fervently. But something happened along the way. You somehow got disillusioned and your heart grew cold. You walked right out of God's presence, being drawn away by the things of the world. Now, you no longer have a desire to spend time with your Father. You no longer have a deep hunger for His Word and a thirst for His righteousness. You are just existing. Life is no longer an exciting adventure. But wait.....I hear your Father saying, "Son, you'll find everything you need right there in the Word." Open it up! There's a blank check for you, signed by Jesus, entitling you to all the riches in glory in Christ Jesus. God has already told you that you'll find everything you need in the Word. Don't be foolish and miss it all due to your neglect!

PSALM 119:162 *"I rejoice at Thy Word, as one that findeth great spoil."*

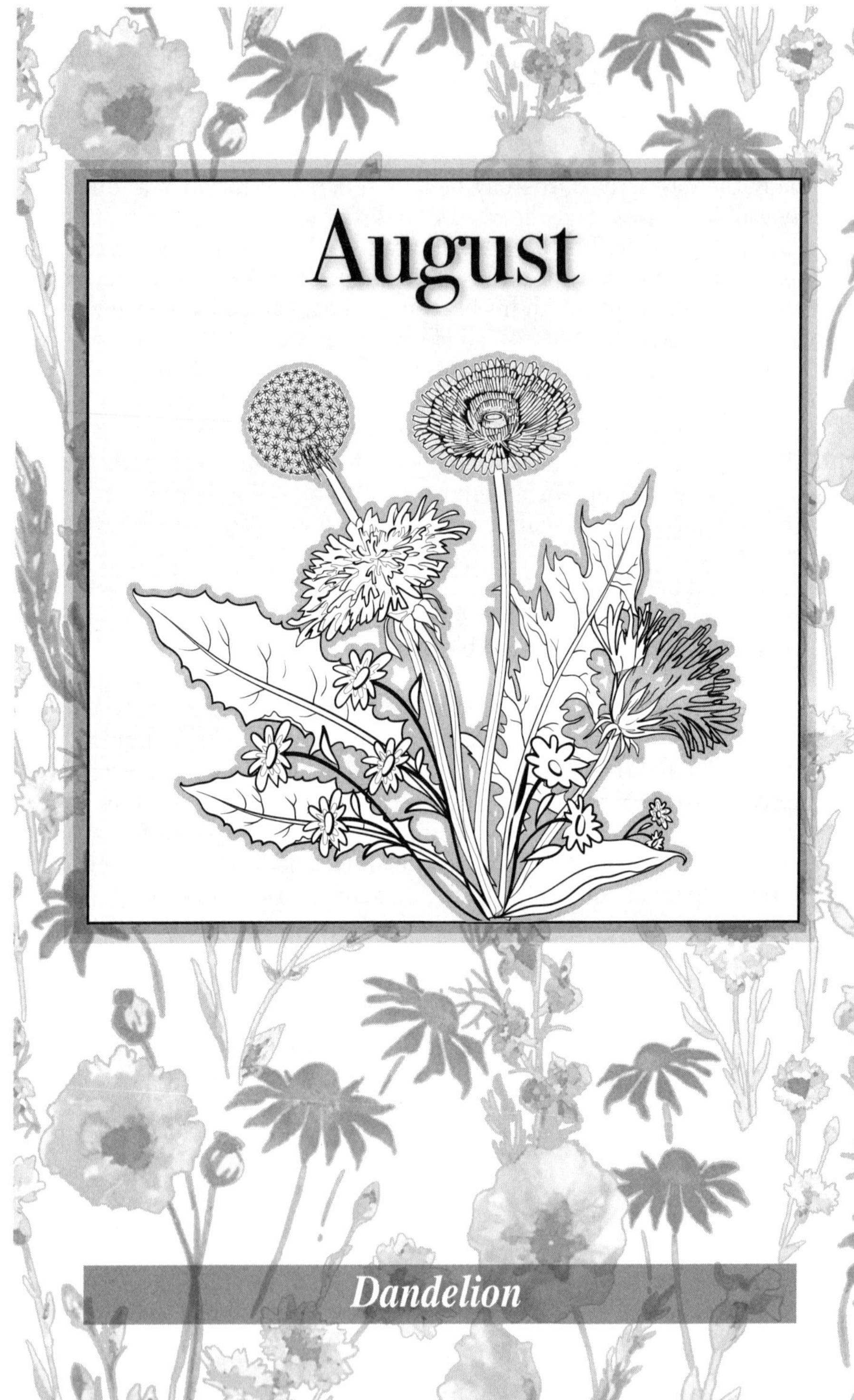

August

Dandelion

August 1

Do you have a pabulum faith?

Most of our modern day faith is really a "pabulum" or "baby food faith." It consists mostly of what God can do or what God will do for us. This makes the focus of our faith chiefly man-centered rather than God-centered. It's a far cry from the faith we see in some of the mighty men of God who have gone before us…men like Daniel, Shadrach, Meschach, Abednego, Paul, and Silas.

When Daniel was facing the lion's den, we don't read of him wringing his hands and trying to work up enough faith to believe God was going to deliver him. In fact, we don't read of him even asking God to deliver him at all. He wasn't trusting in what God would do for him. Rather, he was trusting in God… period! He knew that, whatever God did, it would be the right thing for him and for everybody else concerned.

When Shadrach, Meschach, and Abednego were facing the fiery furnace, we don't read of any concern whatsoever on their parts about the outcome. They weren't down on their knees, begging God to deliver them from the fire. They weren't focusing at all on what God would do for them. Rather, they were focusing on how great their God was! They told Nebuchadnezzar, "*If it be so, our God, whom we serve, is able to deliver us from the burning fiery furnace, and He will deliver us out of thine hand, O king. But if not, be it known unto thee, O king, that we will not serve thy gods, nor worship the golden image which thou hast set up." Daniel 3:17, 18* These mighty men of faith had their focus on God… not on what God would do for them!

When Paul and Silas were in the Philippian jail, we don't read of them being depressed, worried, or wasting any time whatsoever focusing on their own problems. They didn't say, "Why me?" or "I don't deserve this, Lord," or "Get me out of here, God!" They weren't trying to muster up enough faith to believe God for deliverance. Instead, they were praying and singing praises to God at midnight, using their voices to praise their Provider rather than to proclaim their predicament.

What kind of faith do you have today? Are you praising your Provider, focusing your attention solely upon Him and Him alone? Or are you proclaiming your predicament, focusing on yourself and your circumstances? Are you trusting in what God will do for you? Or, are you trusting in God…period?

DANIEL 3:17 *"Our God…is able to deliver us…but if not… we will not serve thy gods…"*

August 2

Gathering an army by subtraction

They were outnumbered four to one and that's not very good odds when you're going to battle. How in the world could 32,000 men possibly face 135,000 of their enemies? And, as if that weren't bad enough, Gideon stood before them with an unusual request. "*Whosoever is fearful and afraid, let him return." Judges 7:3* At this, 22,000 of them took off home, leaving a little measly 10,000 men to face 135,000. Now the odds were thirteen to one. God was gathering the Israeli army by subtraction. He wanted soldiers who dared to believe Him against all odds, soldiers who were not afraid to fight. War is not for the fearful, the unbelieving, or the cowardly.

Leading the 10,000 soldiers to the water's edge for a cool drink, God continued gathering His army by subtraction. He told Gideon to watch how the men drank. Part of the men were "lappers,"bowing upon their knees to drink water. The others cupped their hands, bringing the water to their mouths. According to God's instructions, Gideon picked only those who cupped water in their hands. These 300 "cuppers" were alert. They brought the water to their faces instead of bending down to the water, because they were keeping watch for the enemy even while drinking. God chose these alert, awake, watchful young men as warriors, because war is not for the sleepy, apathetic, unconcerned, or lazy.

Now, with 9700 more men gone, the army was reduced to 300, making the odds 450 to one. Logically speaking, it was an impossibility to win a war with those odds. But, God knew what He was doing. He wasn't interested in odds! He was interested in men that He could use, that He could fight through… because the battle was God's anyway. And, God used these 300 dedicated, determined, vigilant, rapt, resolute men to defeat the vast army of 135,000. There is a war raging in America today, an invisible war between the forces of God and the forces of Satan. God's army is outnumbered drastically. The odds are highly stacked in Satan's favor! However, it seems that God is once again in the subtraction business. He has told the fearful and unbelieving to return, as He cannot use them in this battle. They are scared they might rock the enemy's boat. God wants soldiers who will believe Him in spite of all odds. He has told the "lappers" to return, because He cannot use those who are spiritually lazy. He wants self-disciplined, alert, watchful, determined, prayerful, vigilant soldiers who will take up their cross and follow Him.

Will you dare today to be a soldier for God? Will you believe Him against all odds? He's gathering His army for these last days by subtraction, just as Gideon did. He wants you to be a part of it. So, put away your unbelief, arise out of sleep, put on the armor, and get in there and fight! Don't be one of those subtracted!

JUDGES 7:3 *"Whosoever is fearful and afraid, let him return..."*

August 3

On the damascus road

He was on the road to Damascus to do what he thought was God's work. He was very religious, highly educated, and zealous toward God. He was a self-made man, a man of prominence and prestige. Carrying with him letters to the synagogues from the high priest and elders in Jerusalem, Saul had the authority to bind the Christians in Damascus and bring them back to Jerusalem. Christians were troublemakers, always talking about this One called Jesus, whom they claimed was the only way to heaven. They were constantly trying to convert others to their way of thinking. So, Saul felt good about himself that day as he traveled down the Damascus road with his head held high.

He felt good about himself.....until he met Jesus on that road! Suddenly, all his credentials, all his importance, all his self-assurance melted as a bright light from heaven shone round about him and a voice spoke to him. The first thing he did was to fall to the earth, no longer puffed up with pride. He was now trembling and astonished. He did not pull out his credentials or try to impress the Lord with whom he was. Oh, no! It no longer mattered who he was. It was whose presence he was in that consumed him now.

The first words he uttered were, *"Who art Thou, Lord?" Acts 9:5* His focus was not on himself any more or on the work he was doing for God. Suddenly, his religion of works and accomplishments was swallowed up by the bright light all around. Saul's man-centered outlook had now become God-centered, focused on what Christ had already accomplished and on who Christ was instead of on what he was doing.

The second words Saul spoke were, "*Lord, what wilt Thou have me to do?" Acts 9:6* He did not jump up and ask where he could go to have another thrilling experience like this one. He did not bring out a shopping list and tell God what all he wanted. He did not go around bragging about his great spiritual experience. He did not look for seminars on how to live for Christ. He just got up and lived a Christ-centered, self-denying, self-disciplined life from that day forward.

Today, religion walks down life's highway, centered on man's abilities, man's goodness, and man's accomplishments, thinking it is on its way to heaven. But, when it meets Jesus on the Damascus Road, religion is knocked to the ground. Today, are you religious? Or, have you been on the Damascus Road and met Jesus?

ACTS 9:5, 6 *"And he said, Who art Thou, Lord?"*
"Lord, what wilt Thou have me to do?"

August 4

Nothing you say, or believe, or do

You can call it anything you want…a "wop," a "ning," a "blurg," or any other name, but, it's still the sun! It really doesn't matter what you call it, or whether you even believe it's the sun or not. It still provides light and heat for this old earth. It's still 93 million miles away. It still has nine planets revolving around it. It will still burn you if you stay out in it too long in the hot summer time. So, you can believe whatever you want to believe about it. You can call it whatever name you choose. You can ignore it. Or, you can even pretend it doesn't exist. However, nothing you say, or believe, or do changes one single fact about that big ball of hot gas in our solar system, known as the sun.

Likewise, you can call the Bible anything you want to call it…a "book of fairy tales;" a "book written by man;" a "book containing errors;" or any other name…but it's still the Truth! It really doesn't matter what you call it, or whether you even believe it or not. It still provides light for this old dark world. It still changes lives. It still contains hundreds of prophecies about the end times, many of which are being fulfilled every day right before our very eyes. It still provides help and hope for millions of people. It still shows the Way of salvation. It still exposes sin and shows the severe and devastating consequences of it.

So, you can believe whatever you want to believe about the Bible. You can call it anything you choose. You can ignore its principles. Or you can even pretend that it's not relevant in your life. Nevertheless, nothing you say, or believe, or do changes one single fact about the Bible.

However, your belief does change your response to the Word of God. If you don't believe there's judgment to come and that there are consequences for rejecting the Lord Jesus Christ, you will never be serious about the things of God. You will think you can live your life the way you want and get by with it, rather than having to live the way the Bible says. You will think you can control your own life and things will turn out all right in the end.

But, the Truth is that, unless you receive Jesus as your Savior and Lord and turn your life completely over to Him, you will find yourself in hell the moment you take your last breath. You'll know then that nothing you said, or believed, or did affected the Bible one iota. But, it sure affected you…for all eternity!

PSALM 117:2 *"the truth of the Lord endureth forever."*

August 5

Not a Rolls Royce, but a Cross

In America, we have developed our own strain of what we call Christianity. We have taken the strong meat of the gospel, chopped it up, shredded it, and drowned it in so much watered-down preaching that what we have now does not even remotely resemble true Christianity. Our gospel does not even have enough nourishment in it to keep a baby alive. It is a weak, self-centered, spineless, compromising gospel that we live and preach.

The American gospel says that God wants you healthy and wealthy. It says that you should just live a good life. You can go where everyone else goes, do what everyone else does, enjoy the same things others enjoy.....as long as you live morally and decently. You can live a normal, ordinary, regular life, blending in with the world around you. You should live in peaceful coexistence with everyone, not rocking the boat or offending anyone.

Is this the gospel of the Word of God? Well, look down through the pages of history. All the apostles, except John, were martyred, because they would not compromise and live in peaceful coexistence. They would not hold hands with the enemy, tiptoeing around on egg shells lest they offend him. And even though John died a natural death, he was put into a pot of boiling oil, badly disfigured, and banished to the Isle of Patmos to die alone. Isaiah was sawed in two with a saw for thundering out against the sin, corruption, idolatry, and laxity in his day. The pages of history are red with the blood of the countless martyrs who were burned at the stakes, thrown to the lions, beheaded, etc. for their unyielding allegiance to Jesus Christ.

The gospel of the Lord Jesus Christ is centered on the cross. The cross means death to the flesh. That means death to your desires, death to your comforts, death to everything offensive to Jesus Christ - and the world is offensive! If you are not willing to follow Jesus in suffering and death to yourself, then go find you a leader without a cross, because you cannot follow Him any other way.

Friend, do not measure your Christianity by the American gospel. It will take you straight to hell. The vehicle which carried Jesus to His destination was not a Rolls Royce. It was a cross! If you are planning on making it Home, there is only one way. The way of the cross leads home!

I CORINTHIANS 1:23 *"But we preach Christ crucified..."*

August 6

What will you do with this one?

He was governor of Judaea and had seen many things in his day, but he had never seen anything like this. He found himself face to face with someone unlike anyone else he had ever met. An angry mob had brought this one, called Jesus, to him. They were filled with fierce hatred, all of them like sticks of dynamite with their fuses lit. Judging from the intensity of their anger, Pilate could only assume that this One before him was a heinous, hardened criminal, having committed about the most atrocious acts one could imagine. However, after examining Jesus thoroughly, a bewildered Pilate came to the conclusion, "I find no fault in this man."

What was Jesus guilty of? Why had this angry crowd brought Him to the governor, demanding that He be crucified? What evil had He done? Looking back over Jesus' life, we find an unparalleled record. He healed the lepers, opened blinded eyes, cast out demons, caused the lame to walk, fed the multitudes, cooled fevered brows, healed the sick, and raised the dead. Everywhere Jesus went, He touched people and made them whole again. He went about doing good, as His great heart of love and compassion was poured out on the multitudes. With this record of Jesus' life, how could anyone even remotely consider crucifixion, the most torturous death possible? What fault could this angry mob possibly find in Jesus that led to such utter hatred and rejection of Him?

Today, the angry mob is still around, doing just what they were doing in the days Christ walked on earth. Some blatantly curse Jesus and take His name in vain. They ignore Him, spurn Him, and reject His offer of eternal life. They let everyone know where they stand in regard to Christ. Others are not blatantly against the Lord, but they silently go along with the loud crowd. They, just like everybody else, take their own lives into their own hands, living as they please without ever consulting the Lord and following His plans for their lives. They may not reject Him verbally, but they reject Him by their lifestyles. They watch in silence as He is crucified daily by others in the world around them. Either way, this mob is the same as the one who cried out in the days of Pilate, "Crucify Him."

Today, friend, you are in Pilate's seat. An angry mob has brought Christ to you and is watching to see what your verdict will be. What will YOU do today? What fault do YOU find in Him? Will you be one of the angry mob who just does not want anything to do with Him? Will you cry out that He be crucified? Will you be like Pilate, who finds no fault in Him, but you are too weak to stand? Will you reject Him by your silence and let Him be turned over to the accusers as Pilate did? Or, will you stand for Him, defend Him, believe Him, and trust Him as your Savior? What will you do today with this One, who is called Jesus, the Son of the living God?

MATTHEW 27:22 *"What shall I do then with Jesus, who is called Christ?"*

August 7

What is your 23rd psalm?

In multitudes of American homes today, there is a pot-bellied idol sitting right in the middle of them. Or, at least it appears to be an idol, because folks gather around it often and appear to be mesmerized by it. It has their complete and undivided attention. They will spend as much as two, three, or four hours or more at a time in this idol's presence. However, if you asked them, they would quickly tell you that it's not an idol. But, then, perhaps they've never read Mr. Webster's definition of an idol. (It is any object of ardent or excessive devotion or admiration.) Seems to me that any object you spend two or three or four hours every day with would have to be an object or ardent devotion.

This object in multitudes of homes is the TV set. Since folks spend more time with it than they do with the true and living God, then the TV set is an idol to them. However, it's only just an idol, a false god. It never puts broken marriages back together. It doesn't mend the hearts of wounded, scarred, and battered children. It doesn't solve devastating, personal problems. It doesn't restore dashed hopes. It doesn't lead people to live more holy and righteous lives. It doesn't train up children to be moral, decent, productive citizens. It never visits a hospital, makes a phone call to the lonely and hurting, or writes a note of encouragement to the weary. It doesn't pay the bills, buy the groceries, fix broken items around the house, nurse the sick back to health, care for the aged, hug the lonely, or meet daily needs. It won't be there for you! It doesn't care about you! It's a false idol…it takes your time and gives nothing lasting or eternal in return.

Friend, please stop and analyze the time you spend watching TV. Has it become n idol in your life? Could this be your 23rd Psalm? "The TV set is my shepherd. I shall not want. It maketh me to lie down on the sofa; it leadeth me beside the sensuous and violent waters. It taketh hold of my mind; it leadeth me in the paths of unrighteousness for the world's sake. Yea, though I walk through the valley of decisions, I will fear no evil; for thou art with me; thy pleasure and thy entertainment, they spellbind me. Thou preparest a perverted meal before me in the presence of my children; thou anointest my mind with the oil of secularism; my cup of self-gratification runneth over. Surely, worldly thinking and false doctrine shall follow me all the days of my life; and I will dwell in the house of the idolaters forever."

JEREMIAH 50:38 *"and they are mad over their idols."*

August 8

Cry, Christian, cry!

As he looked around the pasture, he could not find his mama anywhere! Suddenly, he realized he was lost and alone! He hadn't planned to end up like this! The little lamb only took his eyes off his mama for a little while, just long enough to follow some other sheep. What they were doing had looked so intriguing to him that he just couldn't resist following. But, he never intended to get this far! Now, he was mixed in with all the flock and his mama was nowhere in sight. This separation from her left him feeling so scared and so vulnerable. He didn't know where to find her. So, he just stood there on his little wobbly legs and began bleating as loudly as he could. And as he continued crying, his mama heard him, even from afar. She recognized his voice at once and came for him. Once again, he was safely with the one who loved and protected him.

Maybe you are that little lamb today. You got your eyes off the Great Shepherd. You became interested in the things around you and were distracted from following the Lord. You did not mean to get away, but it just happened so subtly. For a while, you were unaware of the separation between your soul and your Savior. You still went to church, prayed, read your Bible, and did other things that good little Christians do.

However, it is like you suddenly woke up and realized that you had left your first love. You looked for Jesus, but He was nowhere to be seen. You no longer could feel the sweet, warm, overwhelming, fresh presence of your Great Shepherd. You were just going through the motions of worship without the presence of the One being worshiped.

Now, here you stand, mixed in with a multitude all around you. You feel scared and unprotected. You want your Shepherd and you cannot get to Him. You have tried.....but you just cannot seem to find Him. Well, little lamb, just start crying after Him. Stand there on your wobbly little spiritual legs and cry and cry and cry after Him. He knows your voice. You just keep crying and He will come for you. When He does, follow Him away from that mixed multitude to the safety and security of Himself....and don't ever leave Him again!

Aren't you tired of wandering out there away from Him? He is waiting on you today. A lamb's bleat always brings its mother. A Christian's cry always brings his Father. So cry, Christian, cry!

PSALMS 34:17 *"The righteous cry, and the Lord heareth, and delivereth them..."*

August 9

Hide and show

Unlike many modern day Christians, he was not too busy, too tired, or too stressed out to spend time alone with his God. He could actually hear from God, since his life wasn't flooded with noise and confusion and turmoil. So, when the word of the Lord came unto him, saying, "*Get thee hence, and turn thee eastward, and hide thyself by the brook Cherith," I Kings 17:3* Elijah heard and "*went and did according unto the word of the Lord." I Kings 17:5*

The first thing God told him to do was to "hide thyself." Elijah needed to be shut up with his God, totally dependent upon Him for everything, in order to be prepared for the ministry that lay ahead. He went to the brook, Cherith, as instructed by his Father. He didn't carry anything with him either...no TV set or radio; no form of entertainment whatsoever; no extra clothes; no supplies; or no food or drink of any kind. In fact, all he carried was himself! However, he didn't need anything but God. God furnished him fresh water to drink from the brook. And, God commanded the ravens to bring bread and flesh in the morning and evening every day for him to eat. Oh, what must have transpired between Elijah and his heavenly Father during those days.

Then, after many days, the word of the Lord came again to Elijah, saying, "*Go show thyself to Ahab; and I will send rain upon the earth," I Kings 18:1*...which, by the way, was very severely needed due to a ravaging drought and famine in the land. Elijah was prepared for this task, one which called for a mighty miracle of God to be performed right before everyone's eyes. Elijah faced 450 prophets of Baal alone and confronted all those lukewarm, mamby-pamby folks who were halting between two opinions. But then, he had been shut up with his God for some time and he was ready to take on the world. He had done according to the word of the Lord. First, God had said to "*hide thyself*," and then He had said to "*show thyself*." That's always the working order in God's business.

We modern Christians desperately need some of this "Elijah" theology. First, we need to "hide ourselves" before we ever try to do anything else. We need to shut ourselves in with God and spend some valuable time in His presence, getting to know Him and to hear from Him. We need to stay there by our Brook, the Lord Jesus Christ, drinking the Living Water and eating the Bread of Life, allowing Him to fill us and change us and prepare us for His work.

Then, after we have spent much time alone with the Lord, we can "show ourselves." We can go to the lost, the backslidden, and the halting ones and we'll be so filled with the Lord that we will make an eternal difference in their lives. So, let's "hide" and then "show." That's God's Way...and it always works!

I KINGS 17 *"...hide thyself by the brook Cherith..."*

I KINGS 18:1 *" ...show thyself unto Ahab"*

August 10

And she did!

Who would like to go to church with me?" asked the Little Red-Hot Christian.

"Not I," said Worldly Wilma. "Not I," said Busy Bob. "Not I," said Procrastinating Pete.

"Then I will," said the Little Red-Hot Christian. And she did…Sunday mornings, Sunday nights, Wednesday nights, and any other time the church doors were open!

"Who would like to surrender his heart and life to Christ with me?" asked the Little Red-Hot Christian.

"Not I," said Worldly Wilma. "Not I," said Busy Bob. "Not I," said Procrastinating Pete.

"Then I will," said the Little Red-Hot Christian. And she did! She gave the Lord total control over her life, asking Him to be her Savior and Lord. She completely dedicated her life to serving Christ.

"Who would like to read the Bible and pray with me?" asked the Little Red-Hot Christian.

"Not I," said Worldly Wilma. "Not I," said Busy Bob. "Not I," said Procrastinating Pete.

"Then I will," said the Little Red-Hot Christian. And she did…early every morning before anyone else in the house arose, every night before she went to bed, and every other opportunity she had during the day.

"Who would like to go to heaven with me?" asked the Little Red-Hot Christian.

"I would," said Worldly Wilma. "I would," said Busy Bob. "I would," said Procrastinating Pete.

"I'm sorry," said the Little Red-Hot Christian. "While I was going to church, reading my Bible, praying, and witnessing, you weren't concerned about the things of God. As I committed my life to serve Christ, you lived yours just to please and satisfy your own selves. You didn't have time for God, for church, for the Bible, for fervent prayer….too many other things took priority over God and His kingdom. You didn't want Him interfering in your life; you didn't want to surrender everything to Him; and you certainly didn't want Him in control. So, now that you've kept your life for yourself, you will lose it. In eternity, you cannot keep what you didn't commit here on earth. If you had only given up your life to Christ, you could have kept it. There's only one place in the universe for you now…a place where God is not! You didn't want Him in life…so you can't have Him in death.

However, I gave my heart and soul to Him. I loved Him and served Him as best I could on earth. Now, I'm ready to go to heaven and be with Him forever!" And she did!

MATTHEW 10:39 *"He that finds his life shall lose it; and he that loses his life for My sake shall find it."*

August 11

He way of Balaam

Balaam was determined to take the path that his heart really wanted. He prayed, asking God what to do, but he already had his mind set on a certain direction all the time. So, God just simply let Balaam have his own way. Balaam was deceived into thinking that, just because God allowed it, it was God's will.

However, three times God tried to stop Balaam by putting an angel in his path. Balaam's deception kept him from seeing the angel, so God used his donkey. The first time, the donkey saw the angel and turned off the path. Balaam beat her to get her back on the road. The second time, the donkey continued on the path, but pressed close to a wall and crushed Balaam's foot, because she was scared to get close to the angel. Balaam beat her again. The third time, the donkey just lay down. Balaam was so angry that he beat her again. All three times, God was giving Balaam the opportunity to turn back. He was trying to show Balaam that this was not His will for him, but Balaam was blinded by his own desires. He could not see the method God was using to stop him. In fact, he even lashed out at the donkey, the very one that God was using to help him.

Balaam had a desire to obey God, but he also had a strong desire for what he wanted. He tried to fit God's will into his own heart's desires. And this same attitude actually led to his death later, because his willful disobedience caused him to be in the wrong place.

Today, maybe you are in Balaam's shoes. There is something you want so badly that you are trying just as hard as you can to make it fit in with God's plans. You are assuming everything that happens is an indication that this is God's will. You are reading things into the Word of God, so you can justify what you want to do. You are turning a deaf ear to the Godly counsel you are receiving from those who walk with God.

Well, Christian, it is time you listen to God, not to your own bent. He may let you go ahead with your way, but you will sell yourself short. You will never get to see the glorious answer God had in store for you. You will have to settle for the best you can do when you could have had the best God could do. And your disobedience could very well cost you your life on down the road. So, Christian, if you're smart, you'll forsake the way of Balaam and follow the Lord Jesus Christ all the way.

II PETER 2:15 *"Who have forsaken the right way, and are gone astray, following the way of Balaam..."*

August 12

Who's responsible for the fruit?

Boy, this orange is delicious! It is probably the sweetest, juiciest, tastiest orange I have ever eaten. I must thank someone for this superb piece of fruit. Should I thank the one who picked it? Or what about the one who ploughed up the ground before the seed was planted? Should I thank the one who planted it.....or the one who watered it.....or the one who fertilized it.....or the one who dusted it for destructive insects.....or the one who packed it.....or the one who delivered it to the store? Ummm, this is really a tough decision!

Since this juicy, tasty, succulent orange is the result of a joint effort by many different people, each doing different jobs, I really don't know who to thank for it! Each one actually had a part in the finished product, so I could thank them all. But, I must thank God first of all, because He was the One who actually grew the fruit. He caused the life to come up out of that seed, break through the soil, and grow into a beautiful tree with oranges. Man couldn't create the life, and man couldn't cause the life to come up out of the ground, but he could cooperate with God in the planting, watering, fertilizing, etc.

The same thing is true in spiritual fruit as well. Someone ploughs up the hard ground to prepare it for receiving seed. They preach, teach, talk, or just live out the Word, which pierces the hard soil of someone's heart and begins to break up those big dirt clods of sin. Someone else comes along and plants seeds of truth and one of them really takes root. Others come along and water and fertilize the soil by talking about the Lord, by sharing Scriptural truths, or by living a Godly life that proves the reality of God. Then, there are others who dust for destructive insects. Their lives of submission to God and walking in the Spirit foster in others the desire to know God and to avoid unholiness. And, finally someone comes along in just the right time and picks the fruit.

Who gets credit for the salvation of a soul then? Why, everyone who has ever had any part in that life spiritually! God is the only One who can impart life, bring that soul out of darkness into the light, and grow fruit...but He uses the labor of many people cooperating with Him to make the final product a reality.

Knowing this, Christian, get busy. Every single Biblical truth you speak, every spiritual thing you do, every lost person you minister to in any way at all contributes to the final product. Each person who has a part in the salvation of a soul gets the reward!So, get out there and start tending to your crop, Christian! You're in the business of fruit production.

I CORINTHIANS 3:9 *"For we are laborers together with God..."*

August 13

Ants in the dog food

Totally oblivious to my presence, they were having the time of their lives. Little did they realize that this fast food would be their last food. As I watched them crawl all around in the bowl of dog food that I had just picked up from the deck, I thought about how foolish the ants were. They were feasting when they should have been fasting. They were eating when they should have been retreating. On the very brink of disaster, the ants were going about business as usual, completely unaware that someone was looking on, preparing to invade their little picnic. As they surfaced from the dog food, I picked them out one by one, making a quick end to the unsuspecting little critters!

Suddenly, it dawned on me how much this scene resembles us in America! Like ants, we Americans are scurrying here and there, always in a mad rush everywhere we go. We are eating and drinking, laughing and partying, frolicking and entertaining ourselves with an unparalleled frenzy. And all the while, the enemy is looking on and laughing at our foolish games, as he picks us off one by one. Willingly ignorant of the enemy's devices, we are so busily engaged in the pleasures of the flesh that we never even see the war that is raging all around us. We have a deaf ear turned to the heart cries of the millions of lost souls on their way to hell. We are so caught up in the urgent that we never even catch a glimpse of the important. We are living for the temporal, for the here and now. We are going for the gusto. We are feasting when we should be fasting. We are playing when we should be praying. We are sleeping when we should be keeping watch. We are burying our heads in the sand when we should be lifting our heads to heavenly places. We have settled into a comfort zone when we should be in the war zone, fighting the battle with everything within us.

Well, the time has come for us to read and heed the prophet, Joel, once again. *"Blow ye the trumpet in (America), and sound an alarm in My holy mountain. Let all the inhabitants of the land tremble; for the day of the Lord cometh; it is nigh at hand." Joel 2:1 "Turn ye even to Me with all your heart, and with fasting, and with weeping, and with mourning. And rend your heart, and not your garments, and turn unto the Lord your God." Joel 2:12, 13*

Oh, friend, quit fooling around in the world's bowl of enticing food before the enemy picks you off! Quit feasting and start fasting! Quit playing and start praying! The party's just about over!

JOEL 2:1 *"Blow the trumpet in Zion, and sound an alarm..."*

August 14

A door between two worlds

The Christian life is not an arrival.....it is a pursuit. Somehow, however, many people mistakenly think that a Christian should "have it all together." They confuse salvation with arrival or perfection, thinking that the salvation experience is the end, rather than the beginning.

Salvation is simply a door between two worlds. There is the physical world, which we can see, hear, smell, taste, and feel. We operate in this world by our physical senses, all of which are connected by channels to our brains. With our minds, we make decisions based on information we receive through these five channels.

Then, there is the spiritual world, which we cannot see, hear, smell, taste, or feel physically. This world is entirely separate from the physical world and we can only operate in it by faith. We get frustrated and defeated when we try to operate our spiritual lives by our physical senses, because the spiritual realm is lived only from the spirit. The spirit is the channel through which God manifests and reveals Himself to us. Then, by faith, we act on these revelations to live in this spiritual world.

When a person experiences salvation, he just simply goes through the door, which is Jesus Christ. He enters a brand new world, the spiritual world, through being "born of the Spirit." This new birth brings him from the darkness of the womb of sin into the glorious light of Christ. But, he is a brand new baby in this spiritual world and has to learn to live in it just like he had to learn to live in the physical world. He must learn how to walk and talk, experiencing many falls as he learns. Each fall shows him what does not work in his new world and he can try again, each time growing stronger and more mature.

The entire spiritual life is a pursuit. A person can never learn all there is to know in the spiritual realm any more than he can in the physical realm. However, he continues to grow and learn and change, always pressing toward the mark for the prize of the high calling of God in Christ Jesus. But first, he must go through the door!

Have YOU been through that door yet into that glorious spiritual world? If not, you have NO idea what you are missing! It is totally awesome! Almighty God, the Creator, is calling you to step through this Door between two worlds. It is open. Come on in!

JOHN 10:9 *"I am the door; by Me, if any man enter in, he shall be saved..."*

August 15

After Marah, there's Elim

They could hardly believe their eyes! Right here in the middle of nowhere was the most beautiful oasis one could imagine. There were twelve wells of fresh, clean water, surrounded by seventy gorgeous palm trees. It was astounding that such a place as this existed out here in the midst of a barren, dry, dead wilderness. The children of Israel stood for a few minutes, gazing in awe at God's miraculous provisions for them. What an appropriate place and time this oasis of Elim was to these tired, worn, thirsty, discouraged children of God!

Elim was an especially welcome sight, because the children of Israel had been wandering in the wilderness for a few days and had run out of water. They had come to Marah, a stream whose waters were bitter and undrinkable. Instead of praying and trusting God to provide, the Israelites began to murmur. Their attitudes were just like the water... bitter! In spite of their unbelief, however, God still provided for them. He had Moses to cast a tree into the waters at Marah, resulting in them becoming sweet and drinkable. God showed them that He can make something sweet out of something bitter. God provided for them at Marah. However, that was not all He had for them, because only six miles away lay the beautiful oasis of Elim!

God had a very valuable lesson that He was teaching the Israelites - and you, too. He wants you to know that after Marah, there's Elim. Often in your Christian walk, you will come upon some bitter waters. These are to test your faith, to grow you, and to teach you to trust and obey God. They are there in your life to help you spiritually. So, do not become bitter like the waters, but instead look to the Lord in faith and trust Him when you do not see any possible answer. God will faithfully provide for you in these bitter waters. And, just hold on, because He has an Elim only six miles away!

Today, Christian, are you in a deep trial? Are you discouraged? Would you love to murmur and complain and just have a big old pity party? Well, DON'T! Just as Moses cast a tree into the bitter waters of Marah, cast your situation on the tree at Calvary. It will make your circumstances sweeter and more bearable. And right up ahead, just around that next bend, right over that next hill is Elim. It will come at the perfect time and in the perfect place. God will not leave you at Marah. Remember: after Marah, there's Elim!

EXODUS 15:27 *"And they came to Elim, where were twelve wells of water and seventy palm trees..."*

August 16

What's that I smell?

The sense of smell is one of the five senses of the human body. It is closely tied with the sense of taste. Just smelling certain things to eat can activate your salivary glands, tantalize your taste buds, and create a desire in you for those things.

Often, the sense of smell can be magnified. Bacon has only a slight smell, but it can be put into a frying pan, and the stimulating aroma will permeate the entire house. An orange has a smell up close, but it can be broken open and its delightful fragrance will quickly fill a whole room. Coffee beans smell if you are near them; but if you put them into a coffee grinder where the beans are crushed, the aroma will be much stronger and cover more territory. Heat, brokenness, and crushing release the confined savor of an object, scattering and propelling its molecules in all directions.

Spiritually, we have a sense of smell, too, and it is closely related to our spiritual sense of taste. The Bible says of Christians that God *"makes manifest the savor of His knowledge by us in every place. For we are unto God a sweet savor of Christ, in them that are saved, and in them that perish." II Corinthians 2: 14, 15* A Christian should be so filled with Christ that His life literally pours forth onto others. All the fragrance of Christ should fill every place a Christian goes, saturating those around him with love, joy, peace, and other sweet aromas of Christ. This will activate the spiritual salivary glands and taste buds and create a desire in them to have what the Christian has.

Often, God wants to magnify the Christian's aroma, to scatter and propel the spiritual molecules in all directions. So, He applies heat, brokenness, or crushing to do so. As the unexplainable sweetness, joy, peace, and love flow from the Christian's life in the midst of all this suffering, the spiritual salivary glands of the lost are stimulated. They begin to hunger after whatever the Christian has that makes him so joyful in trouble. The lost develop a desire to "*taste and see that the Lord is good." Psalm 34:8*

Dear one, are you in the fire today? Is your life being crushed and broken? Oh, child of God, your Father is just simply wanting to manifest the savor of Himself through you to that lost and dying world out there. So, yield to the crushing. Rejoice in the tribulation! Be a sweet savor! Then, perhaps someone will say, "What's that I smell?" and will ask for a taste of what is so satisfying and good to you!

II CORINTHIANS 2:14 *"God...maketh manifest the savor of His knowledge by us in every place."*

August 17

Will you dare to be an Elijah?

The times were wicked! The hearts of the idolatrous people were on everything but the Lord. And the king was no exception. In fact, he did more to provoke the Lord to anger than all the kings of Israel who were before him. He even married a woman who did not believe in God, but was a worshiper of Baal. Ahab was already weak in his faith before this marriage... and this unholy union with Jezebel just finished him off. He did not have the backbone to stand for the God of his fathers. Instead, he succumbed to his wicked wife's idolatry and even built for her a house of Baal in Samaria, the capital city of Israel.

Suddenly, onto the scene of such appalling times, there stepped a man whom the Bible spoke nothing of until this particular moment of time. This man was not famous, not well-known, not prominent. He had not made the "Who's Who" in Israel. In fact, it seems as though he stepped out of obscurity, out of nowhere, right up to the forefront on center stage and became the main actor in God's unfolding drama for the time. This was no ordinary man, however, who came in and went out like a thundercloud! This man did not succumb to the spirit of the age in which he was living. He did not blend in with everybody else, eating and drinking and making merry and living like all the others around him. Elijah dared to be different! He was not afraid to confront the evil of his time. In fact, he even stood before the king himself. He was sold out to God, dedicated, loyal, faithful, bold, uncompromising, holy, and unwavering. He just believed in, trusted, and obeyed God.

This man of faith blazed an unforgettable trail across the pages of history. Led by God, he prayed earnestly that it might not rain...and God shut up the heavens for three and one-half years. During those years of drought, God told Elijah to go to the brook, Cherith, where God Himself sent food twice a day by ravens. By God's power, Elijah raised a widow's son from the dead. He also challenged four-hundred fifty prophets of Baal, all watching as God sent fire from heaven to consume the sacrifice on the altar. And even Elijah's departure was unusual. He was taken, not by death, but by a whirlwind up into heaven.

God is again looking for some Elijahs! He is looking at YOU! Will you dare to be an Elijah, amidst all the idolatry and evil of our day? Will you totally yield to God and allow Him, through you, to blaze a trail across the pages of the times in which you live?

I KINGS 18:46 *"And the hand of the Lord was on Elijah..."*

August 18

So, God did!

She knew that he was God's man, obviously anointed by the Lord for a special work. She had watched him through the years, as God had used him time after time. He had been God's appointed messenger to Pharaoh, being used to lead the children of Israel out of Egyptian bondage. She had been there as the ten plagues fell on the Egyptians, each one being foretold to Pharaoh by this anointed man of God. She had no doubt that God worked through Moses' life to influence others.

Yet, despite her knowledge, Miriam disagreed with her brother, Moses, on a certain occasion and spoke out against him. Instead of taking this to the Lord in humble prayer for Moses, Miriam joined with Aaron in open, verbal dissatisfaction. "*Has the Lord indeed spoken only by Moses? Has he not spoken also by us?" Numbers 12:2*

Miriam had a problem that is still around today - submission to authority. She thought she knew some things that Moses did not know and that he did not always lead in the right way. Miriam felt that not all Moses'decisions were right, so she stepped in to set him straight.

However, the Bible says, "*And the Lord heard it." Numbers 12:2* Moses heard it, too, but he made no effort to defend himself. He was simply trying with all his heart to follow the Lord. He did not think he had all the answers either, but he was certainly seeking God daily for directions and trusting God to speak through him. So, he left this up to God, too. And God Himself called Moses, Aaron, and Miriam to come to the tabernacle, where He set them straight. Speaking to Aaron and Miriam, God said, "*Wherefore, then were ye not afraid to speak against My servant, Moses?" Numbers 12:8* God's anger was kindled against them and, as God departed, Miriam became leprous.

Miriam learned a most valuable lesson that day. God has placed certain people in positions of leadership and it is very dangerous to speak out against them. Miriam could have gone to Moses with a sweet spirit and discussed her disagreement with him. She could have prayed for God to show Moses or show her, whichever was needed. Moses would gladly have listened. But, he could do nothing with her tongue...or with her unwillingness to trust him and follow his leadership. Moses couldn't...so God did!

NUMBERS 12:8 *"Wherefore, then, were ye not afraid to speak against My servant, Moses?"*

August 19

In need of some centurion faith

He was a man with authority. Being a centurion, he had from fifty to one hundred soldiers under his command. When he spoke, the men obeyed. His word was the authority, since it was backed up by the government itself; therefore, he understood about authority. He understood that a word spoken was as good as done. And he knew he didn't even have to be present for his word to be carried out. By just simply speaking it, all those under his leadership must obey.

Therefore, when his servant was at the point of death, the centurion sought out Jesus. He had heard about this man from Galilee who could heal all manner of infirmities. He recognized Jesus as a Man of authority. He believed that the words of Jesus were backed up by God Himself! He believed that any word spoken by this Great Physician was as good as done, even if Jesus weren't present to carry it out.

So, the centurion sent some elders of the Jews to Jesus, asking Him to come and heal his servant. Before Jesus could get to the sick one, the centurion had already sent some friends to the Lord with a message. "*Lord, trouble not Thyself; for I am not worthy that You should enter under my roof. Wherefore, neither thought I myself worthy to come unto You; but say in a word, and my servant shall be healed." Luke 7:6, 7* The centurion knew that Jesus had only to "say in a word" and it would be done! His faith was based entirely on the Word of the Lord, whether Jesus was present or not. He believed that Jesus' Word was sufficient!

At this, the Lord marveled. He turned about and said unto the people, "I say unto you, I have not found so great faith, no not in Israel." Luke 7:9 Could God say that about you? Do you really believe that God is a God of authority? Do you believe He has the power to back up His Word? Do you really believe that He has only to "*say in a word*" and it will be done?

Perhaps today you're in need of some centurion faith. Try it! Just take God at His Word. Start believing that He can "*say in a word*" and it will be done. After all, if you cannot believe God's Word, then what in the world CAN you believe anyway?

LUKE 7:7 *"but say in a word, and my servant shall be healed."*

August 20

Graves covered by grass of good works

Walking to the burial plot was very hard for me. I had been taught as a child that it is highly disrespectful to step on a grave. However, in this particular cemetery, most of the graves were covered with grass, not marble slabs. You couldn't even tell where any of the graves were, other than those that had a little vase of flowers on them, and some that had a marker with the name of the dead engraved on them. I carefully walked where the markers were. As I looked out over this beautiful cemetery, I thought about how camouflaged death is. Thick, rich, pretty grass grew right over the dead. You'd never know by outward appearance that bones lay underneath.

That's how the Pharisees were! Jesus said about them, "*For you are as graves which appear not, and the men that walk over them are not aware of them.*" *Luke 11:44* The Pharisees looked beautiful on the outside. They were highly religious. They did a lot of praying. They carried Scriptures around with them in their phylacteries. They tithed. They fasted. They followed the letter of the law right down to the jot and tittle. Outwardly, they looked like the ones who would make it to heaven!

However, they failed to deal with the inside. They put on outward garments of good works and religious activities, but the inside was full of dead men's bones. They were self-righteous, thinking that their own works could earn them the right to go to heaven. They thought God was smiling on all their good little deeds. What they failed to realize is that God doesn't look on the outward appearance, as man does. God looks on the heart! And underneath the religious exterior of the Pharisees, unseen by human eyes, lay death. They had never been born again. They had never submitted their hearts to the control of the Lord Jesus Christ. They looked good outwardly, but inside they were full of dead men's bones - graves covered by grass of good works!

Perhaps you have been in church all your life. You joined years ago when you were young, because all your friends were doing so. You have been religious ever since, doing good deeds, tithing, praying some, reading a little of the Scriptures, etc. However, you know deep inside that you really don't know Jesus.....and God looks on the inside. You've been a Pharisee far too long, being full of dead bones on the inside, yet covered on the outside by good works. Don't you think it's time to get rid of the camouflage and truly give your life to Christ?

LUKE 11:44 *"For you are as graves which appear not, and the men that walk over them are not aware of them."*

August 21

Woe-lo-go training classes

Never in his life had he experienced anything like this before! He would never, ever be the same again! Of course, he didn't realize at the time that God was preparing him to become one of the greatest of the Old Testament prophets and that this experience was needed to make him the man for the job. God was raising up Isaiah during this time of moral and spiritual decay in Israel to warn the people. They were in a comfort zone, enjoying the blessings of God, thinking they were doing pretty good, when, in fact, God was preparing to destroy them because of their disobedience. Isaiah needed special preparation for this difficult mission; therefore, God put him through a woe-lo-go training class first!

This woe-lo-go training class took place in heaven, where Isaiah was caught up in a vision before God. He saw the Lord sitting upon a throne, high and lifted up. He saw seraphim flying all around the throne, crying, "*Holy, holy, holy is the Lord of hosts; the whole earth is full of His glory." Isaiah 6:3* He saw the posts of the door move at the voice of Him who cried, and the house was filled with smoke. Being in the very presence of Holy God brought deep conviction upon Isaiah of his own utter sinfulness. He said, "*Woe is me! For I am undone, because I am a man of unclean lips..." Isaiah 6:5* When Isaiah saw God properly, then he also saw himself properly...and it was an awful sight! We cannot really see the sinfulness of our sin until we see the holiness of God.

After Isaiah's "woe" training, he was ready for the next step. The seraphim took a live coal from the altar and laid it upon Isaiah's mouth, saying, "*Lo, this has touched your lips, and your iniquity is taken away, and your sin purged." Isaiah 6:7* Isaiah's confession and repentance brought forgiveness and cleansing. He had said, "*Woe*;" the seraphim had said, "*Lo*;" and now God was ready for the final step in Isaiah's training. He said, "*Go and tell this people..." Isaiah 6:9* And for about sixty years, Isaiah did just that!

The church in America today is in desperate need of some woe-lo-go training classes! We've become more concerned with people having a proper view of themselves than we are with them having a proper view of God. We bypass the "woe" training…we don't want anyone to think that God is too hard on their sin. We never get them to real heart-broken confession and repentance, which leads to the "lo" of forgiveness and cleansing. We skip the "woe" and "lo" and just say, "Go;" therefore, the impact we're making on our society in this day and age is negligible!

The Isaiah breed is on the endangered list…it's almost extinct! But perhaps you will be the one to keep the breed going. Enroll today in God's woe-lo-go training class!

ISAIAH 6:5 *"Woe is me! For I am undone, because I am a man of unclean lips…"*

August 22

Need a good fitness center?

In our health conscious society, much emphasis is placed upon taking good care of our physical bodies. We are told to eat properly, to exercise, and to get adequate rest. A body that just eats what it wants, gets little or no exercise, and does not get the rest it needs cannot stay physically fit. It will become run down, making it highly susceptible to sickness and disease. A weakened body is a prime target for viruses and bacteria. But even a healthy body is subject to these invasions if it eats or drinks after someone that is sick. So, a body must take necessary steps in order to remain physically healthy.

It is too bad that we are not nearly as conscious of our soul's health as we are of our physical health. A soul must have the same care taken of it in order for it remain healthy. First, it must get the proper nourishment, which is the Word of God. If it feeds itself on other things, like the junk food of the world, it will become sickly. The Word of God has all the spiritual vitamins and minerals needed for good spiritual health. However, the Word will do the soul no good if it sits on a shelf and is not taken internally on a regular, daily, consistent basis.

Second, a soul must have exercise. There is a spiritual fitness center, where the soul can go to work out. It is called the church. There are weights to lift there...the burdens and cares and heartaches of others. There are aerobics there, as the Pastor leads in stretching and pushing and urging the participants on to a greater spiritual workout through the preaching of the Word. There are showers there, where a soul can get a good spiritual bath by the *"washing of water by the Word." Ephesians 5:26*

Third, a soul must have proper rest. It must spend time with the Lord Jesus Christ in prayer and communion, casting all its cares upon Him. It must draw aside from the world, getting away from the busy and hectic pace, to rest in Him. The soul needs that every day just as much as a physical body needs to withdraw from the world to sleep.

Have you become spiritually run down, catching the diseases of the world? Have you been eating and drinking after the world? Today is a good day to join a spiritual fitness center and start taking care of the one and only soul you have.

JEREMIAH 31:12 *"...and their soul shall be like a watered garden."*

August 23

A Jell-O Christian

Just watch it! Pour it into a container and it will take on the very shape of that container it is in! If the container is round, it will be round. If the container is square, it will be square. If the container is shaped like a star, it will be shaped like a star. And, if you put it into the refrigerator overnight, it will solidify, becoming completely conformed to its surroundings. You can even turn it upside down, take it out of the container, and it will remain in exactly the same shape of the container. It will look just like what it was in! And, the only way you can get Jell-O to return to its original liquid state is to heat it. You can either put it directly on a burner or leave it in the rays of the sun on a warm day. The heat will loosen the hardened molecules and cause them to become liquid again.

Christian, you are like that Jell-O. You will conform to the shape of your surroundings. That's why the Bible says, *"Be not conformed to the world," Romans 12:2 but "come out from among them and be ye separate." II Corinthians 6:17* If you watch all the worldly things on TV, participate in the same things the world does, and live like most everyone around you, you will take on the same mindset and be shaped by that same mold. You will look just like the majority of those around you. And the only way then for you to ever become tender and fluid again is for heat to be applied to your life. You can get in the rays of the Son long enough for the hardness to melt, or God will apply heat through trials and tribulations that will melt down your conformity.

Instead of being conformed to the world, however, you should be conformed to the image of Jesus, being made conformable to His death. But, how can you do this? First, you must spend much time in the Word... reading, studying, memorizing, and meditating upon it. Second, you must spend much time in prayer rather than in frivolous, eternally unrelated activities. Third, you must humble yourself unto obedience to God's will, giving up all your rights, your desires, and your plans for the plans of the Lord. And fourth, you must totally give yourself for others, even denying and crucifying your own flesh to meet others' needs.

How about you today, Christian? You are like Jell-O, in that you are easily conformed to your surroundings. You will become just like what you hang around! So, has your soul been surrounded by the world lately or by the things of God? What shape have you taken on?

ROMANS 8:29 *"...conformed to the image of His Son..."*

August 24

Get up, spiritual glutton

The table is spread! Covering it from end to end are delicious, nutritional foods. There is fried chicken, mashed potatoes, peas, pork chops, salads, banana pudding...why, there is every kind of food you can think of on this huge table. The king of the land has set the table, furnished all the food, made all the provisions, and invited everyone to come. There is enough for all the people in the land!

Seated at the table are all who have responded to the king's invitation. They are busily engaged in eating, passing food to each other, laughing, and talking. But wait, something is terribly wrong here. All around the table, on the ground, under the trees, and in the bushes are many who are dying of starvation. They are so weak that they cannot get to the table. Some do not even know there is a table available. Why aren't the people at the table helping these poor souls? They are eating and drinking and laughing, completely ignoring the plight of those around them. How can they gorge themselves and pass food to one another without taking even so much as a morsel to the dying? What lazy, gluttonous, apathetic, self-centered people those at the table are!

Well, the King of Kings, Jesus Christ, has spread a spiritual table in America. There are churches, Bibles, tapes, videos, conferences, seminars, books...why, there is every kind of spiritual food imaginable. The King has invited everyone to come. There is enough for everyone in the land.

Seated at this spiritual table are all who have responded to the King's invitation. They are busily engaged in eating the spiritual food, laughing, talking, and socializing with one another in the church. But wait, something is terribly wrong! All around the table.....in the jails, on the streets, in the grocery stores, at the malls, everywhere.....are many who are dying of spiritual starvation. They are too weak to get to the table. Most do not even realize the table is there and can help them. Why aren't the Christians in America helping them? How can they come to church week after week, eat the spiritual food, socialize with others who are stuffed just like they are spiritually, and never even take so much as a morsel out of those doors to the lost world?

Have you been at the spiritual table too long? Have you gotten spiritually stuffed, lazy, apathetic, and too self-centered to take any to the dying? Well get up, spiritual glutton, get up! The starving are all around, waiting on someone to feed them!

PSALMS 23:5 *"Thou preparest a table before me..."*

August 25

A nation of cast sheep

He counted them carefully one by one, as was his habit each day. There was one missing. Without hesitation, he left the flock to find that one lost sheep. The shepherd loved his sheep with all his heart and could not bear the thoughts of a single one of them straying away.

With a grieving heart, the loving shepherd searched for his one lost sheep, knowing that every second was crucial. Scanning the horizon, he spotted her. As he reached her side, it was just as he feared.....she was cast! She had lain down and gotten comfortable, causing her to roll over in a slight depression in the earth, from which she could not arise. He quickly set her aright and began rubbing her abdomen and talking gently to her. He knew the gases that built up rapidly in a cast sheep would cause death in a few hours. He rubbed until all the gases were expelled and his sheep was restored. Returning to the flock with her, he reprimanded her for straying away, reminding her of the dangers to herself and of the grief it caused him.

America has become a nation of cast sheep. There are literally thousands of Christians who have been born into the flock of God. At first, they loved their Great Shepherd with all their hearts. They followed Him, adored Him, praised Him, thanked Him, and worshiped Him. As they wanted to stay close to Him, they would never even dream of straying away from the flock.

However, as time passed, they lost some of their zeal for the Shepherd and began looking around at other pastures. They began finding fault with the flock, thereby smothering their desires to be with the rest of the sheep. They wandered off, lay down, and got comfortable. No longer did they have to keep up with the flock or be accountable or responsible to them. And then..... they became cast sheep. The gases of apathy and stagnation began rapidly filling them, rendering them helpless spiritually.

Look across America today. You will see a nation of cast sheep. They are no longer with the flock, but have lain down in their comfortable spots and have succumbed to the gases of apathy. The Shepherd is looking for them… but they're no longer interested in returning to the flock!

What about you, dear one? Are you a cast sheep? Have you settled down into a little comfort zone? Well, the Shepherd has come for you today. Will you return with Him to the flock...or die in your cast state?

ISAIAH 53:6 *"All we like sheep have gone astray; we have turned every one to his own way."*

August 26

Let Egypt go!

Oh, children of Israel, why have you returned to Egypt in your hearts? Why won't you let Egypt go? Sure, you remember the fish, melons, leeks, cucumbers, onions, and garlic that you feasted on! But, don't you remember the oppressive bondage you were under while you were there? Were those Egyptian delicacies that were so good to your mouth really worth the bondage? Look! You have been brought out of Egypt, miraculously delivered by the hand of God. You've gotten out of Egypt…and now it's time to get Egypt out of you!

There are multitudes of Christians today who have done exactly as the children of Israel did. These Christians at one time were in the terrible, oppressive bondage of sin. They were living in their Egypt, with the old Pharaoh, Satan, enslaving them. Their souls were in relentless bondage. They finally became so sick of the shackles that they cried out to God for deliverance. He miraculously saved them and delivered them from the power of Satan, from the bondage and control of this brutal taskmaster. They were very thankful to God at the time for saving them.

However, they quickly forgot the oppressive bondage they had escaped from and began yearning once again for some of the things of the world. In their hearts, they returned to Egypt. They began to live like the world, talk like the world, dress like the world, and act like the world. They began going again to the same places, enjoying the same entertainment, and participating in the same activities as the world.

Oh, children of God, what's wrong with you? Why don't you let Egypt go? The world does not need another just like them. They need dedicated, Godly, holy, committed Christians who can help free them from their bondage to Satan. You are out of Egypt; now get Egypt out of you. Let Egypt go! You do not belong there anymore!

ACTS 7:39 *"And in their hearts turned back again into Egypt."*

August 27

Run! it's a rattlesnake!

A rattlesnake is beautiful, but deadly. He may look pretty, but you certainly would not want to pet him. If fact, you would not even want to be in the area where you know one is crawling around. If you hang around a rattlesnake, stepping over him, walking around him, and petting him, you are assured of getting bit. Knowing the deadly venom could kill you helps your decision making ability tremendously.....you run!

In the physical realm, we have no problem recognizing and retreating from danger. However, in the spiritual realm, we are not nearly as smart. Sin is beautiful, too, but it is more deadly than any rattlesnake ever thought about being. If you hang around sin, stepping over it, walking around it, and petting it, you are assured of getting bit. Knowing that the deadly venom of sin will kill you spiritually should help your decision making ability tremendously. When you see sin, you should RUN!

However, such is not usually the case. Sin clothes itself in beautiful garments, deceiving even the wisest and smartest of human beings. Sin dresses up in clothing that appeals to the fleshly nature and desires. It never takes into account what God's will is or what God's Word says. Instead, it puts on the shiny, showy, glittery clothing of money, prestige, power, materialism, pleasure, popularity, and sexual desires. These are merely outward lures to draw and attract an unsuspecting individual. Once he begins to play with these things, petting them and flirting with them, he gets bit. He then finds himself enslaved to something that he thought was innocent but turns out to be a cruel taskmaster and will kill him spiritually.

Yes, sin is beautiful. There is even pleasure in it.....but only for a season. It looks harmless but it is deadly. The end of sin is ALWAYS death! So, what should you do when you see sin? If you are smart, you will run! You cannot name one good, helpful, home restoring, life-building, people helping thing about sin. It is high time you wake up and quit being deceived by sin. Jerk that cloak off the dressed-up sin in your life and look at the rattlesnake that is hiding beneath it.....and run!

PROVERBS 14:12 *"There is a way which seemeth right unto a man, but the end thereof are the ways of death."*

August 28

Are you in Adullam?

He could have been moping around in the pits of despair, complaining and murmuring and throwing the biggest pity party you've ever seen! He could have been filled with resentment and bitterness...and justifiably so in the world's eyes. He had done nothing but honor, obey, submit to, and follow King Saul; yet, in spite of all this, Saul hated him and was trying to kill him. David, even though he had done nothing wrong, was finally forced to flee for his life, making his dwelling in the cave, Adullam.

While living in this cave, David penned the words of Psalm 57, showing his complete trust and faith in the Lord. What a great attitude he had in spite of his circumstances! "*Be merciful to me, O God, be merciful to me; for my soul trusteth in Thee. Yea, in the shadow of Thy wings will I make my refuge, until these calamities be passed by." Psalm 57:1 "My heart is fixed, O God, my heart is fixed; I will sing and give praise." Psalm 57:7* By praising and honoring God in these adverse conditions, David was paving the way for God to work His Divine will in the situation. Unbeknownst to David or to anyone else, God was building an army during this time. Men began coming to the cave to get help from David..."*everyone who was in distress, and every one who was in debt, and every one who was discontented." I Samuel 22:2* David became a captain over them, numbering about 400 men, and eventually numbering about 340,000. These were men whom God hand-picked to love, follow, and stand by David all the way from the cave to the crown, as David eventually became King of Israel. What a strange way to build an army and what strange recruits to build an army with! But then, God's ways are never anything like man's ways anyway!

Perhaps today, like David, you are in a cave of circumstances that you didn't ask for and feel that you don't deserve. You've been complaining and whining about these circumstances, and you've even felt some bitterness and resentment over them. You've done everything but trust the Lord; therefore, you are still in the cave!

Well, friend, God has a blueprint for your life...and the cave is part of the blueprint. So, why don't you quit grumbling, pack your "Psalm 57" survival kit, and move into Adullam? Who knows what God will do with your life while you're in that cave, as you fix your heart upon Him and sing and praise Him through it all?

PSALM 57:1 *"Yea, in the shadow of Thy wings will I make my refuge..."*

August 29

Then Isaac came!

Then Isaac came! It didn't happen at all like they expected. It just didn't fit in with any of their human plans and ideas. In fact, Isaac came when there was absolutely no way for him to come. All hopes of him coming were vanished...dead...utterly inconceivable. However, it was at the point of outright impossibility that Isaac came!

God had promised Abraham and Sarah a son, through which the Messiah would come one day. As years passed and no son appeared, the couple decided to help God. After all, it WAS God's will for them to have a son and time was running out for them. So, they decided that Abraham would take Sarah's handmaid to himself before he passed the childbearing age. There would be no possible way after that. The son born to Abraham and Hagar was called Ishmael, the progenitor of the Arab race, which has been a thorn in Israel's side ever since. Man always suffers from taking things into his own hands.

Finally, when Abraham was one hundred and Sarah was ninety, they completely gave up. There was nothing left to try. They could not come up with any more ideas for a son. All natural, human means were exhausted, as their bodies were as good as dead. And then, Isaac came!

Isaac always comes after man has given up! God cannot send him as long as man is interfering, trying to do it his own way. God will allow man to try every avenue he can possibly try, every human method he can concoct, every natural means he can imagine until all man's ways are utterly exhausted. Then, when man finally gets to the end of himself, to the grand finale of all his own efforts, God steps in and sends Isaac!

What is your Isaac today? You have a promise from God that you have been clinging to for years. However, you have yet to see the fulfillment of that promise. Perhaps it is because you have been helping God, as if He really needed your feeble help anyway. You cannot keep your busy little hands out of God's business, much less your meddling mouth. You keep birthing Ishmaels because you won't wait for God to send Isaac. Why don't you take your hands off today? Remember: Isaac cannot come until you give up!

GENESIS 18:14 *"Is anything too hard for the Lord? At the time appointed... Sarah shall have a son."*

August 30

Removing your donkeys!

Thinking he was on a mission for his earthly father, Saul set out to find the stray donkeys. In Bible days, donkeys were the "pick-up trucks," used for transportation, hauling, and farming. They were necessities, something which even the poorest families could not do without. Losing these donkeys was similar to the owner of a trucking company finding all his trucks missing on a particular morning!

However, what appeared to be a disaster was simply God's providence, working to accomplish His perfect will in Saul's life. The donkeys weren't really lost...God knew where they were all along. In fact, he was the One who had removed them. This sent Saul on a search for the missing donkeys, but he found a whole lot more than donkeys in the process. God's Divine intervention had really sent him to the prophet, Samuel, to be anointed and crowned as the first king of Israel. So, Saul left his house as an ordinary, unknown, common man on a mission from his earthly father...but became an important, well-known, set-apart king on a mission from his Heavenly Father. Saul thought he was looking for donkeys, but God had a crown for him instead!

Today, friend, perhaps you have "donkey" problems, too! Something terrible has happened in your life, leaving you afraid, bewildered, and confused! It seems that God has removed something from your life that seems so necessary for your survival, leaving you in very dire circumstances. Humanly speaking, there's no way out of your situation, no hope whatsoever on your horizon!

Dear one, your predicament did not catch God by surprise. He didn't look down at your circumstances and say, "Oops!" Have you ever thought that perhaps God is the One who has arranged things as they are today...that this could be God's Divine providence working in your life? Maybe He had to remove your "donkeys" to get your attention, to send you on a search, to get you up and out of that same place you've settled down in for so long! He has plans for your life... big plans...and He had to interrupt your lifestyle to accomplish those plans. You wouldn't let go and let God as long as the "donkeys" were around! You were depending on them rather than on God! So...quit your grumbling...get up out of your pity party...and start thanking God for removing your "donkeys." God never makes a mistake!

I SAMUEL 9:3 *"Take now one of the servants with thee, and arise, go seek the donkeys."*

August 31

A friend of God

Can you imagine being called a friend of God? What an awesome thought to realize that you could be a friend to the Creator of this universe. He desires friends just like you do and He really wants YOU to be His friend!

The Word of God tells us that Abraham was a friend of God. What was it about Abraham that caused God to look upon him as His friend? First, Abraham was instantly and readily available. When God spoke, Abraham heard. He did not put God off or make excuses as to why he could not do as God said. He just simply said, "*Behold, here I am.*" *Genesis 22:1* If Abraham had been in a rush or caught up in worldly things, he probably would have never heard the voice of God.

Second, Abraham was unhesitatingly obedient. God spoke to him and he rose up early the next morning to obey. He did not question what God had said to him. He did not try to figure out how it would work. He did not come up with an alternate plan or try to help God out with the answer. He just simply obeyed!

Third, Abraham had offered himself as a living sacrifice to God. He had given up all rights to himself, his property, his land, his family, and even his own son. We know he had done this, because God presented him with four opportunities. Each opportunity involved a surrender of something most dear to Abraham and all four times he yielded. He gave up his country and his kindred; his nephew, Lot; his plans about Ishmael; and his beloved son, Isaac.

Put yourself in Abraham's place. Could the same thing be said about you? Are you instantly and readily available to God? Are you unhesitatingly obedient to the Lord? Have you offered up yourself as a living sacrifice unto God?

If you haven't made these commitments to the Lord, then you actually are a friend of the world, according to the Bible. However, God wants you to be His friend. He longs for someone to share His great heart with...and you can be that someone in this day, as Abraham was in his day. The choice is up to you! Will you be a friend of God...or remain a friend of the world?

JAMES 2:23 *"...Abraham believed God, and it was imputed unto him for righteousness; and he was called the friend of God."*

September

Flames of Passion

September 1

Oh, if only!

You get up on Sunday morning, trying to decide whether or not to go to church. You are not feeling your best, but you decide to go anyway. You haven't been for about three Sundays now, and you're feeling pretty guilty, so you feel that you really should make an effort today. When you arrive at the church, you find a most startling sight! The parking lot is empty! All the doors and windows are barred. Signs are posted on all doors, saying that all churches have been confiscated by the government and are closed to public worship.

Fear runs through your veins like water. You wonder how in the world this could be happening in free America. This is like a nightmare, only you are wide awake. In fact, you are more awake now than you have been for years. The pages of your mind begin turning, reminding you of so many good times right here in this empty building standing before you. You remember all the sermons, as your Pastor stood in the pulpit with his Bible before him, always faithful to be there and bring God's Word to you. You remember the choir, the special music, the plays, and the programs. Oh, how your heart was touched at times! You remember kneeling at the altar, the tears, and the testimonies. You remember the weddings, the socials, and the fellowships. Stark reality shatters your comfort zone as you realize that it is over. It is all over. Your freedom is gone!

Oh, if only you could turn back the pages of time. You did not realize how precious and dear the freedom to worship God was to you. You took it for granted. You never looked at attending church as being a cherished privilege. You missed many Sunday nights and Wednesday nights, and were not even totally faithful on Sunday mornings. You did not realize that every time you stayed home when you could have been there, you were casting a vote to close the doors. You just expected others to be there and keep the doors open, so you could go when you wanted to. You never realized the importance of prayer either.You never met with others to pray for revival in America, because you just assumed that America would stay free.....you had too much other stuff to do to take time out for prayer!

As you look at your church, you realize that you helped bring this on. You did not join the vanishing remnant in fasting, prayer, and tears for America. You did not even care enough to be faithful. And now, you have lost your freedom. Oh, if only you could go back. Oh, if only...

I CORINTHIANS 7:29 *"The time is short...."*

September 2

The final countdown

10...9...8...7...6...5...4...3...2...1...Lift off! This is the final countdown in the launching of a vehicle headed for space. Now, the decision as to when lift off will occur is made perhaps months before the final countdown. Then, many preparations must be made to get the space craft ready for departure. Each day brings the final countdown one day closer. As the exact time for this preplanned departure draws near, there is much anticipation and excitement in the space center. All the work that went into this project, all the billions of dollars spent on it, and all the time that elapsed in making this craft are over now. It is the final countdown!

There is a final countdown in your life, too. Before you were ever even conceived, Almighty God drew up His design for you. He planned the precise time of your arrival and departure from this earth. Each day brings you one day closer to that final countdown. Just think: today, you are one day closer than you were yesterday. You are drawing nearer to that final countdown every second. Your clock of life is ticking.

Have you been making all the necessary preparations for departure? Are all systems go? Are you prepared for your soul's lift off to eternity, where you will stand face to face with Almighty God, the Creator of the universe, the King of kings and Lord of lords?

If you are unprepared at this moment, you had better get all systems go before that final countdown begins. It will be too late then. You must realize that you are a sinner. You have wronged and offended a holy, all-powerful God. You have lived your own life the way you chose. You have been in control of your own life. You must bow before Him, confessing your sin and rejection of Him, asking His forgiveness, and relinquishing the total control of your life to Him.

Why don't you settle this today? You are closer to eternity than you were yesterday. You're even closer than you were when you started reading this. Friend, the final countdown is getting closer every second.

10...9...8...7...6...5...4...3...2...1...

REVELATION 1:3 *"...for the time is at hand."*

September 3

An issue of blood

She had just about reached wit's end. For twelve years now, she had endured a problem that apparently could not be solved. She had tried everything. She had gone to many physicians and had done whatever they told her. She had even spent all the money she had trying to get well. However, all she tried was futile and, instead of getting better, she only got worse. She had an issue of blood, which no one could cure.

Perhaps one of the doctors had suggested education to her. Through learning more about her condition and studying ways to overcome it, she could get better. Maybe another doctor had suggested that she get the finest doctors in other lands to help her. Still another could have suggested a different diet or better nutrition.

After attempting every plan and method suggested by man, she finally realized the futility of man's efforts. There was only one hope.....Jesus! She went looking for Him, knowing that she would do whatever it took to get to Him. She pushed through the crowd, not allowing the masses of people to discourage her and cause her to turn back. She knew if she could only touch the hem of His garment, she would be healed. Pushing her way through the masses of people, even in this weakened state, she got to Jesus. She reached out and touched the hem of His garment, and immediately her issue of blood dried up.

America has just about reached her wit's end, too. She has an issue of blood, flowing from all the aborted babies and from all the daily victims of murder. She has tried everything the "experts" have suggested in order to find a cure. She has spent untold amounts of money to correct the problem. However, the condition only keeps getting worse. Some think educating the people will help. Some think more money should be spent on research, on welfare, on birth control, on better law enforcement, etc. Others think new politicians are the answer. And yet others think that stricter laws and controls on the people will help.

What about you? Do you think any of these things are the answer? Or do you believe Jesus is our only hope? If Jesus is our answer, then why don't you do whatever it takes to get to Him? Lay aside your self-centered world, get your feelings off your sleeve, and go find Jesus! Our country is fighting a losing battle and will soon die from its issue of blood unless someone gets to Jesus and touches the hem of His garment for America. Do you care about your country? Well, then, you'd better go get Jesus.....time is running out!

MARK 5:28 *"If I may touch but His clothes, I shall be well."*

September 4

Have you died yet?

You stand looking at your outstretched hands, with both palms up. In your left hand, you hold a seed from an orange; and, in your right hand, you hold an orange from a seed. Both contain the life of an orange within, yet how different that life appears in each. The life in the seed is encased in a hard, outer shell. That seed cannot be eaten, would not provide nourishment for anyone, and is not helpful to anyone in that state. It could remain for years in that state, still containing all that life and all that potential within, yet never doing a single soul any good.

The orange, on the other hand, has had its life manifested. It was once a seed, with the life encased within the hard, outer shell. That seed was buried in the earth and life broke through that shell, grew upward toward the sun, broke through the darkness into the light, and formed an orange tree. It took the death, burial, and resurrection of that one seed to produce this glorious, magnificent orange, with limitless possibilities for new life.

There was once a seed of everlasting life. He walked on the earth for thirty three years, with that seed encased in a human body. Then, He was crucified on a cruel cross, His body beaten and pierced and mutilated. That body died and was buried in the darkness for three days. The everlasting life burst forth from its housing, pushed toward the Light, and was resurrected from its grave. This was the first fruits of everlasting life.

This fruit is the Lord Jesus Christ. All who die to their old ways, allow their old natures to be buried, and invite Christ into their hearts will receive this everlasting life. Have you ever recognized that the way to life is death? No seed EVER grows into an orange without being planted in the earth and resurrected. Neither will any person ever be resurrected to see God without first being crucified with Christ. Have you died yet?

I CORINTHIANS 15:36 *"...that which thou sowest is not made alive, except it die..."*

September 5

The last word!

Voltaire was a famous French writer who lived in the 1700's. He was a man of prominence, a man who could be depended upon. However, he made one very grave, fatal mistake. He did not believe in God. In fact, he even predicted that there would be no Bibles in existence one-hundred years after his time. The ironic thing is that, one-hundred years later, Voltaire's home became the property of the Geneva Bible Society...a home filled with the very book that Voltaire had never believed in and had predicted would cease to exist. God got the last word. He always does!

For years, skeptics said that the Bible could not possibly be true, because it told of the city of Nineveh, a city of which there were no historical records in existence. However, in 1845 A.D., archaeological discoveries uncovered the entire city of Nineveh, which had lain buried beneath the earth for 2,457 years. Even the library was uncovered and many historical records were completely intact. God got the last word. He always does!

Other skeptics along the way tried to prove that some of the books of the Bible, like Isaiah, which predicted the birth of Christ, were actually written after Jesus' birth. However, in the mid 1900's, the Dead Sea Scrolls, which had been written long before the birth of Christ, were discovered. In these Scrolls was the book of Isaiah, which paralleled the book in our Bible. Once again, the skeptics were silenced! God got the last word. He always does!

Recently, with the use of computers, many scientists have come to the conclusion that the "Adam theory" is correct after all. According to their information, they traced the genes of the human race back to one man. How strange that it has taken man 6000 years to discover what God said all along, "*In the beginning, God...*" *Genesis 1:1* God got the last word. He always does!

Yes, down through the ages, there have been hundreds of skeptics. Our day is no different. There are scoffers in our day, as II Peter 3:3 tells us there will be. They will walk after their own lusts. They will make light of God's Holy Word. They will live as they please, ignoring the Word of God. Like Voltaire, they will totally disregard the Bible as the Truth. Like the skeptics about Nineveh, they will not believe the Bible because it has not been proven to them. Like the scientists, they will only believe what man can figure out. However, they will end as Voltaire and all the other skeptics did...in a hell they never believed in! God will get the last word. He always does!

EPHESIANS 5:15, 16 *"See, then, that you walk circumspectly, not as fools, but as wise, redeeming the time, because the days are evil."*

September 6

Spiritual forecast

Most people like to listen daily to their local weather report. They want to know if a storm is coming, if a storm is departing, if it will be raining, if it will be snowing, or if it will be sunny. Often, they make plans based on what the weather forecast is.

Spiritually, there is a weather forecast, too. You are either in a storm right now, going into one, or coming out of one. Life is filled with storms and trials... and being a Christian does not remove these in any way. In fact, it often brings them on. These storms cannot be escaped!

So Christian, you might as well make the best of your storms. Just as a wise person prepares ahead of time for environmental storms, so you should prepare ahead of time for spiritual storms. Before hurricanes hit, people put up all loose objects, secure doors and windows, and store up extra food and supplies that may be needed. A wise Christian will make sure there are no loose ends in his life, no unconfessed, unrepented of sins that the devil would use to batter him in a storm. He will deal with all unstable areas of his life, bringing them to Christ, because they will be magnified during a storm. He will make sure he is fortified, strengthened, and protected by the Word of God. He will read the Bible daily, pray, and stay in church to be spiritually prepared for his storms instead of waiting until a storm hits to do something about it.

What is your spiritual weather forecast today, Christian? Are you presently in a storm? If so, just remember that storms don't last forever. There IS an end in sight! While you are in the storm, keep reminding yourself that this is the worst you will ever have it. Heaven awaits you! Think about those lost souls out there in the storms of life. This is the best they will ever have it. Hell awaits them! Surely you can endure for a short time, for your light affliction is but for a moment compared with eternity.

Perhaps you've just come out of a storm. If so, reflect on what you learned during the storm. Use this time to strengthen yourself in the Word and in prayer. Set aside some time to be alone with God, getting filled up once again and ready to take on the world. Examine your life thoroughly and make sure it is lined up with the Word of God. Tie up all loose ends.

Friend, storms are inevitable. But, God will walk with you through them and will use them to do things in you and for you that He could never do otherwise. So, whether you are presently in a storm, just going into one, or coming out of one, remember that you are just passing through this life. The storms will soon be over forever and you won't need a spiritual forecast anymore!

I PETER 4:12 *"Beloved, think it not strange concerning the fiery trial which is to test you."*

September 7

Why float when you can fix?

"It's Friday and I'm so excited! My best friend is coming over for dinner at 7:00. I started having this strong feeling earlier in the week that she would be coming, so I started believing it and claiming it. By faith, I have cooked her favorite foods. I have even baked a cake from scratch. I am eagerly looking forward to the time of her arrival. I just know she will come, because I feel like she will. I have the faith to believe it and I am acting on that faith. I have not doubted at all. I will speak it into existence!"

This kind of faith is a "floating" faith. It isn't based on anything concrete. It isn't anchored to anything solid. It is actually faith in one's own faith and is like a cork bobbing up and down in a choppy lake. It floats from here to there, depending upon the wind currents. "Floating" faith only attaches itself to unstable things, such as feelings, dreams, and visions. This results in a roller coaster lifestyle - up and down, high and low, in and out - unstable as water!

Now, let's rewrite this little story, adding one vital element. "It's Friday and I'm so excited. My best friend is coming over for dinner at 7:00. We have been talking about getting together for a few weeks now, and we decided that Friday would be good for both of us. She said she would be here at 7:00. Since she always keeps her word, I know I can count on her to come. By faith, I have prepared her favorite foods, even a "scratch" cake. I know she will come, because she said she would. I have her word to go on."

This kind of faith is a "fixed" faith. It is based on something concrete, the friend's word. Being anchored to something "fixed," it is unaffected by feelings and cannot be blown about or moved. It doesn't have to be propped up or supported. The fulfillment of the faith rests with the reliability of the friend instead of anything the believer can muster up. The believer simply acts upon the friend's word.

What kind of faith do you have, "floating" or "fixed?" Christian, your faith should be firmly anchored, or "fixed" on God's Word. You don't have to muster up anything. You don't have to speak anything into existence. Just act on what God says. There's no need to "float" when you can be "fixed" to the Word of the living God!

HEBREWS 4:2 *"the word...did not profit them, not being mixed with faith in them that heard it."*

September 8

Jellyfish........everywhere!

There is a giant standing on the horizon. He is a Goliath, a fully armed, well trained, experienced warrior. His deceptive, but venomous attacks have been poured out against nation after nation, to which most have already succumbed. The whole world lies prey to him. And, judging from his past record, anyone coming against him is assured of losing. Soon, he will take over the entire world. He is the spirit of the anti-Christ; the spirit of worldliness: doing your own thing, permissiveness, situational ethics, peaceful coexistence, relativism, and tolerance. In other words, he stands for everything anti, or against, Christ and the Word of God.

Is there any hope? Even rulers and politicians are bowing to Goliath, afraid to stand against him lest they mar their chances for reelection. Christians, as well, have become passive, apathetic, and listless, as they retire to their comfortable sofas to be lulled to sleep even more by the spirit of Goliath coming across the air waves into their living rooms. Everywhere you go, there are jellyfish - people with no backbone, no strong convictions, no firm stand, no rocking the boat. Jellyfish.....everywhere.....the world is covered with jellyfish!

It is time for a David to stand up. He may be young and inexperienced, but he can see the absurdity of this situation. He can look into the glazed, lifeless eyes of those who say they have God on their side and say, "*Is there not a cause?*" *I Samuel 17:29* David will not need the armor of the world nor any weapon the world has to offer. All he will need is one Rock!

Where are you, David? Haven't you gotten sick of the lukewarm, jellyfish Christians who have retreated from the battle? Isn't it a pathetic sight to see soldiers who have the God of the universe on their side shaking and trembling in the presence of one little ole' giant? Pick up that Rock, David, and stand up to Goliath. Tell him, "*You come to me with a sword, and with a spear, and with a shield; but I come to you in the name of the Lord of Hosts...whom you have defied. This day will the Lord deliver you into my hand...that all the earth may know that there is a God in (America.)" I Samuel 17:45, 46* Get that Rock, David, and start slinging! You can take America back with that Rock. He never misses!

I SAMUEL 17:29 *"Is there not a cause?"*

September 9

There's a serial killer loose!

I am an invisible serial killer. No one sees me coming, so they do not know to run and hide. I never carry weapons that anyone can see either, so no one is afraid of me. I am so sly and deceiving that I can do my job quickly and efficiently without anyone even knowing what I am doing. That way, I normally don't even get the blame for it. Usually, no one recognizes me as the killer, for I am the smartest, most deceptive killer there has ever been. I can even get others to help me without them being aware of what they are doing!

Oh, you should see me in action! I just go from one to the other, leaving a trail of destruction behind. Rarely a day goes by that I do not harm someone. I devastate lives, tear up homes, ruin reputations, cause despair, foster discouragement, shatter hopes, create doubt, raise fears, leave open wounds, cause suicides, generate depression, and tear up churches. I am like a mini atomic bomb, only the destruction I cause is generally never overcome.

You know about me, because you have used me time after time to kill someone!I am your tongue. I am the deadliest weapon on planet earth. Since I am an unruly evil, untameable and full of deadly poison, you need to lay me on the altar. God can control me, if you will let Him, but He's the only One who can! Wouldn't you like to have me under control? Do you like using me as a lethal weapon? Does it give you pleasure to criticize others? Does it help them in any way at all? Will it bring them to Jesus or help them live healthier spiritual lives? What good do you accomplish by verbally raping another person's character? Can you name one good, helpful, Christ-centered thing about the negative, caustic stuff that your tongue so often proclaims!

Today, Christian, that serial killer in your mouth is on trial. God's Word is the judge. Your tongue is guilty, as charged. The sentence is life imprisonment. Put that tongue behind bars, in captivity to the Lord Jesus Christ. He is the Warden and is the only One who can control what it does from now on!

JAMES 3:8 *"But the tongue can no man tame; it is an unruly evil, full of deadly poison."*

September 10

Grunting and leaning

Boy, oh boy! Since God already knows my needs and already has the answer, I will just sit back, do nothing, and wait on Him to provide. Isn't that what it means to be anxious for nothing?

Well, not exactly! God provides for the birds of the air, but He never puts the food in their mouths. They are responsible for going after the food He has so graciously put here for them and they are responsible for picking up the food and eating it. God provides…but they must go get the provision.

Similarly, God has already provided everything for us. It is already here before we even have the need. But we, too, must do something. The reality of this hit me while observing Keith, the two year old son of some friends of mine. Keith, up until this point in time, had not been very interested in talking. He just grunted and leaned toward what he wanted, expecting someone to get it for him without him having to say a word. That worked for a while. But, since his parents wanted to communicate with Keith, they couldn't continue providing the things he wanted without him asking. To do so would hinder his learning to talk, which we all know is an absolutely vital part of any relationship. So, my friends taught Keith to ask in order to receive.

Sometimes, we are kind of like Keith. After we are born again and find ourselves in a brand new realm, a spiritual realm, we want to just grunt and learn and expect God to answer. It is so much easier than it is to get down on our knees and spend the time necessary with our Heavenly Father to make our desires known. We had rather just grunt and lean…and have what we want without any cost whatsoever on our part.

However, our loving Heavenly Father cares about us too much to let us grunt and lean. He wants to communicate with us. He wants to hear us talk to Him. He doesn't want us to stay in spiritual babyhood, but rather grow up to love Him and have a sweet, intimate, personal, vital relationship with Him, a relationship which involves much communication, both talking and listening. So, He teaches us to ask in order to receive.

How about you, dear one? Are you still in the grunting and leaning stage? Or are you truly learning to communicate with your Father in heaven? Are you developing a relationship with Him that gets stronger and more precious every day? Are you learning to ask that you may receive?

MATTHEW 7:7 *"Ask, and you shall receive…"*

September 11

By this shall all men know

They were all gathered together in a large upper room to celebrate the Passover. Only Jesus and one other man there knew that this would be the last Passover on earth they would all celebrate together. People knew that these twelve men were Jesus' disciples, because they followed Him and were with Him bodily. But, He knew His departure was near and He would no longer walk with them physically. So, at this last supper, Jesus wanted to leave them a most powerful verbal truth and a living example of that truth. He wanted to leave a way for them and all future disciples to be easily recognized as disciples.

Rising from supper, Jesus laid aside His garments and girded Himself with a towel. He poured water into a basin and began to perform a service that the lowest servant in Jewish households performed. He began to wash the disciples'feet and wipe them with the towel.

The disciples did not know what to say. Here was the King of Glory robed, not with royalty, but with the attire of the most menial servant, doing to them what they should be doing to Him. And then He came to the one man there who knew this would be their last Passover together, because he had already made plans to betray Jesus that very night. Jesus knew about this; yet, He knelt before this traitor and washed and dried his feet with the same tender love and affection as He did the others. Afterwards, Jesus told them, "*A new commandment I give unto you, that you love one another; as I have loved you...By this shall all men know that you are My disciples, if you have love one to another.*" *John 13:34, 35*

Christian, Jesus left you with a powerful example. Rise up from supper. Perhaps you spend too much time at the table anyway. Lay aside your garments of pride, self-centeredness, and selfishness. Lay aside your fleshly desires and earthly pleasures. Put on the towel of humility, the garment of the least of all servants, and wash the feet of others. Give yourself completely for others, even those who have betrayed you. Love others as Jesus has loved you. It will not be convenient. It will not be comfortable. It will not always be enjoyable. But, if you lay down your life for others, suffering with them, taking up the cross for them, and honoring them more highly than yourself, you will honor the Lord. And, by this shall all men know!

JOHN 13:35 *"By this shall all men know that you are My disciples..."*

September 12

A tiny little dew drop

As I sat in the grass, enjoying the time alone with my Savior, just meditating upon the things of God, I spotted it! It was so small I didn't even notice it at first. But then, its gleam caught my eye. It was just a tiny little dew drop, perched comfortably on the top of a single blade of grass. Leaning over to get a better look, I was thrilled by what I saw! In that one tiny little dew drop, I could see the sun and its rays radiating out from it. How awesome, I mused, that something no bigger than a pencil eraser could reflect the sun, a huge ball of gas that is thousands and thousands of times bigger than the earth, and is 93 million miles away! It staggered my imagination that in something as insignificant as a dew drop, one could see something as mighty and powerful as the sun itself!

Looking around me, I noticed that nothing else reflected the sun…not the grass, the dirt, the sticks, the leaves, or anything else in the area…only that one tiny little dew drop. It was the only thing with the capability of reflecting! It just sparkled and glittered. But, then, this little dew drop was clean and pure and clear. Had it been dirty or muddy, its reflecting properties would have been diminished or possibly even negated!

As I sat in awe, this thought floated across my mind. "Oh, Lord, I want to be a tiny little dew drop for You. With all my heart, I want people to look at me and see the Son. Father, I want my life to radiate Christ, to sparkle and glitter so much spiritually that people will look and wonder what's different about me. Then, as You create in them a hunger for what I have, I can introduce them to You! Oh, I know, just like the dew drop, I must be clean and pure and clear to do so; else, my reflecting properties will be greatly affected. Any sin whatsoever in my life will stop others from seeing the Son when they are around me. So, I'm asking You, my Savior, to "*create in me a clean heart and renew a right spirit within me.*" *Psalm 51:10* Show me the sin in my life that I might confess it, repent of it, and forsake it altogether…and I can be "*cleansed from all filthiness of the flesh and spirit, perfecting holiness in the fear of God.*" *II Corinthians 7:1* Make me just a tiny little dew drop for You, Jesus!

Christian, would you also like to be a tiny little dew drop for the Son? Well, you can, because God has created you with reflecting ability. So, get in the water of the Word and take a spiritual bath, confessing and cleaning up your life. There's a lost world out there that needs to see the Son in one tiny little dew drop just like you!

Psalm 51:10 *"Create in me a clean heart, O God, and renew a right spirit within me."*

September 13

You don't need soul power

One of the main characteristics of the end times, of which the Bible warns repeatedly, is deception. There will be many false teachers, false doctrines, and false prophets. People will have itching ears, wanting to hear about power and signs and miracles.....things which are appealing to the flesh.

Now Satan is very sly. He has been practicing on man for 6,000 years, so he ought to know by now what works. Some people can be deceived by false cults, with far-out leaders who can capture men's souls. Some people can be deceived into thinking they can live their lives as they please, being their own leaders. And others, who feel they need to be religious, can be deceived by allowing people who appear Godly to be their leaders. Satan works as an angel of light, even using Scripture, Bible studies, and seminars to draw people away from the cross and the blood of Christ. He will try to interest people in signs and miracles, works, or anything that can divert their attention away from the main thing....Jesus!

Christian, beware! Signs and wonders and miracles do NOT mean it is of God. In the end times, false prophets shall show great signs and wonders and even deceive the very elect, if it were possible. You see, man has not only a spirit, but a living soul. This soul has dormant powers that Satan wants to put to use so man will not have to be totally dependent upon God. Some people tap into these powers. They learn to release these dormant powers, thus deceiving many people.....powers such as hypnotism, telepathic communication, astral projection, trances and visions, predictions, walking on hot coals without being burned, healings, lying on a bed of nails, moving objects by thought, etc.

So, Christian, do not judge something as being from God because you experienced it and it is real. It IS real! Satan is real! So, how can you be safe in this highly deceptive age? Stick to the cross! Determine, as Paul, not to know anything except Jesus Christ and Him crucified. Quit dwelling on power, on signs, on manifestations, or even on your own ministry. Dwell on Jesus Christ! Set your mind and affections on Him and let Him do through you whatever He chooses! You do not need soul power...you just need Him!

MATTHEW 24:24 *"And there shall arise...false prophets and shall show great signs and wonders..."*

September 14

A spiritual Hitler

What do you think when you hear the name Adolph Hitler? You probably think about the millions of Jews that were mercilessly slaughtered under his authority. He was an evil man, feeling that his race was superior and that the Jews were subhuman. He was blind to the Jewish race as really being people. He was calloused and indifferent to their suffering, feeling no remorse whatsoever in putting them in gas chambers, burying them alive, and many other hideous forms of torture and death.

You cannot comprehend anyone doing such atrocious things as Hitler did. Yet, you may be guilty of something far worse than what he did. If you are lukewarm, you are dooming some soul to an eternity in the lake of fire. That soul is watching you, because you claim to be a Christian. That soul is making a determination about what it means to follow Jesus Christ by looking at your lifestyle. If you are conformed to the world, living like everyone else, going the same places, doing the same things, then the world will feel it has no need to change. The world will think it can live like it pleases and still go to heaven. So, in actuality, you are giving false hopes to that soul who is watching you.

How are you going to feel at the Great White Throne Judgment when that soul stands before Almighty God and hears Him sentence them to an eternity in the Lake of Fire? What kind of look will you get from that soul who is doomed to hell because he saw nothing in you that made him want Christ; yet, you knew the truth?

Maybe you think Hitler was awful, and he was! But his actions only caused physical death. Yours may be causing eternal death, which will be forever and ever and ever. You may right this minute be sentencing someone to burn throughout all eternity. That is as bad as you can get!

If you are lukewarm as a Christian, you had better take another look at yourself. God says He will vomit you out of His mouth! He hates lukewarmness, because it damns others to hell. He says He had rather you be hot or cold - yes, even cold - than lukewarm. Do not even name the name of Christ if you are not going to be on fire for Him. Just get out completely and never let anyone even remotely suspect that you know Jesus Christ. That way, at least you will not be hurting anyone. If you are not going to live totally, completely, and wholeheartedly for the Lord, then at least care enough about others to not be the cause of them being in torments forever. Get in or get out! Quit being a spiritual Hitler...you are sickening to God!

REVELATION 3:15 *"I know thy works, that thou art neither cold nor hot..."*

September 15

Roads are built on your knees

God is a sovereign, Almighty God, who can do anything He pleases any time and anywhere. He spoke a universe into existence from nothing; therefore, all things are possible with Him. There is nothing that God cannot do. However, God has placed things in a certain order and He works according to that order, although He could do it many other ways. He could make an apple grow on a pine tree...but that is not the order He has chosen. He could make dogs with wings, people with four legs, and elephants with flat noses. He could make grass pink, the ocean red, bananas purple, and on and on. However, God has an established order to everything He has created and everything works only according to that order.

This is true in the spiritual realm as well as in the physical. God CAN do anything He pleases spiritually, but He has chosen to work through prayer. If you do not plant the crop, God does not send the harvest. Likewise, if you do not pray, breaking up the spiritual soil, planting the spiritual seeds, and watering the unseen crop, God will not send the spiritual harvest. His will on earth is accomplished only through prayer.

Prayer can be looked upon as the roadway of life down which God's will travels. His will only goes where a road has been laid. Now He is the architect. He designs the roadways. He knows where bridges need to be built, where dynamite must blast obstructions away, and where trees must be uprooted. He designs, but we must build the roads. We must come to the Master Designer, allowing Him to put His blueprint in our hearts. Then, we pray all that He puts within us. Sometimes, we must pray for a long time, because it takes longer to build some roads than others. Roads through mountainous terrain take longer to build than roads across plains. Prayer builds these roadways! And, once a roadway is completed, God's will can travel down it to its destination.

Christian, God has chosen YOU to build some roads. There are lots of places He wants to go, but He needs a roadway to travel down. Will you be a road-builder for Jesus? If so, then get down on your knees and start building. Roads are built on your knees!

LUKE 18:1 *"...men ought always to pray, and not to faint..."*

September 16

Leave the cocoon alone

He watched the little butterfly struggling to get out of its cocoon. Its little wings would push against the sides, exerting all the force they could, but to no avail. For what seemed like ages, the butterfly wiggled and pushed and struggled, yet all its efforts were so futile. Finally, the onlooker had stood this painful ordeal as long as he could. He took a tiny pair of scissors and gently snipped the cocoon, thus enabling the butterfly to escape with practically no further effort.

Quickly, the butterfly emerged from its bondage. It floundered around for a short while, but soon met its death. It could not fly. Its wings were not strong enough, not developed to their full potential. They were unable to pick the butterfly up and put it to flight. Sadly, the onlooker realized the value of the struggle. The little butterfly needed every ounce of that struggle to strengthen and develop its wings. It needed the opposition from the cocoon to help it grow properly. The onlooker had good intentions, but he carried out his own will instead of God's in the matter of the butterfly. He interfered in the butterfly's development, and it cost the little butterfly its life.

Friend, perhaps you have been watching a struggle too. One of your loved ones has been battling to escape the cocoon of problems he has become entangled in. For what has seemed like ages, he has been pushing and wiggling and struggling, yet he is no nearer to deliverance than he was when it all started. You cannot bear to watch this struggle any longer. You are on the verge of stepping in and helping your loved one out of the situation he's entangled in. You are ready to cut the cocoon. You don't see any other way out.

Oh, don't interfere! Your loved one needs every ounce of the struggle to strengthen and develop his spiritual wings. He needs the opposition from the cocoon he's entangled in to grow properly. Don't carry out your will in your loved one's life. Oh, precious one, wait for God and seek His will instead. He is working in your loved one's life through the struggle. If you interfere at this time, it could very well cost your loved one his spiritual life. So.....leave the cocoon alone!

II CORINTHIANS 4:17 *"For our light affliction...works for us a far more exceeding and eternal weight of glory."*

September 17

There "ain't" no such thing!

How utterly amazing it is to sit in a church service, listening to folks singing, "Victory in Jesus," and watch those same folks go out the doors to live in defeat most of the time. Do they not believe what they sing? Do they just mouth empty words with absolutely no thought of the meaning behind those words? Don't they realize that it is very hypocritical to sing one way but live another?

Perhaps they should change the wording of the song if they're not going to live what they sing. They should sing it this way. "Defeat in Jesus; my Savior forever. He sought me and He bought me, with His redeeming blood. He loved me 'ere I knew Him, and all my worry is due Him. He plunged me to defeat...beneath the cleansing flood." This would be much more realistic...and much less confusing to the lost world, a world who is watching these defeated, murmuring, downcast Christians saying one thing with their mouths, yet living something completely different. It appears that the Christ they serve has no more power than the gods of the lost world!

The sad thing is that these Christians, by their lifestyles, are bringing reproach and shame to the Savior who purchased them with His precious blood. They proclaim a gospel of victory, of peace, of love, of joy...yet live in defeat, worry, bitterness, and complaining. They live as though their Christianity is something to endure rather than to enjoy. However, nowhere in the Word of God is there anything about defeat in Jesus! There "ain't" no such thing! The Bible says, *"Now thanks be unto God, who always causeth us to triumph in Christ..." II Corinthians 2:14 "This is the victory that overcometh the world, even our faith;" I John 5:4 and "Nay, in all these things we are more than conquerors through Him that loved us." Romans 8:37*

Christian, if you've been living a life of defeat, it's time for you to grow up spiritually and start living out what you say you believe. Start practicing what you preach!Take God at His Word and act accordingly. He says, "*The just shall live by faith" Hebrews 10:38*...not by sight; not by feelings; not by opinions; not by circumstances; and not by anything you can see, hear, smell, taste, or feel. So, quit trying to figure things out, worrying and fretting and complaining all the while. You're not living for victory...you're living FROM it! There "ain't" no such thing as defeat in Jesus!

II CORINTHIANS 2:14 *"Now thanks be unto God, who always causeth us to triumph in Christ."*

September 18

Got an operating room ready, Lord?

You have a skin cancer. You put medicine on it. You wash it and cleanse it and put fresh dressings on it every day. But, it keeps getting worse. No matter what you do, it does not seem to help much. Well, the reason is that you are treating the problem externally, while the roots are internal. You must deal with the internal roots by surgical removal before the external problem can be corrected.

We have no problem recognizing this need on the physical level. However, spiritually, we often mis-diagnose. We see the evil that pervades our land and deal with it by putting a salve on the cancer. We try educating the people, helping them, making it easier for them, finding reasons why they are like they are, etc. Yet, the root of the problem is that the heart is wicked and must be changed by spiritual surgery. Jesus Christ is the Great Physician and is the only One capable of doing this spiritual surgery.

On a personal level, we have many problems that come into our lives and we often make inaccurate diagnoses of them as well. We sometimes get put out and upset with others and often blame them for our actions. We say they pushed us into it or provoked us; therefore, it is their fault. What we fail to see is that it is only an internal problem surfacing. If it were not already in us, then it could not be brought out. So, our problem is a wicked heart, filled with the sin of self. Our little old "self" is full of pride, wanting its own way and demanding its rights. When someone comes along and violates these imagined rights, that "self" rises to the surface and erupts. That person we got upset with was only a piece of "heavenly sandpaper," sent along by God to get the impurities in our lives to rise to the surface where they can be exposed and sanded off.

We should always remember one thing in our relationships with others which will help us tremendously. We cannot fall out with man until we have first fallen out with God. It is IMPOSSIBLE to be right with God and wrong with man. Let's learn to diagnose correctly so the cancer can be removed. Our problem is NEVER external. It is always internal. Our hearts are desperately wicked and the sin must be removed by spiritual surgery done by the Lord Jesus Christ. Got an operating room ready, Lord?

JEREMIAH 17:9 *"The heart is deceitful above all things, and desperately wicked..."*

September 19

It shouldn't be inferior...it should be dead!

Do you have a poor self-image? Are you uncomfortable around most people because you feel inferior? Maybe you feel that you do not look good or that you just do not measure up, so you are intimidated by those who look better than you. Maybe you feel that you are not as educated or polished and that makes you feel inferior. Perhaps you were laughed at throughout childhood, causing you to still feel today that you are somehow less of a person than others. This inferiority complex leads you to be continually trying to prove your worth and gain acceptance from others.

A low self-image can manifest itself in various ways. Some withdraw from others and become loners. Some become clowns, always covering up by acting crazy. Others become critical, putting people down verbally so that they will look better. Still others become proficient in one certain area, putting their whole heart and soul into it, so that at least they can feel worth somewhere.

If you are a Christian and you have a poor self-image, then you have a sin problem. That problem is found in the middle of sin..."I." You are dwelling on your own sad little self, on your inabilities, on your looks, or on your worth instead of on Jesus Christ and who He is! A Christian should not have a self-image. That is what's wrong with the world now...self! Self is at the center of everything! Why would you want a self-image when you have Jesus living inside you? He spoke a universe into existence from nothing. Can you improve on that? He is the Highest you can get. There is nowhere to go beyond Him... and He dwells in your heart. Isn't it rather dumb to try fixing up and improving self? Why don't you instead work on crucifying your self? Nail that old man to the cross and allow Jesus Christ to live through you.

From now on, when inferiority creeps over you, recognize it immediately as sin!You are dwelling on "I." Put self back on the cross! Self shouldn't be inferior... it should be dead! Cross it out and let Jesus be Jesus in you. Then it will be "..*not I, but Christ that liveth in me.*"

GALATIANS 2:20 *"I am crucified with Christ: nevertheless I live; yet not I, but Christ liveth in me..."*

September 20

Confession opens it!

Let's try a little experiment. I lay a plain piece of notebook paper on the floor. I say to you, "Now, I am going to put my foot on one end of this paper. I want you to face me, putting your foot on the other end. And you will not be able to touch me at all when we do this." Of course, you do not believe this, so we try it. As you come toward the paper, I pick it up, go out the door and close it, and slip the paper under the bottom of the door. You can stand on one end and I can stand on the other, but you cannot touch me, because a door is between us.

God says, "*But your iniquities have separated between you and your God and your sins have hidden His face from you, that he will not hear." Isaiah 59:2* Do you ever pray and feel that your prayers are getting no higher than the ceiling? You pray and it is as though your prayers are vanishing into thin air, just as your breath does outside on a cold morning. You pray and pray, yet rarely see any real answers. In fact, you have even gotten to the point where you pray and do not even expect any answers. You get down to pray, yet never feel the warmth of His presence, the overflowing joy there is in His presence, or the assurance and peace of knowing He has heard. Your spiritual life has become an empty shell. You are just going through the motions of being a Christian like some robot with no life and soul and heart.

Well, Christian, perhaps you have taken the paper and have slipped it under the closed door. There is a wall of separation between you and your God. That wall is called sin! You put it up...God didn't! Sin ALWAYS separates! You cannot be living in rebellion against God's Word, doing your own thing, living as you please, and still have a sweet, intimate relationship with Him. Sin is the closed door.

How do you open the door? Remove the sin! Set aside some time alone with the Lord. Get in His Word, open your heart, and ask Him to reveal all the sin in your life. As He reveals sin, no matter how small, confess it as sin against Him, forsake it, and make restitution where needed. Claim I John 1:9 over each sin. Stay before Him until He finishes. If you have time for anything, surely you have time to make things right with God. Is there anything more important to you than that? Just remember: sin closes the door, but confession opens it. God is waiting. He is tired of standing on that paper with the door closed. Aren't you?

ISAIAH 59:2 *"But your iniquities have separated between you and your God..."*

September 21

Lord, I need a heart shop!

"Here's my heart, Lord! It has been shattered into a million pieces. I thought I was strong. Yesterday, I felt like I could conquer the world. Oh, I was singing songs of praise and victory and living on top of the mountain. Yesterday, I would have told you that nothing could touch me, that I was a victorious warrior. Yesterday, I was invincible! Yesterday, I was more than a conqueror through Jesus Christ.

Oh, but yesterday's gone. And here I stand today, Lord, in the valley. I gave my heart to someone, someone I thought it would be safe with. I trusted them with my heart. I thought they would treat it gently and tenderly and take care of it. Oh, but Lord, they walked all over it. They crushed it. They broke it, and it didn't even bother them at all. So, here it is Lord! It's shattered! Can you put it back together again? I don't know anywhere else to take it. There's no heart shop around that can fix a broken heart."

"Yes, My child. Please give it to Me. It will be safe here in My hands. I will very tenderly and lovingly mend it. After all, I am the One who made it in the first place. You can trust Me, dear child. I am not like everyone else - I am Almighty God! Whatever you give to Me, I will take care of. I will never disappoint you or leave you or forsake you. But, little one, you must let go when you give Me your heart. I can not fix it with you holding onto it.

Here are My outstretched hands, little one. Just place your broken heart right here. Now, you run on along. You go on back up that mountain and start singing and praising. You ARE victorious! You ARE more than a conqueror! Nothing is going to touch you!You have brought your heart to My heart shop. I love to fix shattered hearts! Leave it here, little one. I've NEVER seen a heart I couldn't fix. I'll make it as good as new!"

PSALM 61:2 *"From the end of the earth will I cry unto Thee, when my heart is overwhelmed; lead me to the rock that is higher than I."*

September 22

Heavenly taste buds

When you were born, you came into the world with a set of taste buds. God gave them to you for a reason. One of the purposes for them is for enjoyment of the food your body needs for growth and development. If you had no taste buds, eating would never be pleasurable or enjoyable, thereby causing you not to get proper nourishment. The basic need of your body for food would often go lacking. Besides giving enjoyment of food, your taste buds are also used for discerning things not meant for consumption. Taste buds tell you what to spit out and reject and also what to eat.

At birth, your taste buds are not fully developed. A young child will put anything in his mouth. He cannot discern the good from the bad. His parent must guide him as to what his body needs. Then, as he matures, he will be able to discern for himself.

When you are born again, you come into the spiritual world with a set of heavenly taste buds. God gives them to you for a reason. One of the purposes is for enjoyment of heavenly things, things you need to grow and develop as a Christian. Your heavenly taste buds will love and enjoy the food of the Word of God. Your spiritual mouth will water over the things of God, like going to church, fellowshipping with other Christians, praying, spending time alone with the Lord, etc. Your heavenly taste buds will also tell you things to spit out and reject, things that are not beneficial to your spirit.

At your spiritual birth, your heavenly taste buds are not fully developed. You will put anything in your spiritual mouth. That's why a baby Christian needs a strong, mature Christian to teach him the good from the bad until he can discern for himself.

How's your heavenly taste buds today? Don't allow the devil to put spiritual novocaine in you and deaden your taste buds to spiritual things. God gave you these taste buds for a reason. Use them as God has designed!

I PETER 2:2,3 *"As newborn babes, desire the pure milk of the Word, that you may grow by it, if so be you have tasted that the Lord is gracious."*

God is too good to send anyone to hell!

Have you ever heard anyone make this statement, "God is too good to send anyone to hell?" That would be like saying, "That is such a good mother. She loves her child so much. She is too good to send her child to the stove and burn his hand nearly off." Now, the fact is that the mother DOES love her child with all her heart. She has made every provision, including changing the knobs on the burners, to provide safety for her child. She has warned her child repeatedly about the stove, telling the little one about all its dangers and how to avoid getting burned. She has even allowed mild doses of touching hot things to impress the reality of the danger on the child's mind. Yes, the mother does love her child! Yes, she is a good mother! And, no, she would never burn her child.

However, the fact remains that the child has a free will. In spite of all the love, in spite of all the teaching and warnings, in spite of all the obstacles placed in the way, the child can still freely exercise his will. He can ignore all that his mother has told him and burn himself badly on the stove. If so, did the mother send her child to the stove to get burned? Of course not! The child did so through disobedience!

Likewise, we have a God that loves us with all His heart. He could have created us as robots, pulling a string and making us say, "I love You, God." But, who wants forced love? So, He gave us a free will, which means we are equally as free to reject Him as to accept Him. He has made every provision for us to be with Him in heaven, even suffering death on the cross to pay for our sins. He has given us His Word and repeatedly warns us of hell, telling us how to avoid it. He even allows us little tastes of it here on earth through the suffering and pain we experience. He has put every obstacle in our way to keep us from going there.

However, the fact remains that we have a free will. So, we can live a lifestyle that says, "No, I do not want You, God. I do not believe Your Word and I do not have any place for it in my life right now. I do not want You running my life. I will run it myself." If we live like this, then one day God will let us have exactly what we want - an existence without Him. He will finally leave us alone and let us go to the only place where He isn't...hell!

Yes, God is too good to send anyone to hell. But, you can send yourself! Choose Him now, and you will live with Him forever. Reject Him now, and you will live without Him forever. If you don't want Him now on earth, what makes you think you would ever change your mind?

JOHN 10:11, 27 *"I am the Good Shepherd...My sheep hear My voice, and I know them, and they follow Me."*

September 24

It's not an earthworm...it's a cobra!

What would you do if you came upon a king cobra, who was poised and ready to strike? You would be suddenly shaken to reality, gripped with fear, and would probably run for your life. You would not hang around disaster, flirting with it, holding hands with it, and hoping everything would be all right. But, if it were an earthworm instead of a cobra, you would have no fear! You would just go right on as though nothing is wrong!

Sin is worse than a deadly cobra. It is poised and ready to strike at all times. However, in our modern age, we have renamed sin. We don't call it a cobra anymore. We call it an earthworm! Homosexuality is no longer a sin. It's an alternate lifestyle. Alcoholism is no longer sin. It's a disease. Gossip is no longer sin. It's therapy. Watching anything you want on TV is no longer sin. It's relaxation. Gluttony is no longer sin. It's a result of my childhood. Since we have renamed sin, we no longer fear it. We flirt with it, hold hands with it, and hang around it until it gets us! Preachers in America are no longer crying out from the pulpits any more about sin. They are too afraid they might offend some of the more influential and affluent members. There are no Jeremiahs, walking up and down the land, crying, "*Oh, that my head were waters, and mine eyes a fountain of tears, that I might weep day and night for the polluted of the daughter of my people.*" *Jeremiah 9:1* Wonder what Isaiah or Jeremiah would do if they were suddenly brought back to life and walked into one of our modern day churches? Do you think for a second that they would get up in the pulpit, pat folks on the back, tell them how much God loves them, and dismiss them back to the cesspool of sin that's wrecking their homes, devastating their lives, and alluring them away from holy living?

No wonder our land is in such a mess! We in the church have been mesmerized, duped, and deceived along with the lost world. We are sleeping sentinels, no longer warning others of the approaching enemy. There's no fear of God and no intense hatred of sin. We are holding hands with the world, the flesh, and the devil. It's time to wake up and realize that it's not an earthworm. It's a cobra...and he's about to strike for the last time!

ISAIAH 30:1 *"Woe to the rebellious children, saith the Lord, who take counsel, but not of Me; and who cover with a covering, but not of My Spirit, that they may add sin to sin."*

September 25

Mission himpossible

Standing on the edge of the Grand Canyon, they were all prepared. The first one backed up quite a distance from the edge, got a good running start, and leaped out over the Canyon as far as he could. However, he only made it about ten feet before he fell to the Canyon floor. The second one backed up even further, got a better running start, and leaped as far as he could. He made it a little further, about twelve feet, but he, too, crash landed at the bottom. Then, the world's champion pole vaulter backed up, with his pole in his hand, ran to the Canyon's edge, and vaulted about twenty-five feet out over the huge chasm. However, he also fell to his death at the bottom just as the others had. All of them tried to jump over the Grand Canyon. Some got further than others, but none of them made it across. Their efforts, no matter how good or noble, still fell short of the mark. This was a mission impossible.

Trying to make it to heaven by human efforts is just as foolish and futile as trying to jump the Grand Canyon. Humanly speaking, it is a mission impossible. The standard by which one reaches heaven is not good works; not baptism or confirmation or church membership; not keeping the Ten Commandments; etc. The standard is perfection. God says, "*Be ye holy, even as I am holy.*" *I Peter 1:16* Therefore, in order to make it to heaven, one must be totally and completely perfect and holy. He must have absolutely no sin on his account… not even one! Now, some may do a little better than others. Some may sin a whole bunch…even to the point of murder, rape, adultery, drugs, etc...and miss the mark, thus falling headlong into hell. Others may not sin quite as much, only being guilty of such things as lying, taking some things that don't belong to them, and covetousness…but they nevertheless miss the mark of perfection and plunge into hell at their death. And then others may be really pretty good people. They may help others, do lots of good things, and be model citizens; yet, they are guilty of occasionally telling a little "white" lie, fudging on income tax, and not always having the best attitude. However, even with all their goodness, they still miss the mark of absolute perfection and plunge into the bottomless pit the same as the most wicked sinner.

Making it to heaven is a mission impossible…impossible, that is, without Him, the One who is totally perfect and holy. Jesus came to earth, lived a completely sinless life, lived the standard of absolute perfection, and then died as our substitute. Accepting Him as our Savior means accepting His perfect life in the place of ours, accepting His standard of perfection rather than our standard of imperfection. He didn't miss the mark!He made it all the way!

So, dear one, don't try to make it to heaven by your own efforts. That is more foolish than trying to jump the Grand Canyon by your efforts. Instead, trust in Him and your mission impossible will become a mission Himpossible!

HEBREWS 12:14 *"Follow peace with all men, and holiness without which no man shall see the Lord."*

September 26

Be still

Our modern, fast-paced society is characterized by ceaseless, busy, time-consuming activity. In this rat race, we have somehow lost the art of being still and knowing that He is God! We race around frantically, living as though each moment must be filled with some kind of project. We fill our time, not only with our endeavors, but with endless noise. We always have a radio or TV or some kind of sound around us to fill the deafening silence we seem to fear. We are a people who do not know how to be alone with God.

When is the last time you spent quality time with the Lord Jesus Christ? This does not mean the times you ran in, got on your knees, and told the Lord what you wanted! Nor does it mean the times you read or studied the Word because you knew you should. It means a time when you laid everything else aside, turned everything off, got totally alone somewhere with your Savior, and spent time with Him. It was a time when you weren't in a rush and had no deadline to meet. It was a time when meeting with Him was the most important and desired thing on your agenda. It was a time when you spent sharing your heart with Him, listening to Him, enjoying His sweet presence, getting to know Him, and sharing His heart and His burdens. It was a time when you could hardly bear the thoughts of anything interfering with or interrupting your intimacy with Him.

Have you EVER spent time with Jesus in this way? Do you even know how to do this, or is your time with Him mechanical, routine, and ritualistic? If it is, you are missing the greatest joy on the face of this earth - time alone with Him! Today, that can change. Plan a time when you can get completely alone, away from all interference. You may have to get up much earlier than everyone else in your household in order to do so. Make sure it is peaceful and quiet. Talk to Him as though He were standing right there, for He is! Treat Him as your dearest friend, for He is! Express your love, appreciation, praise, and devotion to Him. Be still and allow Him to speak to you.

Today, God is waiting for you! He has been waiting a long time, yearning for time with you. He has been watching as you have rushed around. He has been calling you. He has been hurt as you have flippantly and haphazardly come to Him. Listen! What's that I hear? Be still! I think I hear God calling you right now!

PSALM 46:10 *"Be still and know that I am God."*

September 27

What is Jesus worth to you?

Most everything in your life holds some kind of value. Some things are worth a lot, while others are worth very little. Your car, your home, and your possessions are all worth a lot to you. However, they could all be bought for a high enough price. Their worth is only transitory and fleeting. Your family and your best friends are worth a lot to you, too. In fact, there is no price tag that can be placed on them. Their worth is infinite and eternal. They could not be bought for any price.

Well, what is Jesus worth to you? Is He worth your love? Do you tell Him? Do you show Him by the way you live and by your devotion to Him? Can others tell that you love Him by your passion and consecration to Him and to Him alone? Can others see that He is worth everything to you? Do you enjoy spending time with the Lord and is every minute you spend with Him sacred and precious to you? Do you love reading His Word and praying? Do you faithfully attend all services in your church to worship Him and learn of Him? Is He the number one priority in your life, above all other relationships, above all material things, above your job, and above everything else in your life? Is He your all-consuming passion and desire?

Is His worth to you infinite and eternal, bearing no price tag? Or, is there a price tag that can buy your love and time from Him? Perhaps unknowingly you have a price tag. Maybe TV is that tag in your life. You spend much more time in front of it than you do in front of your Savior.You had rather it captivate your mind than have your mind upon Him and upon heavenly things. Or perhaps your flesh is your price tag. It is greedy and insatiable, offering you comfort, ease, rest, and pampering in place of taking up your cross and following Him. It will subtly buy your time and entice you away from your Savior. Or it just could be that some other relationship is your price tag. There is someone you love so much that you had rather spend time with them than with Jesus. You will talk with them for hours, yet talk with the Lord only briefly. Communication with that person is more important to you than communication with Jesus.

Today, exactly what is Jesus worth to you? Whatever He's worth shows by your life. You may deceive yourself, but others know. Just ask your children or your spouse, "As you watch my life, what do you see is the most important thing in the world to me?" They will tell you, especially your children, and you might just be in for a shock. You might find out what Jesus is really worth to you!

I PETER 2:7 *"Unto you, therefore, who believe, He is precious..."*

September 28

Married......or not?

"Oh, honey, I love you and I do want to marry you. But, I just want you to know that I have another lover, too. I will only go and stay with him on weekends. I will stay with you all week. I will love you, cook for you, clean for you, and tell everyone that I am your wife. No one will ever know that I have this other lover. I really do want to be your wife. I want your name. However, I cannot completely and totally give myself to you. I will be your wife, but his occasional lover. I say "Yes" to your proposal of marriage."

Now, what man in his right mind would marry someone with a divided heart?Every man wants a wife who will love him only and will give him her total, undivided affections and loyalty. He wants her to be completely his. There is no way he would marry her if she would not willingly give up all other lovers for him.

Today, there are thousands of people claiming to be Christians, claiming to be married to Christ. The Lord Jesus came along and stirred their hearts, drawing them to Himself and giving them a desire to be His. They did want to be saved. They wanted the name of Christ upon them and wanted an entrance into heaven. So, they said yes to His proposal. However, they wanted another lover, too - the world. They wanted to marry Christ but still have the world also. They thought they could spend a little time with Jesus, reading their Bibles occasionally, praying a few minutes each day, and coming to church as they pleased. But, they still wanted to partake of worldly amusements and indulge in a love affair with the world and all it has to offer.

These people said "yes" to Christ's proposal, thinking they said "yes" to the marriage vows. In reality, they said "yes," but Jesus said "no." He did not take them as His bride. He is a jealous God and will have NO other lovers beside Himself. So, they think they are saved, but are not really married to Him at all.

Today, friend, examine yourself. If you have another lover, if your affections belong to anyone or anything else other than Christ, you may not be saved at all. You cannot be married to Christ and the world. You cannot serve God and mammon. Have you truly given yourself to Him and Him alone? Are you married.....or not?

I JOHN 2:15 *"If any man love the world, the love of the Father is not in him."*

September 29

Where does the problem lie?

You have always been an honest, dependable, reliable, loyal person. You have always kept your word, being of the old school that your word is your bond. How would it make you feel when someone you loved very much just didn't believe you? How would you feel if you gave them your solemn word on something and they did not trust you? It would probably hurt you very deeply. It would grieve you immensely that someone you loved enough to give your life for would ever doubt you.

Trust is one of the most important things in our lives. It is one of the basic, foundational building blocks of a person's character. If you can say you trust someone, truly trust them even with your life, that speaks volumes about that person's character. It would really be better for people to say they trust you with all their hearts rather than love you with all their hearts. You can love someone without trusting them, which is devastating. But, you cannot really trust someone with all your heart without loving them. Love does not necessarily have to be earned.....trust does!

You really do want to be trusted, don't you? Well, how do you think God feels?God is the Creator of the universe. He is the One who spoke it all into existence; the One who holds it all together by His Word; the One who has always taken care of you; the One who should have earned your total, wholehearted trust by now. Yet, you doubt Him. He has given you His Word, even having it all written down for you, but you still don't believe Him! You are walking around murmuring, complaining, fearful, and doubting. Why, you might as well slap Him in the face, because your life says to Him and to others that He cannot be trusted! What an insult, what a grief, what a hurt that is to your Heavenly Father that you do not trust Him!

What have you found in God that causes you to doubt Him? Is He unworthy of your trust? Has He not earned your respect and trust completely? If you doubt, then there's a problem. Either God is unworthy of your trust and incapable of coming through for you. Or else, you have an evil heart of unbelief. So, where does the problem lie.....with God or with you?

HEBREWS 3:12 *"Take heed, brethren, lest there be in any of you an evil heart of unbelief, in departing from the living God."*

September 30

As a little child

Do you feel like you are poor in prayer? Do you ever listen to the prayers of others and feel like you just don't know how to pray? Do you measure yourself spiritually by others and feel that you come up short, causing you to be shy and inward?

Well, dear one, if these feelings describe you, you have missed a very important truth in the Word of God. The Bible says that we are to come to God as little children. How do little children come to their loving parents? They come bankrupt, with nothing to offer. They come asking, even begging. They KNOW that they cannot supply what they need or want, but their parents can.....so they ask! They figure it won't hurt to ask, because they just might get what they are asking for. They do not worry about fancy words or how they sound. They just simply tell their hearts to their parents.

Is this the way you come to God? Do you realize that all of us are just children to Him? Did you know that the ground is level at the foot of the cross? Have you ever realized that, when you kneel before God, you are on equal grounds with every saved person who has ever lived? You have just as much access as did Moses, Abraham, David, Elijah, or Paul. Everyone MUST come to God through Jesus. They must come bankrupt, with absolutely nothing to offer. They must come asking or begging, because they cannot supply their own needs or wants. If they could, they would not need the Lord! They can come without fancy words.....they can just simply come and tell their hearts to Him.

Today, just come to Him as a little child. The child asks and the Father answers. The child cannot supply the answer.....that is why he must ask. Quit worrying over how you sound and trying to figure out all there is to know about prayer. You CAN'T! Just come as a little child. He is waiting!

MATTHEW 18:4 *"Whosoever, therefore, shall humble himself as this little child, the same is greatest in the kingdom of heaven.."*

October

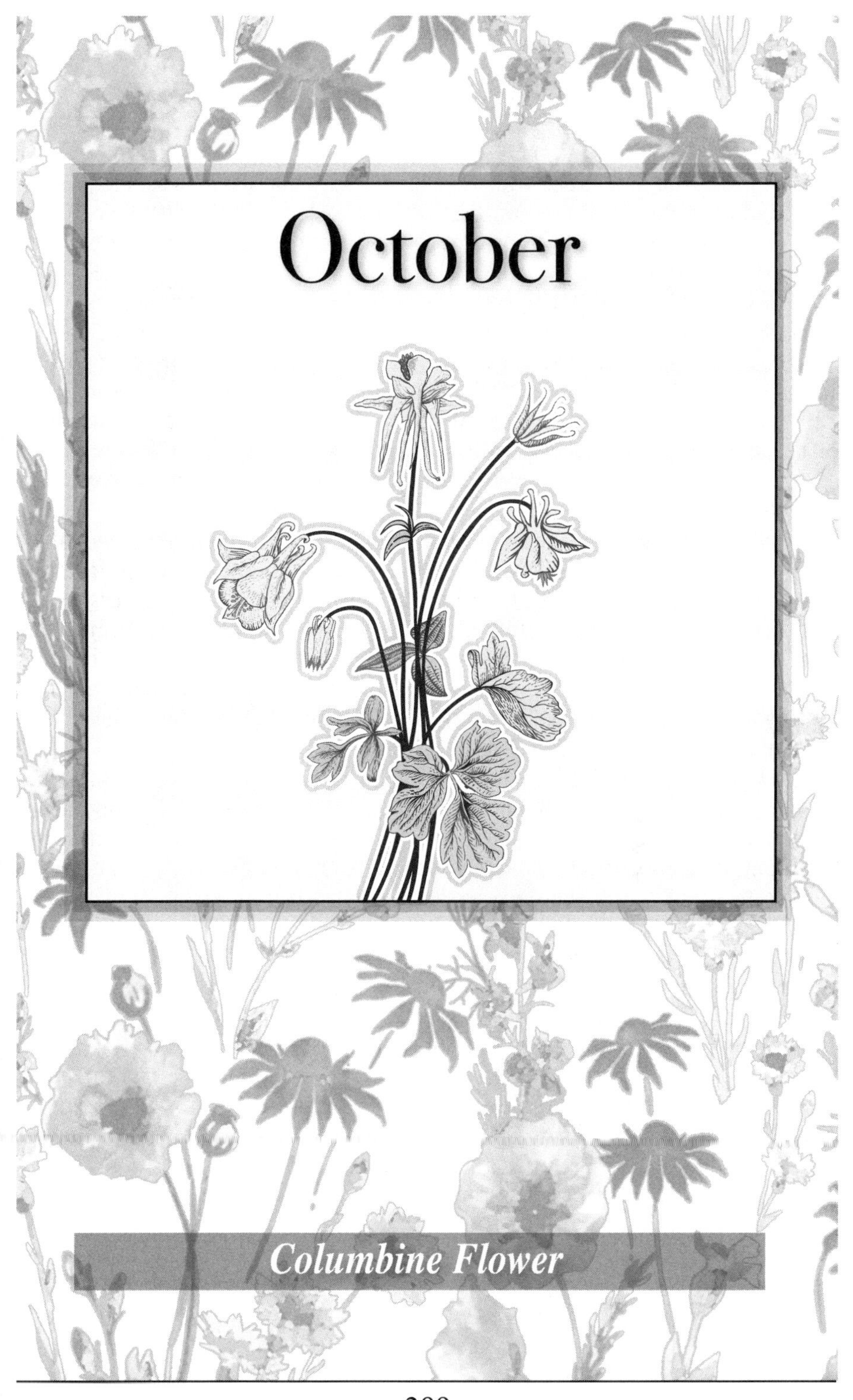

Columbine Flower

October 1

When night falls

At noon, the sun hides the stars in the sky. Likewise, prosperity often hides God's promises. But when night falls, the deep dark night of sorrow, a host of God's promises begin to shine, bringing forth God's blessed hope and comfort from His Word.

It wasn't in the sunlight that the Apostle John received the visions of his Redeemer and wrote the book of Revelation. Rather, it was on the Isle of Patmos...exiled because of his Christian faith, alone, old, forgotten. What appeared to be a deep dark night of the soul to the old Apostle was actually a blessing. It was during this "night" that John was transported to heavenly places in his spirit and received all the wonderful visions about the end of the ages. Without this dark time, this "Isle of Patmos," there would be no book in the Bible called Revelation.

It wasn't in the sunlight that Joseph became second in command over all of Egypt and was able to save his entire family from starvation. Rather, it was in the deep dark night of his soul...sold into slavery by his own brothers; taken to a foreign country away from family and comforts and familiarity and sold to someone else as a slave; falsely accused and imprisoned for something he did not do; and finally, after twenty years, reunited with his family as their earthly savior. Without Joseph's dark time, his years of bondage, the Jewish race might have perished.

It wasn't in the sunlight of Jacob's life that his name was changed to Israel. Rather, it was during a dark period in his life, a time when he was preparing to face his brother, Esau, who had expressed intentions of killing him. Jacob was all alone at the ford, Jabbok, having sent his wives and his children ahead. Facing the night by himself, he wrestled with an angel the entire night. About daybreak, he told the angel he would not let him go until he blessed him. The angel said, *"Thy name shall be called no more Jacob, but Israel; for as a prince hast thou power with God and with men, and hast prevailed." Genesis 32:28* Without this literal night of Jacob's life, he would not have become known as "Israel" and he would never have been used mightily by God.

Friend, perhaps you are in a deep dark night of sorrow. If so, just remember that photographs are always developed in the dark. God is simply trying to develop the image of his Son in you. This "Isle of Patmos" in your life could be one of the greatest blessings you have ever received. So, just look up. You may see many stars of promise that you never noticed in the brightness of the good times.

PSALM 63:6-8 *"On my bed I remember You; I think of You through the watches of the night. Because You are my help, I sing in the shadow of Your wings. My soul clings to You."*

October 2

Polluted bread

In Malachi's day, there was a spiritual cancer in the house of God, yet the priests did not even recognize it. They were still going through the motions of serving God, but God was not accepting them. They were an abomination to Him, nauseating to Him; yet, they lightheartedly carried through with their worship as though everything was great. Their practice was right, as Malachi said, "*Ye offer...*" *Malachi 1:7* They WERE offering to God! Their place was right, as Malachi said, "*upon Mine altar.*" *Malachi 1:7* They were still coming to God's house and making an offering to Him. But, their procedure was an absolute slap in the face of Almighty God, as Malachi said, "*polluted bread.*" *Malachi 1:7* Can you imagine the nerve of those priests to come to the house of God and offer polluted bread upon the altar? They were giving God the leftovers, keeping the best for themselves. They offered the blind, the lame, and the sick, although God required a pure offering. Why, they would not even have done the governor of the land that way! They would have set the best before him..... yet, they gave God the worst.

God asked, "*If, then, I be a father, where is My honor? And if I be a Master, where is My fear?*" *Malachi 1:6* They were calling God their Father and telling people He was their Master, when other things were actually more important to them than God. They did not take the worship of God seriously.

Friend, you could be in that same boat! You are saved, so you call God your heavenly Father.You say He is your Master, so you still come to church on a regular basis. You are offering upon His altar. But, what are you offering Him? Are you giving Him your leftovers? Do you give Him the first part of each day when you are fresh...or do you give Him what is left over at the end of the day? Do you give Him the first of your increase, or what's left over after you have spent on your own needs and wants? Do you give Him your spare time or do you give it to the TV or newspaper? Are you taking the worship of God seriously, giving Him the first, the best, the pure of all that you have? Is He your number one priority?

Dear one, perhaps today your practice is right, because you are offering. And maybe the place is right, as you are a regular church attender. But, is your procedure right? Are you offering God the best of yourself on the altar.....or are you offering polluted bread?

MALACHI 1:7 "*Ye offer polluted bread upon Mine altar...*"

October 3

A degree in kneeology

They all graduated from the same college. They all held the same degree. And they all used their degrees in life. You've probably heard of all of them..... Abraham, Moses, Samuel, David, Jonah, Isaiah, Jeremiah, Elijah, Elisha, Paul, Peter, James, John.....just to name a few. They all impacted many lives for eternity with their hardearned degrees.

These men all graduated from the school of experience with a degree in "kneeology." Elijah, being one of the graduates, used his degree repeatedly. He found it to be better than a degree in economics and aviation, because it provided meat and bread daily to him during a famine.....flown in on the wings of ravens. He found it to be better than the degree of meteorologists, because it enabled him to call down fire from heaven and call down rain after a long drought. He found it to be better than the degree of a forensic specialist, because it enabled him to raise a widow's son from the dead.

Moses was another graduate with a "kneeology" degree. And he used it often. He found it to be better than a D.D., because he used it to obtain Miriam's healing from leprosy. He found it to be better than a geologist's degree, because he used it to bring an earthquake, swallowing up those who had provoked the Lord. He found it to be better than a chemist's degree, because he used it to bring forth water out of a rock. And he found it to be better than the degrees of all the court of Pharaoh, the king of Egypt. He used it to bring ten successive plagues upon the Egyptians.

You can attend the same school as these great men and you can graduate with the same degree. "Kneeology" is the most desired degree anyone can receive. With this degree, one has immediate and unhindered access to any place on earth at any time whatsoever. One has access worldwide to king's castles, the White House, the Taj Mahal, the U.N., the Supreme Court, etc. If we only had more "kneeology" instead of "theology," we, too, could impact our world today for God!

LUKE 18:1 *"that men ought always to pray, and not to faint..."*

October 4

Start breaking up those tiles

They had heard that Jesus was in Capernaum. What exciting news this was...to realize that He was nearby and they could actually get to Him. They wasted no time in making preparations to go. Their friend was paralyzed with palsy, for which there was no cure or help. He could not get to Jesus because of his condition, but they could take him!They knew there was no other help under the sun - no doctor, no medicines, no diet, no exercise, no other way for their friend to be helped. He needed Jesus!

Carrying their friend on a small bed, the four friends made their way to Jesus. He was preaching the Word to many gathered in a house in the town. The crowd completely filled the house, making it impossible for the four to get to Jesus. But, they were determined to get to the Lord, no matter what it took, because they knew that He was the only One who could help. So, they went up on the roof and broke up the tiling, making an opening large enough for the bed to go through. They lowered their friend right down into the presence of the Lord Jesus Christ. When Jesus saw THEIR faith, He first touched the man's soul, forgiving him of his sins. Then, He touched the man's body and healed him instantaneously.

There is someone in your life that you are gravely concerned about, someone very dear and close to you. You have tried talking to this one about his condition - only to no avail. You have done everything you know to do, but nothing has worked. Your friend needs Jesus! You are wasting your breath and efforts, because YOU cannot do a thing. Realize that your friend is paralyzed spiritually and cannot get to the only help available, which is Jesus. In fact, your friend probably does not even want to get to the Lord. But, YOU can take him! Put him on a cot of your prayers and carry him straight to the Lord. Do whatever it takes to get your friend to Him, no matter how long it takes. It may take years to break up all the obstructions that are blocking entrance to Jesus' presence. But, do not give up! Keep on praying! Keep on believing! You get that bed up on that roof and start breaking up tiles through persistent prayer. One day, that last tile will be removed and your friend will finally be in the presence of the King of glory. Perhaps when Jesus sees YOUR faith, He will touch your friend's soul and body. Time's wasting! Start breaking up those tiles today!

MARK 2:5 *"When Jesus saw their faith, He said...*
Son, thy sons are forgiven thee."

October 5

The valley of achor

"I am now going to allure her, and bring her into the wilderness, and speak tenderly unto her. And I will give her her vineyards there, and the Valley of Achor for a door of hope; and she shall sing there, as in the days of her youth, and as in the day when she came up out of Egypt." Hosea 2:14, 15 Wow! What a strange and unusual verse! In the first place, a wilderness is not normally a place where you would find vineyards and it is certainly not a place to which you would allure a loved one. Yet, God is telling Israel that He is going to allure her and bring her into the wilderness where He will speak tenderly to her and give her the vineyards there.

Could it be that God allures us, like Israel, to the wilderness, the desert areas of life, the lonely places of isolation, so that we can find the true riches of life? Maybe it's because we just don't really want Him or seek Him as long as we are on prosperous territory. We get so busy with our toys and trinkets and entertainment that we just do not have the time for Him any more and can no longer hear His voice. He must allure us to the wilderness so He can speak tenderly to us...and so we can have receptive ears once again.

Once in the wilderness, we find ourselves in the Valley of Achor (which means troubled). This valley of troubles often leads us back to God. In our desperation in this valley, we cry out for His help and deliverance and find that the Valley of Achor is actually a "door of hope," leading us, not only to the vineyards, but to the Vinedresser Himself. As our wonderful Vinedresser provides for us miraculously in the desert of our lives, we rediscover Him and fall in love with Him all over again. And, believe it or not, He so spoils us in the wilderness that we might not even want to come out of it.

Friend, I don't know about you, but I'd much rather be in the wilderness with my Vinedresser speaking tenderly to me and giving me His vineyards than to be anywhere else in the world without Him. It is in the Valley of Achor that I will sing, as in the days of my youth, for there is always a song of joy and peace and victory in the presence of the Vinedresser! So, give me the Valley of Achor, Lord...it is there that I will find my "door of hope!"

Hosea 2:14 *"I am now going to allure her, and bring her into the wilderness, and speak tenderly to her. And I will give her her vineyards there, and the Valley of Achor for a door of hope..."*

October 6

You cannot conquer your Midian

For seven years, the children of Israel had been under oppression from the Midianites. They were powerless against this huge number of nomads, who would encamp against them and destroy the increase of their land. These Midianites would use the Israelites' pasture lands for their own herds and flocks and would take the produce of the children of Israel for themselves. Relentlessly, year after year, the Midianites would come upon them, never allowing them to get ahead. In fact, the children of Israel even made themselves dens in the mountains and caves, hiding themselves and what little they had from the raiding nomads.

Out of this fearful, weak, retreating band of Israelites, God called one man, named Gideon, to deliver them. Gideon was the least in his father's house, not having a reputation as a prominent and mighty warrior. He was hiding from the Midianites, too. In fact, he was in hiding, threshing wheat, when God called him. However, he responded to the call and prepared for battle, according to the Lord's instructions.

What a strange battle this was! Here was a leader that would probably never have been voted "Most Likely to Succeed." To add to this situation, God required Gideon's army to be drastically reduced. As they went forward to battle, there were only 300 men going against 135,000; their weapons were trumpets and pitchers and lamps. Humanly speaking, victory was impossible! They had an inexperienced leader, they were outnumbered 450 to 1, and they had no weapons with which battles are normally fought. But, they had God... and God is all that anyone needs! They won! God had first stripped them of every ounce of human ability and effort until their total reliance was upon Him and Him alone. And, then He secured the victory for them!

Perhaps there is a Midianite situation in your life today. It is oppressive, relentless, and overwhelming. It robs you of things dear to you.. It seems hopeless, causing you to retreat and withdraw. You are outnumbered, having no strength of your own to conquer it. You have no weapons with which to fight. You are on the verge of giving up. Well friend, God is simply trying to strip you of every ounce of self-reliance so you can trust Him! You cannot conquer your Midian. But, God can...and He WILL, if you will let Him do it His way instead of yours!

ISAIAH 26:4 *"Trust ye in the Lord forever; for in the Lord God is everlasting strength."*

October 7

A spiritual couch potato

To develop a strong physical body requires effort. Strength is never made from laxity and indifference. Muscles are developed and strengthened only through proper nourishment and exercise. Just fail to feed your muscles properly and they will grow weak. Quit exercising them and they will atrophy. The course of least resistance is NOT the course your body needs to take. It will result in you being a fat, lazy, couch potato, having barely enough energy and stamina to function.

The body has a strong tendency to take the easy route. It likes to be pampered, not pushed. It had rather swim with the flow than against it. It had rather ride the bike downhill than uphill. It had rather rock than run. However, strength is not developed on the downhill side, nor on going with the flow, nor on rocking. Strength requires effort. When you see a muscular body-builder, you know he did not accidentally fall into it. It took effort!

It takes effort to be spiritually strong, too. When you see a strong Christian, you can rest assured that he did not get that way accidentally. It came through much effort! Spiritual muscles are developed and strengthened only through proper nourishment and exercise. They must be fed with the Word of God. The TV, newspapers, and magazines will NEVER feed your spiritual muscles. Only the Bible contains the spiritual vitamins and minerals your soul needs for good health.

Besides feeding your spiritual muscles, you must exercise them or they will atrophy. You must obey the Word of God, which requires much effort on your part. The Word pushes the soul rather than pampers it. It requires commitment, dedication, and persistence! It is NOT the course of least resistance. It is hard! However, spiritual strength is not developed on the coasting side. It never comes out of laxity and indifference.

Today, God is looking, not for body-builders, but for some strong, spiritually muscular soul-builders. There is much spiritual work to be done; yet there are very few soul builders around to do it. There are too many couch potatoes…too many spiritually fat, lazy Christianettes, always following the course of least resistance.

If you're a spiritual couch potato at the present time, shame on you! Get up off that sofa, get out from in front of the TV set, and start you a daily spiritual workout. It won't be long before you'll begin looking like a spiritual soul-builder and will be useful in the kingdom of God.

I CORINTHIANS 16:13 *"Watch, stand fast in the faith, quit you like men, be strong."*

October 8

Shop-aholics in the devil's workshop

You buy a beautiful diamond ring. Before you purchase it, you thoroughly check it out for imperfections and flaws, but you find none. The jeweler takes it back to his workroom and, unknown to you, substitutes a cubic zirconium in place of the diamond. What you have looks good to the untrained eye, but it is only a worthless substitute. You have been unknowingly deceived and are falsely satisfied with your new purchase.

The devil is that jeweler. His workshop is filled with beautiful jewels, which he delights in showing to you. And he is a clever, topnotch, master salesman! When he finishes with his sales pitch, you are hooked.....persuaded that this is just what you need! However, you fail to recognize that the devil only carries worthless substitutes in his workshop. They are all beautiful to the eye but they are worthless. You will leave his workshop with a false satisfaction over your purchase.

One of the devil's favorite target markets is the church. There are many educated and enlightened church leaders of our day who have become shop-aholics in the devil's workshop. They have gone on shopping sprees, buying all kinds of programs, methods, music, and ministries to draw people in and grow their churches. Now, these things look good and sound good. In fact, they ARE good.....but they are only substitutes. These leaders are depending on substitutes to draw people into their churches and make them want to be a part of the church. In reality, they are saying that they need something else besides Jesus to draw people. Is Jesus alone not enough? Remember: what you get people with is what you have to keep them with.

Church leaders have shopped and bought the idea that times have changed, so the church must change in order to get and keep people. Yes, times have changed, but Jesus NEVER changes! If Jesus alone is what the church is drawing people with, then times have absolutely nothing to do with it.

It is time we get out of the devil's workshop and go shopping in God's market. Let's buy some fasting, some weeping, some old-fashioned preaching on sin, and some agonizing and travailing and prolonged prayer to get people in and keep them. That's what Jesus did! It worked then.....and it will still work now!

DEUTERONOMY 11:16 *"Take heed to yourselves, that your heart be not deceived..."*

October 9

I was one of those kittens

On the news, there was a story of a fire in a vacant building. As the firemen arrived at the scene, they noticed a cat. She kept going back into the fiery inferno, each time returning with a kitten. She did this five times, until she had saved all her little ones from their burning graves. The firemen had wanted to help her but could not locate the kittens. The mother cat was the only one who knew where they were and could rescue them. As she faithfully went back into the fire five times, her fur was burned off and her eyes were swollen shut.

What made this cat perform such an unselfish act? No animal would even think of going into a fire, not even once, much less five times. However, this cat had only one reason, a reason that was greater than she, and a reason that drove her beyond fear, beyond pain, and even beyond concern for her own life. That one reason was love!

Oh, what a picture of our Lord and Savior, Jesus Christ. I was one of those kittens! I was a lost sinner, dying in my sin and wretchedness. I was on my way to hell, that everlasting fiery inferno, where the flames are never quenched. Unable to rescue myself, I needed a deliverer. There I was, in utter hopelessness and despair. No one knew where I was. No one could help!

As I cried out in despair, my heavenly Father heard my cry. He left heaven and came down to earth, knowing He would suffer unbelievably in order to save me. But, He did not care! He had a reason greater than He, a reason that drove Him beyond fear, beyond pain, and beyond concern for His own life. That reason was love! His love for me caused Him to be beaten unmercifully, until the skin on His back hung in bloody ribbons. His love for me caused His beard to be plucked from His face, leaving it swollen beyond recognition. His love for me caused Him to be mocked, spit upon, slapped, rejected, and crucified on a cross, the slowest and most torturous death conceivable. His love for me put Him on the cross to pay the penalty for my sin and to rescue me from eternal damnation.

Thank You, Jesus, for Your love for me! I cannot ever repay You for what you did for me, but I can certainly abandon and surrender my life totally to You. From this day forward, I have decided to be a dedicated, consecrated, devoted, faithful, loyal, completely trusting, appreciative follower. You gave Your life for me…and now, I give mine to You!

HEBREWS 12:2 *"Looking unto Jesus...who for the joy that was set before Him endured the cross."*

October 10

Broadcast from on high

Can a TV program that's being filmed live in America be seen in China while it is in progress? In bygone days, this was impossible, because of the curvature of the earth. A TV signal could not go from the USA to China, because the world lay between the two. But in this modern age, TV signals are beamed up to a satellite hovering above the earth, and then beamed down to other places, even on the opposite side of our planet.

This is just as true spiritually as it is physically. We have spiritual messages that we so desperately want our loved ones and friends and all those around us to receive. So, we try talking to them, showing them, and anything else we can think of to give them the message. But, we are sending messages horizontally and the world lies between us and them. Therefore, they don't get the message at all. It is time we learned that we first must pray. We must send our spiritual messages to our Heavenly Father; we must communicate back and forth with Him who sits enthroned in the third heaven, far above this earth. Then He, and He alone, can broadcast this message into the person's receptacle, their heart. He is the only One who can get past the world and implant the message; otherwise, it just vanishes into thin air.

Hudson Taylor, the great missionary to China, whose life impacted thousands of Chinese, said, "I am determined to move men through God by prayer alone." Others have said, "You can do a whole lot more talking to God about them than you can talking to them about God." Our problem is that we find it easier to talk to them than to God. We want to spend five or ten minutes a day in prayer; yet, we want God to save our loved ones, bless our families, and heal our land! A TV program involves hundreds of hours of preparation, commitment, dedication, grueling work, self-denial, agony, etc.....all to get out a message. What an utter shame that we who have the message of eternal life aren't that committed to getting our message out!

Whether you have realized it or not, you are a broadcaster. You have a Divine message that everyone needs to hear. But, that message must first be vertical. You must communicate with the Lord in prayer. Then, He will send His message down through you and out to the lost! Remember: the world stands between you and them, so the message must be broadcast from on high.

PSALM 109:4 *"...but I give myself unto prayer."*

Pulling groceries off the shelves and spitting

You are in the grocery store. Coming down the aisle toward you are a father and his two children. The children are pulling groceries off the shelves, spitting on each other, and running around wildly. Do you go up, grab the children, and begin to administer discipline to them? As much as you'd love to, you cannot do that, because the children aren't yours. If they were your children, it would be different!

Maybe you look at the world around you and see many people just running wild. They are arrogant, having little regard for others. They will do anything to get ahead, including stepping on anyone they can to advance. They live as they please and are prospering. Everything they touch seems to turn to gold. You wonder how they can continue in such prosperity when they aren't living like they should. Why doesn't God stop them?

Well friend, you must realize that they do not belong to God! They are NOT His children! Just as Jesus said to the Pharisees, "*You are of your father, the devil, and the lusts of your father you will do,*" so He would say to many today. Before you get upset or jealous or frustrated over those who prosper in their wickedness, just remember to whom they belong and where they are going when this life is over. You would NOT be angry, jealous, or frustrated if you could only see their final end. You would try to win them to Christ instead!

Quit trying to measure yourself by the world around you. They have a different father than you do. Your Father loves you and has guidelines and boundaries for your life. When you disobey, He administers discipline. He loves you too much to let you run wild, do your own thing, hurt yourself and others, and bring shame and disgrace to Himself. He has a big woodshed, which you will often visit as a child of God. When you do, then humbly accept His loving discipline. Repent of your wrongdoing and be thankful that you have a Father who won't let you run wildly down the aisles, pulling groceries off the shelves, and spitting. Discipline is painful, but it certainly is a blessing when you think of the alternative!

HEBREWS 12:6 *"For whom the Lord loves He chastens and scourges every son whom he receives."*

October 12

Playing possum

King Jehoshaphat and the children of Israel were surrounded by enemies. The armies of Ammon, Moab, and Mt. Seir had come against them, making the situation look pretty grim! In fact, there was NO way to defeat such overwhelming odds! So, what did Jehoshaphat do? He called the entire nation to prayer and fasting. He did not try to figure out any military strategy; he did not have a conference with the mighty warriors; he did not even try one single human method. It was too late for that! Unless God supernaturally intervened, they would be destroyed! Their only hope was a Divine interruption, and the only way to get that was through prayer and fasting. They did it and it worked!

America is surrounded by enemies. They have invaded our homes, our schools, our government, our economy, and even our churches and have almost taken over. The situation in our country looks pretty grim. In fact, there is NO way humanly to defeat such overwhelming odds, because it is intertwined into the very fabric of our society. It would take years to unravel the mess we have made. It's too late for us to do anything!

But, wait! What did Jehoshaphat do? He knew his ONLY hope was a Divine move of God. He put aside every attempt to change things and began fasting and praying until he heard from the Lord. Would it work for us? Well, God hasn't changed one bit! He's the same yesterday, today, and forever. He says if His people, the Christians, would humble themselves and pray and seek His face and turn from their wicked ways, He will heal their land!

Christian, is that what you're doing? Are you fasting and weeping for your dear land? Are you praying real agonizing and travailing prayer for America? Or, are you usually thrown up in front of the TV set, on your back instead of on your face? Are you playing possum, rolled up in your little smug, comfortable, uncommitted ball, hoping danger will go away? Well, it's NOT! Playing possum won't save America.....but fasting, agonizing, travailing prayer will! Will you join me down on your knees in calling America back to God?

ISAIAH 19:20 *"...for they shall cry to the Lord because of the oppressors... and He shall deliver them."*

October 13

Commit self-icide

Yep, this is it…the final straw, the one that broke the camel's back. I am throwing up my hands! I'm giving up! I quit! I just cannot take it any longer. This maze of circumstances, these black clouds of doubt and despair, and all these endless problems have finally pushed me to the brink of desperation. I have landed on the shores of wit's end. The harder I have tried, the worse things have gotten. And I am sorry, but I am not gonna try any more. I am just plain tired and worn out! The fight is all gone out of me. I have really had it this time. There is only one solution that I can think of…and that's out! I want out and I am getting out. I am going to go commit self-icide!

Yoo, hoo, self! Come here! Quit all your wiggling and squirming. No use running either…you are NOT going to rule me any longer. I am nailing you to this cross. I am putting you to death. You have whined and complained about your circumstances and blamed everybody else for them until I am sick of hearing it. You have worried over your situation day and night, planning and scheming and thinking of every possible human solution. You have always been determined to have your way, never allowing anyone to rest until you get what you want. You have been in control of me most of the time. But, let me tell you something…as of today, self, I am taking you out of the driver's seat, turning everything over to the Lord Jesus Christ, and giving Him full control of my life. I have finally gotten it through my thick head that I have a choice. And I choose Jesus rather than you!

Friend, perhaps you too are having problems with "self." Maybe you are suffering from repeated "self attacks," which leave you spiritually weak and impotent. "Self" is generally in control of you, making demands of your time, your energies, your monies, and really your very life itself. These "self attacks" are draining you and robbing you of your vital relationship with the Lord Jesus Christ. And as long as you allow "self" to reign on the throne of your life, you will never live a victorious, abundant, fruitful Christian life.

However, there is good news for you! There is an answer to your dilemma. Every time your flesh rises up to have its way, just determine in your heart to commit "self-icide." Put that "self" on the cross, kill it, and let Jesus be Jesus in you!

GALATIANS 5:24 *"And they that are Christ's have crucified the flesh with its affections and lusts."*

October 14

Jerk the devil's needle out of your arm!

Ordinary. . .humdrum . . .repetitious . . .unexciting . . . boring . . . predictable. . . stale... just barely existing! Does this describe your life? Have you become so apathetic and listless that your spiritual speed would even embarrass a snail?

Friend, you are a prisoner! The devil has taken you captive and is holding you in chains of your own choice. He is your anesthesiologist, keeping you sedated and unresponsive to the reality of God, keeping you in a twilight state spiritually, and keeping your mind dulled with temporal things. You are just lying there, letting him keep that old needle of lies flowing into your arm.

Well, it's high time you jerk the devil's needle out of your arm, rip off those chains he has enslaved you with, get up out of that prone position, and LIVE! You are a child of God! Your Father is the King of all kings, the Lord of all lords, and the Creator of the whole universe. He is the supernatural, all-powerful, Almighty, everlasting God. He is the mighty Conqueror, having defeated death, hell, and the grave. He has overcome the world. He says you are His heir and joint-heirs with Christ. He says you are more than a conqueror through Christ, who loves you. He says all things are possible to him who believes. He says you can do all things through Christ, who strengthens you.

Then, how come you are living like you are? You are believing anesthetic lies instead of believing the life-changing truths of God's Word. Get that needle out of your arm and get in the Word of God. Get in it with enthusiasm and excitement, just like it's the million dollar lottery and you just won it. It's worth far, far more than any million dollars could ever even hope to be. Read it and every time you come to a promise, believe it! Get up and start acting like it's so, even when it isn't so, and watch it become so in front of your eyes. You'll get excited then! Start living out what God's Word says. It's a supernatural book, surpassing all natural laws and reasonings and opinions. It's God's Word! It promises abundant, overflowing, joy-filled, exciting life to those who read, believe, and heed. Jerk the devil's needle, filled with his anesthetic lies, out of your arm and start believing God's Truth instead!

MARK 9:23 *"If you can believe, all things are possible to him that believes."*

October 15

Spiritual termites

You are worried! Bills are due, money is short, and time is not in your favor right now. That frequent, unwanted visitor has invaded your life again, giving you the sinking feeling of being pressed down by a weight of a million pounds. Worry is a relentless, hounding, unwelcome intruder, robbing you physically, mentally, emotionally, and spiritually. It goes with you everywhere, even to bed at night. And once those spiritual termites of worry gain access into your life, they will silently gnaw and eat away until even once strong areas in your life begin to crumble.

As a Christian, you know you are not supposed to worry. So you try not to worry, but that's about like trying not to breathe. After all, it's in your genes and you just cannot help it. And besides, this is reality! You cannot just bury your head in the sand and pretend that all is well. That will not work either!

Well friend, you cannot get rid of termites unless you know what you are doing. You have been dealing with the fruit and not the root. Worry is the fruit. The root of your problem is unbelief. You do NOT believe God! By your worry, you are calling God a liar. You are saying that He cannot take care of you, so you must try to figure it out yourself. So you spend all this time figuring out ways to solve your problem instead of spending that same amount of time in earnest prayer and communion with the Lord Jesus Christ. Oh, you do pray some, but your whole focus even then is man-centered. Your focus is entirely on your problem, so you stay wrapped up in your little, bitty perspective. Get your focus on God! Start praising Him and thanking Him and meditating on His awesomeness and grandeur. As you stand in the light of His presence, your problem suddenly melts into nothingness.

After being with Him and being filled with His Spirit, then His wisdom takes control and attacks your problem, like the Orkin man does termites. Friend, get alone with God and focus on Him. His presence drives away spiritual termites... and His presence will keep you from making those rash decisions in the future that brought in the spiritual termites in the first place. God is the Expert! Call 911-O'HEAVEN today for help!

PHILIPPIANS 4:6 *"Be anxious for nothing, but in everything by prayer and supplication, with thanksgiving, let your requests be made known unto God."*

October 16

LSD trip

He was with them when it all happened. It was the most awesome series of events he had ever seen. They had been wandering in the wilderness for years, fed with manna straight from heaven. He knew God would provide, as he had witnessed supernatural provisions with his own eyes day by day. Then, they had come to the Jordan River, which stood between the wilderness and the land of Canaan. He had watched the waters roll back until they had all passed through to the other side…on dry ground, nonetheless. He had living proof that his God was all powerful! And, if all that wasn't enough, he then stood with them at Jericho and watched as walls that were twenty-five feet high and twenty feet thick in some places just crumbled to the ground. He saw first-hand that God meant what He said and that obedience to God's Word always worked.

Oh yes, he had been there through it all. But being an eyewitness of the supernatural miracles of God did not make him a devout believer. Achan instead took an LSD trip...lust, sin, death...even after having great experiences with the God of his fathers. He SAW some things that were appealing to him after entering the land of Canaan, some things that God had forbidden. His glance turned into a longing look, as he COVETED these things. Temptation now turned into sin, as he TOOK them. And, then he did what sin often times leads us to do...he HID them. When his sin was uncovered by God (*"Be sure your sin will find you out), Numbers 32:23 he and his family were all stoned to death for direct violation of God's Word. "But every man is tempted, when he is drawn away of his own lust and enticed. Then when LUST has conceived, it brings forth SIN; and sin, when it is finished, brings forth DEATH." James 1:14, 15* LSD trip!

Friend, just because you have had some supernatural, mountaintop experiences with God, that does NOT assure you of faithfully following Him. Do not ever underestimate your own flesh. Within your flesh dwells NO good thing! Experiences are wonderful, but do not ever base your Christian walk on them. Your experiences and your feelings can change from day to day. They come and go. But God's Word never changes, so base your Christian walk on it. Realize that the great experiences of life are like spiritual desserts. They are good. It's great to have them occasionally…but they will not sustain life and they will rot your spiritual teeth. You need the strong meat of God's Word for a healthy, vibrant spiritual life.

JAMES 1:15 *"when lust has conceived, it brings forth sin; and sin, when it is finished, brings forth death."*

October 17

Is hell real?

Do you believe that hell is real? You might be thinking to yourself that you have never seen it, or you have never known of anyone coming back from there to tell you, so it is not really real in your mind. Well you have never seen wind either, but wind is real. You have never seen thought, but thought is real. You have never seen gravity, but gravity is real. There are many things that are real that you have never seen.

How do you know what these things are if you cannot see them? How do you know what gravity is? How do you know that wind is what moves leaves on trees instead of some little invisible being from another planet? You know because scientists and other experts have told you. You have studied books written by these experts. Everything you know concerning your physical world you have learned through what others have told you.

Well isn't it strange that you would believe what other men have written down about our universe, yet you wouldn't believe what God has written down? You believe there are nine planets in our solar system. You believe our sun is ninety-three million miles away. Do you know that for sure? Have you personally measured the distance to the sun?Or, are you accepting by faith what someone else has said? Well, if you accept by faith what scientists tell you, why can't you accept by faith what the Creator God tells you in the Bible?

Friend, the Bible speaks of a literal hell. Jesus Christ Himself spoke more about hell than about heaven. Now, if the Bible is a lie, you have nothing to worry about, because you will just cease to exist when you die. But, if the Bible is true, then you will either go to a literal heaven or a literal hell when you die physically. It does not matter what you feel or what your opinion is. God's Word is truth, and truth is never changed by what anyone thinks or feels.

According to God's Word, there is an everlasting, burning lake of fire. Everyone whose names are not recorded in the Lamb's Book of Life will go there in eternity. Are you absolutely, positively, 100% sure that your name is in that Book? You do not have to guess! You can know! God's Word tells you how to be saved and to know it beyond a shadow of a doubt. You believe scientists...why don't you try believing God?

REVELATION 20:15 *"And whoever was not found written in the book of life was cast into the lake of fire.."*

October 18

Only vippies can get in to see the king

A V.I.P. always gets preferential treatment everywhere he goes. He gets the best seat, the best table, and the best service. He is recognized and looked up to, being treated differently than the average person. People make over him, stand in line just to get his autograph, and roll out the red carpet for him. And because of his V.I.P. status, he often can go places into which the common person would not be allowed entrance.

Well maybe you are not a V.I.P. here on this earthly terrain, but you ARE on heaven's soil. If you are saved, you have been purchased by the King of all the universe. He paid the most expensive cost that could ever be paid, the royal blood of His dear Son, to redeem you. That makes you of priceless value to Him! You are His purchased, valuable, precious, dear, treasured possession!

Wow! Talk about a V.I.P.! That's as Vippie as you can get! You belong to the King of all kings, the Lord of all lords. You have access to His throne room twenty-four hours a day. His throne room is an unbelievable place. The unsaved cannot go there. Only V.I.P.'s in heaven have access to this glorious place... Vippies like you. You do not even have to have an appointment. You can go into His throne room any time day or night and He is always there waiting for you. He is always glad to see you. In fact, He will even roll out the red carpet for you. You can go crawl right up in His lap and tell Him whatever is on your heart. He will give you grace and mercy to help in your time of need. He will give you His wisdom for your trials. He will fill you with His joy, His peace, His forgiveness, and His love. All the unsearchable riches of Christ are there in that throne room, too. They are yours...free...if you will just come in and spend some time there.

How often do YOU visit heaven's throne room? How long do you usually stay?You see, you have an adversary who wants to keep you out of that throne room, because he knows what's in there. So, he will put all kinds of interruptions and diversions in your way to detour you. Today, why don't you go into that throne room to spend some valuable time with your King? His royal blood has bought you and made you a Vippie, giving you access to His throne room both now and eternally. Only Vippies can get in to see the King!

HEBREWS 4:16 *"Let us, therefore, come boldly to the throne of grace that we may obtain mercy and find grace to help in time of need."*

October 19

Peach tree oil

Growing up, I received quite a few doses of "peach tree oil," as my Mother called it. Now, I wasn't fond of "peach tree oil" at all. In fact, I trembled when it was mentioned. It was always used in connection with my disobedience. When I didn't mind my Mother, she told me she was going to give me a good dose of "peach tree oil." Then, while I watched numbly, she headed for the peach tree in the back yard, where she proceeded to break off a nice, long, limber peach tree switch. As she entered the house, I held my breath in anticipation of the dose of "peach tree oil," which she promptly administered to my bare legs.

You'd think, as much as I disliked "peach tree oil" that I would never disobey again. Disobedience ALWAYS brought on that dreaded switch! However, I still continued to get into trouble fairly often in spite of the peach tree. Gradually, as I grew older, I finally learned that disobedience does not pay and is certainly not worth the consequences.

Today, I am so thankful for the "peach tree oil." I learned as a young child that, what my parents said, they meant. If I was told I'd get a spanking, then I got one. I was never threatened or yelled at. I was just simply told what to do and what not to do and disobedience always brought discipline. That sure has made it easier for me as an adult to believe God. I just believe God means what He says.....I was brought up that way! And I believe that disobedience, or sin, always results in the peach tree. Since I wasn't raised on the second, or third, or fourth chance principle, then I believe that God brings swift and immediate discipline. He has a great big peach tree, and He never fails to administer a good dose of "peach tree oil" when I don't mind Him!

Parents, don't threaten your children. Just tell them one time.....and discipline them if they disobey. It will sure help them to believe God when they grow older. If they don't believe you mean what you say, then they won't believe God does either. If you tell them more than once, they will figure God will too. And boy will they ever be in for a shock. Sin is ALWAYS followed by a big dose of God's "peach tree oil." You can teach that to your children now.....or they can learn it later when the consequences are much more severe!

HEBREWS 12:10 *"but He for our profit (chastens us) that we might be partakers of His holiness.."*

October 20

Raise those blinds all the way to the top

Are there blinds on your windows? If so, you have reasons for them being there. Blinds keep the light out. They block the sun's rays from entering the room. You may want the rays to come in at times, but there are other times, especially if you are trying to sleep during the day, that you would want to block out entrance of the light. Not only do blinds keep light from entering a room, they also keep what is in a room from being seen on the outside. You close your blinds when you do not want someone seeing in. You are the one who controls the blinds. You open or close them by an act of your will, at your own discretion.

Spiritually, you have blinds on the windows of your soul. You can open or close them any time you choose. You are the one who controls these blinds. Sometimes, you close them to block the Son's rays from entering your soul. The Word of God is sharp, powerful, cutting, and brings death to your flesh. You do not always want to hear it, because it brings deep conviction. So, you close the blinds. You hear with your ears but block entrance of the words into your soul by your independent spirit. Pride, rebellion, stubbornness, unbelief, stiffness, hardness, self-centeredness, idolatry, and a host of other things all close the blinds to the windows of your soul.

Then, there are occasions when you close the blinds deliberately and do not even go back to open them. You put the Word of God on a shelf and leave it there for days, or perhaps even weeks. You have totally blocked out the Sons' rays, leaving your soul dark and cold.

Sometimes, you close the blinds to keep people on the outside from seeing what's on the inside. You are spiritually undressed and don't want anyone to know. You are not open and free and loving with others, because you have closed the blinds. You try to put up a front, making everyone think things are fine on the inside when, in reality, you are dying within.

Dear one, why don't you raise those blinds all the way to the top today? Let your soul be flooded with light from the Son. Let everything within be visible to the outside world. Your soul needs the light and warmth from the Son. It also needs to be real and genuine with others. Open up and let the Son shine in!

II CORINTHIANS 4:4 *"In whom the god of this age has blinded the minds of them who believe not..."*

October 21

Would the real reason please stand up?

Would the real reason please stand up? Who is behind all this madness? Why is it that a young teenage girl cannot get her ears pierced without her parents' permission, yet she can have an abortion without them even knowing? Why is it that someone would get all up in arms over baby seals being killed or over lobsters being boiled, yet see nothing wrong with a baby being pulled apart within its mother's womb? Why is it that condoms would be distributed in public schools, condoms which have no guarantee of AIDS prevention; yet abstinence, a 100% effective prevention, is never promoted? Why is the family being redefined as Adam and Steve instead of Adam and Eve? Why is it that criminals who attack someone and get shot in the process can sue the victim for shooting them?Why is it that a child in the womb is different than that same child at the moment of birth?If a mother had a seven-month preemie and then took its life, she would be tried for murder. Yet, if a doctor cuts that same seven-month preemie up inside her womb, or sticks a needle in the base of its brain, collapses its head, and then sucks all those body parts out, it is considered lawful. What is the difference in the preemie in these two cases? Why is one considered a baby and the other just tissue?

Would the real reason please stand up? Who is behind all this madness? Oh, it's you! But.....you look like an angel of light. You are so educated and polished and refined. You are enlightened. Your words are smooth as butter. How could it be you? But, wait! Is that a mask you have on? Yes, it certainly is. Why you're.....you're the devil!

"Yes, I am the reason. I am Satan. Boy, have I done a first class job. My plan has indeed worked well! My first priority was to get God's Word out, because those Bible believers always measure everything by that troublesome book. I just simply began to cast doubt on it...and people fell for it! After that, it was a piece of cake. I went after people's minds by gradually introducing them to new ideas through TV and the media. I reshaped their thinking. Simple... when people no longer believe the truth, then a lie is all that is left to believe! If people stand for nothing, they'll fall for anything.

Yes, I am the real reason. I am proud of it, too! I have fooled an entire generation of people. And, I'll continue to do so, because most people don't know...and besides that, most of them don't even care!"

II CORINTHIANS 11:14 *"And no marvel; for Satan himself is transformed into an angel of light."*

October 22

Spiritual leprosy

He first noticed a small patch of skin that had become discolored. As he daily watched in fear, it slowly began to spread. Surely, it could not be true. Surely, it couldn't happen to him. Horror filled his soul as the greatest fear experienced by people in his day became a reality in his life. He had leprosy!

Before long, his face and body became covered with spongy, tumor-like growths. His hands and feet became deformed, as the leprosy literally ate away the good tissue. His nerve endings were so damaged that he could no longer feel heat or pain. All this was horrible enough, but the worst thing of all was separation from those he loved. He was forever separated from his family, his companions now being only those who also suffered from leprosy. Everywhere he went, those who saw him would cry out those soul-wrenching words, "Unclean, unclean," and would avoid him at all costs.

There was no hope...no help...no cure! Nothing could remove leprosy. No medicines or doctors could even touch it. And then.....he met a man called Jesus, who could work miracles. He believed this compassionate man with all his heart. He knew somehow deep in his soul that this man could help him. So, in complete faith, believing what Jesus said, he followed Jesus'instructions… and was healed immediately. With a grateful heart, he returned to thank this wonderful Healer and Savior!

Leprosy is a picture of sin. It starts as a small patch, when a person dabbles in a forbidden area, even though that area doesn't really look so bad. However, once it is allowed, it will begin to spread. Before long, it will eat away spiritual nerve endings, leaving the person dead to any warmth or feeling from the Lord. He becomes unresponsive and uninterested in spiritual things. Through the years, he becomes harder and harder. His spiritual hands and feet, his work and his walk, become deformed.

Humanly, there is no hope, no help, and no cure for his sin. Nothing can remove it! Ultimately, it leads to death and separation from his saved family forever in a place called hell, where those who suffer from spiritual leprosy will be. Only clean ones can enter heaven!

But, just as with the physical leper whom Jesus healed, there IS hope also for spiritual lepers. There is One who can heal. There is One who can remove the spiritual leprosy of sin and make the sinner clean. His name is Jesus!

Today, if you've never been cleansed from your sin, why don't you come to Jesus for healing? Give your heart and soul to Him and allow Him to cleanse you from your spiritual leprosy, make you whole, and take you to His heavenly home when you die?

LUKE 17:19 *"Arise, go thy way; thy faith hath made thee well."*

October 23

Mistletoe christians

It looks pretty, with its little green leaves and its appealing white berries. You would not know by looking at it that it is really a parasite. It attaches itself to a tree and can draw off so much of the tree's rich sap that the tree will die. Now, mistletoe plants DO contain chlorophyll and actually could make their own food. However, they prefer to steal water and minerals from the trees on which they live. It is easier to depend upon the tree. It doesn't take any effort, nor does it cost the mistletoe anything to do that.

Besides being parasites, mistletoe berries are highly poisonous and cause acute stomach pain and heart failure if consumed. You always find them high in the tops of trees. They get there by birds. Birds eat the white berries, each of which contain a seed. The berries are digested, but the seed goes through the bird's digestive tract and is deposited on the limb of another tree. Then, that seed produces more mistletoe.

Well, mistletoe isn't only found in the physical realm…it's also found in the spiritual realm as well. There are many mistletoe Christians. They pretend to be disciples of Christ. They are big workers in the church, which makes them look real good. However, they spend very little, if any, time alone with the Lord. Instead, they live off what the preacher or other Godly folks say. They are too lazy to get in the Word and dig and study for themselves. They had rather be parasites, living off the spiritual sap of dedicated Christians. It doesn't take any effort, nor does it cost them anything to do that.

And, just like physical mistletoe, spiritual mistletoe can often be found in high places also. Pastors and teachers, choir directors, youth leaders, deacons, and other leaders in the church can be actually living off what others have said about Christ, rather than having a personal relationship with Him themselves. Then, they spread their seed to others, which produces churches filled with mistletoe Christians.

However, there is one tree that is able to resist the destructive power of the mistletoe. That is the incense cedar tree. How interesting that, in the Bible, incense represents the prayers of the saints. So, in the spiritual realm, as well as in the physical, there is only thing that is effective against the destructive power of mistletoe…..incense!

How amazing it is that God has messages for us in all His creation! The devil tries to keep us from learning these truths, so he counterfeits everything that God does. He even used mistletoe as a counterfeit to the Passover. Occult worshipers hung its boughs over the door posts to protect those inside.

We need to learn from the mistletoe. We must get in God's Word for ourselves, get on our knees, and follow Jesus. The devil's mistletoe is everywhere!

I JOHN 3:7 *"Little children, let no man deceive you…."*

October 24

You can't fall when you're on your knees

It certainly wasn't planned. In fact, it was not something I had expected or had even given a thought to. It just happened anyway. Hurrying through the kitchen, with my mind completely on something else, I suddenly discovered my feet going up and my body going down. Splat…right there in the kitchen floor! Just about as quickly as I had fallen, I sprang up, looking to make sure all my appendages were still attached and in working order. Nothing had been damaged but a little piece of my ego, which needed some major whittling down any way.

As it had not been my habit to fall, it really shocked me into reality. It dawned on me how easy it is to fall and how quickly and subtly it can happen, especially on slippery surfaces and even more so if one gets careless and thoughtless. Falling is not something one plans to do and hopefully not something one will do. However, falling is always a possibility!

In the spiritual realm, the same thing is also true. One doesn't sit down and plan to fall, mapping out the strategy it would take to do so. He doesn't deliberately sit back and say, "Um-um-um, I think I'll just slow down gradually on my Bible reading until one day I will no longer read it at all. I am going to make my prayers shorter and shorter, with less and less heart in them, and eventually I will completely quit. And, I think I will start missing a church service here and there and ultimately get out of church altogether."

Falls never come by planning. They come by neglect. They start when one begins stepping out on slippery surfaces and neglecting safe ones. "Just missing one church service won't hurt anything!" "Oh, I can read my Bible tomorrow." "I'm just too tired tonight to pray." "I can hang around these same friends and be a witness to them." "Everybody else is doing it." Oooo, these are slippery surfaces! Any avenue that leads to pleasing self instead of obeying God is a slippery one! And if you walk long enough on a slippery surface, you're bound to fall.

So, friend, the best thing to do is to stay away from slippery surfaces! Walk circumspectly, cautiously, keeping your mind on the Lord Jesus Christ. Stay in the Word every day. Come to church every time the doors are open. And, get on your knees, especially the knees of your heart all day long. That's the safest place in all the world to be…because you can't fall when you're on your knees!"

I CORINTHIANS 10:12 *"Wherefore, let him that thinks he stands take heed lest he fall."*

October 25

Weighed in the balances

His motto could have been, "Eat, drink, and be merry" or "Go for the gusto." Life was good! He was wealthy, having all life's toys and trinkets that he desired. Secure in all his material possessions and in the control he had over his own life, Belshazzar held a great feast to a thousand of his lords. They drank wine from golden vessels. They laughed and talked. The world was at their disposal, as they reveled in all the gold and silver, the shining trinkets, the bright lights, and all their worldly possessions. What a feast they had, as frivolity, food, wine, and laughter flowed like a river!

Suddenly, the frivolity came to a screeching halt, just as abruptly as a radio being turned off. A man's hand wrote upon the plaster of the palace wall. The interpreted message was for Belshazzar. *"God has numbered your kingdom and finished it. You are weighed in the balances and are found wanting. Your kingdom is divided, and given to the Medes and Persians." Daniel 5:26-28* That very night, Belshazzar was slain. All his gold and silver could not deliver him when God spoke. All his authority and power could not help him. Belshazzar had laid up all his treasure here on earth, which was powerless to deliver him in the day God weighed him in the balances.

Maybe you are living like Belshazzar and have never realized it. Most all your thoughts are on worldly things, things you need and want. You constantly think about money, as it really controls your life. You are living for yourself, buying this trinket and that toy, eating and drinking, investing in fun and enjoyment for yourself, laying up all your treasures here on earth. You are feasting on the world.

Friend, you can get by with this for a while, just as Belshazzar did. But one day, just as quickly as a radio is cut off, God will weigh you in the balances and you'll be found wanting. Your money, your pleasure, your toys and trinkets, your control, your frivolity will NOT be able to deliver you in that day. You will have heaped together treasure that cannot help you when God speaks. So, why don't you give your heart to Jesus today and begin laying up treasure in heaven before you are weighed in the balances and found wanting?

DANIEL 5:27 *"Thou art weighed in the balances, and art found wanting."*

October 26

One gold nugget's coming up!

He kept the fire going under the big pot. He could not accomplish his work without the fire. The goldsmith sat in front of the vessel filled with liquid gold, dipping off impurities as the fire drove them to the top of the liquid. The process took time, but he patiently continued to watch and dip. He kept peering over into the hot liquid. He would know it was pure when he could see his reflection in it.

God is a goldsmith, too, only He is working with human gold. He is not interested in a cheap, flimsy, worthless, weak substitute. God wants gold that is strong, durable, and priceless, gold that is of such high quality that it will be of eternal significance in His work here on earth. One pure nugget of human gold is more precious and valuable to Him than thousands of impressive gold boulders that are unrefined.

Today, heaven's Goldsmith has His eyes on you! He wants YOU to be that one pure nugget. In order to accomplish this, He must take you through the refining process, removing all impurities, dross, and sediment. He must free you from all that is imperfect, man-centered, selfish, independent, prideful, self-righteous, and worldly. There are many impurities in you that must rise to the top so they can be exposed, confessed, forsaken, and forever removed. These things lie buried deep within you and only the fiery trials of life can drive them to the surface.

So, guess what? God is going to apply the fires of life to you in order to make YOU that one pure gold nugget. He will patiently sit and watch, keeping the fire going and dipping off all those impurities as they surface. He is in no rush, for He has all the time there is. He will do whatever it takes to purify you in order that He may see His reflection in you!

If you are in the fire today, then rejoice! That means you have been chosen to be a gold nugget for God. Just sit back and relax. The Goldsmith knows what He is doing. Get your focus off the fire, off the gold, and onto the Goldsmith! No telling what you will be when He gets through with you if you will quit resisting and start yielding to the refining process. Hallelujah! One gold nugget's coming up!

I PETER 1:7 *"...the trial of your faith, being much more precious than of gold that perisheth..."*

October 27

Can good works save you?

The rich young ruler had heard about Jesus, about His healing power and about all His mighty, wonderful works. He was interested in meeting this carpenter from Galilee, whom he had heard was such a good teacher. He came to Jesus asking, *"Good Master, what good thing shall I do that I may have eternal life?" Matthew 19:16*

The young ruler came to Jesus with all his credentials. He was proud of himself, feeling good about his accomplishments. He felt he was a good person, having kept the Ten Commandments from his youth up. He somehow thought that his goodness would give him an entrance into heaven. As he stood before the Lord, the rich young ruler expected to hear words of commendation and praise from Jesus. He thought he would get a pat on the back for his righteous lifestyle. He asked Jesus what good thing he could do to have eternal life, feeling confident in his heart that he had already done whatever Jesus would say.

As Jesus answered him, the young ruler's confidence and self-assurance were suddenly melted into dismay. Instead of praising him, Jesus simply showed him that he was far from meeting the righteous standards of the law. Jesus reminded him that one of the commandments was to love your neighbor as yourself. Therefore, Jesus said, *"If thou wilt be perfect, go and sell what thou hast and give to the poor...and come and follow Me." Matthew 19:21* The young ruler's heart sank as he realized that he really did NOT love his neighbor as himself after all, because he was unwilling to sell his possessions, give all he had to others, and follow Jesus.

Are you like that rich young ruler? Are you depending upon your good works to get you to heaven? If you are, then you must meet ALL the law, which includes loving your neighbor as yourself. Do you? Would you sell all that you have, give it to your neighbor, and follow the Lord?

Friend, you cannot meet all the standards of the law any more than the young ruler could. That's why you need a Savior. That's why He came and died in our place. Why don't you get down on your knees today, confess your sin, and ask Jesus to come into your heart and save you? Good works are not your Savior...but Jesus will be if you will let Him!

MATTHEW 19:21 *"Thou shalt love thy neighbor as thyself."*

October 28

Faith's object

"Lord, You certainly do have a sense of humor," I thought as I sat there stunned! "Most of the time You want me to live out what I teach in Sunday School, but this experience really takes the cake! My ladies are going to get a big kick out of this one!"

As I removed myself from the hole in the bottom of the chair, I was thinking back over the past three Sundays in Sunday School. I had been teaching on faith. One of the verses I had stressed repeatedly was *Mark 11:22 "Have faith in God."* I had told them that my faith is to be in God period…not necessarily in what God is going to do; not in how my situation is going to turn out; not in whether my prayers are answered or not; but faith in God period. That means that I believe God no matter what happens, no matter how my situation turns out, no matter what direction my path takes. I just believe God period. I know that He never makes a mistake…that He has everything planned down to the smallest detail…that nothing ever takes Him by surprise…that He will ultimately work everything for my good…and that He is totally in control.

Repeating again that we are to "*Have faith in God*," I stated that the most important thing about faith is not how much we have, but rather what our faith is in. In other words, the object of our faith is critical! If the object of our faith is defective, then ultimately our faith, no matter how strong, will fail. For three weeks in a row, I had used the same illustration. I pointed to two chairs that I had put in the center of the room. I went on to explain that, if one of the chairs were defective and messed up under the bottom, then it wouldn't matter how much faith I had in the chair. The ability of the chair to hold me up would be defective…and the rest would be history.

Little did I know that I was going to go out on my deck the following week and sit down in one of the chairs that I had trusted in for four or five years and actually live out my lesson. That chair had always held me up. That chair had never let me down before. And I had great faith in that chair…so much, in fact, that I never even entertained any thoughts about the chair's ability. So, I plopped down in the chair rather hurriedly. And…I received the shock of my life as the vinyl straps, which had dried out through the hot sun, just snapped in two and I fell through with a jolt!

Picking myself up, I realized a valuable truth. Everything on this earth that we are trusting in will one day fail. It may work for years and years, but eventually it is bound for failure, because everything on earth decays, weakens, and breaks. Therefore, we had better be trusting in God alone. He is the only One and the only thing that will never fail!

Today would be a great day for a "faith" check up. Remember: it's not how much faith you have that matters, even if it's not more than a grain of mustard seed. Rather, it's the object of your faith that counts! Friend, what is your faith's object?

MARK 11:22 *"Have faith in God.."*

October 29

If they itch, scratch them with the cross

"For the time will come when they will not endure sound doctrine but, after their own lusts, shall they heap to themselves teachers, having itching ears; And they shall turn away their ears from the truth, and shall be turned into fables." II Timothy 4:3, 4 That time has come! We are living in that age the Bible speaks of when the church will have a form of godliness but will forsake or deny the power. The church is now in that state, a state of apostasy, where it has departed from the true faith, but not from the outward profession of Christianity.

The American Christian is spoiled rotten! He wants to go to church to be entertained, to have a good time, to please his flesh. He wants the Pastor and teachers to spoonfeed him the Word. He goes to seminars and meetings and groups, but then he does nothing with what he has learned. He does NOT take it to the streets, to the jails, to the highways and byways.....that would be too hard! He never fasts or stays up all night praying and weeping over the lost world around him. He doesn't burn the midnight oil in study of God's Word. He has too many other things to do. He only has a few minutes a day for the Bible.

In addition, the American Christian has itching ears, wanting to hear a pleasing message of how God loves him and wants to bless him. He likes a message centered on himself. So, he gathers those kinds of teachers and self-proclaimed prophets who will tell him a good message from God, so that he will NOT have to get in the Word and dig for himself. He doesn't want Biblical prophets either, prophets like Isaiah or Jeremiah, or any of the others, because theirs was a message warning of sin and judgment. He doesn't want a teacher like Jesus, for Jesus'words were strong and powerful, convicting of sin and promoting a Godly, holy lifestyle. This spoiled Christian believes God gave the Ten Blessings instead of the Ten Commandments.

Christian, wake up! Jesus said, *"If any man will come after Me, let him deny himself, and take up his cross daily, and follow Me." Luke 9:23* This says nothing of blessing. It is hard! That's why many in Jesus'day turned back. Examine YOUR ears today. If they itch, scratch them with the cross!

II TIMOTHY 4:3 *"For the time will come when they will not endure sound doctrine but, after their own lusts, shall they heap to themselves teachers, having itching ears..."*

October 30

Do not disturb!

He was facing a grave situation. Speaking the truth could enrage Herod and could put John the Baptist in serious jeopardy of his own life. He did not actually have to lie, because no one had asked his opinion. He could just go on about his business, remaining silent about the situation. However, he was committed to proclaiming the truth and could not sit in an apathetic state, ignoring sin and pretending that everything was fine. He knew that sin carried with it severe consequences; therefore, he MUST speak up in warning.

John the Baptist, without hesitation, told Herod that it was not lawful to have Herodias, for she was the wife of Herod's brother, Philip. Perhaps some of the religious folks of the day jumped on that, telling John that he must not be judgmental of others. John, however, knew that he wasn't the judge...God's Word was! He knew that obedience to that Word brought blessing and disobedience brought destructive results. So, he spoke the truth to Herod and it DID cost him his life, but John the Baptist never once flinched in the face of adversity. He was a strong, dedicated soldier of the cross, standing for truth no matter the consequences and warning people of the sin, which would riddle and ruin lives.

What would YOU do if you were in John the Baptist's shoes? Would you just mind your own business and passively live with the sin around you, not partaking of it, but not exposing it either? Or would you speak up? What kind of soldier for the Lord are you? Have you retired from the battle like most other church folks? Have you settled into a comfort zone, putting up your "Do Not Disturb" sign? Has the church become a social club or an entertainment center to you instead of a battlefield?

One good way of rating yourself as a soldier for Jesus Christ is to examine the persecution you get. God's Word says, "*all that will live Godly in Christ Jesus shall suffer persecution.*" *II Timothy 3:12* This does not say "all that will live good." Anybody can live good, even the lost. This says, "Godly." If you are not suffering persecution, you are NOT living Godly. Perhaps you have settled into a respectable Christianity, which does not expose sin or bring conviction in the lives of others. It's time to throw your "Do Not Disturb" sign away. You won't need it any more. There's a battle to be fought against sin!

II TIMOTHY 3:12 "*Yes, and all that will live Godly in Christ Jesus shall suffer persecution.*""

October 31

The wind, the earthquake, and the fire

Oh, God, it's dark! My path's so dark!
The way I cannot see.
I feel as though I'm drowning, Lord!
Why don't You rescue me?

Where are You, Lord? I'm so alone!
I'm lost in deep despair!
Have You just forgotten me?
Or are You even there?

I pray and cry aloud to You,
But the heavens seem like brass.
I know my prayer's not getting through,
So I wonder, "Why even ask?"

You sent a wind into my life.
It blew so fierce, so strong.
But I somehow managed to survive
And even kept my song.

And then You sent an earthquake.
It shook my entire world.
I held on to everything I could
As my life was being hurled.

Then, out of nowhere came a fire.
I thought this was the end.
How could You do this to me, Lord ?
I thought You were my friend!

So, here I stand now, stripped and bare
And wonder what to do.
Should I just throw the towel in,
Or keep on serving You?

All around me, it's so dark.
The way I cannot see.
But, wait...I hear a still, small voice
That's speaking right to me!

"My child, I've not forsaken you.
I've been right by your side.
Have you so soon forgotten
That it was for YOU I died?

I sent a wind into your life
To blow away your pride.
But you stood in self-sufficiency
Instead of drawing to My side.

And so, I sent an earthquake
To rend your lukewarm walk.
But you still clung unto the world
Instead of coming to Me to talk.

At last, I had to send a fire
To burn up all that dross;
To strip you, child, of everything
In your life.....except the cross!"

Oh, Lord, my God, as last I see.
The way seems now so clear.
You sent this all into my life
So, to You, I would draw near.

Thank You, Lord, for stripping me.
In You, I'll now abide.
I'll love You, serve You, trust in You,
And stay forever at Your side!

I KINGS 19:12 *"And after the fire, a still, small voice."*

November

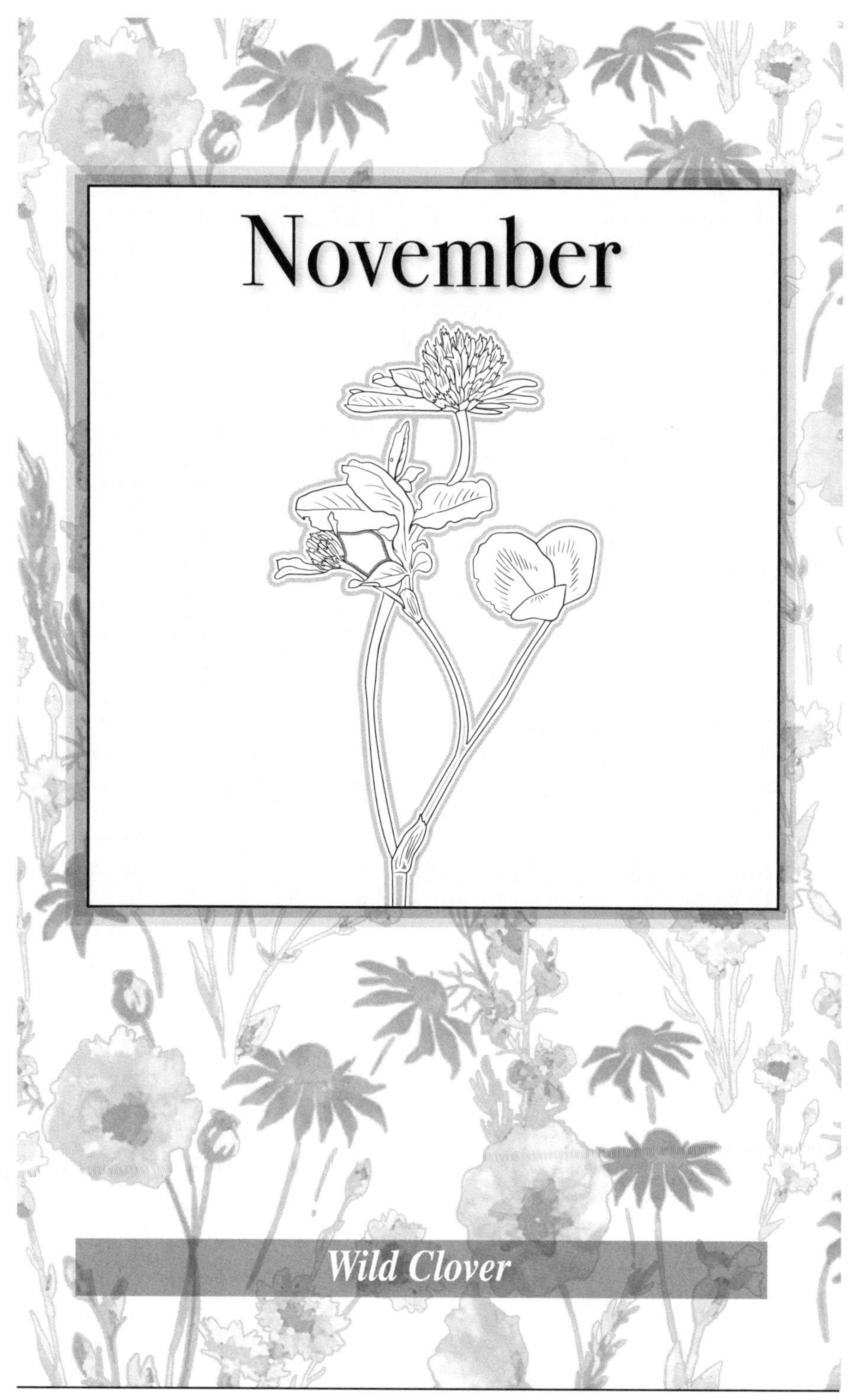

Wild Clover

November 1

Come in, come out, come up!

Justified; sanctified; glorified...what in the world do all these big words mean? I hear them being tossed around in Christian circles, but I am not sure I understand them real well myself. Is there a simple way to understand these vital principles of the Christian faith so that I could explain them to someone else?

Jesus' definition of these terms would be simple enough for even a child to understand. Perhaps He would explain them by saying, "Come in," "Come out," and "Come up." First, He would say, "Come in." He invites everyone to come into His glorious kingdom. He extends the invitation to "*whosoever will.*" *Revelation 22:17* Jesus died on the cross as a sacrifice for the sins of the whole world, personally paying the wages of sin, which is death. Through His death on the cross, He became the "Door" to Heaven, the only Way in. He says, "*I am the Door; by Me, if any man enter in, he shall be saved...*" *John 10:9* When a person enters through the "Door," his sins are then all washed away and he is justified (just if I'd never sinned.)

Once a person has "Come in," then Jesus says to him, "*Come out.*" "*Wherefore, come out from among them, and be ye separate saith the Lord, and touch not the unclean thing...*" *II Corinthians 6:17* In order to serve Christ, a person must "come out," living a life separated from the world and separated unto Christ. It's all right for a Christian to be in the world, but it's another thing for the world to be in the Christian. The Bible says, "*No man can serve two masters.*" *Luke 16:13* A person cannot live for Christ and for the world simultaneously. In fact, once a person is saved, he will no longer even want to live for the world. He will be sanctified, or set apart, for the furtherance of God's kingdom as long as he is breathing this earthly air.

And then one day, when the justified, sanctified person's allotted time on earth is fulfilled, Jesus will say to him, "Come up." His spirit will go to be with the Lord in heaven, while his body will remain in the grave for a time. At the rapture of the church, Jesus will say to all those alive at the time and to all the bodies in the graves, "Come up." At that time, all those living and all those raised will receive new bodies. These bodies will be changed in a moment...from corruptible to incorruptible, from mortal to immortal. They will be glorified at that time!

Today, dear one, make sure you have "Come in." If so, then "Come out," and one day you will hear your Lord say to you, "Come up."

ROMANS 5:1; 15:16; 8:17 *"...being justified by faith..." "sanctified by the Holy Spirit..." "...that we may be also glorified..."*

November 2

Snares and traps, scourges and thorns

Snares and traps, scourges and thorns.....that's what they were to the children of Israel. However, God had very explicitly warned the Israelites about them. He had told them, *"come not among these nations, these that remain among you; neither make mention of the name of their gods, nor cause to swear by them, neither serve them, nor bow yourselves unto them. But cleave unto the Lord your God." Joshua 23:7, 8 "Take good heed, therefore, unto yourselves, that you love the Lord your God. Else if you do in any way go back and cling to the remnant of these nations, even these who remain among you, and shall make marriages with them, and go in unto them, and they to you, know for a certainty that...they shall be snares and traps unto you, and scourges...and thorns..." Joshua 23: 11-13*

Very foolishly, the children of Israel did not heed God's Word. They mixed and mingled with the people around them, thinking that just a little mingling wouldn't hurt. The devil always makes us think that just a little sin won't hurt us. That's like telling a fish that one bite of the lure won't hurt him. It only takes one bite to ensnare. That's why God warned the Israelites beforehand not to bite the bait. They did.....and what looked so innocent turned out to be snares and traps, scourges and thorns. The very things they refused to separate themselves from eventually enslaved them!

Today in America we need to take heed to these same words that God spoke to the Israelites. He has the same message for us. In *II Corinthians 6:17*, God tells us Christians, *"Wherefore, come out from among them, and be ye separate, saith the Lord, and touch not the unclean thing; and I will receive you, and will be a Father unto you, and you shall be My sons and daughters, saith the Lord Almighty."*

Christian, don't mingle with the world, thinking you can embrace its lifestyle and serve God at the same time. No man can serve two masters. If you bite the devil's enticing bait, you'll get hooked, reeled in, and captured. The very things you refuse to separate yourself from will eventually enslave you. They will become snares and traps, scourges and thorns, not only to you, but to the generations succeeding you. So, Christian, come out from among them and be separate! Your children are at stake!

II CORINTHIANS 6:17 *"come out from among them and be ye separate,
saith the Lord, and touch not the unclean thing;
and I will receive you, and will be a Father unto you.."*

November 3

Dead things don't make any noise

What would you do if someone came to your door, bearing the news that you had just won a million dollars? In all probability, you would show some kind of emotion. You would probably be grinning from ear to ear, laughing, crying, shouting, jumping around, and carrying on. You would most likely give an enthusiastic cheerleader a run for her money. Great excitement and joy tend to loosen our inhibitions!

Generally, we think nothing of people getting excited or becoming highly emotional at winning money or other prizes or at winning a sports event, especially in a close race. Yet, we look at people like they have some kind of a plague when they show any emotion at all in church. It must be awfully sad to our Savior when people get so excited at a ball game that they shout and jump and cheer the players on...but come to church where He is proclaimed and sit as dead as a stump, looking like they just lost their best friend!

Hey, if there is anything in the world to get excited about, it is Jesus! He has bought you by His own blood and snatched you from the pits of hell. He has translated you from darkness into the light. He has made you an heir of God and joint-heirs with Himself. He is preparing you a place in heaven and He's coming back for you soon. He has scored the winning touchdown...He defeated death, hell, and the grave...eternity to zero! He is King of kings and Lord of lords and He has chosen YOU!

Since you have such an awesome Father Who has chosen you and made you His heir, then how in the world can you sit like a knot on a log with your face dragging the ground? You look like you have something to endure rather than enjoy. No wonder people don't want what you have! The world shows more enthusiasm and joy over temporal things that will pass away than you do over the eternal riches of glory. Christian, what is wrong with you? Why don't you get your focus on God and start praising Him, jumping around, shouting, or whatever else you do when you get excited? Folks will say you're in the flesh. They're right. You are! That's all you have to praise Him with is your flesh. But, they're in the flesh, too, only theirs is dead. Dead things don't make any noise and dead things don't move. What does that tell you about the church of the Lord Jesus Christ?

I PETER 1:8 *"...ye rejoice with joy unspeakable and full of glory..."*

November 4

Let's go to the ant!

They don't waste even one second of time! Apparently, they live in a state of preparedness, for the whole colony of them will respond immediately to an intrusion by an enemy. Many times, I have purposely stepped on one of their colonies, ground my foot into it, and then stood back, watching as thousands of them poured out of the anthill and went to work. As soon as my foot touched their dwelling place, the ants rose to the challenge, some moving their larvae to a safer place and some immediately starting the rebuilding process. They didn't sit back in their recliners, watching their ant TV shows, ignoring the foot of the enemy that had come against them. They didn't gather together and hold conferences on what to do, debating over the most effective means of rebuilding. They didn't discuss all the reasons why this had happened…perhaps they had built in the wrong place; perhaps their anthill was too conspicuous; or perhaps their anthill should have been much stronger! It didn't matter the reason. All that mattered now was that the foot of the enemy had come against them and they didn't waste time doing something about it.

As God's Word so plainly tells us, *"But ask now, the beasts, and they shall teach thee; and the fowls of the air, and they shall tell thee. Or speak to the earth, and it shall teach thee; and the fishes of the sea shall declare unto thee." Job 12:7, 8* It's too bad that we humans don't look to the animals for many valuable lessons we need to learn. We could certainly learn something about dealing with the enemy from the ant…if we'd only watch!

Today, the foot of the enemy has come down on America! He has stepped on our homes, ground his feet into them, and is literally tearing them apart. And, there's much talk about everything that is going on. Men and women gather together and hold conferences on what to do, debating over the most effective means of handling the situation. They discuss all the reasons why they think this is happening, especially as they keep up with the latest intrusions by the enemy on the news. But in the meantime, while they hold their educational, pompous, theoretical discourses, the enemy is laughing his head off and having his heyday in our country.

Well, it's time for us to quit speculating and start supplicating! It's time to quit reasoning and start requesting revival! It's time to get off our ease and onto our knees. We're in a battle in America, a spiritual battle, and it can only be fought with spiritual weapons. So, like the ant, let's get to work immediately… the real work…which is prayer for our nation. Let's rebuild our country on our knees! Prayer never fails!

Job 12:7 *"But ask, now, the beasts and they shall teach thee; and the fowls of the air, and they shall tell thee."*

November 5

C.R. and the "last straw" point

You are totally frustrated! It feels like every nerve in your body has been tied in a knot in the middle and frayed on both ends. You have reached the "last straw" point, where you are going to do something drastic. Here you are, living for the Lord, serving Him faithfully, and getting your life straightened out...and C.R. is driving you crazy. C.R. won't change!

You have tried everything you can think of to change C.R., but nothing has worked! You have told him what the Bible says, but it goes in one ear and right out the other. Your life has changed dramatically, and it looks like C.R. would notice and would want to change, too. However, he just continues on the same day after day. You have asked, begged, threatened, cried, and even tried to embarrass and force C.R. to change; yet, C.R. won't budge! Nothing you try has any effect whatsoever!

As frustration has grown greater with each failure, it has driven you to a point called the "last straw." You are not happy at all. You are depressed, discouraged, defeated, weary, and worn out! You stay upset with C.R. all the time. C.R. keeps your life in a turmoil and you cannot take any more. You are ready to throw up your hands and give up!

Great! Now, you're getting smart! That's exactly what you need to do... give up!Give up C.R. to God. You have been trying to change him yourself, instead of letting God do it. You thought God needed your help, your input, and your words. You have interfered and stuck your big mouth in the picture time after time. Oh, you prayed often, asking God to change C.R., but you got right up off your knees and got busy trying to figure out ways to accomplish it yourself. You haven't trusted God! You haven't turned anything over to Him! So, give up! God does NOT need your help!

Give up all expectations of C.R. to God! Expect nothing.....then anything C.R. does at all would be a blessing. As you put all your expectations into God's hands, it will release the control C.R. has on your life. If you don't expect anything, then nothing C.R. does can affect you. Give up and let the Lord Jesus be your focus, your joy, your love, and your everything. Let Christ, rather than changing C.R., be your life! When Christ is your life, C.R. (Close Relationship) can no longer affect you and drive you to the "last straw" point!

PROVERBS 23:26 *"My son, give Me thine heart, and let thine eyes observe My ways."*

November 6

Imitation crab meat and Christians

What does imitation crab meat, instant potatoes, powdered milk, and most American Christians all have in common? They are not the real thing! Americanized Christianity has been processed, refined, diluted, tenderized, artificially colored and flavored, and mixed with so many ingredients to make it more palatable and chewable that it does not even remotely resemble the real thing any more.

Wonder what Isaiah or Jeremiah or Ezekiel would think if they sat in on one of our so-called "worship services" on Sunday morning? These three guys thundered out against the sin in their land, bringing a message of repentance. They would probably vomit at most of the messages in America today, messages proclaiming how God will bless and love and prosper a people who are sitting comfortably in their smug, self-righteous, lukewarm, apathetic states. These men probably would not believe their ears as they listened to the watered down, diluted, mushy pabulum coming from the pulpits, messages easily digested by fat, spoiled, lazy, Christian babies.

Or wonder what Jonathan Edwards, one of the great preachers of the 1700's, would think if he sat in and listened to one of our Sunday morning services? In his day, he would stand, weeping profusely as he preached "Sinners in the Hands of an Angry God" to a people who were not nearly as immoral and ungodly as we are now! Or, what about David Brainerd? Wonder what he would think of the modern Christian, who reclines in front of a TV set, eats too much, sleeps as much as he can, and is scared to death to get alone for a few days in fasting and prayer, seeking God for his family, his church, and his nation? Mr. Brainerd would spend long hours in prayer, spitting up blood from his tuberculosis, and weeping over the lost North American Indians. He would probably think our Christianity a joke, as he would see a people eating, drinking, marrying and giving in marriage, and making merry.....with no tears, no brokenness, no concern over their own sin or the sin of their nation, and no burden for the lost.

It is time to throw out the artificial color and flavor, the tenderizer, and the mixture of the Americanized spiritual diet. It's time to get rid of the imitation crab meat sermons and get back to the real thing! It's time to call sin "sin" again. It's time to preach hell-fire and damnation. It's time to tell the people that it's a fearful thing to fall into the hands of the living God. It's time to call America back to the cross, to repentance, to brokenness, to crucifixion of the flesh, to separation from the world, to walking the straight and narrow path. Let's get back to real Christianity once more in our country, the Christianity that produced pray-ers, not party-ers!

JEREMIAH 6:16 *"Stand in the ways, and see, and ask for the old paths..."*

November 7

Goodbye, wilderness, goodbye!

For forty years, they wandered in the dry, barren, deserted wilderness. They wore the same clothes, traveled the same paths, and ate the same thing day after day.....manna! Life to them was like a merry-go-round. The children of Israel were always on the move, but they didn't go anywhere. Life certainly didn't have a whole lot of purpose, meaning, or excitement to it. After all, what could be exciting about a wilderness?

The sad thing about it was that the land of Canaan was just in sight! It was a land flowing with milk and honey, a land where even the grapes were so large that one bunch had to be carried on a pole across the shoulders of two men. That land was just across the Jordan River, only eleven miles away from where they were. Possibly, they stood on Jordan's stormy banks, casting a wistful eye over at that promised land. But, they didn't figure they could ever go there, because they had listened to that negative bunch that told them all the reasons why it couldn't be done. Somehow, they never believed God, who had very plainly told them that the land was theirs...and all they had to do was to go in and take it. But, because of their unbelief, they wasted their years in the wilderness, eating manna rather than meat; roaming rather than resting; enduring rather than enjoying; and were depressed rather than delighted! They made their choice.....and it was the wrong one!

Well, today, I woke up and found myself in the wilderness, too. I've been listening to the wrong crowd lately...that negative bunch in the majority that's always running down the church and the pastor, that bunch that won't ever go over into Canaan. And, just like them, I've been living off spiritual manna, just barely existing in my spiritual life......without joy, enthusiasm, excitement, or real purpose! And it's dry and barren in the wilderness. It's discouraging. It's the same old drudgery day after day and week after week and I'm tired of it!

Today, I stood on Jordan's stormy banks and looked over into the promised land, the abundant Christian life, that my Savior told me I could have. I wondered what in the world I am doing in the wilderness, living as a spiritual pauper, when my Father is the King of Glory and has told me I'm an heir... and everything that's His is also mine! I must be stupid! I don't have to live in this wilderness! I'm not going to live in it any longer. I have a choice. So, today I'm doing away with my duds of doubt, shedding my shoes of straying, fixing my faith on the Father, and crossing over Jordan into Canaan! Goodbye, wilderness, goodbye!

Hebrews 3:19 *"So we see that they could not enter in because of unbelief."*

November 8

A silent battlefield

What a fierce battle! It rages on ruthlessly. The enemy never tires of his endless attacks, nor ever takes a break from the war. He is always on the battlefield, persistently trying to win one more victory. He uses only invisible weapons. He fires only silent ammunition. He camouflages himself so cleverly that he is rarely ever spotted. As an experienced warrior, he is often conqueror on this silent battlefield of your mind.

On this battlefield, the enemy recklessly hurls thought bombs through the air. He buries unforgiveness mines everywhere on the battlefield. He propels resentment grenades at unsuspecting victims. He fires judgmental darts and critical bullets at every available target. And he never runs out of ammunition. He can make up a fresh batch any time from the inexhaustible supply of excuses, self-pity, self-righteousness, personal rights, laziness, apathy, love of pleasure, love of self, etc. lying strewn over the battlefield.

The victory on this battlefield depends upon one lone warrior, who ultimately decides the outcome in each battle. This warrior is your will. Your mind is just simply the battlefield; your will actually fights the battle. It decides in each attack what it will do.....believe God or believe the enemy, the devil. Your will can ignore the invisible, silent attacks. It can remain passive, just allowing the enemy to run rampant through the mind. That is the easiest route, the one of least resistance. It's the route that is painless and effortless. However, the will can also launch an offensive attack. It can deliberately capture all thought bombs, bringing them captive to the obedience of Christ and thus allowing Him to deactivate them. It can allow Christ to dig up all forgiveness mines and disarm them. It can bring all resentment grenades and all judgmental darts and critical bullets to the Word of God, where they are shattered, as a hammer breaking a rock into pieces. The will can retire in its comfort zone and be conquered - or it can fight in Christ's victory and be the conqueror!

Christian, your mind is a battlefield, where the forces of God and the forces of the devil contend for the victory in your daily life. Your will is the warrior that decides the outcome in each battle.....and there are many. So, gird yourself up, will, and prepare to fight. There are many, many lives besides your own that are at stake on this silent battlefield!

PSALM 18:39 *"For Thou has girded me with strength unto the battle..."*

November 9

Two of the most dangerous words

An unbridled, wild stallion is a beautiful creature, but he is of no use to man in that state. He must be tamed and brought into submission, which is a process that takes time. The longer he runs wild, living as he pleases, the harder he is to bring under control. A good trainer knows that, if a horse is left to himself, he will never be useful. Therefore, he daily and consistently works with the horse, bringing his will into subjection.

When we are born into this world, we are born with a free, unbridled, untamed will. The will is like that of a wild stallion, being absolutely of no use to God in that state. The will is in rebellion against God, always wanting to do what it wants, live as it pleases, and control its own self. The will doesn't want anyone telling it what to do. It always reserves the right to make the final decision in every situation, which is what rebellion really is. "I will" make the final decision. "I will" be in charge. "I will" are the very words which caused Lucifer's fall, as he said these two dangerous words five times in *Isaiah 14:13, 14.* "I will" are the words which sent the rich fool to hell, as he said these two dangerous words four times in *Luke 12:18, 19.* "I will" are two of the most dangerous words in the world. Every child is born with these two words on his lips.

As each child enters the world with an unbridled will, God provides him with a trainer, which is usually his parents. It is the parents' job to see that this child's will is trained, tamed, brought under complete control, and bridled, so that he may grow up to be useful to God. The older the child gets, the harder this is to accomplish. While he is young and pliable, the parents can train him daily, consistently, and purposefully to bring that will under reins. If the parents do not do this, the child will grow up unbridled, doing exactly what he wants, being his own boss, and making all the final decisions. Then, as an adult, accustomed to always saying, "I will, " he will say those same two dangerous words to God.....only this time, he cannot get away with it.

If you have a problem disciplining your child, just remember that, if you cannot control your child, then God will not be able to either. If the child rebels against you, he WILL rebel against God! Practice makes perfect! Bring his will into subjection now......before he stands in God's face one day and says the two most dangerous words man can say, "I will."

LUKE 12:18 *"And he said, This will I do..."*

November 10

Are you a Zedekiah Christian?

Apparently, he must have wanted to believe in Jeremiah's words and in his prayers, for he solicited them on more than one occasion. He had even asked Jeremiah once to "*Pray to the Lord our God for us.*" *Jeremiah 37:3* However, King Zedekiah didn't like the message Jeremiah proclaimed, because he wanted a religion that wouldn't cost him anything. Jeremiah somehow just never said what the King wanted to hear. However, as Jeremiah's prophecies began to occur, Zedekiah called for him once again, saying, "*I will ask thee a thing; hide nothing from me.*" *Jeremiah 38:14* He was asking for the truth.....but he didn't really want to hear it!

Jeremiah told the King that Babylon would besiege Jerusalem and that he, Zedekiah, was to go forth unto the king of Babylon's princes. If so, he and his family would live and the city would not be burned with fire. If not, he would be taken and the city would then be burned with fire. King Zedekiah had now heard the truth from the Word of God out of the mouth of the prophet. Obviously, he had wanted to believe the word from God, but when it didn't match up to what he felt, based on the circumstances, he decided to go with what he felt was best! And the outcome, of course, was just as Jeremiah had predicted. Zedekiah was captured, all of his sons were slain, his eyes were put out, he was bound with chains, the houses were burned with fire, and the walls of Jerusalem were broken down! Oh, the cost of disobedience!

There are multitudes of Zedekiah Christians today! They dabble around with the Truth, showing somewhat of an interest in knowing the Word of God. They attend church, join Bible studies, go to seminars, read books, listen to audio tapes, and a host of other things that teach the Word. However, the Word goes in one ear and right out the other, for they can hear a sermon and walk out the church doors without ever putting into practice what they just heard. And, when the Word doesn't line up with the way they want to live, they disregard it and go with what they feel is best. The outcome, of course, is disastrous. They are captured by Satan, their children fall prey to the enemy, their spiritual eyes are put out, they're bound with chains of their sin, their homes are destroyed, and their walls are broken down. Oh, the high cost of disobedience!

Friend, are you a Zedekiah Christian, dabbling around in the things of God, but not really wanting to totally trust and obey God? Or do you hear and heed every word that proceeds out of the mouth of God? You have a choice in your life today...you can either be a Zedekiah Christian or a zealous Christian. It's all up to you!

Jeremiah 38:20 *"Obey, I beseech thee, the voice of the Lord...*
so it shall be well with thee..."

November 11

It's not that you can't.....it's that you won't!

Easy...easy...easy! You are just downright easy! Why, you are not even a challenge! I led you around by the nose and had you eating from my hand. Then, it was no problem to snap those old chains of bondage on you. Now, I have you and you cannot get away. It is so much fun watching your frustration with me, as you declare time after time that you are through with me. You always say you are giving me to the Lord, but I know better than that. You get up off your knees and take me right back again.

Boy, do I have you fooled! I have convinced you that you cannot get rid of me. You have even told the Lord that, if He wants me out of your life, then He will have to do it Himself! You noodle! You are so weak-willed that you do not even have enough backbone to say "No" to me; yet, you are calling God a liar! You tell Him you can't, when His Word says that you can do all things through Christ who strengthens you. Guess you think that verse doesn't apply to you, huh?

Oh, I think I have this thing all figured out. The problem is not that you can't. It's that you won't. You see, you really like me and want to hold onto me. You don't really want to be rid of me. You know God is not pleased with me and He wants me out of your life. You know I am a hindrance to your Christian walk and a weight that keeps you from running the race effectively. You feel guilty because of this; yet, you are determined to have me anyway, regardless of what God says. You give in to me and then make flimsy excuses as to why I am still in your life. If you really loved God more than me, you WOULD get rid of me!

By the way, my name is "stronghold." I have been deeply entrenched in your life for a long time. You keep waiting on God to miraculously get me out of your life. Well, you'll be waiting a long time, friend. God has already done everything He is going to do. He won the victory at Calvary. He has overcome the world and made you more than a conqueror. He has already given you the power over me. Now, you must stand in the victory that He has won. YOU must lay me down! YOU must put off the old man! YOU must cleanse yourself from all filthiness of the flesh! YOU must say no! Remember: it's not that you can't.....it's that you won't!

Hebrews 12:1 *"...let us lay aside every weight, and the sin which does so easily beset us."*

November 12

Wars aren't won with pillows

Come over here and lie down! Here's a nice, soft, comfortable bed for you. Just lay your little head right here on this pillow and I'll pull the covers up over you. There!Now, you go to sleep and don't worry over the war that is going on around you. Don't fret over your friends and loved ones who are being taken captive. Just ignore the approaching enemy, the blazing bullets, and the numerous casualties. What's important is that you remain comfortable and undisturbed.

Can you imagine the foolishness of someone acting this way in a time of war?Well, spiritually, this is exactly what we are doing in America! There is a war going on in America, only it is an unseen war. It is a war between the forces of good and the forces of evil, between God and Satan. It is a war for the souls of men and women, boys and girls all across our land. The enemy, Satan, and all his demonic helpers are rapidly taking over more territory every day. They are hurling their fiery missiles and are hitting the bull's eye of their targets..... human souls. There are casualties too numerous to count. Thousands are being taken captive.

Meanwhile, the army of God, the church, is asleep. Pastors and teachers are lulling them into a comfortable bed of easy Christianity, teaching mostly on the love of God and ignoring the wrath. They are using the Word of God as a soft pillow, upon which the Americanized Christian can lay his little spoiled head. It seems that modern leaders have forgotten that the Word of God is like a hammer that breaks a rock into pieces. It is sharper than any two-edged sword, piercing even to the dividing asunder of soul and spirit and of the joints and marrow. The Word is not meant to make folks comfortable and undisturbed. It is meant to make soldiers in the army of God!

So, get out of that bed, church! This is war and the devil is having a field day. God has called you to a battlefield, not to a social event. A good soldier does not entangle himself in the affairs of this world. He must deny himself of many of the pleasures of life. He must not cling too tightly to relationships. He has a battle to fight. He has a war to win. You've slept long enough! It's time to get up and fight for your life and the lives of those you love. Trade that pillow in for a sword! Wars aren't won with pillows!

JEREMIAH 23:29 *"Is not My Word...like a hammer that breaketh the rock in pieces?"*

November 13

A screeching halt!

Everything was going great! They had a beautiful home, a brand new car, more than enough money to pay all the monthly bills, and a healthy and successful family. They worked hard on weekends on their house and yard, always keeping them in topnotch appearance. They made sure their kids were in every kind of sports, spending hours on ball fields, in practice, and in games. They went on numerous trips, watched a lot of TV together, went to movies often, and talked frequently about making money and being successful in this life.

Then one day, without warning, they were in a horrible automobile accident. Their entire world came to a screeching halt. He was killed on impact. The rest of the family was hospitalized, all in critical, life-threatening condition. In a split second, he was hurled from the comfort of this life into the jaws of hell. It was a raging, fiery inferno, with flames that engulfed and burned his body, which was now indestructible. The pain was so intense it was unbearable. The noise of the millions of unending, torturous screams was deafening. The stench of burning human flesh was nauseating. He was falling...falling...falling...no place to ever set his foot in this bottomless, eternal lake of fire.

Oh, now he had all eternity to ask himself the same questions over and over. Why did he waste his life? Why did he have his priorities so mixed up? What good was his beautiful home and his new car? They certainly couldn't help him here. What good was all his money? It couldn't buy his way out of hell! It couldn't buy him any comfort or pleasure here in this horrible place. What benefit was all the hours spent in sports, on vacations, watching TV, engaging in idle talk? None of these things prepared him or his family for eternity. Oh, if only he could go back! He would spend time with the Lord Jesus Christ. He would read God's Word, attend church, and serve God with all his heart. He would spend time with his family, teaching them the Word of God and involving them in eternal matters. His priorities would change from the temporal to the eternal. But.....it was too late now.....forever and ever too late!

There are thousands of Americans today who are living for this world, storing up their treasures here on earth. They are rushing here and there in a frantic pace to make more money, accumulate more things, go more places, and be more involved in more things. They are busy...busy...busy...so busy, in fact, that they have little or no time for a relationship with the Lord Jesus Christ!

Where are your priorities today? How are you spending your time? What are you doing with your life? Would you be adequately prepared if your life today suddenly came to a screeching halt?

LUKE 16:23 *"And in hell he lifted up his eyes, being in torments..."*

November 14

Those same two pivotal words

Listen! Do you hear that? It's a clarion call, coming through the maze of voices and confusion in the world, coming form the portals of glory. Those words have a familiar ring. They are the same words spoken to Peter and Andrew, as they were fishing on the Sea of Galilee. They are the same words spoken to Matthew, as he sat at the tax office; to Philip in Galilee; to the rich young ruler who didn't want to part with his possessions; and to Peter, when he became concerned over what John would do.

Yes, I hear that same call, only this time the words are being spoken to me. My heart hears those words distinctly, even though they are spoken softly. They are powerful, life-changing words, *"Follow Me." Matthew 4:19* My heart is pounding, as I realize that this is no ordinary call. The King of Glory has spoken these two little, but pivotal words to me. He is waiting for my response.

My mind reels as I count the cost of responding affirmatively to this call. It must be immediate, as the disciples straightway, without hesitation, followed Him at His beckoning. It must be alone, just as the disciples left their families to follow Him. Each individual must decide for his own self to answer this call. It must be empty-handed, just as the disciples left their nets and their jobs to follow. The rich young ruler was told to sell all his possessions, give to the poor, and then follow Him. It must be single-minded, as Peter was told to follow and not to worry about what John was going to do.

As I look around, I see the call has gone out to many, but few have responded. Oh, they think they are following the Lord...but they are deceived! They have not forsaken all; therefore, they cannot be His disciples. They are still holding onto material things, money, jobs, relationships, pleasures, and other things of the world. And He says that we cannot serve God and mammon. That's impossible!

Oh, there's the call again. I hear those same two pivotal words, "*Follow Me.*" I've counted the cost and made my choice. I will follow Him! And now, the call is being extended to you, too.....yes, you. What are YOU going to do?

MATTHEW 4:19 *"And he saith unto them, Follow Me."*

November 15

Won't somebody go after the Lord?

Her daughter was lying at the point of death. Can't you just see that precious mother now...holding the sick child in her arms and waiting anxiously? Perhaps she told the twelve year old girl, "Honey, just hold on a little while longer. Daddy has gone after the Lord." Probably like most mothers, she kept looking out the window, hoping any time to see Jairus coming back with Jesus! The only thing on her mind was getting her dying daughter to their only hope in the whole world, the Lord Jesus Christ!

Can you imagine her response if some long-tongued busybody had come over that day and said, "Mrs. Jairus, have you heard what's going on down at the house of God?Have you heard what that preacher did? Do you realize what a mess they're in down there?" Mrs. Jairus would have told her right quick, "Look, Mrs. Floppy-Tongue, I could care less right now about what's going on down there! My daughter is dying and I've got to get her to Jesus! I don't have time to discuss all the problems at the house of God. The problem right now is down at my house! My house is the one in need of Jesus!"

Well, today, we too have a lot of sons and daughters lying at the point of death... spiritual death! We have a lot of brothers and sisters, mothers and fathers, aunts and uncles, cousins, and friends that are lying at the point of death! Oh, we again need somebody to go after the Lord and bring Him to our house! Our house is the one in need of Jesus! Sure, there may be lots of things going on down at the house of God, things we might not understand and might not necessarily agree with. But, if we get our minds off the gossip and onto our lost sons and daughters, and onto our lost family members, and onto our lost nation, we won't have the time or the interest to be listening to the long tongued busybodies that are always hunting a listening ear. We'll have one thing and one thing only on our minds... getting the dying ones to Christ before it's too late!

Friend, if you're that long-tongued busybody, you need to get your tongue on the altar, cause it's wrecking havoc in the church of God! Why don't you run after Jesus instead of running your mouth? Get on your face and stay there until you get God on your life...cause your church needs Him more than they need anything else! Won't somebody go after the Lord today, cause we're in a mess and He is the only Answer!

Mark 5:23 *"My little daughter lieth at the point of death...come and lay Thy hands on her, that she...shall live."*

November 16

Phew! if you stink, you need a bath!

Dumb dog! She puts up a fight every time she gets a bath. She tries to hide when she knows a bath is imminent. Then, she refuses to stand under the water, wiggling and squirming to get away. It looks like she would just cooperate and get it over with. But, no!It's the same old fight every time, in spite of the fact that she desperately needs a bath!

Boy, she's dumb! She forgets the benefits of the bath from one time to the next. In the first place, she stinks! Surely, she ought to take that into consideration and not want to be around her loved ones stinking. Secondly, her fur gets matted and unsightly and uncomfortable. A bath frees her from those things and makes her fur fluffier and softer and shinier. Thirdly, when her fur gets dirty, it itches. A bath cleans her up and she feels much better. Why, she goes crazy after a bath, too, running around like a chicken with its head cut off. It looks like she would want a bath the way it makes her feel afterwards. But, unfortunately, that never happens. She always puts up a protest!

Dumb Christian! She puts up a fight every time the Lord comes after her for a bath. She refuses to stay in the water of the Word, thinking of every excuse in the world to get away. It looks like she would just cooperate and get it over with, because her protests are not going to stop God from coming after her.

Boy, she's dumb! She forgets the benefits of the bath from one time to the next. In the first place, she stinks! She is not fooling anyone. They can smell her rotten spiritual life a mile away. Just like the dog, she is the only one who cannot smell her own self. Secondly, her life is tangled and matted with worldly things that hinder her walk. And thirdly, when her life gets spiritually dirty, it leads to anger, frustration, judgmental attitudes, pride, depression, selfishness, and a host of other things that affect one's feelings.

A good spiritual bath in the water of the Word washes the stink away, gets rid of all the sin and hindrances, and cleans the life up. It feels so good when it's over. Christian, when is the last time you got in the Word and in prayer and stayed there long enough to get cleaned up? If it has been awhile, you may have to soak for a LONG time for it to do any good. Do I smell something? If it's you stinking, then you need to take a bath!

EPHESIANS 5:26 *"That He might sanctify and cleanse it with the washing of water by the Word."*

Spiritual botulism

What do you devote more time to: your body or your soul? Think about the time you spend each day in preparing your body for the day. You shower, wash and fix your hair, brush your teeth, and dress. You would not think of going off to work stinking, never having taken time to correct offensive problems. You would not think of going off to work naked, either.

However, spiritually you go through your day without devoting an equal or even greater amount of time to your soul. You will not shower in the Word of God, brush your spiritual teeth with the prayers coming across your lips, or dress in all the provisions of God's Word. You go out that door each morning spiritually dirty, matted with worldliness and carnality...and naked. You are spiritually offensive to God and to everybody else. There's no sweet savor of Christ in your life. You stink! No wonder people do not want what you have!

What would you do today if the whole church was praying the prayer for you that John prayed for Gaius? "*Beloved, I wish above all things that thou mayest prosper and be in health, even as thy soul prospereth.*" *II John 2* Wow! Would that ever change your priorities! Your soul would now become more of a priority than your body. You would want to feed it properly. Your spiritual diet would be the pure Word of God, instead of the junk food of secular, worldly stuff that you have been feeding it. You would realize that the contaminated food of this dirty world causes spiritual botulism, better known as food poisoning, and is fatal to the soul. You would also want to drink the Living Water, since the world's drinking fountain is polluted. How careful you would be now about the things you take in through the channels of your eyes, ears, and mouth!

Besides feeding your soul properly, you would want to give it a good workout every day. You would exercise your soul in eternal matters, leaving off much of the temporal stuff that you now do. Without proper nourishment and exercise, your soul would not be healthy. What kind of spiritual diet are you on? How much spiritual exercise do you get every day? Are you taking care of your soul as well as you are your body? Would you want to prosper and to be in physical health in direct proportion to the prosperity of your soul? If not, it's time to make a visit to the Great Physician, determine the state of your spiritual health, get on a good spiritual diet, and start exercising spiritually every day! You only have one soul - better take good care of it!

III JOHN 2 *"Beloved, I wish that...you may prosper and be in health, even as your soul prospers.."*

November 18

A "what about" problem

Carefully watching the bird, the spider thought to himself, "What shall the bird do?" As he watched the bird flap his wings and take off through the air, the spider decided that this is what he must do also. He perched on a limb, began flapping his hairy legs, and sailed off into the blue. As he plummeted to the ground, he wondered what went wrong. So, he tried it again...and again... and again. He was finally so frustrated at his futile attempts that he just gave up. He sat down in the dirt and threw the biggest pity party you've ever seen. He was worthless, no good, useless! Why, if he couldn't fly like a bird, he certainly would never amount to anything!

As he groveled around in the dirt, he overheard two passers-by talking. Of all things, they were talking about spiders. One was saying how thankful he was for spiders because, if it weren't for them, the world might be overrun by flies. The other was talking about how beautiful and intricate a spider's web is. He was marveling at a spider's ability to design such a delicate work of art.

The spider's ears perked up as he realized that he could do something the bird could not do. He had never seen a bird spin a web! Why in the world had he become so depressed and so downhearted when he DID have a purpose after all? He got up, determined to let birds be birds and to be the best spider he could be!

Have you ever looked at another Christian with this question in mind, *"Lord, what shall this man do?" John 21:21* Peter did! He was concerned over what John would do and expressed this to the Lord. Jesus' reply to him was, *"If I will that he tarry till I come, what is that to thee? Follow thou Me." John 21:22* In other words, Jesus was telling Peter to get his eyes off John and what John was doing and follow Him regardless of what anyone else was doing.

Jesus is saying that same thing to you today. You have a "what about" problem just like Peter did. You are always asking "what about" this person or "what about" that person. But, Jesus is asking you today, *"What is that to you? Follow thou Me."* Forget about what others are doing. Some are spinning; some are flying; some are digging. But, none of these may be the purpose for which God created you! He wants you to get your eyes upon Him and Him alone, quit looking at others and comparing yourself to them, and follow Him! From now on, just concern yourself with, "what about" Jesus?

JOHN 21:22 *"...what is that to thee? Follow thou Me."*

November 19

Until the stink is removed

Suppose you are a salesman for a newly formed, growing company. You come to work one day with your clothes torn, dirty, and wrinkled. Your hair is matted and greasy. Your shoes have holes in them, with your toes protruding through some of them. You stink so badly that folks have to hold their breath to even talk to you.

Now, when you walk into the presence of your boss, what do you think is the first thing he would say? Would he put his arms around you, put you in his favorite chair, and begin to tell you how he wants to use you? Would he laugh and talk with you, sharing how the company wants to bless and prosper you? Or, would he tell you to go home and take a bath? Would he make it clear that he is highly disappointed and grieved with you, as you are a very poor representative of his company and are a shame and reproach to the company's name in your present condition? Would he let you know without question that the company cannot use you like that?

Obviously, no boss would ignore a filthy condition of one of his salesmen. Until that problem was corrected, things could proceed no further. The boss would not have much to say until the dirt and stink were removed! Well, spiritually, the same thing is true. People come to church on Sunday, after having walked all week in a dirty world. Many of them have had little or no time for the Lord all week, as their schedules were filled with work, chores, obligations, TV, ball games, and the like. They walk into church, having spent no time in repentance, confession of sin, and cleansing during the week. Therefore, they walk in spiritually dirty. But, it isn't long before they are singing, praising the Lord, and enjoying themselves. They listen to how God wants to bless them and prosper them and use them. They feel goose bumps and get very emotional, saying, "Boy, we had church!" They say they have been in the presence of God!

Friend, don't be fooled! They have NOT been in God's presence! They may have had goose bumps, but they weren't from God. If they had been in the presence of the Holy, Almighty God, they would have been on their faces in repentance and confession. God would have let them know they were poor representatives of Him and a shame and reproach to the name of Christ. He would have made it plain that He could not bless and prosper anyone in that condition! He would have told them He dwells with those of a contrite and humble spirit. He would have made it plain that, until the stink is removed, He could do nothing further.

ISAIAH 57:15 *"I dwell in the...holy place, with him also who is of a contrite and humble spirit."*

November 20

A walk into death

In Old Testament times, people sometimes made blood covenants with one another. They would split the sacrificial animals in two, laying half to the right and half to the left, leaving a path of blood between the pieces of the sacrificial animals. The two people making the covenant would then walk between those pieces in a figure eight, representing infinity, as an eight has no beginning and no end. As they stood between the pieces, they would repeat the terms of the covenant. They would exchange robes, weapons, belts, and names.

The two people entering a covenant together were bonded to one another in a closer relationship than even family ties. They each gave up the right to themselves, as their two wills literally became one forever by the covenant agreement. The exchange of articles meant that each was becoming the other, taking the identity of the other person; therefore, whatever affected one, affected the other. They promised to love, support, defend, protect, honor, and care for one another for life. If either one broke this covenant, he would be saying, "May I be as these sacrificial animals." In other words, "May I die." Covenant was a very serious, eternally binding agreement.

Our God has initiated an eternal blood covenant with us. He willingly chose to come to earth as a man, called Jesus Christ. He literally became the sacrifice for our sins, as the blood of the Lamb of God was poured out on Calvary. Today, our God stands at the sacrifice, the Lord Jesus Christ, ready to make a covenant of salvation with you. He initiated this covenant and has already made the sacrifice. Now, all you have to do is to take His hand and walk through the sacrifice, the blood of Jesus, with Him. You do this by completely yielding your life to Christ. Your will is merged with His and the two wills become one. You give up all rights to yourself, as you give Him your robe of sin, your defense of yourself, your provision for your own life, and all the decisions you will make from now on. Salvation is a walk into death...death to your own self, your own will, your own desires, your own plans. In exchange, you take His life, His desires, His plans, His weapons, His protection, His provision...all of Him! If you break this covenant, you are saying that you will be as the sacrifice.

Have you ever entered this covenant with the Lord? It gives you His eternal life, but requires completely giving yours up first. Covenant is a serious, eternally binding agreement. But...to whom do you want to be bound eternally anyway?

HEBREWS 13:20 *"Now the God of peace...through the blood of the everlasting covenant."*

November 21

Get under the umbrella

"I'm getting soaked! There's not a dry thread anywhere on my body. My hair, my clothes, and my shoes have all been drenched in this downpour. And, look at you! Why, you're high and dry! It's all your fault that I am soaking wet. You should have done something. You knew I was out in all this rain. Why didn't you help?"

"Friend, I tried to help. I told you the rain was coming. I offered you an umbrella to cover and protect yourself with, but you were too busy to take time for that. The sun was shining brightly at the time and you saw no need for an umbrella. Then, when the rains started to fall, you had nothing to cover yourself with. So, friend, it's your own fault. An umbrella was available, but you didn't take it!"

Does this describe you? At one time, you were standing in the sunshine of life. Things were going pretty good, for the most part. Your life was busy, filled with activity from sunup to sundown. Between your family, your job, and your hobbies, every minute of every day was pretty well taken. There just wasn't much time for reading and studying the Word of God. And prayer was always a rushed and hurried duty, too. You just mumbled a few words here and there, mainly out of guilt. And Sundays…well, you were so exhausted from the rest of the week that you felt you had to rest. After all, Sunday was your only day for this!

But then, the rains came! There was a downpour in your life, as one problem after another bombarded you. Your whole world was suddenly filled with thunderclouds and violent storms. And now, you are standing here drenched, bewildered, and depressed. You feel so vulnerable, so unprotected, and so helpless, as the rains continue to saturate you.

Well, friend, you need to go stand under the umbrella. You didn't take the umbrella while the sun was out, so you've been without any protection. But, if you will look, you will see that the umbrella is still open, just waiting for you to come and get under it.

That spiritual umbrella is God's Word! It is the only thing that will protect you during the storms of life. Open it, read it, memorize it, meditate on it, and keep it near your heart daily. It won't stop the storms, but it will certainly keep you dry while the rains are falling. Friend, the choice is yours! You can get drenched...or you can go get under the umbrella!

PSALMS 119:165 *"Great peace have they who love Thy law, and nothing shall offend them."*

November 22

Pipeline from glory

It had been there all the time, lying buried beneath the earth's surface. No one knew or even suspected that it was there. For centuries, people had walked on top of the ground, not knowing that this sea of liquid gold was underneath their feet. Some had lived like paupers, when wealth was just a few feet away. And then, one day, the oil was discovered underneath the cold Alaskan soil.

However, the discovery of the oil presented a new problem: how to get it from its source in Alaska to other destinations. Just knowing the oil was there was not enough! The oil did no good underneath the ground. It must be extracted from the earth and transported to other places. The best method of doing so was through a pipeline. What an important place the pipeline plays in getting the riches below the ground to places above the ground, where it can be used to help millions of people.

Dear one, have you yet discovered the vast riches that are in glory? Maybe you have been walking around for years as a Christian, but you have never discovered the sea of God's eternal riches that are there in heaven. Perhaps you've been living as a spiritual pauper, when all God's riches were just a belief away. They have been there all the time, just waiting to be claimed and distributed here on earth.

Well, Christian, God is looking for a pipeline to get these riches from glory to earth. You are that pipeline from glory. You are a channel, through which the liquid gold of God can flow to others here on earth. That's why you need to keep your channel unclogged, free from sin, so God's unsearchable riches of Christ can flow freely through you. God wants to touch the lives of the people around you, and He wants to do it through you! He has chosen to work ONLY through His children, which are His pipelines from glory.

Sometimes you may feel so insignificant that you think your little bitty pipeline won't matter. After all, you are one small person in this vast world. But just remember: how many pipelines does it take to get oil from Alaska to another destination? It only takes one! Likewise, Christian, it only takes one pipeline from glory to earth...and that pipeline is you! God is the unlimited source. You are just simply the channel.

How do you get this treasure of heaven down here and into the lives of others?You do this by prayer. God COULD work any way He chooses, but it just so happens that He has chosen prayer. He will not move here on earth except through prayer. So, little glory pipeline, get in the Word and find out all the riches that are there. Then get busy praying them into being here on earth. Remember: you are God's pipeline from glory!

II CORINTHIANS 4:7 *"But we have this treasure in earthen vessels..."*

November 23

Drop the sugar days

It wasn't "road rage" that was bothering me! This was "kitchen rage!" Boiling up from somewhere deep inside me was a river of frustration, ready to break the dam and flood everything in its path. Why, I didn't have time for this interruption! I was already rushed, already out of time, already pushed to the limit. This certainly wasn't the time to drop a five pound bag of sugar on the floor and watch it scatter from one end of the kitchen to the other. However, regardless of whether I had time or not, the sugar did drop, making a great big mess…and I had no choice but to clean it up!

As I was whining and grumbling and vacuuming, a small, still voice said to my heart, "If you had spent time with Me this morning like I asked you to, this wouldn't have happened. You didn't think you needed My help today, so you never asked…and you've been on your own." Suddenly, like a vapor, my "kitchen rage" just vanished. Whereas I had grumbled, now my heart was instead humbled under the convicting power of the Holy Spirit. I had been getting up early each morning for several years to spend time alone with the Lord. But, for the past few days, I had gotten lax and had punched the snooze button every morning…and punched…and punched. And, by the time I finally got around to getting up each day, there was just no time left to spend with my Savior.

Well, I learned a valuable sugar-coated lesson that morning: I need Jesus more than I need sleep. I have too much to do to substitute extra time in bed in place of extra time with my Savior. And besides, I had much rather Him be in control of my day than for me to be in control. He can certainly handle things a whole lot better than I can…if I'll only let Him. I found out that, if I'll tend to His eternal business down here on earth, He will tend to my earthly business up there in heaven…and my life will go much smoother, without nearly as many interruptions and interferences!

How's your life today? Are you putting Jesus first or last or not at all? Are you beginning each day with Him, turning the controls of your life over to Him, yielding yourself totally to Him, and going out filled with the Spirit? Are you taking care of eternal business and leaving earthly business up to Him? If not, what are you waiting on? How many "drop the sugar" days will it take before you ever learn?

Matthew 6:33 *"But seek ye first the kingdom of God and His righteousness; and all these things shall be added unto you..."*

November 24

Elijahs of the Lord God

There was a deathly silence! Not one single soul spoke a word…or nodded… or gave an affirmative grunt…or responded in any way whatsoever. It was as if an Arctic wind had blown across their mouths and had iced them shut. Elijah was waiting for their response, as he had just given the invitation to the multitude gathered on Mt. Carmel that day. "*How long halt ye between two opinions? If the Lord be God, follow Him; but if Baal, then follow him. And the people answered him not a word.*" *I Kings 18:21*

Yet, just a few hours later, those same people, who did not respond to Elijah's earlier invitation, fell on their faces, saying, "*The Lord, He is God; the Lord, He is the God.*" *I Kings 18:37* They would have all gone home that day just exactly like they came…except for one thing. The fire fell! They had a real, genuine demonstration of the power and presence of God! When they showed up on the mountainside that day, they didn't just hear another lesson that gave them a warm, fuzzy feeling and sent them home satisfied and content with themselves and with the status quo. They didn't just hear about God that day…they met Him for real!

Apparently, the people in Elijah's day weren't seeing anything real and genuine. They didn't know who the real God was any more, because they saw no power, no fire, no reality, no difference in the lives of those who claimed to know God, and no demonstrations of the Word. They had heard about God's power…how He had parted the Red Sea; how He had sent manna from heaven; how He had sent water from a rock; how He had closed the mouths of lions; how He had delivered three men out of the fire. They had "heard," but they had never "seen." It was just words on a page to them until the fire fell!

Well, in America, we're halting between two opinions just like they were in Elijah's day. We go to church and hear and hear and hear all about God. But… we don't ever see Him! We don't come away visibly shaken with the power and presence of Almighty God. In fact, we pretty much come away just like we went, only with maybe a little more Bible knowledge each time. Well, God hasn't changed…we have the same "Lord God of Elijah." What we need then, are some "Elijahs of the Lord God," men who will stay shut up with God until His power is upon them and who can call down the fire on our Arctic Christianity!

I KINGS 18:21 *"How long halt ye between two opinions? If the Lord be God, follow Him; but if Baal, then follow him. And the people answered him not a word."*

November 25

Trade your "L" for an "R"

There is an invisible war going on. Because we cannot see the enemy or see literal fiery missiles being hurled, we have a tendency to forget that we are in an unending battle. We are often oblivious to the enemy's advances and unaware of new territory being taken over by him. He is so sly and devious that he can gradually conquer ground right out from under our noses, while we contentedly smile and play our little religious games.

If we do not recognize and see a battle going on, then we will not fight. We will lay down our weapons and start playing. So, one of the devil's main tactics is to convince us that things are fine. He offers us comfort and ease. He dangles pretty toys of the world before us to entice us. He lures us with all his glittering bait, which is always appealing to the flesh. Everything he offers centers on us... on what we want, on what pleases us, on what feels good to our flesh. He knows that we easily give in to our flesh and we will end up bathing in the world's sweet-smelling delicacies instead of in the sword-piercing Word of God and in the soul wrenching agony of prevailing prayer. Who will pray when it's much more fun and much easier to play?

Another tactic of the devil enticing us to play instead of to pray is to convince us that God has not heard our prayers and will not answer. This leads to discouragement and finally to giving up on our part. We fail to realize that EVERY prayer prayed in faith by a heart in right relationship to God and according to the will of God IS already answered in heaven. But, that answer must reach earth! God generally works through people and will send the answer through one or several chosen vessels. However, Satan sees that the answer is on its way and he does everything in his power to hinder the answer from arriving. If he can discourage the person who is praing, then that one will give up in defeat and the answer will never arrive. Just as Daniel in Daniel 10:11-13 prayed and the answer was delayed by Satanic opposition, so likewise are our prayers often hindered by the same.

Christian, it is time for you to get serious about prayer. You have had it easy long enough! Trade your "l" for an "r" (play to pray) Your loved ones and your nation are at stake. Grow up! Quit being distracted by every temporal toy. This is warfare! Get in the battle and pray until the answers arrive. Pray, Christian, pray!

I JOHN 5:14 *"...if we ask anything according to His will, He heareth us...."*

November 26

From henceforth thou shalt have wars

He knew what it was to trust the Lord. A mighty army of a million men had come against his 580,000 men, making the odds about two to one. He cried unto the Lord, saying, "*Lord, it is nothing with Thee to help, whether with many, or with them who have no power. Help us, O Lord, our God, for we rest on Thee, and in Thy name we go against this multitude." II Chronicles 14:11* Because of his trust in God, King Asa's army unquestionably defeated the Ethiopian army.

And now, Asa, the king of Judah, was facing trouble with Baasha, king of Israel. Somehow, Asa had forgotten about his former victory, won by faith, and relied instead on human means. He appealed to the king of Syria with silver and gold out of the treasuries of the house of the Lord to help him overcome Baasha. God was not pleased at all with this decision and spoke to King Asa through a seer, named Hanani. *"Because thou hast relied on the king of Syria, and not relied on the Lord thy God, therefore is the host of the king of Syria escaped out of thine hand." II Chronicles 16;7 "Herein thou hast done foolishly; therefore, from henceforth thou shalt have wars." II Chronicles 16:9*

Christian, there have been times in the past when you totally relied upon the Lord for victory, just as King Asa did against the Ethiopians. Your situation seemed such an impossibility humanly; yet, God came through miraculously for you, because you were depending upon Him completely, using no means of your own. But now, you are facing a situation which looks hopeless and you have been trying every human idea conceivable to fix it. You are relying upon human strength, human ability, human methods, and human plans. Oh, you have prayed, but you still get up trying to do it yourself.

Maybe God has spoken to you what He did to Asa, "*from henceforth thou shalt have wars.*" Perhaps that is why there is so much conflict and turmoil in your life. It seems like a battle raging inside you. Your home stays in an upheaval. There is no peace anywhere to be found. Well, Christian, get up and start trusting God again. Change your mind's dwelling place, from your problems to God. Then, He will change His Word to you by simply removing one word and substituting another in its place..."from henceforth thou shalt have peace."

II CHRONICLES 16:9 *"Herein thou hast done foolishly...*
from henceforth thou shalt have wars."

November 27

If Jesus knocked

It is Friday afternoon. As you are finishing preparations for the evening meal, the doorbell rings. What a shock you receive as you open the door to discover the Lord Jesus Christ standing there. He tells you that He has come personally to spend the weekend with you. He says that, since you have invited Him into your heart to be your Savior and Lord, He would like to be a guest in your home also, so He can bodily be a part of all that is going on in your life.

How would you feel if this happened to you? Would you be embarrassed, wishing you had known ahead of time, so you could have prepared? Would all the reading materials you have lying around be suitable? Would you mind if Jesus picked any of them up and read through them? Or would you have some things you would like to hide before He sees them?

What about the conversation at your house if He were there? Could you just continue normally as you usually do, or would His presence make a difference in the talk at your house? And would His presence change your activities any? Would you have Him to sit down and watch all the same things on TV that you usually watch? Would you show Him the movies that you rented earlier that day? Would you take Him to all the places that you had planned to go that weekend? On Sunday, would you take Him to that outing your family had planned, or would you take Him to church?

Is there a relationship in your life that would embarrass you in His presence? Would you try to hide that relationship or could you just go on as you always do, acting the same, talking the same, and living the same?

Friend, if Jesus came knocking at your door today, what would you do? Perhaps you would want to do as Adam and Eve did in the Garden of Eden.....cover up your sin. Maybe you, too, have a fig leaf religion. It's good enough for others, but it sure wouldn't stand up under the scrutiny of the Lord Jesus Christ!

II PETER 3:11 *"what manner of persons ought you to be in all holy living and godliness..."*

November 28

What's your mind's address?

From the moment you entered earth's atmosphere, you have occupied some spot on planet earth. Your body takes up a space somewhere. This space is called your address. It is an exact, pinpointed location that singles you out of the billions of others and tells where you live. Someone in China can write a letter to you here in America and it will be delivered to you by your address. Your address is where you can be found!

Your mind has an address also. It stays somewhere. Perhaps your mind's address is your job. You think about your job continually. Even when your body goes home at night, your mind stays where you work. You worry and fret over all the things going on at your job, over all the people there, and over your plans and hopes for the future. Your mind can usually be found dwelling at the place you work. Its address could be: #1 Work Blvd.; Worry, U.S.A.

Maybe your mind's address is materialism. You constantly think about things. You are always wanting new things, deciding how and when to buy the next new thing you want. Your mind is always occupied with either taking care of the things you already have or planning for the ones you are going to get. The address of your mind could be: 4 My Things Street; Want It All, U.S.A.

Or perhaps your mind's address is a relationship. You think about that person all the time. Everything you do revolves around that person. Even when you pray, your mind dwells on that one, as that is mostly what you pray for. To find your mind, someone would go to this address: #1 Idol Road; Obsessed, U.S.A.

If your mind's address is your job, or materialism, or a relationship, then that explains why you are always negative...or discouraged...or worried...or dissatisfied...or hurt...or restless...or without peace and joy. You need to move! Your mind needs a new address: 4 Jesus Only; Praise Blvd.; Heaven. Pack the bags of your mind and move out of this old world. There's nothing here but heartache and disappointment and sorrow. Move in with Jesus! Your body's address may still be here...but your mind's address will be Heaven.

ISAIAH 26:3 *"Thou wilt keep him in perfect peace whose mind is stayed upon Thee."*

November 29

Severed fingers cannot survive alone!

What a sad burial service! Poor old finger! He thought he could do without the rest of the body. So, he just separated himself from the body.....and he died! If only he had realized how much he needed the rest of the body, this would never have happened.

At first, he was part of the body. He thought it was neat how the eyes worked, how the feet walked, and how the knees bent. But as time went on, he began to get critical of the other body parts. He resented the mouth telling him what to do. He didn't like all the places the feet went. He didn't care for some of the things the hands held. He just picked every member of the body apart. All he had to do was to see one thing he thought was wrong about a member, and he never saw anything good after that. He completely discounted them from then on. And finally, he became so disgruntled that he just separated himself. When he did, he died! He could have been an active, participating, contributing, important member of the body - but his caustic, critical attitude severed him from his vital, life-support system, thus bringing about an early death.

Many a Christian is just like this poor old finger. He got saved, thereby joining him to the rest of the body of Christ. At first, he was excited about coming to church and being around the other members of the body. He thought it was neat how the preacher preached, the teacher taught, the singers sang, etc. But as time went on, he began to get critical of the other body parts. He resented any spiritual authority telling him what to do. And, even though he had had a messed up life, he would not listen to someone else whose life had been productive. He picked every message and every messenger apart. He judged every act of his fellow members. If he saw even one thing that he thought was wrong in another member, he completely wrote them off forever!

Finally, the disgruntled Christian separated himself from the rest of the body, thereby becoming a severed finger Christian. By doing so, he separated himself from the very thing that Christ loved, gave Himself for, and established Himself the head of. Severed finger lost his joy, his peace, his love for others, his zeal for God, etc., literally becoming an unproductive, useless, dead Christian. Severed fingers cannot survive alone!

EPHESIANS 5:25 *"as Christ also loved the church, and gave Himself for it."*

November 30

The buck stops here

It started in the Garden of Eden and has not stopped since. Adam passed the buck to Eve. Eve passed the buck to Satan. And the buck stopped there! Of course, Satan does not mind the buck being passed to him at all. He will gladly take the blame, because that will keep a person from facing his own responsibility and doing something about it. If someone else is to blame, that lets a person off the hook!

The devil doesn't care to whom you pass the buck, just as long as you don't let it stop with you! He loves for you to pass the buck to your parents...or your spouse...or your circumstances...or even to him. If your attitude is, "The devil made me do it," you become the laughing stock of hell, for you have swallowed the devil's lying bait hook, line, and sinker.

Has it ever dawned on you that the devil can NOT make you do anything? He does not have that kind of power. You have a free will and YOU are the one who chooses your own course of action. The devil is responsible only for the temptation, but you are responsible for your reaction to that temptation. Don't ever blame the devil or anyone else for what you do. No one can make you do anything you don't want to do. Now, they may entice you or tempt you, but you choose to listen to them and act accordingly, or to listen to God and do as He says.

Why does Satan play "Pass the Buck" with you? He does it because it works! You like to play that game, never realizing its destructive powers. It keeps you away from the root of your problem, which is your own sin. Sin enslaves and imprisons you, keeping you bound and ineffective spiritually. If Satan can keep you fooled into staying in that state, you will never be any threat to his kingdom of darkness. However, if you let the buck stop with you and acknowledge your sin and responsibility, you will be set free. The Bible says "*You shall know the truth and the truth shall make you free." John 8:32*

Uh, oh, here comes that buck again! What are you going to do with it this time?Are you going to pass it to someone else...or are you going to let it stop with you? Let's see if you are a pathetic wimp or a triumphant warrior!

LEVITICUS 5:5 *"When someone is guilty, "he shall confess that he has sinned in that thing."*

December
St. John's Wort

December 1

Verbal tongue lashing

"You're no good." "You can't do anything right." "You don't deserve anything." "You're not as good as everybody else." "You're not as smart as others." "You had a bad upbringing." "If everybody finds out what you're really like, then nobody will like you." "You have done some awful things in the past." "You're dumb...you're ugly...you have no self esteem...you don't measure up... you have nothing important to say...you're a nobody."

Does any of this sound familiar? Chances are, the devil and his demons have paid many a visit to you and gave you some of this verbal tongue lashing. And perhaps you just swallowed that big pot of verbal trash hook, line, and sinker. It soured in your spiritual stomach, gave you spiritual indigestion, and drained your spiritual tank, leaving it dead on empty. It left you defeated, discouraged, depressed, and incapacitated in prayer, Bible study, and the Lord's work.

Well, friend, it's high time you start believing the Word of God! According to it, the moment you accept Jesus as your Savior and Lord, you are saved from your sin, from the wrath to come, and from your own self. Those things are over and done with. When you get well from a disease, you don't dwell on the disease any more. You forget it and press on. Well, you have been made whole, friend, so quit dwelling on past sin, on negatives, and on your own self. Rather, you should "*press toward the mark for the prize of the high calling of God in Christ Jesus." Philippians 3:14*

Therefore, when the devil comes around the next time with his verbal garbage, you can reply, "Oh, no, devil...it's not that I'm no good. I'm dead! I don't even exist any more. I've been cancelled out! The Lord Jesus lives here now, so you'll just have to take this up with Him. He is the owner of this property, so just unleash all your filthy verbal tongue lashing out at Him, the new tenant, Jesus Christ. If you're looking for me, you'll find me at my new address. "N Heavenly Places; Christ Jesus, Heaven."

I CORINTHIANS 6:19 *"What" Know ye not that your body is the temple of the Holy Ghost...and you are not your own?"*

December 2

Cranking up the engine of your belief

Out of the multitudes, there came a man in the throes of desperation and exasperation, bringing his son with him. The boy had suffered for years from epilepsy, causing him to fall and get hurt time and time again. The father had tried everything he knew to help his boy. He had even brought his son to the disciples, thinking they could help, but they couldn't do anything for the boy either.

In a last ditch effort to get help, the father knelt down before the Lord Jesus Christ, begging Him for mercy for his son. Jesus, summoning the child, healed him that very hour. Dazed, the disciples wondered why they had been unable to help the boy. They came to Jesus later and asked Him why they had failed. To this, He replied, "*Because of your unbelief; for verily I say unto you, If you have faith as a grain of mustard seed, you shall say unto this mountain, Move from here to yonder place and it shall move; and nothing shall be impossible unto you. Howbeit, this kind goeth not out except by prayer and fasting." Matthew 17:20, 21*

What was wrong with the disciples? Had not Jesus given them power against unclean spirits, to cast them out, and to heal all manner of sickness and all manner of disease? Yes, He HAD given them power, but that power was like that of a lawn mower engine. It must be cranked up first. They had failed to turn the power on, the power of faith. Jesus rebuked them for their unbelief, for their lack of faith.

As they listened to the words of Jesus, the disciples were again perplexed. They DID believe! They DID have faith! So, how come their faith did not crank up the engine of power? As Jesus continued talking, suddenly the eye-opening words from His lips pierced their hearts, "*Howbeit, this kind goeth not out except by prayer and fasting.*" Now, they understood. They HAD been given this power, but not a license to use it as they pleased. God had put a safety valve on the power, lest they crank up the engine and mow the wrong lawn. This safety valve was prayer and fasting. They could now see that there were steps to take before the power could be used appropriately. They must first fast and pray, seeking the mind and heart of God. Then, God would begin to infuse them with His thoughts, His plans, and His will. As God placed His will and His faith inside their hearts, that cranked up the engine of belief, thereby turning on the power. That power was then used to carry out ONLY the will of God!

Perhaps, today, like the disciples, you have also been unable to help others. You know that you are a Christian and that Jesus' power dwells within you. Yet, you have just settled down into believing that other Christians can exercise this power…but not you!Believer, you are living in unbelief! You need to have your engine of belief cranked up. Jesus would say the same thing to you that He said to those disciples back then, "*This kind goeth not out except by prayer and fasting.*" Maybe it's time for you to push back from the earthly table and sit down at the heavenly table. Out of all the multitudes around, some will come in the throes of desperation and exasperation. Will you be able to help them?

MATTHEW 17:21 *"Howbeit, this kind goeth not out except by prayer and fasting."*

December 3

Selling glory products

You have decided to make a change in your life. You are getting older now and your face is beginning to need some help. You decide to try some new makeup, which could hide many of the blemishes and give you a more youthful, radiant look. So, you go to the mall to one of the makeup counters and begin talking to the saleswoman about her product. However, you notice that her makeup is splotched, pallid, and drab. It looks terrible. There is no glow, no healthy radiance, no life to her face. She is a poor representative of her product, thereby leading you to the definite conclusion that you certainly don't want the makeup she is using and selling.

Leaving this counter, you move on to a makeup counter in another store and begin talking with the saleswoman there. Just one look at her face tells you something. Her makeup looks so fresh and clean. In fact, it is almost flawless. She has a youthful, appealing glow, even though she is a middle-aged woman. Of course, it doesn't take long for you to decide which product you want. The representative made the difference in your decision!

Christian, you claim to be saved, so that makes you a representative of the Lord Jesus Christ. Folks cannot see Him, so they are going to judge whether they want Him by what they see in His representatives. Perhaps you are a representative from the first makeup counter. You are always down and discouraged.....no joy, no excitement, no enthusiasm. You hardly ever smile, much less laugh. Much of your conversation is grumbling and complaining.... just always down in the mouth. You are dull and drab. There is no glow of Christ on your life. You are not fresh. Judging by your life, folks would think that God is dead. They certainly would not believe that a supernatural, all powerful, victorious, overcoming, wonderful, almighty God lives inside you! You surely don't have anything they want. So, they will move on to the next counter.

Hopefully, you are a representative from the second counter. You are selling glory products. You have a boss who is the best there is. He has bought you for His own and is abundantly supplying all your needs. The benefits of working for Him are out of this world. He has provided an eternal life insurance policy for you, paid in full. He is preparing a mansion for you on the golden shores of glory when you retire from working for Him. You are so excited about being His representative that many folks want the same glory products that you say are yours!

What kind of representative are you? Folks will be watching you today, so you had better put on your Christ-like makeup. You are selling glory products. Will anyone want what you have by looking at your life?

II CORINTHIANS 5:20 *"Now, then, we are ambassadors for Christ..."*

December 4

Better check the oil!

He had bought the car of his dreams. Oh, it was a beautiful machine and he was so proud of it. Every day, he washed it. He polished it often, keeping it just as beautiful as the day he bought it. He would not even let the tires get dirty. His car was spotless outwardly. But, he neglected the inward parts of his car. He never checked the oil, he never had a tune-up, and he never inspected the brake system. He spent all his time and efforts on the external, to the complete neglect of the internal. Things went fine for quite awhile. However, one day, his car ran out of oil and blew his engine. How foolish he had been to take care of the outside while neglecting the inside!

Perhaps you are thinking that no one could be that stupid. Probably not when it comes to cars.....but, there are many who are that foolish when it comes to their own lives. They take really good care of the exterior. They work out, they eat right, they dress good, and they keep themselves clean and polished. They spend much time in caring for the outside and in making it look good, but they spend very little time on the inside. They do not put fuel in, as they read little or none of the life-giving Word of God every day. Their oil supply is ignored, as they do not spend the time alone with the Lord Jesus in order to be filled with the oil of His Spirit daily. They never have a tune-up, either....a time when they get before God in confession and repentance and allow Him to clean them up and fine tune their spiritual lives. They never inspect the brakes or add brake fluid, as they don't hide God's Word in their hearts, thus enabling them to put the brakes on sin!

Our society has degenerated from the highest level of living, which is spiritual, to the lowest level, which is physical. Everything is geared to the lowest, taking care of the external. Listen to the talk around you - all about the body. Watch anything on TV. It's all sex, violence, eating, body-building, etc. Even the music gravitates to the body, emphasizing the beat rather than the melody or the words. People are caring for the external to the complete neglect of the internal.

Friend, the car will run awhile without taking care of the internal, but it will not run forever. If you've been working out at a fitness center, eating health foods, and doing everything you can to take care of your physical body, but you are doing practically nothing for your spiritual life, then your oil is probably getting pretty low.Your spiritual engine may be about to blow!

MATTHEW 25:4 *"But the wise took oil in their vessels with their lamps."*

December 5

Some folks die in Moab

Because of the famine in the land, Elimelech was afraid for his family. He saw no possible way to provide for them in his homeland of Bethlehem-judah. So, after trying to figure out what to do and coming up with no solutions, he decided that his only answer was to move his family to another country where food was more plentiful. Reluctantly, he packed up his wife, Naomi, and his two sons and moved to Moab.

Elimelech's decision proved to be fatal. Since it was based entirely on the circumstances rather than on the Word of God, it was doomed from the beginning. In the first place, Elimelech's name literally means, "My God is King." His decision said the opposite…that his God was not King…that his God could NOT take care of them in a famine…that he needed to make a logical decision, based on common sense. In the second place, Moab was an ungodly place, coming from the descendants of an incestuous relationship, and worshiping the idol, Chemosh. It was not a place to take a family, even if food were scarce. Elimelech left the place of God's blessing in a time of barrenness for a more profitable place. He never returned home again.....never came back to the place of God's blessing. He and his two sons died there in Moab.

Christian, you are in a spiritual famine right now. At one time, God was moving in your life and it was so exciting all the time. You felt like shouting to the world, "My God is King." But, it's not like that now. You wonder if God is anywhere to be found. It is dry and barren. Nothing you do is producing any fruit whatsoever. You are thinking about moving. Logical common sense tells you to give up what you are doing and move on to something more profitable. You have cooled off in your Bible reading and prayer. You have been skipping some church services, worshiping the idol of "Do what you want."

Oh, Christian, wake up! Famines are to prove your faithfulness. God wants people who will remain faithful, steadfast, and committed at ALL times. He will allow occasional famines to see if you will remain where He put you. Even a wimp can be faithful in abundant times, but only a warrior will remain true in times of famine. Christian, seek God. Do not leave the land of original blessing. You may never return again. You cannot always get back to Bethlehem-judah when you move to Moab. Some folks die in Moab!

REVELATION 2:10 *"Be thou faithful unto death, and I will give thee a crown of life."*

December 6

Will the true church please stand up?

Upon this Rock I will build My church, and the gates of hell shall not prevail against it." Matthew 16:18 What powerful words coming from the lips of the Lord Jesus Christ! In the first place, He says, "Upon this Rock." That Rock is Jesus! The church is built upon the Lord Jesus Christ Himself - not upon sinking sand, not upon some weak foundation, not upon shifting earth. The church is built on Jesus Christ, the Solid Rock, Who is unmovable, unchangeable, firm, steadfast, everlasting, all powerful, and strong!The Solid Rock cannot be shaken or overtaken! He cannot be rooted up or booted out! He cannot be defeated or go unheeded! He IS the Rock, the Solid Rock, the Rock of Ages!

In the second place, He says, "*I will build.*" Jesus, the carpenter from Galilee, the Creator of the Universe, is the One building the church. The Divine Architect drew up the blueprint for the church, designing it exactly as He wanted it. It is according to His perfect specifications. He designed it and He is building it. Now, men may design and build buildings and try to grow churches, but the Lord Jesus Christ is the One who is building the true church!

Thirdly, He says, "*My church.*" The church does NOT belong to anyone else. It is not the Pastor's church, not the deacons' church, not the trustees' church, and not the members' church. The church belongs to Jesus. He set it up. It is His business - and He is the One who is supposed to be running it. The reason churches are in such a mess is that they have forgotten whose church it is!

Fourthly, He says, "*and the gates of hell shall not prevail against it.*" This means that all the power of hell itself, represented by the importance and strength of gates, shall not be strong against the church. Hell is powerless against the true church, since it is founded upon The Rock, built by the Divine Architect, and belongs completely to the Lord of Glory! It is high time for the true church to stand up, push back the gates of hell, go on the offensive, run the devil and his bunch off, and reclaim our territory! We're the church!

MATTHEW 16:18 *"Upon this Rock, I will build My church..."*

December 7

Can the crooked be made straight?

Have you ever thought about why creeks and rivers are crooked and twisted and have so many bends in them? It is because they follow the path of least resistance. When they come to an obstacle, they simply go around it, rather than remove it or overcome it. Often, especially in small creeks, debris builds up in some spots and will actually alter the course that the creek has taken for years. All this debris and all these obstacles then stand as visible witnesses that they won over the body of water that they stood in the way of - unless, of course, a mighty flood comes along with the power to wash these obstacles away.

Friend, perhaps you are like that creek! Your life is crooked and twisted and bent. You have always followed the path of least resistance, going around every obstacle rather than removing it or overcoming it. As you stand on the banks of your life, looking back over its past course, you see all those obstacles and all that debris standing as visible witnesses that they overcame you rather than you overcoming them. You have tried in your own power to straighten out your life, but you have come to the conclusion, as did Solomon, *"That which is crooked cannot be made straight." Ecclesiastes 1:15*

You want your life to change. You're sick of it! However, the course ahead of you is an obstacle course that no one can conquer. You see three major obstacles that you have always faced and have never overcome: the world, the flesh, and the devil. You absolutely CANNOT make this obstacle course. It's too hard for anyone, especially for someone who has already proven such a repeated failure!

But, wait! There stands an old rugged cross, from which a voice speaks to your heart, *"I will go before you and make the crooked places straight." Isaiah 45:2* Suddenly, you realize that there is One, and only One, who walked the straight path, overcoming everything, including death, hell, and the grave! There's only One who can take a crooked, bent, messed up life and make it straight again. There's only One whose blood can flow like a flood through your life and wash away all the debris of sin that stands as a visible reminder of your failure. There's only One who can do it. His name is Jesus. So, just put your hand into His, give Him control of your life, and follow Him! He will make the crooked places straight!

ISAIAH 45:2 *"I will go before thee, and make the crooked places straight..."*

December 8

Does your walk match your talk?

For the first time, you meet your new neighbor, who tells you he works for Sunbeam Bread. Of course, you accept his word at face value. But, as days go by, something does not add up. You see him pull up in his driveway in a Colonial Bread truck. You go over to his house one day and are surprised to see Colonial bread, Colonial buns, Colonial break cakes, etc. So, you secretly follow him to work one day and he goes straight to the Colonial factory.You are bewildered! Your neighbor says one thing with his mouth, but he is living another.

Sadly, there are thousands of Americans who are just like this neighbor. They say they are saved, which means that God is their Master, their employer, their boss. This means they are working for God because, according to the Bible, no man can serve two masters. Everyone is serving either God or the devil. These are the only two spiritual employment agencies in existence!

So, here's a person who says with his mouth he is saved. Yet, when you look at his life, something just does not add up. He rarely ever goes to church, of which his professed Boss is the head. He seldom ever reads the Holy Bible, which is his Boss' manual of instructions for life. You never see him talking to his Boss, down on his knees in prayer. He never weeps over or witnesses to the lost, which is his Boss' explicit instructions to His co-laborers. If you follow this person around for a while, you see that he says one thing with his mouth but lives another.

This person is completely deceived! He claims to work for God, but instead he is working for the devil and doesn't even know it. He is living a lie, believing the father of lies himself. He has been deceived into believing he is saved and on his way to heaven when, in actuality, he is a lost man on his way to hell.

Does this describe you? If you are truly saved, your life WILL show it! Folks won't be shocked by what they see in you after hearing what you say. If they followed you for a month, they would see that your walk lines up with your talk. However, if you say one thing but live another, friend, you need to get saved today! You need to change your boss, your spiritual employment agency, your line of work, and your destination! Make sure your walk matches your talk!

ISAIAH 2:5 *"Let us walk in the light of the Lord."*

December 9

To plant or not to plant

Look at this! I hold in my hand a small acorn seed. It is not very big or impressive. It really won't do me any good like it is. I can put it on a shelf somewhere or continue holding it and looking at it, and it will always remain just an acorn seed. But, if I get down on my knees in the dirt, plant the seed, and water it, it will one day grow into a mighty oak. It is not the size of the seed that matters. It is what I do with it that counts. "Mighty oaks from little acorns grow".....that is, if the acorns are planted and watered.

One day, the apostles were talking to Jesus and they asked Him to increase their faith. He replied, *"If you had faith as a grain of mustard seed, you might say unto this sycamine tree, Be thou plucked up by the root, and be thou planted in the sea; and it should obey you." Luke 17:6* Jesus was trying to show the apostles that the size of their faith was not the determining factor of spiritual success. It was what they did with their faith that mattered. To plant or not to plant.....that was the real question!

You see, the Word of God contains thousands of promises. All these are spiritual seeds. Each seed has the life of God within it, just as an acorn houses the life of an oak tree within. But these promises, like the acorn, will not do you any good by just reading them or talking about them or claiming them. They must first be planted. You must get down on your knees and pray, for prayer is the soil into which the seeds of God's Word are planted. As you continue to pray daily, you are watering and tending to the seeds. God is responsible for bringing the life out of its shell and into the light. But, He will not do that unless the seed is first planted. God does not work without prayer.

Christian, you have the Word of God, housing all the seeds of truth. You have the soil of prayer to plant those seeds of truth in. But, you need one more vital ingredient...faith! Faith is the motivator that causes you to plant or not to plant. Faith gets you on your knees, because faith believes that prayer works! Even a mustard seed faith will cause you to pray, believing; the prayer of faith gets God's ear; and God brings the results!

Today, this question is before you. To plant or not to plant...what will YOU do?

LUKE 17:6 *"If you had faith as a grain of mustard seed, you might say unto this sycamine tree, Be thou plucked up by the root, and be thou planted in the sea; and it should obey you."*

December 10

Needed desperately - Aarons and Hurs

His arms felt like they weighed a million pounds. It was all he could do to continue holding them up. With sheer, dogged determination, Moses mustered up every shred of energy he had. As he stood on top of the hill, he could see the troops fighting in the valley. As long as he held his arms up, the Israelites would prevail over the Amalekites; but, when he dropped his arms in exhaustion, the Amalekites would prevail. He realized all the lives that were at stake, all the lives that were literally in his raised or lowered hands. He could not afford to even slack off, much less quit. But, he was so tired that he just could not go on any longer.

Recognizing their leader's need for help and support, two loyal men, Aaron and Hur, came to Moses' aid. They put a big stone under him and had him to sit on it. Aaron got on one side of Moses and Hur got on the other, and they held up Moses'arms until the going down of the sun. The children of Israel vanquished Amalek and his people with the edge of the sword. The victory was won because of the faithful and loyal support that Aaron and Hur gave to their leader!

Christian, you might not be a Moses, but you can certainly be an Aaron or a Hur. How can you sit so contentedly and watch your Pastor and your teachers fight the spiritual battle alone? Can't you see that your leaders desperately need your support and loyalty? Has it ever dawned on you that your leaders get so tired that they don't feel they can go on any longer? Maybe you're lying back in a hammock spiritually, taking it easy. Well, your leaders aren't! They are studying and preparing to teach you! They are praying and weeping over you! They are burdened over your problems! They are distressed over your shallowness and sin, as you argue with them and pick them apart, when they are only trying to teach you the Truth! They are grieving over your nonchalant attitude about coming to hear and study the Word, especially after they have spent hours in preparation and you do not care enough to even come and support them. Your lack of loyalty is killing your leaders! They are fighting for you; yet, you let them fight alone! You certainly do not want it to cost you anything!

Why don't you get your eyes off yourself, O lax one, and become an Aaron or a Hur? Your leaders need you! They are getting awfully tired in the relentless battle, in which the enemy, without doubt, seems to be winning But, if you'll get behind your leaders, praying, encouraging, supporting, helping, and holding up their spiritual arms in battle, we can run the devil off and win this battle! Together, we can vanquish the enemy!

EXODUS 17:12 *"Aaron and Hur held up his hands...until the going down of the sun."*

December 11

Jesus is looking for failures

As he stood there before all the multitudes of people, this rugged, uneducated, seemingly unqualified fisherman lifted up his voice to everyone in the crowd. He began to expound Jesus unto them, at which time many were pricked in their hearts. In repen-tance, they gladly received his word and were saved and baptized. That same day, three thousand souls were added to this first church.

Continuing daily to teach and preach Jesus, Peter astounded people everywhere he went. When men saw his boldness and perceived that he was an ignorant and unlearned man, they marveled and took notice that Peter had been with Jesus.

Could this possibly be the same man who, only a few weeks earlier, had been a complete failure? He had been with Jesus in the Garden of Gethsemane, when his beloved Master was in such agony and distress of soul that the small capillaries under His skin burst and oozed blood from His pores. Yet, Peter was asleep in this hour of his Master's great agony. He was there at the time of Jesus' arrest and he was resisting the will of God while Jesus was submitting. As Jesus was arrested and carried away, Peter followed afar off. He sat down among his Lord's enemies and even went as far as to deny Jesus and the faith. Wow! Talk about a failure!

Well, what happened to transform such a failure into a mighty man of God? Judging by his track record, he could have given up in despair and called it quits. However, Peter gave up to victory instead of giving up to despair. He WAS a failure! He that. But, then, Jesus wasn't looking for successes, because anyone who could succeed without Him did not need Him in the first place. Jesus was looking for failures! He needed failures who would give up.....not to defeat and despair, but to Him! Peter gave himself totally to the Lord. He quit trying to do it and let Jesus do it through him.

Today, maybe you're a failure! That's great! Jesus is looking for failures, so you qualify! You have the best reason in the world to turn your life over to Him completely. You need to give up today - not to despair, but to Jesus!

ACTS 4:13 *"Now when they saw the boldness of Peter and John, and perceived that they were ignorant and unlearned men, they marveled; and they took knowledge of them, that they had been with Jesus."*

December 12

Hoarded grain for abundant gold?

According to an old legend in India, a poor beggar was standing by the roadside when a wealthy Rajah passed by. Holding out his bowl, which contained a few grains of rice, the beggar was hoping for a handout from this one who had so much to give. However, much to the beggar's surprise, instead of giving him a handout, the Rajah asked for some of the rice. Very reluctantly and begrudgingly, the beggar gave the Rajah one grain of rice. Then, the Rajah asked for another grain. This really upset the beggar, for he wanted to hold onto every single piece of rice. After all, those few grains were all he had in the whole world. He could hardly bear to give his last few possessions to this wealthy man. He unwillingly gave it all!

As the Rajah rode away, the beggar sadly looked down into what he thought was an empty bowl. Much to his surprise, the bowl was no longer empty. In the place of each grain of rice that he had given to the Rajah, there was one grain of gold. How blessed and excited the beggar was, as he realized he had given everything he had, only to get much more in return!

Perhaps today, friend, you are that beggar before Almighty God. You came to Him, praying and beseeching Him to supply something that you felt an urgent need for. However, instead of answering your petition, He asked something of you. He pinpointed a specific area of your life, an area that He wanted you to surrender totally to Him. When you refused to turn that thing over to Him, He then began putting pressure on you. Everything in your life started falling apart. Not only did He refuse to give you your desire, but He even began taking things from you as well. At this point, you certainly didn't understand what was going on, so you got angry with God. Everybody else appeared to be getting along fine, making it look as though God was picking on you. So, you concluded, "Well, He is Almighty God and He can do anything He chooses. He could have stopped all this from happening to me, but He didn't! Therefore, I believe He must be punishing me for some reason, even though He's blessing all those others around me who aren't even faithful to Him like I am. It's just not fair!"

Dear one, like the Rajah, God is passing by today. Why don't you undo your clenched fist and surrender to Him that last grain of your life that He's asking for? Do some trading on the Heavenly stock market. Invest one grain of your life...and, in return, He will give you one eternal gold nugget. Quit your whining and blaming God. He is only trying to replace your hoarded grain with His abundant spiritual gold!

MATTHEW 10:39 *"...he that loses his life for My sake shall find it...."*

December 13

Don't look at the lions!

Pulling back on his father's arms and digging his heels into the ground, he just refused to go any further. Very patiently, his father squatted down and put his arm around his small son. "What's wrong, son? Don't you want to see the lions? I thought that was the main reason you wanted to come to the zoo today." "No, daddy, I'm scared. Listen to all those big old lions. I'm afraid of them. Daddy, why aren't you afraid?" "Well, son, you're looking at the lions...but I'm looking at the cage!"

Dear one, perhaps you are like that small son. You have pulled back on your Father's arm, dug your spiritual heels in, and refused to go any further. You have heard the roar of many "what ifs!" You have seen a lot of ferocious looking circumstances up ahead, just waiting to pounce on you and rip you to shreds. You're afraid to go forward in the direction your Father is taking you, even though He's holding your hand. Somehow, even though you know your Father is all-powerful and has never failed you, you still cannot bring yourself to believe that He is going to handle this particular situation for you. You're afraid that the circumstantial lions will really get you this time.

So, you have balked on God. You've come to a spiritual stand still in your life. You're not going forward and you certainly don't want to go back where you came from. Well, it's high time to get your eyes off the circumstantial lions and look at the cage instead. The enemy may roar and he may look quite intimidating, but you must remember that he's on a chain. He can only go as far as your Father will let him. And besides, if you'll just look in his mouth when he lets out a big roar, you'll find that he has no teeth. He's all bark and no bite...just a big bag of hot air, trying to scare you and intimidate you. Your Father has already rendered him powerless. Jesus *"disarmed the powers and authorities. He made a public spectacle of them, triumphing over them by the cross." Colossians 2:15*

Today, why don't you take your Father by the hand and go with Him? The loud roar of the "what ifs" will be silenced as you go. The circumstantial lions will tuck their tails and flee. You needn't be afraid. Don't look at the lions, my friend. Look at the cage instead!

COLOSSIANS 2:15 *Jesus "disarmed the powers and authorities."*

December 14

Infected with a Laodicean virus

Inside your body is an army of little dedicated soldiers, all dressed in white. They stand ready for battle day and night, never sleeping and never laying down their armor. They are on call twenty-four hours a day. As soon as the battle cry is sounded, they rush to the scene of the conflict, even giving their lives for the victory. They work together as a mighty team, surrounding and attacking the intruder and eventually killing him. They are relentless! They will not give up until the battle is won!

These little soldiers are called white corpuscles. As soon as any foreign intruder invades your body, thousands of these little soldiers rush to its defense. They attack and destroy the foreigner, losing their lives in the process. That's what "pus" is. It is all those cor(pus)cles who gave their lives to kill the invader!

It's too bad that the body of Christ does not work equally as well. Inside the body of Christ is an army of little soldiers, all dressed in white robes of righteousness, having been washed clean by the blood of the Lamb. These soldiers should be standing ready for battle day and night, never sleeping spiritually and never laying down their armor. These soldiers should be on call twenty-four hours a day. As soon as a foreign intruder invades any member of the body of Christ, these little soldiers should rush to the scene of the conflict, even giving their lives for the victory. They should give their lives in prayer, in fasting, in weeping, in concern over the wounded member. They should work together as a team, surrounding the wounded with the love of God, with phone calls, with cards and letters, and with encouragement. They should be relentless, not giving up until the battle's won.

The body of Christ today has been invaded by a Laodicean virus and mortal infection has set in. But, something has gone awry in the body. The message of corruption is not getting through from the Head to the corpuscles. The Pastors are suffering from the "all is well" syndrome. They are not preaching on sin and judgment, so the soldiers do not know to fight. They are playing while the body is decaying, because no alarm is being sounded! Oh for an injection of some Holy Ghost, spirit-filled, status-quo shattering messengers into the blood stream of the body of Christ, who will call all soldiers to battle until this Laodicean virus is destroyed!

PSALMS 18:39 *"For Thou hast girded me with strength unto the battle..."*

December 15

Yield to the pruning shears

"Ouch! That hurts! What is going on? I have been a good little branch this year. Why, I bore fruit for my master, and now look what he's doing! He is cutting me mercilessly. There's not going to be anything left if he keeps cutting. Oh, he is killing me! This is so painful! I don't understand. I just don't understand."

"Little branch, I know you don't understand, but just trust me. Haven't I always been a good vinedresser? Just look at all those older branches who have much fruit on them. Oh, how many times they have been through this same process, but it took that to get them where they are - a bearer of much fruit. You see, little branch, I want you also to bear much fruit. But, in order for that to happen, you must be pruned. Each year, you get too much branch, too much of yourself, and all the nourishment from the vine then goes to you instead of to the fruit. That's why I must prune you!

So, little branch, just yield gratefully and thankfully to what I am doing. I could chop you off, you know, and work on the other branches instead. Not all of them are whining and complaining like you are! But, I see great possibilities in you. Oh, you are going to have much fruit when growing season comes, and you will be a delight to me, your vinedresser. Everyone will know what an awesome vinedresser I am as they see, not you, but all that fruit.....and they will praise me for it!"

Christian, you are that little branch and God is the Vinedresser. Maybe you are going through the pruning process right now and you just do not understand it at all. It is so painful! You feel like you cannot take any more. You have been whining and complaining and even questioning the Vinedresser, as though you know what you need better than He does! Well, stop it right now! You had better thank your heavenly Vinedresser that He cares enough about you to even fool with you at all. He could just chop you off, you know!But, He is lovingly, patiently pruning you so you can bear much fruit. There is way too much self in you that must yet be pruned before fruit bearing can occur. So, little Christian, yield gratefully and joyfully to the pruning shears of your heavenly Vinedresser. It won't be long before growing season comes again!

JOHN 15;2 *"...every branch that beareth fruit, He purgeth it, that it may bring forth much fruit."*

December 16

Bringing into captivity every thought

Just suppose that a very strange phenomenon has happened in your body. Your thoughts, instead of being contained silently within the confines of your head, suddenly have become audible. As soon as you think something, it is spoken at the same time for all to hear. Now, suppose that everyone else can hear your thoughts audibly, except you. You do not know that your thoughts are being verbalized.

As you sit in church comfortably, unaware that people can hear you think, what would they be hearing? What would they find out about your opinion of the Pastor, or the people around you, or the message? How much would they learn about Jesus from hearing your thoughts? Would they hear your judgment of sin in others, or your brokenness over your own sin? Would they hear your derogatory remarks about others, or your genuine grief over their spiritual condition? Would they hear your love of the world, or your love for Jesus?

When you go about your daily business, what would the cashiers hear as they rang up your merchandise? What would the people in line hear? What would your co-workers hear? What would your customers hear as you waited on them? What would your spouse or family hear as you were around them? What would the lost people around you hear as you passed them daily?

Wouldn't it be an awful thing if people could hear what you're thinking? Well, friend, God does! He knows every thought you think. He even knows the motives of your heart. Everything you think is passed through the council halls of heaven. God hears audibly what you think silently. Knowing this, you should learn to bring your thoughts captive to Christ instead of letting them wander anywhere they choose. You should determine to train and discipline your mind, to keep it on things above rather than on things on earth. You should today begin to take control of your thoughts. Remember: others may not hear what you think...but God does!

II CORINTHIANS 10:5 *"Casting down imaginations and every high thing that exalts itself against the knowledge of God, and bringing into captivity every thought to the obedience of Christ."*

December 17

Luke Warm, Wurl Lee, or I. M. Busy

Satan hates God! Since he cannot physically do anything to hurt God, he has found other ways of attack. One such way is accusation. He goes before God day and night, as Job 1:6-12 and Revelation 12:10 tell us, to accuse God's children of not caring about him or loving Him. This hurts the heart of our great God!

Let's imagine one such conversation of Satan with the Lord. "Well, here I am again, from going to and fro in the earth. You say Your children love you. Ha! Ha! They don't care a thing about You. Why, just consider Your servant, Luke Warm. He claims to be a Christian, but he does not even care enough about You to come to Your house every time Your children meet to honor and worship You. He is too tired...or he must run off to the lake or to a game with his family... or he needs his sleep. If he really loved You, he would be there with bells on, anxious to meet with You, to hear from You, and to learn about You!

And, just consider Your servant, Wurl Lee. You cannot tell that he belongs to You. There is certainly NO family resemblance. In fact, he resembles the world. He goes where they go, dresses like they dress, and talks like they talk. Oh, he goes to church fairly regularly, but that does not mean much. He is accepted and loved by the world. He just "loves" everybody, embraces their sin by his silence, and treads Your blood under his feet by a lifestyle that is good, but not holy, devoted, passionate, and fervent for You! Wurl Lee is quite worldly!

Oh, and just consider I. M. Busy. He only gives You fifteen minutes a day. That's all the time he has after he has worked all day, attended ball games and socials, taken care of his daily needs, read the newspaper through, and watched T.V. It is a joke if You think he loves You! Why, he loves me more than he loves You! You can tell that by the time he spends doing what I want him to do in comparison with the time he spends doing what You want him to do."

Christian, are you a Luke Warm, or a Wurl Lee, or an I. M. Busy? If so, it is time to change your name to I. M. His. Jesus bought you with His own blood and loves you with an everlasting love. Why don't you start showing Him your love and devotion by being on fire for Him, coming out from among the world and being separate, and stopping some of your busyness to spend time alone with Him? Show Satan that he's wrong when he tells God that you don't love and adore Him!

REVELATION 12:10 *"...the accuser of the brethren is cast down, who accused them before God day and night...."*

December 18

A little dab'll do ya!

"No one has ever seen me, because I am invisible to the human eye. But, that does not stop me from working. I am one of the most powerful things in the whole universe. I have destroyed lives, wrecked homes, put people to flight, stopped armies, and rendered millions of people helpless and homeless. It is absolutely astounding how little old invisible me can cause such destruction!

You cannot see me. Oh, but you know me well! I have stalked you since birth, and I will continue to do so until you're lying cold in your grave. I hound you day and night, twenty-four hours a day. I will never leave you alone. I jump on your back...and you usually give in to me. I love weaklings!

Now, you may hate me, but Satan loves me! We are bosom buddies. Of all the things he uses to influence people with and to hurt God with, I am his most effective and his favorite. In fact, I am the one he used in the Garden of Eden to cause the fall of the human race. And, what is so amazing is that it only takes a pinch of me to do the job. Guess my motto should be, "A little dab'll do ya!"

Hell has enlarged herself for me. In fact, everyone who will spend eternity there will do so because of me. Some people think that murder, rape, child molestation, robbery, or some of the other evils are what sends people to that fiery inferno. But, oh no, it's me!I am the one responsible. I fill the whole of hell, from end to end. Yes, hell is my home and I am going to carry as many there as I can. I must work now while I can, for I will never get to see heaven. I will never be in the presence of the Holy One. There is NO place for me in heaven!

There is only one thing that scares me. It is that one Christian who does not go by his feelings; that one who is not controlled by his circumstances; that one who crucifies his flesh and yields to the Lord; that one who loves the Word, stands on it, and does everything according to it! HE is the one who scares me! He won't give in to me! Oh, by the way, my name is doubt...in case you haven't guessed by now!"

Christian, wise up! When doubt starts to sprout, get it out! Recognize it and do NOT give in to it! Believe God's Word instead!

MATTHEW 14:31 *"O thou of little faith, why didst thou doubt?"*

December 19

Eighteen inches

You work for a huge corporation that has locations all over the United States and even in a few foreign countries. You are a very conscientious, hardworking employee. You do your job to the best of your ability. You follow all the rules of the company, stick right to the guidelines, and endeavor to make your company successful. You have worked for this same corporation for years; yet, you have never one time seen the top dog, the president of the corporation. You know his name. You know quite a lot about him. In fact, you even know what he looks like, because there are pictures of him hanging in some of the offices. Yet, you are not intimately acquainted with him. You have no personal relationship with him whatsoever, even though you work for him.

So, you see, it is entirely possible to work for someone - and work well - without knowing them. Knowing about someone is not the same as knowing them! It is one thing to know information and another to know the person. If you know enough information about someone, you could fool others into believing you know that person intimately. But, the truth is that you have only head knowledge.....not heart knowledge.

The same thing is true of many people who profess to be saved. They work for the Lord. They are very conscientious and hardworking. They do their jobs to the best of their abilities. They follow the Ten Commandments; they are moral and good people; and they endeavor to further God's kingdom. They may even have been working religiously for years.....yet, they have never come into contact with the Head of it all, the Lord Jesus Christ! Oh, they know His name. They know quite a lot about Him from reading the Bible and from listening to others. However, they are acquainted with Him only headwise...not heartwise!

So, you see, it is entirely possible to work for God without knowing Him intimately. Being a worker in church, attending faithfully, and learning about the Lord do not necessarily mean that you have a personal relationship with Jesus. You could miss heaven by eighteen inches.....the distance from your head to your heart.

Where do YOU stand today? You can fool others and you may have even been fooled yourself. But, you cannot fool God. Why not ask Him to reveal your true spiritual condition to you? He knows.....and He will!

ROMANS 10:10 *"For with the heart man believeth unto righteousness..."*

December 20

Leftover basket faith

They had never seen anything like it! They had just watched Jesus perform a miracle beyond description. He had taken five loaves and two fish, blessed them, broke them, and fed five thousand men, plus women and children with them. And, if that weren't enough, the fragments that were left over filled twelve baskets, one basket for each disciple. As they stood there in complete amazement, the disciples should have realized that the word "impossible" is NOT in Jesus'vocabulary! It should have dawned on them that, when man places what he has into the hands of Jesus, the Lord will bless it and break it - and then the leftovers will be more than man started with initially. Even division is multiplication with Jesus.

But, instead, the disciples must have placed their belief in the leftover baskets, for they certainly did not carry what they learned with them. They left the scene of this mathematical miracle, having been constrained by the Lord Jesus Christ to get into a boat and sail to the other side of the sea. Jesus remained behind, as He wanted to spend time alone in prayer.

So, here they were in the midst of the sea. It was now dark. In fact, it was the fourth watch, somewhere between three and six A.M., the darkest hours of the night. The waves had become contrary. The ship was being tossed about like a toy. The disciples began rowing as hard as they could, but their efforts were not getting them any closer to land. Man's efforts will never get him to the other side! They were in an impossible situation! Jesus could NOT get to them, because He had no boat. Isn't that just like man's logic?

Suddenly, the troubled disciples saw someone walking on the sea. Not expecting Jesus, they cried out in fear, because their faith was back there in those leftover baskets. They peered through the darkness, thinking it must be some sort of spirit. It was He - Jesus! He had come at the darkest hour. He always does! And, as soon as He came aboard, the winds ceased, for His presence always brings complete peace!

Are you facing an impossible situation today and it's the fourth watch of the night already? Well, get your faith out of those leftover baskets and trust Him! Look across those troubled waters. Is that Jesus I see coming toward you?

LUKE 18:27 *"The things which are impossible with men are possible with God."*

December 21

Are you possessing your inheritance?

Suppose that a near relative of yours passed away, leaving you an inheritance of one billion dollars. You place this inheritance in banks for safe-keeping. Now, all this is your inheritance, but you do not have it all in your possession. When you need part of your inheritance, you go to the bank and make a withdrawal. You take into your possession what is already yours. If you never go and make withdrawals, then all the inheritance is still there and is still yours, but it's as though you don't even have it. Inheritance is what is legally yours. Possession is what you claim and take for your own out of the inheritance.

This same principle is true spiritually as well. When you are saved, you are adopted into the royal family of God, making you an heir of God and a joint-heir with Christ. Legally, according to the law of God, your inheritance is everything that is Christ's. That means that every promise in the Word of God is yours; everything that Jesus has access to, you have access to; everything God has given Him, He has given you! Saved friend, that means you are spiritually wealthy. You are a spiritual billionaire. All the "*unsearchable riches of Christ: Ephesians 3:8* are yours.

Now, this inheritance is yours, because God says it's yours! It's yours legally, not because of your worth, not because of your ability, not because of your good works, and not because of your feelings. It's yours because of Christ. However, this inheritance is in the Bank of Heaven. It is all recorded for you in the last will and testament of the Lord Jesus Christ, the New Testament, and was brought into force by the death of the Testator. You can read your Bible to find out what all is legally yours, go to your Heavenly Father in prayer, and make withdrawals from Heaven's Bank. The inheritance is all yours by spiritual birth...but the possession is by an act of your will.

Wouldn't it be a shame to be a spiritual billionaire, yet live as a spiritual pauper? To live a life that is anything less than what God tells you in His Word is a shame and reproach unto His Holy name. To go by your feelings, to mope around in unworthiness, to live defeated is to call God a liar! Christian, get up and live out what God says you are!It's high time you start possessing your inheritance!

GALATIANS 4:7 "*...thou art...a son; and if a son, then an heir of God through Christ.*"

December 22

Maybe you have YOJ!

You can mix up the letters any way you want - yoj, yjo, ojy, oyj, or jyo - and you have no purpose for them. They don't mean anything. They bring confusion. But, when you put them in the proper order, you have the word "joy." The letters must be in that exact order; else, you'll have something besides joy, something with no purpose!

Maybe that's what is wrong with your life. You have absolutely NO joy in your life! You have no purpose for living. Life is boring, mundane, routine, unexciting, drab, blah! You are really just existing; yet, you keep thinking that there MUST be more to life than this! Well, friend, in all probability, you have yoj!

You see, you have life backwards. Yourself (Y); Others (O); Jesus (J) - YOJ! You devote most of your time, most of your thoughts, most of your attention to yourself. You are always fretting over what you are going to eat, how much you are going to sleep, what you are going to do, how you can be entertained, and how your flesh can be pleased and satisfied. Then, if it doesn't put you out any, you might consider doing something for someone else. Of course, you don't want it to cost you too much. You would NOT want to give up your TV time or your sleep or your nice meal to help someone. And, last of all, if there is any time left over at the end of the day, you might try to squeeze Jesus in there somewhere!

Dear friend, you will NEVER have joy that way! You cannot get joy out of yoj. The letters absolutely must be in proper order. It is a necessity that Jesus Christ be first. He must be first in all your thoughts, first in all your time, first in all your attention, first in each of your days. If you will seek HIM first, all the other things you are looking for will be added! Then, after you have sought Him and spent time with Him, you will be effective in dealing with others. He will minister through you, love through you, and touch others through you. And, last of all, after putting Jesus first and others second, you can consider yourself! However, you will find that you will get so excited over Him and over helping others that your problems will have melted away in the process and you won't have much to ask for yourself. If you put Jesus (J) first, others (O) second, and yourself (Y) last, guess what? That spells JOY!

PSALMS 16:1 *"In Thy presence is fullness of joy; at Thy right hand are pleasures for evermore.."*

December 23

Fire...flame...flicker...forgotten!

Have you been praying for someone for a long time and nothing seems to have changed? Perhaps you got discouraged somewhere along the way and quit praying. Your relentless adversary kept whispering in your ear that this person would never change...and you believed him. Somehow, the enemy tricked you into looking at the giant instead of at the God who is bigger than the giant. You forgot to Whom you are praying. Friend, remember that your prayers are all "*unto God*." You are speaking to the One who created a universe from nothing; so, do you honestly believe that the person you've been praying for is any problem at all to Him?

Or, maybe the enemy has somehow convinced you that, since you haven't seen an answer yet, God does NOT hear your prayers! You have been deceived into getting the focus on yourself - on your unworthiness, on your spiritual condition, on your poor service, on your inabilities. You have developed spiritual myopia, or nearsightedness, which enables you to only see up close, namely yourself! Maybe it's time to visit the Heavenly Optician. He will remove those distorted, self-centered glasses that you're wearing and fit you with a pair of spiritual eyeglasses for single vision.....Christ alone!

Friend, you started out at one time praying with fire for that lost loved one. However, months passed without an answer and the fire became a flame..... then a flicker.....and then forgotten. Oh, unfaithful friend, listen to the prophet Samuel. "*Moreover, as for me, God forbid that I should sin against the Lord in ceasing to pray for you." I Samuel 12:23* Or, listen to the Apostle Paul. "*...without ceasing I make mention of you always in my prayers." Romans 1:9*

Oh, soft and lax one, so slow of heart to believe, have you forgotten that there is a real hell and it's forever? Can you not see your loved one dangling over that eternal lake of fire by a thin thread? Can you really afford to quit praying? Get that forgotten prayer out of the closet of your heart, ask the Holy Spirit to ignite the wick, and allow Him to blow that flicker into a flame and into a fire again!

I SAMUEL 12:23 *"...God forbid that I should sin against the Lord in ceasing to pray for you."*

December 24

The Million-Mile club

The airplane taxis down the runway and lifts off. As you sit with your seat belt on, you feel only a slight apprehension. You have committed yourself to this airplane and you are trusting in it and its captain to carry you safely to your destination. For a while, the flight is so smooth that you cannot even tell you are in the air. You get so comfortable that you even doze off.

Suddenly, however, you are jolted out of your comfort zone. The plane encounters a storm, with high and turbulent winds. It seems as though the airplane will break apart. Your feelings quickly change from peace and trust to fear and doubt, becoming as turbulent as the weather. Your frantic button has been pushed! Maybe you should just bail out!

Meanwhile, beside you sits a seasoned veteran of the air, a million-miler. He has encountered many storms through the years of flying. He sits undisturbed, calm, at perfect rest. He realizes that his feelings have absolutely nothing to do with the flight. His feelings did not get the plane off the ground and they cannot keep it in the air. He has committed himself to the airplane and he might as well enjoy the ride. His life is in the hands of the pilot and in the ability of the plane.....his feelings change nothing!

Oh, Christian, when will you ever learn this principle? When you first got saved, it was a smooth, comfortable ride. However, it wasn't long before you hit turbulence. At times, it felt like your life would come apart. Sometimes, you even wondered if God was there at all. Your feelings changed from peace and trust to fear and doubt, kind of like a roller coaster ride. You often pushed the frantic button!

Dear one, haven't you become a seasoned veteran by now? It's about time you joined the million-mile club! You have committed yourself to the Lord Jesus Christ as the pilot of your life. He is the One carrying you to your destination. You might as well realize now that you will encounter many storms along the way. And, mark it down permanently that your feelings have absolutely nothing to do with the trip. They don't change a thing. So, why not just enjoy the journey? The Captain will get you there safely! Trust Him!

II CORINTHIANS 4:8 *"We are troubled on every side, yet not distressed."*

December 25

God's little Lamb

God did have a little Lamb.
His heart was white as snow.
And everywhere that God did lead,
The Lamb was sure to go.

He followed Him to Bethlehem,
No room to lay His head.
So, in a lowly manger,
The Lamb did make His bed.

He followed Him through dusty streets
To touch and love and heal.
Yet, the Lamb was scorned and hated
Because man's sins He did reveal.

He followed Him to Calvary
Where His life He freely gave.
The Lamb became a sacrifice
So man, our God could save.

He followed Him out of the grave
Back up to heaven's shore,
Where all who follow this dear Lamb
Will live forevermore.

And one day, every knee shall bow
Before the great "I Am."
And all, with one accord, shall sing,
"Worthy is the Lamb!"

JOHN 1:29 *"Behold, the Lamb of God, who taketh away the sin of the world."*

Sorry……no room!

"Knock, knock!"
"Who's there?"
"Joseph and Mary. Can you give us a place for Jesus, the savior, to be born?"
"Sorry…..no room!"

"Knock, knock!"
"Who's there?"
"Joseph and Mary. Can you give us a place to hide our son? Herod is killing all the children under two years old."
"Sorry…..no room!"

"Knock, knock!"
"Who's there?"
"Jesus. Can I come into the temple to teach you the ways of the Father?"
"Sorry…..no room!"

"Knock, knock!"
"Who's there?"
"Jesus. It's my birthday. Can I come into your home and celebrate my birth with you? Can't wait to see what you got me for my birthday this year!"
"Sorry…..no room!"

"Knock, knock!"
"Who's there?"
"It's me, Lord. my life is over. Can I please come into your home and live with you forever?"
"Sorry…..no room!"

December 26

Yea, hath God said...?

In the Garden of Eden, we find the first recorded words of Satan, "*Yea, hath God said...?*" *Genesis 3:1* Satan's very first attempt at deceiving mankind was to cast doubt upon the Word of God, to fool man into thinking that God did not really mean what He said and that He would not deal with sin as His Word had strictly decreed. This attempt worked! Mankind fell for Satan's lie instead of believing the truth of the Word of God.

Six thousand years later, Satan is using the same tactic, and it's still working. Perhaps he has used it on you. He has whitewashed your sin..... and you let him, because you really wanted to hold onto it anyway. He has fooled you into believing that it's not really sin; and, even if it were, God will not deal as harshly with it as His Word says. So, you have justified your sin and your lifestyle. That way, you will not have to obey God and change. Your lifestyle shows whether you really believe the Word of God or not.

Oh, dear friend, all your rationalization and justification still do NOT change the Word of God! It is still the holy, inspired, inerrant, infallible, unchanging truth! Listen to the Apostle Peter in II Peter 2:4-6. He tells us that God did not spare the angels that sinned, but cast them down to hell, and delivered them into chains of darkness, to be reserved unto judgment. Lest you forget.....these angels had not committed murder, rape, theft, adultery, etc. They had the sin of pride, wanting to be their own boss instead of following God. Peter also tells us that God did not spare the old world, but saved Noah, a preacher of righteousness, bringing in the flood upon the world of the ungodly. Only Noah's family, eight people, were saved out of the multitudes, who were all eating, and drinking, and marrying, and giving in marriage, disregarding the laws of Almighty God. And Peter also tells us that God turned the cities of Sodom and Gomorrah into ashes, condemning them with an overthrow, making them an example to those that after should live ungodly.

Hebrews 2:2,3 tells us, "*For if the word spoken by angels was steadfast, and every transgression and disobedience received a just recompense of reward, How shall we escape if we neglect so great salvation?*" Where does that leave you today, dear one? Are you living for God, loving Him, obeying Him, and serving Him? Just remember: God's Word hasn't changed. God STILL hates sin! His judgment is still just as severe on sin as it ever was! And Satan is still deceiving folks by asking the same old question, "*Yea, hath God said?*" Don't fall for Satan's lie!

HEBREWS 2:3 *"How shall we escape, if we neglect so great salvation..."*

December 27

Let go of that ledge!

All night long, he clung to the window sill, fearing for his very life. He knew that, if he let go, he would plunge to his death to the ground below. However, when the first rays of the morning light began to break over the horizon, Senor Panza discovered that his feet were only inches above the ground. Red-faced and near exhaustion, he realized that his unfounded fears had held him captive when he could have been sleeping soundly and safely all night in a comfortable bed. If he had only known the truth, he would have been free from all his fears and worries about his situation.

Perhaps you are a window sill Christian...holding onto that ledge of self control, afraid to let go and let God. You don't really trust God to handle your situation if you give the controls to Him. You are so afraid that He won't do things the way you want Him to, afraid that your own hopes and plans will plunge to their death to the ground below. Therefore, since you are plagued with fears and doubts about the outcome, you spend most of your waking hours thinking of ways to fix your situation yourself. And, you find yourself in a continual struggle. There's not much peace or joy to be found hanging onto that window sill.

Friend, you need to turn loose of that ledge. Quit clinging to it. Quit struggling to hold on. It's high time you just give up all control, let go, and let God! Get in the Word of God and watch the light breaking over the horizon of your situation. Then, you'll see that your fears and worries are unfounded. You'll see that you have been held captive by these enemies when you could be resting comfortably in the Lord Jesus Christ. You'll see that there is no need to fear...for underneath are the everlasting arms. There's no way to crash land with Jesus in control, for He never fails! He never makes a mistake! He is never wrong!

So, today, dear one, why don't you stop resisting and start resting? Life's too short to spend it worrying and fretting over everything. The Lord wants you to enjoy your journey down here below...not just endure it. He has great plans for your life.....but you must let go of that window sill and trust Him! So, let go, my child, let go!

DEUTERONOMY 33:27 *"...underneath are the everlasting arms..."*

December 28

There's no middle ground

There are three wills on earth, all of which are always actively at work. There is the will of God, the will of Satan, and the will of man. The will of God is always good, for God is good and there is no evil in Him at all. His will is truth, for God cannot lie. His will is light, for God is light and in Him is no darkness at all. God's will is life, love, joy, peace, hope.....it is everything that God is!

Satan's will, on the other hand, is diametrically opposed to God's will. Satan's will is always evil, for there is no good in him whatsoever. His will is a lie, for he is the father of lies and there is no truth in him. His will is darkness, because only God is light and everything else is darkness. Satan's will is death, misery, hate, anger, turmoil, despair.....it is everything that Satan is! Satan hates God and is out to destroy everything that is of God. Ultimately, his diabolical plans are to get people to worship him instead of God, to bow down to him, to follow and obey him, all without people even being aware that this is what they are doing.

Now, we have God's will, which is always good and never changes. We have Satan's will, which is always evil and never changes. And, we have the third will, the will of man, which can go either way. Man has a free will to choose, but he only has two choices: God's will or Satan's will. He cannot act apart from either of these. The Bible says that no man can serve two masters, so everyone alive is either serving God or the devil. There is no gray area, no middle ground, no straddle-the-fence service. It is God or Satan, white or black, good or evil, light or darkness, truth or lie.

In every decision of life, man has these two choices. In fact, life is a series of choices and decisions between God's will and Satan's, between good and evil. You see, these two forces are in an unending battle, each desiring to accomplish his will on earth. However, both accomplish their wills through people, thus making man's mind the battlefield. God wants you to obey Him, and Satan wants you to obey him. God gives you His Word, the truth. Satan gives you his word, a sugarcoated, enticing lie. But, it is up to you whom you obey. Just remember: there's no middle ground. So, will it be God's will or Satan's? You decide!

JOSHUA 24:15 *"Choose you this day whom you will serve..."*

December 29

What kind of "tater" are you?

Churches must be part of the vegetable kingdom, because they are all full of "taters." You can find a variety of "taters" in any given church. Just walk in and look around. It will not take you long to spot them. Perhaps you are even one of them.

First, there is the agi-tater. He is always causing problems. No matter what is going on in the church, he always puts in his two-cents worth. Rarely do you ever hear an encouraging, kind, or uplifting word coming from him. He's a bitter "tater." He complains and grumbles, points a finger, accuses, and gossips. This "tater" has a tongue so long it will not even fit on the altar. He can tell you everything that is going on.....and a lot that is not going on. This "tater" loves a stink, because he's always stirring up one. Pastors, teachers, and other leaders hate to see this "tater" coming. Nothing stinks much worse than a rotten "tater."

Second, there is the spec-tater. He comes to church on a pretty regular basis, but he comes to sit and soak. He is quite a selfish "tater," as he is always just thinking of himself. He never offers to help others carry the load. He doesn't join in the battle; rather, he leaves his fellow "taters" to fight the battle alone. He doesn't want to be bothered. In fact, he puts out his "Do Not Disturb.....Tater at Rest" sign. He's on church welfare, letting others do the work while he enjoys the benefits. He's a lazy, useless, "tater" to the church.

Third, there is the resusci-tater. He is at church every time it meets. He is a very loyal and dedicated "tater." He is always concerned about the life of his church. He finds ways to strengthen the weak, to encourage the discouraged, to uplift the fallen, to love the unlovable, to mend broken hearts, to comfort the afflicted, etc. This sweet "tater" brings life everywhere he goes. He helps carry the load of his church, supporting the welfare recipients. His sign is always out. It says, "Tater at Work!"

Besides these "taters," there are other varieties, such as the meditater, the ro-tater, the hesi-tater, the couch po-tater, and the regurgi-tater. There are hungry people coming in your church doors each week, looking for something good. If what they see is spoiled, rotten, and useless, they will probably never come back.

What kind of "tater" are you?

II TIMOTHY 2:20 *"But in a great house there are vessels... some to honor, and some to dishonor."*

December30

The just shall walk by faith

He had prayed and prayed about the situation; yet, there had been no answer from God. He was quite perplexed, as he thought about the circumstances from his human point of view and could come up with absolutely no logical conclusion. Deeply burdened over this puzzling state of affairs, he prayed, "*O Lord, how long shall I cry and Thou will not hear! Even cry unto Thee of violence, and Thou will not save! Why dost Thou show me iniquity and cause me to behold grievance?" Habakkuk 1:2,3*

Habakkuk was sorely distressed over his land of Judah. The people seemed to have no conscience, no desire for holiness and righteousness, and no heart to serve God. It seemed that the Godly suffered affliction while the ungodly prospered. Habakkuk was puzzled about this; yet, he was even more puzzled as to why God had seemingly turned a deaf ear, overlooking all this wickedness, and allowing things to continue as they did.

Habakkuk decided to stand, set, and watch. He determined to stand upon the Solid Rock, set his mind and affections totally upon the Lord, and watch for the Divine answer. As is always the case when anyone diligently seeks the heart of God, Habakkuk received an answer from God.

The answer contained one of the simplest, yet most profound statements in the entire Word of God, an answer which is one of the central themes of the Bible. "*The just shall live by his faith." Habakkuk 2:4* As Habakkuk listened to the Lord, he realized that there are many things we do not understand. Our little finite minds are so limited. There is no way we can comprehend a God who is so awesome He could just speak an entire universe into existence from nothing. Habakkuk realized that we do not have to understand. All God asks is that we walk by faith, trusting Him completely, even when reasoning fails us. Habakkuk concluded the whole matter with this powerful, life-changing statement, "*Although the fig tree shall not blossom, neither shall fruit be in the vines; the labor of the olive shall fail, and the fields shall yield no food; the flock shall be cut off from the fold, and there shall be no herd in the stalls; Yet will I rejoice in the Lord, and I will joy in the God of my salvation." Habakkuk 2:17,18*

Have you been trying to figure things out all your life? Well, why don't you change that? You have a brand new year right around the corner. Make up your mind to walk by faith and adopt Habakkuk's life-changing statement as your motto.

HABAKKUK 2:4 *"...but the just shall live by his faith."*

December 31

Back up, pack up, and clear out!

Back up! Pack up! And clear out! I have had enough of you! You have harassed me, tempted me, lied to me, deceived me, hounded me, put fear in my heart, plagued me with doubts, and bullied me around long enough! I have allowed you to put a hook in my nose and lead me around for years. But, things are going to change! I have finally realized some very important truths that I intend to practice from now on!

Hey, devil, the truth is that you are defeated! Jesus Christ defeated you two thousand years ago when He shed His blood on Calvary, was buried, and was resurrected by the power of God! He won the victory over death, hell, and the grave, making a show of you openly and triumphing over you. Hey, devil, let me remind you of how much authority you have.....none! You cannot make me do one thing, not one single thing. I do not belong to you, I do not have to mind you, and I do not even have to listen to you. Back up, pack up, and clear out!

Oh, and evil one, let me tell you one more thing. You have always intimidated me, forcing me to retreat and withdraw from the battle time and time again. I have consistently felt powerless against you, as the fears and doubts you hurled at me overwhelmed me to the point of resignation. But, I have learned something valuable. My struggle with you is not a power struggle.....it's a truth struggle. You have known that all along. All you have had to do was get me to doubt the Word of God. Then, I got all down and depressed and afraid and defeated my own self. Hey, I know better now! All I have to do is believe the Truth, stand on it, and act accordingly, regardless of how I feel. I understand that my feelings do not matter. The Truth is still the Truth, whether I feel like it or not. Once I stand on the Truth, in spite of my feelings, the battle is all over. There is nothing else you can do. The Truth is what makes me free. So back up, pack up, and clear out!

Right now, I resolve to go into this next year with some changes. I plan on being a "Word" Christian and a "knee" Christian. I want to bathe and soak in God's Word. I want to be saturated with Jesus, so He pours out everywhere I go. I am coming after you this next year, Satan. So, you might as well just back up, pack up, and clear out!

PSALMS 119:30 *"I have chosen the way of truth."*

Personality
INSIGHTS
PRESS